Peter Watt has spent tim...
trawler deckhand, build...
salesman, private investigator, police sergeant, surveyor's
chainman and advisor to the Royal Papua New Guinea
Constabulary. He speaks, reads and writes Vietnamese and
Pidgin. He now lives at Maclean on the Clarence River
in northern New South Wales. He has volunteered with
the Volunteer Rescue Association, Queensland Ambulance
Service and currently with the Rural Fire Service. Fishing
and the vast open spaces of outback Queensland are his
main interests in life.

Peter Watt can be contacted at www.peterwatt.com.

Author Photo: Shawn Peene

Also by Peter Watt

The Duffy/Macintosh Series
Cry of the Curlew
Shadow of the Osprey
Flight of the Eagle
To Chase the Storm
To Touch the Clouds
To Ride the Wind
Beyond the Horizon
War Clouds Gather
And Fire Falls
Beneath a Rising Sun
While the Moon Burns
From the Stars Above

The Papua Series
Papua
Eden
The Pacific

Other
The Silent Frontier
The Stone Dragon
The Frozen Circle

The Colonial Series
The Queen's Colonial
The Queen's Tiger
The Queen's Captain

Excerpts from emails sent to Peter Watt

Praise for *The Colonial Series*

'I wanted more! No superlative would be sufficient to describe your work.'

'I second every comment your fans have shared . . . for me your craft has awoken a long-lost belief in the art of storytelling.'

'These are extraordinary books and I look forward to reading everything you have written . . . Thank you for writing books to take us away to different times with a great combination of fiction/fact.'

'I found the novels so interesting and enjoyable to read I couldn't put them down . . . thank you from a very happy reader.'

'Peter, I have never written to an author before but I felt compelled to write thanking you for this great story [*The Queen's Tiger*]. Can't wait for the next chapter with our Captain Steele – hopefully he gets his life sorted out!'

'[*The Queen's Captain*] was definitely worth waiting for as the book is certainly in the category of "I can't put the bloody thing down". It was a most interesting, emotional and compelling read, so congratulations on another fantastic book!'

'I like the way you include characters of the time (William Russell and Florence Nightingale for instance) and true-life events (the Crimean War and the pillaging of the Russian baggage train) from the period bringing a healthy dose of realism to the reader. One of my enjoyments is to take events from stories such as yours and research them independently to enhance my knowledge and enjoyment.'

'I have just finished [*The Queen's Captain*] and just couldn't put the book down. You just seem to get better with each book . . . I have no doubt [the next one] will be just as riveting. Keep up the excellent work, cobber!'

'Congratulations, I believe that your stories rank with John Grisham and David Baldacci and their ilk. I recommend your books to anyone who will listen.'

'Some years ago a friend recommended I try reading a novel by a new author by the name of Peter Watt. I have read every one of your books since and enjoyed every one, amazed at your ability to create such fascinating stories intertwined with Australian and world history. I have just read [*The Queen's Captain*], another triumph!'

'You're a master storyteller and researcher. It's amazing how you can put so much actual content and storyline in your work. Your readers learn so much . . . Thank you so much for a fantastic read!'

The Colonial's SON

PETER WATT

MACMILLAN
Pan Macmillan Australia

Pan Macmillan acknowledges the Traditional Custodians of country throughout Australia and their connections to lands, waters and communities. We pay our respect to Elders past and present and extend that respect to all Aboriginal and Torres Strait Islander peoples today. We honour more than sixty thousand years of storytelling, art and culture.

First published 2021 in Macmillan by Pan Macmillan Australia Pty Ltd
1 Market Street, Sydney, New South Wales, Australia, 2000

 A catalogue record for this book is available from the National Library of Australia

Typeset in 13/16 pt Bembo by Post Pre-press Group

Printed by IVE

The map on page viii is from *River of Gold* by Hector Holthouse, first published in 1967 by Angus & Robertson, this edition published in 1994. Permission granted by HarperCollins Australia Pty Limited.
The map on page ix is from the *Illustrated London News*, 7 August 1880, www.britishnewspaperarchive.co.uk

For Naomi

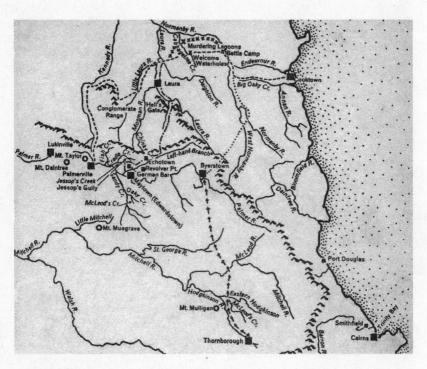

Palmer River Goldfields and surrounding areas, Queensland, in the late 1800s

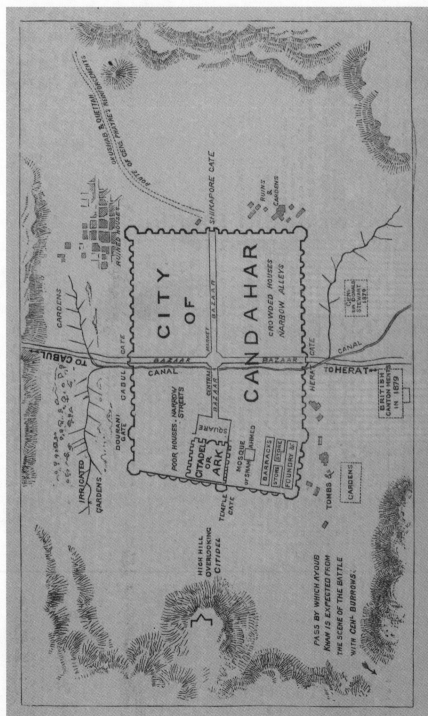

THE WAR IN AFGHANISTAN: PLAN OF THE CITY OF CANDAHAR.

PROLOGUE

Sydney Town

The Colony of New South Wales

1873

A pall of acrid smoke lingered in the air from the ten buildings burned down in George Street. There was speculation the uniform height of the houses, almost as old as the rapidly growing British settlement in the colony of New South Wales, was to blame for the speed of the flames. The newer buildings, built of sandstone quarried from local resources, instead rose in multiple levels. From the sprawling harbourside mansion where he stood, thirteen-year-old Josiah Steele could see the progress too, the transition from sail to steam evident in the many ships from distant lands moored at the piers. He too was growing, entering a new stage of life where he was no longer a boy but a young man.

The blistering southern hemisphere summer continued to bake the world outside, but inside the house was cool and silent. The servants moved about like ghosts, with only the occasional clip-clop of a horse's hooves outside breaking through the ambience of death.

Turning from the window, Josiah returned to the doorway of his mother's bedroom. His father, the former Captain Ian Steele, was kneeling by the bed, holding his mother's hand. Josiah had never seen his stoic father shed a tear before and was shocked to see silent sobs racking his body. Tears rolled silently down Josiah's cheeks; his beloved mother was finally dead after her long, cruel battle with cancer. He could see his mother's wan face against the pillow, skin covering a skeleton. The terrible disease had continued too long, painfully prolonging her inevitable death. Only the opiates administered by the family doctor had taken away much of the pain in Ella Steele's final days.

Josiah did not know if he should go to his father's side and kneel with him so they could mourn together, or let his dear father sit in his private grief.

Josiah's siblings, Samuel and Rebecca, aged only seven and six, were in the care of their nanny downstairs, and Josiah wondered if they could even understand the concept of death. It had never been conceivable to Josiah that his mother was not a permanent part of his life; how could the little ones possibly understand?

A hand touched Josiah's shoulder and he turned to see the heavily bearded face of the family doctor, Parkins.

'I am sorry, Master Steele,' he said. 'Your mother is now in a better place.'

What better place? Josiah wiped away the tears with the back of his sleeve. What place was better than with her loving family?

The doctor walked past Josiah and bent to speak softly to his father. The doctor turned back to Josiah standing in the doorway and gestured for him to step forward.

Josiah walked slowly to the bedside and placed his hand on his father's shoulder, gazing down at his mother's face. It was as if she were asleep and in that, Josiah found a tiny fragment of solace.

'She is gone, son,' Ian said, wiping the tears from his own face with a handkerchief as he rose. 'You must watch over her, act as *shomer*. I will speak with her rabbi and arrange the funeral.'

With that, he clapped his son on the shoulder and departed with the doctor, leaving Josiah in a daze, alone with the body of his mother. The most important person in his life, gone forever. The gentle love Josiah had known in his traumatic early years had been that of his mother.

He slumped to his knees beside the bed. There was no world outside the room, this gloomy, tiny part of the universe. Again, the tears flooded down his cheeks and he was racked with grief.

Josiah thought about his father, who had offered comfort in the only way he probably could. He had always shown his love in a stiff, formal way. Josiah knew his father was a man highly respected and liked by the important people he mixed with from colonial society. Josiah had heard whispered fragmentary stories of his father's courage on many battlefields, fighting for the Queen in distant parts of the Empire. He felt the shadow of his illustrious father on him, and Josiah so desperately wanted the gentle and intelligent man to be proud of him. But following his father's advice to one day take control of the family enterprises was not the way to win that pride. At thirteen years of age, Josiah Steele already knew where his destiny lay – and that his father would not approve of his choice.

Part One

Cooktown: Gateway to the Palmer River Goldfields

The Colony of Queensland

1875

ONE

It was a nightmare.

Through the telescope, fifteen-year-old Josiah Steele stared across the river inlet at the giant, prehistoric beast slithering down the riverbank into the tropical waters. He gripped the coastal steamer's handrail with white-knuckled intensity as it docked at the newly established port of Cooktown, catering to the thousands of people who had arrived from every part of the world to seek their fortunes at the inland Palmer River Goldfields.

'Look, Father!' Josiah passed the telescope to the man beside him: Ian Steele, former British army officer who had served under the assumed name of Samuel Forbes through campaigns from the Crimean War to the New Zealand Wars. He had also led his company of infantrymen across the deserts of Persia and fought in the Indian Rebellion with courage and distinction. He was in his mid-fifties yet had the appearance of a man much younger, retaining the bearing of a soldier. His hair was greying but his eyes were clear. Ian's body was still hard from his active life and his shoulders still had the broadness of a man who had learned his trade as a blacksmith in the colony of New South Wales as a mere youth.

'Gator,' Ian grunted as the great beast slid beneath the waters bordered by a mangrove embankment.

'No,' his son corrected. 'The colony does not have alligators. The creature is a crocodile and has a fearsome reputation as a maneater. I wish Samuel and Rebecca were here to view the beast.' Josiah sighed. His siblings were under the care of an army of nannies and servants back in Sydney, while Josiah had been allowed to accompany his father north on an adventure. For Josiah, his life had changed dramatically when his father and mother, who had crossed the world and the colonies in search of him after he was spirited out of England as a child, had finally found him. Now he had his dear brother and sister and an outstanding academic record at his prestigious private school, but still carried a keen sense that it could all disappear at any moment, like they had lost his mother. The grief had been overwhelming for his father and siblings, and while Josiah had felt the pain, he suppressed his feelings with stoic resolution as time progressed. He sensed that his father knew of his grief and the sea journey to northern Australia was intended to provide a form of therapy.

'Ah, I think I can see our welcoming party,' his father said, leaning forward on the railing to gaze across the wharf, busy with men preparing to unload the precious cargo of luxuries transported from Sydney and Brisbane.

The sun beat down and a haze of heat and dust rose from the landscape which only a week earlier had been mud at the end of the wet season. Josiah was taken by the primitive appearance of the timber buildings lining the main street just up from the wharf, such a contrast to the relative sophistication of civilisation in Sydney. He could also see that some of the rough-looking would-be miners carried firearms and was reminded of stories he'd read about the American frontier. He also noticed many ragged men clamouring at the wharf, crying for a berth to anywhere out of Cooktown. It did not bode well.

The gangplank clattered to the wooden wharf and Josiah followed his father onto dry land. Ian Steele pushed his way through the crowd on the docks to a short, solidly built man with broad shoulders. His hair was a dark red with a flowing red beard to match. Like his father, the man with the ruddy face was wearing a suit despite the tropical heat. He was also beaming from ear to ear.

'Major Hamish MacDonald, how the devil are you?' his father said, thrusting out his hand.

'It is grand seeing you again, Captain Steele,' Hamish replied, accepting the handshake. 'And who would this young laddie be?' the major added with a twinkle in his eye as he turned to Josiah. 'It could not be Master Josiah, because the last time I saw him he was but a wee lad.'

Josiah stepped forward and accepted a handshake. 'It is, sir,' he replied politely. 'My father has spoken highly of you, Major MacDonald.'

'Your father must have taken more than a wee dram to say nice utterances about me,' Hamish laughed. 'But a lot of it must have been true.'

Josiah had been told about the former British major, who had served with a Scots infantry unit that had fought alongside his father's own British regiment in the Persian campaign and on India's north-western frontier. The captain and the major had become firm friends and renewed their friendship when both men had left the service of Queen Victoria. Hamish had a small family fortune in Scotland and had chosen the Australian colonies to further his investments, now running his own establishment in Cooktown.

'I will have your luggage fetched and we will adjourn to my hotel,' Hamish said. 'Time for a good meal and dram of whisky. I read that the *Gothenburg* hit a reef off the coast and over a hundred poor souls were lost at sea. I feared you were a passenger on the steamer.'

Josiah felt a warmth for the Scotsman and could see why his father had befriended him. As they moved towards the main street, Josiah was intrigued to see so many Chinese people, and an equal number of prosperous-looking Chinese stores alongside the European merchants. They were passed by the occasional horse-drawn cart or bullock wagon heaped with stores destined for the many goldfields. The long, dusty road was called Charlotte Street, a marriage of East and West.

The three men made their way to a double-storeyed wooden building with a sign above the main entrance giving the hotel's name. A grander building of similar construction sat next door, and Josiah could not help but notice the group of scantily dressed young women who stood on the second-storey veranda there, gazing down at them across the dusty, hard-packed earthen road.

Josiah asked Hamish, 'Who are those ladies?'

Hamish turned to Josiah with a broad grin. 'Ask your father,' he replied as he stepped onto the porch. Josiah turned to his father and noticed his frown.

'Not now, lad,' Ian growled. 'I hope you are still too young to understand.'

'It is said that we have fifty-four hotels on Charlotte Street – and fifty-five houses of ill repute,' Hamish said, stepping inside the cramped main bar, where smoke, sweat and the smell of alcohol were in equal quantity in the stifling air. It was mid-morning, and the bar was packed with the tough-looking men of the northern frontier. A couple of men were asleep in the corner, probably left over from the early-morning rush.

'There is a dining room of sorts,' Hamish said, stepping over one of his sleeping customers who was still gripping an empty bottle. 'I have a room for you two upstairs, and we can meet in my office at the back when you are settled in. Your luggage will be safe. I have a couple of boys working for me to see nothing gets taken from customers. My hotel has a reputation as a safe place for the prospectors to get drunk and sleep it off.'

Josiah and his father were shown to a room at the back of the hotel by a burly Irishmen. The room was small but clean, with two iron cots and no other furnishings, not even a window to the outside world.

Josiah kept thinking of the women he had seen leaning over the veranda railings next door. From his father's reaction, he felt that he should not enquire too deeply, but he was curious as to who they were.

Once they had settled in their room, Josiah and his father were escorted to Hamish's small, stuffy office at the rear of the hotel. He was not alone. A wiry, weather-beaten man of indeterminate age stood beside Hamish, who sat behind a tiny wooden table on which was a bottle of whisky and two tumblers. Hamish indicated to his visitors to pull up a couple of rickety chairs. He poured the whisky, handing one to his old friend and passing Josiah a glass of tonic water. 'Sorry, laddie, but your father would shoot me if I tempted you into a life of drunken debauchery. This town should have been called Gomorrah, and not in honour of the great navigator Captain Cook that it has been. I should introduce Mexican Jack, one of my employees. Jack will not tell me his real name so I suspect that he may be wanted in his home state of Texas by certain law enforcement agencies, but he is a good man in a tight spot.'

'Pleased to meet you,' Jack said, nodding.

'I believe Captain Cook's ship was run aground for repairs in the river,' Josiah commented, airing his knowledge of the history of northern Australia.

'You are a learned young man,' Hamish complimented him. 'I doubt that any of the drunken prospectors in my bar would have known that. Gold is all they know, and many die trying to fulfil an unobtainable dream.'

'But you have an idea to make the dream of gold come true,' his father said. 'That is why my son and I are here.'

Before answering, Hamish shifted slightly in his chair, taking a swig of the whisky. Sweat ran down his face in the oppressive heat of the small, windowless room. 'The rush for gold nuggets just lying around on the surface has long gone,' Hamish said. 'John Chinaman has moved in and scrapes the meagre alluvial remains. But a geologist friend of mine has assured me that the real gold deposits are still in the Palmer fields, buried deep in quartz veins. What is required is the use of proper mining equipment to recover the gold from the seams, and crushing equipment to extract it from the rich veins. What we need is a ten-stamper driven by a twelve-horsepower engine that can crush ninety tons a week. That requires capital, and someone who is prepared to gamble on the outcome.'

'Hamish, you know I am not a gambling man,' Josiah's father replied. 'From what I know about the terrain around here, it would be exceedingly difficult to move such machinery.'

'Think about those times in your past when all the odds said you would not survive. You took chances and now you share my fine whisky in this godforsaken place of drunks and harlots. It has already been done. One such machine has already reached Maytown.'

'You said your geologist was currently in Maytown when you wrote to me,' the former captain said, leaning forward. 'I will make my decision to possibly back you in the venture after we speak with him.'

'A sensible idea,' Hamish said. 'Carry out a reconnaissance before opting to commit to the battle. I thought you might do so and have prepared for the three of us to travel to Maytown at first light tomorrow. But I should warn you, the trail is fraught with danger. The local Merkin tribe are known to be warlike and are said to be cannibals. Many a prospector has been ambushed and murdered by them coming back down the track with gold.'

'I am prepared for that.' Josiah saw his father smile grimly.

'Do you still carry that brace of Colts?' Hamish asked.

'Yes, and Josiah is a crack shot with the Snider I purchased for him.'

As Josiah listened to his father, his chest filled with happiness. His father treated him more like a man than a callow youth. He loved this tough but gentle man who rarely raised his voice at him or his younger brother. Needless to tell, his sister was a princess in his father's eyes and could do no wrong. Rebecca knew this and got away with everything mischievous around the sprawling mansion on the harbour, often to the detriment of her two brothers.

'A prized weapon out here,' Hamish said. 'Big .577 calibre for knockdown power, and breech loaded with those new brass Boxer cartridges. Wish we had them when we saw our service in India. I know of men who can fire up to ten rounds a minute with the Snider.'

'Josiah is able to match that rate,' his father said with a hint of pride.

'Let us hope we do not have the opportunity to see how good Josiah is with the Snider,' Hamish said, rising from behind his desk. 'Mexican Jack has had firsthand experience with the Merkin last year. He can tell you about it.'

Mexican Jack pulled at his flowing grey beard and squinted, as if trying to recollect the moment. 'I was with a party of Chinese and other prospectors when we were first alerted to the darkies in our area near a creek. We stood to in the night, but nothin' happened. It was on first light when they attacked. They came at us, big, bronze-coloured men wearing war paint like Kiowas back home in Texas, a-hootin' an' a-screeching their war cry like the black cockatoo. Their spears fell like rain in our camp from every side. They were hiding in the dry grass and scrub. The Chinese with us grabbed pick handles, shovels and bamboo poles and huddled in the centre. We snatched up our carbines and pistols and manned the barricade we had built the night before. The police officer in charge gave the order to hold our fire. I was mighty nervous as the Merkin came at us like true soldiers. Big and well-built warriors. They were almost on us when we got the order to fire. When the smoke cleared and we were desperately reloading, I saw about twenty bodies – some still alive. Then they came at us again and we fired another volley. Before we could reload, another wave came against us, and we had to fight man to man as they overwhelmed us with their numbers. Luckily, some of our native police and a few prospectors were able to reload, and that decided the fight. They finally fell back, leaving a few of us with spear wounds. We thought it was

14

over when we saw them stuffing dry grass tufts in their dead and wounded warriors' bullet holes. I guess they thought the wounds were inflicted by invisible spears. Then we once again came under a hail of spears from other Merkin who had crept in close, using the long grass for cover. A few of them got amongst our hobbled horses and tried to separate them from us. Damned if they did not act like soldiers,' the Texan sighed. 'They had guts – like any white man I know.'

Josiah listened with fascinated interest to the American's account of the skirmish. This was a violent and savage frontier, a long way from the cloistered halls of his sedate private school.

★

That evening, the three dined at the prestigious restaurant known as French Charleys, located just opposite the wharf. Ian was impressed with the luxurious decor and the pretty, bare-shouldered young ladies wearing silk and satin who spoke English with French accents and attended the bar where champagned flowed freely. This oasis in the middle of the dirty, brawling town had been the idea of a Frenchman, Charles Bouel, who had trained his girls to talk with a French accent to give an exotic touch to his fine establishment. The cancan was also performed, and if a miner had enough gold, they could retire with the pretty girls of Bouel's staff upstairs for the night. Josiah was wide-eyed at the ambience of forbidden delights he was yet to experience. The three were escorted to a table in the dining room by a male waiter – also with a French accent, and a hefty amount of Gallic arrogance. When they were seated at the table decorated with a vase of wildflowers and candles, Hamish recommended the local fish topped with an oyster sauce. Ian complimented Hamish on his choice of places to dine and Hamish laughed that if anyone was visiting

Cooktown with a need to be impressed, French Charleys was the place to do it. Imported English beer washed down the meal, while Josiah was forced to continue with tonic water as he listened in awe to the two older men exchange stories of their times campaigning for Queen Victoria on far-flung battlefields. Josiah already knew a lot about his father's past from the gardener at their residence, a former corporal who had been a rifleman in Ian Steele's regiment and served from Crimea to India. Corporal Will Bowden had emigrated from England to find his old company commander, and Ian had immediately offered him a small cottage and job tending the gardens. Ian had also paid the fare for his wife and three children to join him.

Josiah had befriended Corporal Bowden's son, who was the same age as himself. His name was George and the two boys often sat in the garden, listening to the stories Will Bowden told of the campaigns he had served under the command of the legendary Captain Forbes – as Ian Steele had been known at the time – but who was affectionately referred to as the Colonial by his men, who were prepared to follow him through the very gates of hell for his outstanding leadership and genuine concern for those who served in his company. The former British corporal's stories had quietly inspired Josiah and he knew where his destiny lay, despite his father dismissing the glory of war as a myth. Josiah sensed that his father would be strongly against any military career for his eldest son, as he was mentoring him to become the next head of their many enterprises. Josiah had remained silent of his desire to seek adventure, glory and fame on another path.

The waiter bent over and whispered in Hamish's ear. 'I think we should retire,' Hamish said. 'The cancan is about to be performed and I would suggest that Josiah is not of an age to experience such carnal entertainment.'

Ian agreed, and a bitterly disappointed Josiah followed his father and the major back out onto Charlotte Street, now alight with kerosene lamps and Chinese lanterns in the shopfronts. The sounds of laughter, yelling and music drifted all along the street as they strolled back to Hamish's hotel, and Josiah was very much aware that he was in a world so far from the life of the southern colonies.

★

Before sunrise the following morning, Josiah and his father met Hamish behind the hotel stables. Three horses had been saddled, with two more carrying supplies for the journey. Tea, sugar, flour, rice, canned sardines and smoke-dried beef were amongst the staples along with the much-valued pipe tobacco and a good supply of rum and gin.

'We'll get a good start travelling west on the Macmillan track before the sun is at its hottest,' Hamish said, tightening the girth on his saddle. Josiah was a good rider, having spent his school holidays on one of his father's many rural sheep properties in the colony of New South Wales. The production of wool was a lucrative income, as was his father's investment in beef. He had forecast that a successful way of freezing animal carcasses was just around the corner and one day, meat from the Australian colonies would grace the dinner plates of Britain.

'Here, son,' Ian said, passing the Snider to Josiah. 'You carry this on our journey inland.'

Josiah accepted the weapon with pride. It was not as if he would need it but the fact his father considered he was man enough to go armed meant a lot. Josiah slid it cautiously into a leather holder attached to his saddle. He knew it was loaded and was careful to keep his hand away from the trigger.

Hamish set out to guide them and the three men rode in single file out of Cooktown as its residents awoke to face another day. The small party trekked their way along a well-worn track, occasionally passing gaunt-looking men stumbling back from the goldfields who hailed them with pleas for any spare food or tobacco – and in some rare cases, offers were made to purchase the desired products with small gold nuggets. But Hamish knew the long and hard trek southwest through forest-covered hills would require all the supplies they had and that these were more valuable than the precious metal.

For three days and nights, the journey was uneventful, but on the fourth day, while navigating a tangle of ridges, Ian signalled a halt and glanced at Hamish.

'Do you smell that?' he asked quietly. Josiah understood the putrid stench of death from his time spent on one of the sheep stations, but this smell was different. He noticed both his father and Hamish dismount, the latter with his double-barrelled shotgun, while Ian drew his two big Colt revolvers. Josiah slid his rifle from the leather bucket.

'Stay with the horses,' Ian commanded his son. 'Be alert.'

Both Hamish and Ian climbed the last few yards of the track to a small plateau. Nervously, Josiah gripped the rifle in his lap.

'God almighty!' Hamish swore at the sight of four bodies sprawled in the dry grass. 'Merkin warriors.'

Ian was so familiar with the putrid smell of bloating human corpses that he did not bother to cover his nose. A thick cloud of flies covered the bodies that Ian could see had been shot to death. He also immediately noticed that there were no weapons beside them, as he had been made aware that the Aboriginal warriors usually carried long, barbed reed-like spears.

'What do you think happened here?' Ian asked.

'Damned if I know,' Hamish replied, removing his broad-brimmed hat to wipe his brow. 'The demise of these men means one less threat to our journey, but we will need to be even more careful.'

Both men returned to Josiah and mounted their horses. They moved forward cautiously, scanning the surrounding scrub and trees. Josiah paled when he looked down on the dead warriors, fighting to overcome the stench of their rotting corpses.

Soon, they were past the place of the killing and descending into a wide gully. That night, they took turns to stand guard and the following morning, they continued along the well-beaten track. At midday, with the sun blazing down, the familiar stench of human death assailed their senses once more. This time, they came across two European travellers riddled with spears. Both bodies were burned by the sun and beginning to bloat. One was a young man in his late teens, the other an older man with a beard. Both bodies had been stripped naked and lay on their backs, staring with sightless eyes at the blue sky above.

'Merkin spears,' Hamish said. 'Most probably from the party we passed yesterday.'

'It does not make sense that any warrior would leave his main weapon behind,' Ian mused, gazing down at the two bodies, blackened and swelling in the tropical heat. He dismounted and squatted by one of the dead prospectors. 'This man was shot,' Ian said, noticing a mark on the younger man's chest. 'It appears that spears have been thrust into gunshot wounds, but they missed this one. I know a gunshot wound when I see it. Besides, how is it that they have spears in them if they are stripped of their clothes?'

'If they were killed by the darkies, it does not make sense that they would leave perfectly good meat behind,' Hamish mused. 'I have heard rumours in the hotel bar from prospectors that they fear a gang is ambushing returning miners and making it look like they were killed by the local warriors.'

'I think I know why we did not see any spears back amongst the Merkin,' Ian said, rising from his squatting position by the body of the young man. 'White men with guns are far more dangerous than darkies with spears. I think it is right that we should bury them off the track. From what I can see, they appear to be related. Maybe father and son – or brothers.' Hamish nodded his agreement. They would not be the last Europeans discovered with spear wounds before they eventually reached the administrative capital of the Palmer River Goldfields, Maytown.

Sweating, Hamish and Ian scraped out a couple of shallow graves in the dry earth, while Josiah stood guard with his rifle. The bodies were lifted into the graves and earth thrown on them. When finished, Josiah found a couple of termite-riddled sticks and thrust each one into the hard ground at the head of the graves. No one expected the sticks to remain for long, but it was a gesture of respect. No words were said, and the three mounted their horses to continue their trek to Maytown.

As they rode, Ian tried to dismiss the terrible thought he'd had; that the men they'd buried could have been father and son. The former soldier shuddered. On this wild frontier, it could have been he and his beloved son being buried by strangers. Had it been a mistake to invite Josiah on this journey into the wild lands of the colony of Queensland?

TWO

After a week, the trio came to a large flowing river swollen by the wet season. It was decided they would camp near a point that showed signs of being a crossing, from the numerous tracks left by Europeans and Chinese. Ian felt the river crossing was too exposed to any observers, so they set up a hundred yards away, in the bush.

A campfire was lit and a tent pitched, then Ian took the water canteens to refill at the river, careful to have his Colts primed.

He was filling one of the canteens when he noticed mud swirling in a footprint not far from where he knelt. When he surveyed the scene, he noticed many more and could see they were not made from a boot but bare feet. The hair on the back of Ian's neck stood up but he did not show any signs of his observations in case he was being watched. They could be Chinese workers, he considered, but they had not seen any in the last couple of days and these footprints were fresh.

Very carefully, Ian rose, slung the string of water canteens over his shoulder and reached down to rest his hand on one of his Colts, aware of the warning by seasoned bushmen that the local warriors could hurl one of their deadly spears a good eighty feet with accuracy, and that was outside the efficient range of a revolver.

Ian reached the camp safely and could see Hamish bending over the fire, baking flour for damper. Josiah was sitting on a log, cleaning the Snider.

'I have a strong feeling that we may be attacked,' Ian said calmly when he was in the camp. 'I saw fresh prints down by the river.'

Immediately, Hamish picked up his double-barrelled shotgun and Josiah reached for a bandolier of rifle cartridges.

'They usually make their attacks at dawn,' Hamish said. 'But we have to keep vigil during the night in case they try to take the horses.'

'I agree,' Ian replied. 'Now I wish that I had brought a spare carbine along. It is about time I got my hands on one of those Yankee repeating Winchesters.' He turned to Josiah. 'Keep the Snider loaded at all times,' he said. 'I am hoping that they will see we are well-armed and move on to easier prey.'

Hamish finished making their meal and the three men ensured that they did not have their backs to the scrub around them. The story told by Mexican Jack echoed in Josiah's thoughts and he gripped the rifle to him, praying that if they were attacked, he would be able to answer the challenge to their lives. Josiah also reflected on the fact that his father, sitting a short distance away with an enamel mug of rum, had so often faced death and survived. It was a reassuring thought as he obeyed his father's order to keep a distance between them while the flames flickered. If a hail of spears were thrown, sitting all together would make them an easy target.

They took turns remaining awake, alert to the sounds of the bush. Just after midnight, Josiah sat with his back to a log under a beautiful moonless sky of twinkling stars. His father and Hamish were not sleeping in the tent, as Ian considered their foe may take it for granted that they were. Instead, he had made a small, low wall of saddles and logs to provide an improvised fortification.

Hamish crawled in the pitch darkness to Josiah via a rope that had been placed to guide them to their sentry position. Josiah had fought sleep during his sentry duty and the distant howling of dingoes miles away had helped him stay awake.

'Get some sleep, Josiah,' Hamish whispered softly. 'Just follow the rope to a log about ten yards away and settle in.'

Josiah thanked him and slithered along the ground until he found the fallen log, where he lay down and quickly dozed off, despite the fear he felt.

*

The screeching sounds of black cockatoos awoke Josiah just before dawn. This was followed by a hissing sound and the rattle of spears striking the tent.

A blast from Hamish's shotgun followed, soon joined by Captain Ian Steele's twin revolvers, shattering the peace of the rising sun. Josiah heaved himself into a position where the log acted as a shield. He could see no threat, but a spear thudded into the dry earth inches from his leg. Suddenly, a painted warrior a good six feet tall emerged with a battle-axe raised above his head. Josiah fired but, in his fear, he missed. He suddenly realised that he would not be able to reload before the white and yellow striped warrior was on him, but the warrior had not advanced two steps before he spun around, dropping his weapon. Josiah realised that a bullet from his father's Colt had caught the man in the shoulder and the Merkin tribesman was smart enough to disappear back into the scrub.

A silence fell as the smoke from the firearms drifted in the still air of the tropical morning. Josiah quickly reloaded, his eyes wide as he stared into the grey-green foliage.

'I think they have had second thoughts,' Hamish said, reloading his shotgun. 'I know I got one of them.'

Ian had also recharged his cap and ball revolvers, crouching behind his son so as not to make himself a bigger target.

Josiah found that his hands were shaking uncontrollably and he was desperately thirsty. He noticed the battle-axe with its wooden handle but metal, curved edge. Hamish picked it up and held it out to Josiah. 'You can see that horseshoes are in great demand by the darkies,' Hamish said. 'Any iron they lay their hands on is fashioned into spear tips and blades for their axes. I have been told by some of my patrons that they have come across wagons where all the metal is stripped away. You can keep it to remember your first battle with the wild men of the north.'

Josiah took the weapon, in awe of the ingenuity of Stone Age and modern technology combined.

'How are you feeling?' Ian asked, placing his hand on his shoulder.

Josiah looked up at Ian. 'A bit scared,' he replied. 'Is this what it was like for you, Father?'

'No. I remember I was outright terrified when I faced the enemy. A bit scared is good by comparison,' Ian replied with a slight smile.

'I was so scared that I did not take aim when that Merkin warrior came at me,' Josiah said, turning over the instrument that had been meant to end his short life.

'Don't chastise yourself. From what I saw, it all happened in a mere second or two,' Ian said. 'The main thing is that we are still here, and I feel that we were fortunate that only a small war party chose to attack us. The big man I wounded may have been their leader. By now, I hope they are off licking their wounds somewhere. It seems a good time to cross the river and continue our journey.'

Josiah rose, controlling the shaking in his legs, and went to their horses hobbled a short distance away in the bush. Within a half hour, they were cautiously wading across the river at the established crossing. The water rushed by them at waist level, but they safely traversed the river to reach the other side.

When Josiah mounted his horse, he had trouble getting the image of the painted warrior charging towards him from his thoughts. It would form part of the nightmares that haunted him for the next few nights.

The land surrounding the river crossing was green with pasture and the horses were grazed before the trio departed. Ian could see from his compass that they had changed course south, and for the next few days, they crossed barren plateaus. The lack of fodder for their mounts was beginning to show until one mid-morning, they saw a range of craggy peaks ahead that appeared impossible to pass.

Hamish warned Josiah and Ian that a place called Hells Gate lay just ahead of them and its name was well earned. There was a very narrow cut in the granite cliffs, and Hamish led the way upwards, weaving through huge boulders until they finally reached the fissure. Josiah could see human bones bleached by the sun scattered in the vicinity of the opening. Scattered remains of Chinese tools, clothing and small personal items indicated that this party had been ambushed. There were also the bones of packhorses which had finally died from exhaustion. It was a grim sight to those attempting to pass through the gates of hell.

'Damned dangerous place for an ambush,' Ian said gloomily, surveying the entrance between steep cliffs.

'We will have to dismount and lead the horses,' Hamish said. 'It is so narrow that a stubborn horse can close the journey from both ways.'

The three dismounted and led the horses into the notorious passage. All three kept their weapons close, silently manoeuvring between the steep, narrow cliffs. Ian could see how easy it would be to rain down rocks or spears on the unwary traveller.

They came to a tight bend, emerging to the sight of rock steps and small plateaus rising before them.

'The Devil's Staircase,' Hamish muttered. This was his second trip to Maytown, and it appeared it had not got easier. 'We are almost out.'

They eventually came onto a summit with a view of the track ahead. It was a desolate ride as they passed through a land of dry scrub, great, detached rocks and deep, dark gorges on either side of the track. As the sun dipped down to the horizon they set up camp for the night.

'Last year, the Merkin attacked a well-armed party led by Sub-Inspector Clohesy with five white and two black troopers. Hann was also with them. They were escorting a gold shipment of several thousand ounces from the Palmer. I heard there were hundreds of warriors and the police party was almost overwhelmed. But they fought back and got out alive.'

They sat around the campfire, the shower of sparks rising

into the serenity of the starry night. The major's recounting of the attack was a reminder that they must be aware of the ever-present danger around them in this hostile country. Neither Josiah nor Ian needed to be reminded.

The next day, they journeyed without incident, occasionally seeing the rotting remains of Chinese workers abandoned by their comrades. When they camped, they were ever vigilant to a sudden, blood-chilling screech of the black cockatoo which fortunately did not come.

The next day, they reached their destination.

★

The three travellers rode into a town of canvas, timber and corrugated iron, with the occasional bark hut.

Ian was surprised how busy the small town was. There were hotels, butchers, bakers, a blacksmith, a chemist, even a lemonade factory, printer, saddler and two banks. The European stores were outnumbered by those catering to the Chinese miners. There was also a distinct absence of women, with the streets teeming with dust-covered prospectors seeking the shade of the few scraggly trees and verandas. Many carried rifles, shotguns and pistols.

'Our man has a small office just down the street,' Hamish said, leading them to a small wooden building displaying a sign above the door that indicated the inhabitant purchased gold and his name was Beauregard Connors.

The three men dismounted and hitched their horses to a rail outside the office before they entered. The small space was occupied by a table and one chair for visitors. Behind the table sat a man with a long, pointed grey beard and flowing grey hair, and he was perusing a folder of papers on his desk. He glanced up and broke into a broad smile when he saw Hamish.

'Ah, Major. It has been some time since we last met. It is grand meeting you again.' Ian noted the distinctive American drawl, most probably from the south.

Hamish introduced Ian and Josiah, and when Beauregard rose from his chair, Ian could see that the man had a wooden leg as he leaned on a walking stick to support himself.

'Colonel Connors lost his leg at the Battle of Missionary Ridge,' Hamish said.

'I presume from your accent that you wore the grey,' Ian said, extending his hand. 'I had a dear friend who also lost a limb at the same battle, but he was wearing the blue.'

'A bloody mess,' Beauregard replied, his grip firm. 'But that was more than a decade ago and I hold no ill feelings towards the Yankees. My life is here now in this Limey colony. Hamish has told me in the past that you had quite a fighting history of your own. As a man of action, I know when you meet the Dutchie geologist, you will be impressed with what he has to propose. But time to close the office and find him before the sun goes down.'

Josiah sensed that he stood in the company of men not unlike his father — who had faced death on battlefields scattered across the world. His own father had always had the ramrod bearing of a soldier and still carried the physical and mental scars of war. Sometimes, when they retired to their bedrooms at night, Josiah heard the desperate cries from his father's room. They were frightening noises of a soul in torment crying out to dead soldiers.

Beauregard led them on foot along the dusty street to the edge of the small town, where a cluster of canvas tents were located.

'Hey, Dutchie!' Beauregard called, and a bespectacled middle-aged man poked his head out of one. He had rheumy eyes and close-cropped hair.

'Vot you vont?' he growled.

'Our esteemed visitors have arrived.'

Dutchie opened the tent flap and gestured for his visitors to enter. Josiah and the three men crammed inside the stifling confines of the tent.

Dutchie introduced himself. 'I am Gustaf von Kroth *und* Prussian, *kein* Dutchman.'

Ian knew that the Americans often referred to those of German blood as Dutchmen. Dutchie produced a bottle of schnapps from a wooden crate that also acted as his desk. Apart from this only a camp stretcher furnished his tent, though a shotgun leaned against the canvas wall.

Hamish accepted the schnapps bottle, taking a swig before passing it to Ian.

'So, you are Captain Steele,' Gustaf said, eyeing Ian. 'I served in the war against the Froggies recently vif our Prussian artillery. It appears ve are all men who have faced the enemy and lived to find our fortunes in this place that God forgot.'

It was Ian's turn to swig from the bottle of fiery clear liquid. It had a bite that Ian knew from his time fighting in Crimea when they had captured a supply from the Russians. At the time, it was an unusual windfall as the Russians were infamous for their heavy consumption and love of vodka.

'Major MacDonald has informed me that you have completed a geological survey of the area and believe that the main sources of gold ore are underground.'

'*Ja*,' Gustaf replied, rifling through the wooden crate before producing a battered ream of papers. 'I haf written a report with survey maps. If ve haf heavy mining tools, ve can make a fortune. Major MacDonald says you haf capital for this venture.'

'I would need to peruse your report,' Ian said, and Gustaf passed him the papers.

'*Gut*,' Gustaf said, rubbing his brow and squinting. 'I haf need to sleep, so you take report und tell me in the morning.'

The visitors could see that the Prussian had dismissed them and left the tent.

'The Dutchie will sleep off last night and make his way to the nearest hotel when the sun goes down,' the American commented as they strolled back to his office. 'I have arranged a tent for you to stay in tonight. It is better than trying to get any sleep in one of the hotels. I have made sure that you have lanterns and bedding. We can discuss your opinions on the project tonight.' Ian was impressed by the Yankee's organisation. They were shown to their tent on the edge of town, away from the noisy hotels filled with drunken revellers and those drowning their sorrows.

Hamish went back into town for supplies, returning with a haunch of fresh beef and fresh-baked bread.

'Cost the price of a gold claim,' Hamish grumbled. 'The only people making a fortune out here are the thieving merchants.' That evening, they ate well of the beef, roasted in a heavy cast-iron pot, washed down with bottles of imported beer.

By the gentle light of the campfire near their tent, Ian sat staring at the sky. Josiah sat beside him, sipping from his bottle of lemonade that Hamish had found on his excursion to the shops.

'What do you think about the report you read this afternoon?' Josiah asked.

'It is feasible,' Ian mused. 'I think that we should invest.'

Josiah nodded. His father had proven to be an astute businessman who had swelled the coffers of the many family enterprises.

'I have noticed that there appears to be something on your mind,' Ian said, poking the campfire with a stick. 'You have been reluctant to talk since the attack on us by the Merkin.'

Josiah hesitated before answering his father. 'It was rather horrible.'

'It was reminiscent of what you experience on a battle-field,' Ian said quietly, staring into the flickering flames. 'There is no glory in war – just what you observed back along the track. Rotting bodies of what were once fine young men in their prime, the gut-wrenching stench of death and the cries of the wounded who have no hope of ever going home.'

'Then why did you remain a soldier for so long?' Josiah countered.

Now it was his father who hesitated in replying. Ian needed time to look deep inside himself for the answer.

'It was complicated, and I do not have a clear answer to your question. But I do know I would never want you to live the life that I did as a younger man. I know that you are destined to inherit all that I have strived to establish for you and your brother and sister. It is what I know your mother wanted for you.'

'Father, I am not a businessman like you. I would rather travel and see the world.'

'That is possible as a businessman,' Ian said.

'But I wish to travel as a soldier,' Josiah replied, and saw his father suddenly tense at his statement.

'That is foolish,' Ian replied, shaking his head. 'You already had a glimpse into the world of death and danger. I could see that you were troubled by what you saw and experienced. I suspect you have foolish dreams of glory fighting for the Queen and Empire. I had the same dreams at your age and lived to regret my decision.'

Josiah listened to his father under the star-filled night. He did not answer as he had already made up his mind.

★

It was hard to keep any secrets in Maytown. Alcohol loosened tongues and the hidden was revealed.

Five tough-looking men sat around a table in the precious space of the Maytown Hotel, avoided by those packed around them. Their reputation for violence was well known and whispers circulated that the gang were responsible for many prospectors not making it back to Cooktown.

'He's goin' to smuggle a batch of gold out tomorrow,' the leader of the group said in a low voice to the other four, who were straining to hear above the din of the drunken noise around them. The leader was a man in his thirties with a scarred face under a thick black beard. Charlie Goodson had travelled north after serving time in the infamous Moreton Bay prison, where he had been incarcerated for armed robbery. Charlie Goodson was nothing like his family name and now held a bitter grudge against the society he lived in.

'How do ya know this, Charlie?' asked Martin Donahue, his second-in-command.

'Got the news from the store owned by Wang, where I have someone listening out,' Charlie replied. 'The Yank is probably goin' to get those three dandy men who rode in today to shift it for 'im. The Yank don't like payin' taxes an' keeps the gold he buys hidden.'

'We don't like payin' taxes either,' one of the other gang members quipped, which elicited a twisted grin from Charlie.

'What do we do?' Martin asked.

'We finish this round of drinks an' head out tonight with

supplies to welcome the escort party up the track,' Charlie said, swilling down his rum, then his men followed him out into the night.

★

Two days later, having toured the goldfields with Gustaf and asked all the questions he could, Ian was satisfied and ready to return to Cooktown. Before the sun rose, Hamish, Ian and Josiah had saddled up with fresh provisions from the Maytown stores in packs on the carrier horse.

'We need to make some distance before last light,' Hamish said. Ian noticed that the Scotsman had two heavy satchels slung over his saddle and his shotgun was gripped in one hand, ready to be used.

'Are we expecting trouble?' Ian asked.

'You saw the bodies up the track,' Hamish said, hefting himself into the saddle. 'Never can be too careful.'

'What is in the bags?' Ian casually asked.

'We are just doing a small favour for the Yankee,' Hamish replied, and Ian immediately guessed that they were smuggling gold back to the coast to avoid colonial taxes.

'No one else knows,' Hamish said quietly, urging his horse forward.

'I pray you are right,' Ian said, straddling his mount and glancing back at Josiah, who took up the rear of their file, leading the packhorse. They struck out in the heat of the rising sun along the track bordered by dry, scraggly trees. Ian had an uneasy feeling. From the size of the bags, they must have contained a considerable weight of gold, and secrets were hard to keep. Ian had witnessed the brutality on this far-flung frontier where it was so easy to disappear without attracting any interest from the law, and he instinctively touched the butts of his big Colt powder and ball revolvers as reassurance of their presence. For a moment, he experienced a dread for the safety of Josiah and glanced over his shoulder at his son. The memory of the young and old prospectors they had found on the track flashed through his mind.

Ian kicked his horse into a walk, and soon Maytown was behind them and the scrub on either side fell silent – there were no birdcalls or any other signs of life. They rode slowly, picking their way through the spindly trees until near midday, when Ian's soldier instincts warned him that the curve on the track ascending a ridge was a perfect ambush site.

'Hamish, I think we should call a short halt,' Ian said in a low voice that just carried to Hamish a short distance in the lead.

Hamish swung around in the saddle with a frown. 'We need to keep going,' he answered irritably.

Ian slid from his mount. Josiah followed his father's example, Snider in hand. Josiah had a belt of rounds across his chest and felt prepared but nervous. Something was wrong if his father had said so.

★

'What they doin'?' Martin Donahue hissed from his position on the low crest overlooking the three men below on the track. 'You think they seen us?'

The men lay side by side in the desiccated grass with their old Enfield rifled muskets. The former weapon of the British army was extremely accurate and fired a deadly Minie projectile. Charlie had two more of his men positioned twenty yards away, covering the track below in an L-shaped ambush. He calculated the range from the three men he hunted as approximately seventy-five yards. His rifle was accurate enough to engage the three travellers, but he only had the edge of one other armed man in his ambush. It was a ratio of four to three, and Charlie could see that the men they were about to engage were well armed. The first man to dismount appeared to be cautious, as if he had faced danger before. It was now or never. Charlie raised his rifle to take a sight on the man still on his horse.

★

'What is it, Father?' Josiah called softly to Ian, who had now retrieved his revolvers from his belt.

Hamish saw Ian's action and quickly slid from his mount, shotgun in his hands, just as a cracking sound came from the shimmering heat, and a round clipped his collar.

'Damn and damnation!' Hamish swore, falling heavily to the earth. 'Bloody bushrangers!'

The first sound was followed by a ripple of rifle fire, but all incoming rounds missed their marks.

Josiah was suddenly frozen with fear, transfixed by the deadly situation that had erupted in the heat and dust of the track. He heard his father roar, 'Get down!' and Josiah obeyed, still confused by the violence. When he looked up from the earth, he saw his father sprinting into the dry scrub alongside the track. The fact that his father was running towards the source of the danger flitted through Josiah's mind and he experienced a sharp surge of absolute fear. Although he knew distance was safety, Josiah's primal instinct was to follow his father as he placed himself in dire peril. Josiah heaved himself to his feet and ran.

★

'Charlie, the bastard's goin' after Tom an' Pete!' Martin uttered in disbelief as he rolled over and hastily reloaded the Enfield.

35

Charlie was already on his knees, scanning the thick scrub for the crazy bushman, his rifle ready to fire again.

★

From the corner of his eye, Josiah saw the figure rising from the dry grass, rifle levelled at his father. Josiah swung his own weapon at the kneeling man and took a quick sight on him, firing a shot. The man on the rise jerked and fell back. Josiah snapped the breech open and rolled the rifle to allow the cartridge case to fall out. He was already reaching for a fresh round to reload.

★

Charlie felt the impact of the lead projectile like a sledge-hammer blow to his hand. He cried out in his pain, dropping his own weapon.

'You bin shot!' Martin gasped.

'Got to get out of here,' Charlie groaned as the pain from the vicious wound to his shattered hand began to overwhelm him. He had no chance of operating his rifle. 'The bastards know what they are doin'.'

His second-in-command agreed and the two men wriggled their way back along the slope, leaving their two comrades to an uncertain fate as the man wielding a Colt in each hand charged the cover of the ambushers.

★

Ian noticed the movement in the grass only twenty paces from him and saw the two men rise slightly for a better view of their attacker. Ian commenced firing volleys of shots into the would-be killers and was pleased to hear cries of pain as the two men fell back into the cover of the long, dry grass. He had not lost his skills as a soldier, and with rounds to spare, he stalked cautiously towards the last position he had seen the men fall. When he was on them, Ian could see that one of his bullets had taken one of the men in the head, while another round had gone through the other man's shoulder at such an angle that it would have ripped into his lung. He looked up with dying eyes at Ian standing over him with his two smoking Colts.

Ian fired a shot into the wounded man's head, killing him instantly. It was both an act of mercy and revenge for placing Josiah's life in danger.

THREE

The distant sound of two horses galloping away could be heard as Ian turned his back on the two bodies and walked back towards Josiah and the major.

'Damned if young Josiah did not save us,' Hamish exclaimed, struggling up the slight slope to Ian. 'My gun did not have the range to help us,' he continued to explain. 'So, I stayed low and saw one of the blighters take a bead on you when you carried out your assault. He might have finished you off if it had not been for Josiah shooting him first. Damned good shot if I may say so.'

Ian looked at his son, whose expression was a mixture of worry and relief. Ian did not doubt the Scotsman's account of the swirling seconds of sheer danger. Ian nodded to his son, acknowledging his critical intervention, bemused that it was Josiah who had saved him when it had been his role to save his son in the ambush.

'I think that we have foiled any intentions of robbing us,' Ian said, guessing the sound of hoofbeats meant the survivors had fled. 'But I also think that we should make as much distance as we can from this place while we have daylight.'

The three men mounted their horses and continued their journey along the rugged track to Cooktown. At one stage, Ian brought his mount level with Josiah's. 'I am just enquiring if you are well,' he asked quietly.

'I am well, Father,' Josiah replied.

'I don't think you slew him,' Ian commented. 'But from what Hamish told me, your shot wounded the bandit.'

'I should have slain him,' Josiah said. 'He might have done you some mischief.'

'I pray that is the last time in your life that you ever have to fire on another human.'

Josiah heard his father's words and wondered if they rang true in his own heart. Was it possible not to kill if one became a soldier? But that was a question he knew he could not ask his father at this time. For now, they were still in danger as they navigated the rugged track to the coast.

★

The Chinese store in Maytown exuded the exotic aromas of Asia. It was a place Charlie Goodson knew well from his dealings of stolen goods. The Chinese entrepreneur who controlled the labour force recruited from Southern China was able to sell on the ill-gotten property of murdered prospectors without a link to the gang responsible. The Chinese were the ghosts of the goldfields, resented but tolerated to an extent by the European population who had left them to find any small amounts of gold in the worked-over claims. Desperate Chinese peasants had been drawn to

Sin Chin San – the new mountain of gold – from their villages in southern China. They had little, and the sight of them jogging wearing only broad conical hats made of straw and loincloths while balancing bamboo poles containing pots of essential supplies was familiar to all on the Palmer fields.

Charlie was in extreme pain from his shattered hand, now a mangled piece of useless flesh. The opium had taken away some of the pain as he lay on a table in the depths of the gloomy Chinese shop.

'Wang knows what he's doin',' Charlie's compatriot said to reassure the wounded leader of the gang, sucking on the opium pipe.

The Chinese man known as Wang stared down at the shattered hand with a frown. He was in his mid-forties with the traditional ponytail down his back. He lifted Charlie's arm and laid it away from his side.

'What's the Chinaman doin'?' Charlie asked in a dreamy voice as the opium took hold.

'I dunno,' Martin replied and caught a glimpse of Wang holding a meat cleaver. Before he could make another utterance, the cleaver came down on Charlie's wrist, and his startled scream filled the small storage room. Charlie's hand fell from the table onto the hard earthen floor and before Charlie could struggle to sit up, Wang was pouring alcohol on the raw stump before producing a swathe of bandages to seal the amputation.

'Charlie lives,' Wang grunted, wiping the blood from his hands with a clean cloth.

Charlie fell back against the wooden table, panting from the shock. Sweat poured down his face and Martin was at a loss to react.

'I'm gonna kill the bastard who caused this,' Charlie gasped through gritted teeth. 'So help me, if it is the last thing I ever do.' Not only had the men they had planned to ambush and murder for their gold caused the loss of his hand but also the deaths of half his gang. It would take time to find ruthless men like himself to recruit for future ventures of death and destruction.

'You gotta get some rest, Charlie,' Martin said.

'I've got to get some rum,' Charlie replied, sitting up and placing his feet on the floor. From the corner of his eye, he could see the amputated hand at his feet, and he looked away. No matter what it took, he would wreak his revenge on those responsible for the trauma he had suffered.

'What are we gonna do now?' Martin asked.

'We are going to Cooktown,' Charlie replied. 'I know some lads there who I think I can convince to join us in a new gang. With any luck, we might find the bastards who are responsible for our losses here.'

'They are probably gone by now.' Martin shrugged.

'No matter,' Charlie said, wincing from the throbbing pain. 'We gotta get to Cooktown.'

★

Ian chose a thickly forested ridge for their campsite and ensured they were in a good position for all-round defence. The clash had shaken them, but they also knew they had won the skirmish and inflicted damage on the would-be bushrangers and Ian felt they were secure enough to establish a campfire.

Hamish heaved off the saddlebags containing the bags of gold dust and small nuggets and placed them at his feet. 'I should have told you, Ian,' he said apologetically. 'But I thought that the secret was safe.'

'That part of our venture was never brought up,' Ian growled. 'It could have cost my son his life.'

41

Hamish crouched down to check the bags for any damage. 'Josiah was as resolute as I have seen you under heavy fire,' Hamish said. 'You are fortunate to have such a brave young lad as a son.'

Ian accepted the praise for Josiah with a slight nod. His son had committed himself as bravely as any soldier Ian had once commanded. He glanced at Josiah standing a few feet away, gripping his Snider rifle. In these few days in the northern colony of Queensland, his son had seen the horrors of violent death and fought in a dangerous skirmish, saving Ian's life.

'Why are we conveying the gold?' Ian asked.

'Because we have to get it to a Chinese Tong in Cooktown,' Hamish replied.

'What in hell is a Tong?' Ian questioned.

'They are a Chinese secret society who have their hands in any illegal venture that produces wealth. The Tong at Maytown are rivals to the Cooktown Tong.'

'I have read that the Chinese emperor prefers silver to gold,' Josiah piped up.

'Ah, that is true, Josiah, but they also appreciate the value of gold if they can get their hands on it,' Hamish replied. 'I have learned from my time in Cooktown that the Tongs are not people you want to cross, and they put a great stake in loyalty. Mine is to Zhu in Cooktown.'

Ian stared with a frown at the former Scottish officer. How little he knew about Hamish, he mused. 'How did you get tangled with the Chinese?' he asked.

'I was approached by Zhu. He speaks passable English, and we had an interesting conversation. He struck me as a very astute and intelligent man, and he was able to convince me that he needed a European partner in some of his ventures. I should also add he is honest and generous in his dealings. We will receive handsome pay for delivering his gold.'

'We?' Ian queried. 'Since when has it been "we"?'

'You have shared the risks of this delivery and I feel as old friends that you should also share the rewards,' Hamish said.

'You mean share the same crimes,' Ian said with a bitter note in his voice. 'If we get caught with this obviously large amount of undeclared gold in our possession, we might end up in prison.'

'Not much chance of that,' Hamish said. 'Zhu gets the gold back to China almost on the same day we deliver.'

'I know that Customs are zealous in inspecting every nook and cranny in ships arriving and leaving,' Ian said. 'They are fully aware that the Chinese smuggle gold out of the Palmer.'

'Zhu smuggles the gold in the bodies of his workers who have died here,' Hamish said, crouching to poke a stick at the flickering flames of the campfire. 'Even Customs have not woken up to that yet. He oversees arranging their coffins for shipping back to their villages in China. Customs have searched the coffins without any success but are not aware of the gold carefully concealed inside the bodies. I can assure you that there is little to no chance of us being caught.'

Ian slumped down on a fallen log and stared at the dancing flames of the open fire. 'You could have told me before you took delivery,' Ian finally said.

'I know you established your own fortune from the spoils of war,' Hamish said mildly. 'It was hardly a secret that you and your men looted the Russian baggage train back in the Crimea in '54. It was a crime to not declare your finding then.'

'That was a long time ago and I was desperate for funds.'

'You have always taken on great risk and yet here you

are today as one of the most respected men in the colonies. What we are doing is a lot better than when you put your life on the line for the Queen.'

Josiah listened with fascination to the words being exchanged between the two former officers. He was hearing of a side of his much-loved and respected father's past life that surprised him. Captain Ian Steele had always been a man beyond reproach by his upper-class peers, despite the rumours of colourful stories from his time as a commissioned officer with the British.

'Just this one time,' Ian sighed. 'Then we return to the original plan to get heavy mining equipment to the fields.'

Hamish stood up and extended his hand. 'My promise as a former gentleman officer to another former gentleman officer.' Hamish grinned. Ian accepted the gesture with just a slight hesitation. It was only his concern for Josiah that gave him pause. But when he glanced at his eldest son, he thought for a moment he was looking back into the past at himself at the same age.

And he had to admit, life had grown a bit dull since he had left his old life behind.

★

They trekked onward without incident under the harsh tropical sun, meeting the occasional prospector walking up the track with a gleam of hope in their eyes and passing the would-be prospectors with little hope in their expressions as they stumbled back to Cooktown. They crossed the desolate regions and camped by the occasional lagoon, now muddied by the European and Asian strangers who desecrated the traditional hunting and fishing grounds.

They were only a day's ride from the seaport, riding along a steep ridge covered in tall rainforest trees, when

Ian suddenly stood in his stirrups, gazing around the bush. Something had attracted his attention, and his hand slid to one of the big Colts in his belt.

'What is it?' Hamish asked, bringing his mount up to Ian.

'Listen!' Ian hissed.

'*Hilf mir!*'

'I know what that means!' Josiah suddenly exclaimed. 'It is German for "help me".'

Both Hamish and Ian turned to Josiah, who had brought his mount up to join his father. Ian knew his son had a strong knowledge of French and German from his language studies at his prestigious private school. His mother had also taught Josiah Yiddish when he was younger, to assist him in his religious training at the synagogue.

'It could be some kind of trap,' Hamish said, sliding the shotgun from his leather rifle bucket.

The cry came once again, and the three could hear the note of pain and desperation in the foreign language. Josiah immediately slid from his saddle and snatched up his rifle before the two men could stop him. He ran to the side of the ridge, disappearing over the edge into the steep, scrubby gully beside the track. Hamish and Ian exchanged a glance then followed.

As soon as Ian reached the edge, he could see the over-turned covered wagon about a hundred feet below, entangled in small trees. Josiah was carefully making his way down with the agility of a strong young man. By the time Hamish and Ian reached him, they were out of breath and scratched up from the surrounding scrub. Ian immediately noticed a young woman lying against a tree with her head at an impossible angle. Ian knew she was dead, her opaque blue eyes staring without seeing the world around her. He carefully stepped around the wagon, gripping nearby small trees to prevent any further fall. A little further down, Ian saw that a horse, attached by a harness to the wagon, was also dead. Hamish and Josiah were kneeling beside a handsome young man crushed between the large wooden spoked wheel and a rocky ledge. From the way he was dressed, Ian guessed he was not just a poor immigrant in search of his fortune in this desolate part of the world. Josiah had a canteen of water and was assisting the man to sip from it. In a pain-racked voice, he spoke to Josiah and gripped his hand.

'What's he saying?' Ian asked.

'He said his wagon went over the edge at daybreak. He wants to know where his wife and daughter are.'

Ian looked his son in the eyes and shook his head.

'What do I tell him, Father?' Josiah pleaded.

'He is not going to live long,' Ian said bluntly. 'I have seen the same injury kill men in minutes after they have been crushed by wagons. We release him and he will die.'

Josiah turned to the trapped man and spoke. Ian could see a wave of relief sweep over the doomed man's face and knew his son had lied, the only comfort they could offer now.

'I found the mother,' Ian said softly to Hamish. 'She is dead, and I suspect that the daughter is also dead, further down the gully. Poor bastards.'

The slight sound of movement behind Ian made him grip one of his Colts. He spun around with the revolver levelled . . . at a girl, staring in shock at the scene before her. She wore a tattered dress, and her pretty face was smeared with dirt. A cut to her hand dripped blood onto the earth. Ian was taken by the blue brightness of her eyes, complemented by her long, golden hair; she was a younger version of the woman with the broken neck.

'God almighty!' he swore under his breath, lowering his pistol. 'This must be his daughter!'

The dying man broke into an agonised smile when he saw the young girl. She stumbled towards his outstretched arms, which enveloped her and held her as she sobbed. The three men were touched by the embrace of father and daughter.

'What do we do?' Josiah asked.

'We have to take the girl with us to Cooktown,' Ian said. 'There we can work out what we can do for her.'

'What about her father?' Josiah asked, glancing back at the German gripping his daughter in his arms.

'Nothing we can do for the poor bastard,' Ian said. 'I want you to take the girl up to our horses while the major and I release her father from under the wheel. We will not do that until the girl is out of sight. Tell her father that we will look after his daughter and find her a safe place with . . .' Ian paused. 'Tell him his daughter is with his wife.'

Josiah understood and turned to the dying man. He spoke and the man nodded his head. It seemed to Ian the man knew what was to happen.

'He says there's a satchel with important papers in the wagon, that they will need them,' Josiah said as the man pushed his daughter away from him. She protested in a shrill voice, but Josiah gripped her gently and assisted her up the steep ridge to the track above even as she cried out for her mother and father. When Ian was satisfied his son had reached the track with the girl, he turned back to the father.

Hamish took one side of the heavy wheel and Ian the other, and with all their strength they wriggled it off the man's stomach and legs, which Ian could clearly see were crushed. Ian reached out with his water canteen as the man continued to speak in German words neither Ian nor

Hamish understood. And then his eyes slowly closed. The toxins released from the crushed muscles had done their deadly work.

Without a word, both men made their way back to the track, leaving all behind except for the leather satchel of family papers the German had mentioned, which Ian found in the wagon and hoped might assist with the future of the girl. Ian had made the choice not to retrieve and bury the bodies while they had the young girl in their care as he felt it would only add to her grief.

Death was something both former soldiers were too well versed in. The discovery of the bodies would be duly reported to the police troopers in Cooktown, but Ian knew there was little they could do as their story was all too common on this wild and dangerous frontier.

FOUR

The young girl silently rode behind Josiah on his horse. Josiah attempted to question her as to her name in his basic German, but she appeared to be in a catatonic state, obviously aware of the fates of her parents.

They camped for the night not far from Cooktown and Ian issued the last of their rations as a billy of tea heated over the small campfire.

'Has she told you her name?' Ian asked Josiah as he leaned forward to pour the black brew into enamel mugs for all, including the forlorn girl, who sat on a log staring at the tiny trail of sparks rising into the night sky.

'Not a word,' Josiah answered. 'I think the satchel of papers might assist us.'

Ian retrieved the leather satchel with its official-looking documents. One was obviously a birth certificate and Josiah was able to decipher it.

'It seems that the girl is called Elise. She was born in Bavaria and is fourteen years old. Her parents were Anna and Paul von Meyer. I remember my German teacher informing us that the inclusion of "von" in the name indicates birth of some noble repute.'

'All that money I spend on your private education is paying off.' Ian grinned. He already knew that his son was at the top of his class academically and had proved himself an athlete in the boxing ring, as well as on the rugby field, but to see it play out in real life was very special.

'What will happen to her when we reach Cooktown?' Josiah asked, glancing up from the documents.

Ian took a sip of his black tea with a frown. 'I suppose we take her to the troopers when we report the death of her mother and father. Elise is an orphan now, so I suppose they will find an orphanage for her.'

Josiah turned to look at Elise sitting alone on the log, her expression vacant on her dirt-smeared face. 'Poor girl,' he said softly. 'Why don't we take her back to Sydney? I am sure there are better places there that can take her in. I doubt Cooktown has such an establishment as an orphanage.'

'You could be right,' Ian agreed. 'I am hoping you are able to convince Elise to eat and drink. Hopefully we will be able to outfit her with a new dress before we steam back. I am sure Major MacDonald will have contacts to that end.'

'Thank you, Father,' Josiah said, retrieving a can of sardines and some hardtack biscuits from their bag of supplies. He walked over to Elise, kneeling before her with the offering of the sardines on the biscuits, as well as a mug of black tea to wash them down. At first, she simply stared, but eventually, to Josiah's relief, she accepted the meal. Although it was a breakthrough, Josiah also sensed that it was not the time to initiate a conversation in his limited German.

Elise slept wrapped in a blanket by the fire. Just after midnight, the three men were woken by her sobbing. Josiah immediately went to sit beside her, softly using all the soothing German words he could remember. It seemed to work, and Josiah stayed by her until she eventually slipped back into sleep. He was still beside her when the sun rose over the tree-covered ridges of Queensland's northern frontier.

*

They rode into the bustling little township on the mouth of the Endeavour River mid-morning. Ian felt that after the solitude of the rugged bush Cooktown could almost pass for civilisation.

The first stop was the troopers, to report the tragic accident that had claimed the lives of Elise's parents. They assured him that they would send out a patrol to retrieve and bury the bodies. Then the travellers headed straight to the hotel Hamish owned for a proper wash and a big meal of roast beef with potatoes and gravy washed down by imported English beer. Elise and Josiah had lemonade with their meals.

Elise remained silent although she ate with better appetite, but she also attracted a little too much interest from the rough men eating in the pub's dining room for Ian's liking.

'That meal was worth the wait,' Hamish said, leaning back in his chair and patting his stomach. 'I think that I have an idea for our young guest,' he continued. 'The woman who runs the establishment next door is a friend . . .'

Ian looked sharply at Hamish. 'You don't mean what I think.'

'No, no!' Hamish hurried to interrupt what he knew was coming. 'Gertrude runs a more discerning house, and she has been a reliable source of information for me in the past. She can be trusted.'

Ian frowned. 'Elise would be exposed to some very unsavoury men.'

'I will explain the tragic circumstances surrounding Elise, and Gertie will be well paid to ensure that our young lady comes to no harm. Gertie has her own private accommodation on the premises, and we can explain it will only be for a couple of days until you travel south. I am sure Gertie will be able to arrange a decent dress and anything else Miss Elise may need.'

'Swear on the colours of your old regiment that Miss von Meyer will be safe,' Ian said, leaning menacingly forward over the table.

'I swear,' Hamish said. 'It is better that she does not stay here. I am not exactly set up for young girls of a tender age – you can see that when you look around.'

Ian nodded. 'We meet your lady friend now and temporarily settle Elise until Josiah and I depart. Then we rid ourselves of the goods in our possession as soon as we can, as they make me nervous.'

'That will be done before the sun goes down,' Hamish reassured him. 'I agree with you that while we are in possession of said goods, we are at risk.'

With the meal finished, the four left the dining room of Hamish's pub and stepped into the baking sun. Ian could see clouds billowing into tall columns and recognised the harbinger of a tropical storm. He would welcome the heavy rain to wash away the humidity and heat of the day.

Then they went into the establishment next door and he met Gertrude Wilson.

★

Josiah could not help noticing anew how little the young ladies were wearing when they entered the neighbouring building. He had heard whispered rumours in the corridors of his elite private school of carnal acts provided by women in the back alleys of Sydney, but nothing was specific. Now he had a clearer picture as men in different stages of intoxication followed the ladies upstairs.

'I have a favour to ask, Miss Wilson,' Hamish said politely as the four stood before a tall, regal woman with her arms crossed. Her face had been pretty once, but that was twenty years ago, and a bad choice of men had left visible scars.

'Ah, Major. You wish me to find a young lady for the handsome young man accompanying you?' Gertrude said, looking at Josiah. 'Or is it that you have a recruit for my stable of belles?'

'No, no!' Hamish said hurriedly. 'I would like to introduce Captain Steele and his son Master Josiah. The young lady is the survivor of a tragic accident on the track to Maytown, Miss Elise von Meyer. Her parents' wagon went over into a gully about a day from here and both were killed. She appears not to speak any English, but Master Josiah – who speaks some German – was able to discern she is Bavarian and fourteen years of age. We need to provide her a place to stay for the next forty-eight hours and will pay well for her care. She also needs a new dress. As you can see, the one she is wearing was damaged in the accident.'

Gertrude looked down at Elise, and Ian saw her stern visage soften noticeably. 'Young lady, you need a good wash and a new dress,' Gertrude said directly to Elise, who appeared puzzled. Josiah immediately translated and Elise looked to him. For the first time, she spoke in a torrent of words Josiah found hard to follow.

'What is it?' Ian asked his son.

'From what I can understand, Elise does not want to be separated from us.'

'Tell her that it is only for a couple of days, and then she will be travelling with us to Sydney,' Ian said. Josiah translated, but Ian could see from the expression on Elise's face that she was not convinced.

Then, to everyone's surprise, Gertrude spoke to Elise in halting German. Elise stared at her with round eyes before nodding.

Gertrude met Hamish's stare with an arched brow. 'When you run an establishment such as mine, you get all nationalities as customers. It pays to know a bit of their language.'

'You are truly a remarkable lassie, Miss Wilson,' Hamish said admiringly.

'The young girl will be safe with me,' Gertrude said, placing an arm around her shoulders. Ian was pleased to see that Elise did not appear frightened in the brothel owner's care and breathed a sigh of relief.

'Time to deliver the goods,' Hamish reminded Ian. 'But I think it might be wise to leave Josiah here for the moment until our business is completed.'

'I am happy to remain with Elise,' Josiah said. 'I will have an opportunity to speak with her about the circumstances that brought her to the colony.'

Satisfied that both his son and the orphaned girl would be safe, Ian departed the establishment with Hamish, frowning as the many young ladies in skimpy attire openly ogled his tall and handsome son.

'That boy of yours will break many a young lady's heart in the future,' Hamish said with a grin.

'I think he has already,' Ian replied.

★

Hamish led Ian down seedy back streets into a quarter obviously occupied by the Chinese. Above the stench of raw sewage they could detect the aromatic scents of opium and exotic Asian spices. Men with long traditional pony-tails tracked them with curious and sullen stares from the shanty-like buildings.

'More Chinese here now than the white men,' Hamish said. 'It's causing a few grumbles from the patrons at my pub.'

'They don't seem to be bothering anyone,' Ian said.

'That's because the local Tong has a firm grip on their behaviour,' Hamish said. He halted at a timber-plank building with a large sign over the front entrance written in Chinese. A tall, heavily built Chinese man stood with his arms folded at the entrance. He had a menacing expression on his scarred face which softened slightly when he saw Hamish.

'Zhu,' Hamish said, and the man stepped aside, allowing them entry into a dimly lit room cluttered with bales, boxes and coffins. Ian kept his hand on one of the pistols tucked into the belt of his trousers.

'Major Hamish,' a voice said from the dark recesses of the room. 'You have brought the package.'

Ian saw a middle-aged Chinese man step into the shaft of light allowed by the open door. He wore a western-style suit of good quality, and his English was particularly good, with hardly an accent.

'This is Captain Steele,' Hamish said, placing the heavy satchel on a wooden table. 'It is because of his help on the track down from Maytown that I was able to make the delivery. We ran into a bit of trouble, and if it were not for Captain Steele, the gold would have been in others' hands.'

Zhu looked at Ian, nodding his appreciation. 'We will ascertain its value,' Zhu said, opening the leather satchel and spilling the small chamois bags onto the table, along with a few gold nuggets. He placed each bag of gold dust on a set of scales, moving beads on his abacus as each bag was weighed, sliding the counters in a way that fascinated Ian. Then it was time to weigh the small nuggets, and Ian was aware that the big man who had been at the entrance was now in the room and standing behind them. Zhu finally finished, writing down a figure on a sheet of paper. Ian could see that Hamish was tense as he waited for Zhu to speak.

'Your share is two thousand guineas, Major,' Zhu said. Ian was stunned at the small fortune. 'Do you wish payment from the gold?'

'That would be good,' Hamish answered. 'It has a better feel than paper.'

Zhu pushed aside a small proportion of the gold nuggets into a pile and Hamish scooped them up into an empty chamois bag.

'I know about your incident with Goodson's men,' Zhu said. Hamish glanced up, surprised.

'How could you know?' he asked.

Zhu smiled for the first time. 'Our intelligence system is superior to that of you Europeans,' Zhu replied. 'I was informed this morning. I must warn you, Major, that Mr Goodson has vowed revenge for the loss of his hand. I was informed that he will be travelling to Cooktown to raise more men for his bandit gang. You must be very wary if you remain here. He is a dangerous man with much blood on his record.'

'Thanks for the warning,' Hamish said, pocketing the bag of gold. 'We will be careful.'

Hamish and Ian left the Chinese quarter and returned to Hamish's establishment.

'Zhu speaks exceptionally good English,' Ian said, sitting down at the small wooden table in Hamish's office as Hamish pulled out a bottle of gin and two glasses.

'He grew up in Hong Kong and worked for an English bank there,' Hamish answered, 'but felt that the Palmer fields offered more opportunity than working for the English bankers. I suspect that he is actually selling off his share to the same bankers in Hong Kong for a tidy profit. Needless to say, your share is half of what I was paid. You earned it. Zhu needs me as his contact here as it makes life easier for his Tong when I deal with the Europeans. As a matter of fact, I helped him purchase a European-owned hotel for the goodly sum of eight hundred pounds.'

Hamish placed the cotton bag on the table and spilled out the nuggets. He divided the pile into two relatively equal parts. 'You choose,' Hamish said.

Ian scooped up one of the piles. 'I remember in our soldiering days that there were rumours about you too,' he said with a smile, pocketing the nuggets.

'All probably true,' the Scotsman said, taking a long swig of his gin. 'I sold my commission before the army caught up with my dubious dealings and here I am. But you were no saint, if I remember rightly.'

'Touché.'

'I missed the danger we once faced and find that it is all here on this wild frontier,' Hamish sighed. 'Except this time, I make a lot of money. You know that there is no man I trust more than you as a partner.'

'I have a family to care for,' Ian said with some reluctance. 'And I have to return to them in Sydney.'

'Next time you return to see how our mining operations are proceeding, you might consider my offer of a partnership in other opportunities.'

'I will risk money but not my life,' Ian said. 'I have my two sons and a beautiful daughter who is so much like her mother. That is worth more to me than all the gold the Palmer might produce.'

'Getting to know Josiah, I can see that he is his father's son,' Hamish said. 'He too has a strong spirit for adventure.'

Ian grimaced. Hamish was uncomfortably perceptive and that worried Ian, who had a dream that his firstborn son would inherit the family enterprises and lead a life of comfort and safety.

★

It was with great relief that Ian stood at the stern of the small coastal steamer, watching the shoreline of tropical north Queensland recede in the early morning. The seas were calm, and the gentle breeze was a relief from the humidity of the coast. The last vestige of Cooktown was the smoke from cooking fires rising lazily over the river town. Ian was joined by his son, still stunned by the gift his father had given him the night before at Hamish's hotel – gold to the value of five hundred guineas.

'You earned it,' Ian had said as Josiah held the precious metal nuggets in his hand. 'You risked your life,' and then he had told his son how much it was worth.

It was a huge fortune, and Josiah had wondered if he was dreaming. Tears of gratitude had filled the corners of his eyes, and he had spluttered a thank you, both for the small fortune and for the fact the man he loved and admired had recognised his contribution as an adult in the grand and exciting adventure on the Palmer River.

'I am hoping that you understand it is your payment to be invested for the future,' Ian had continued. 'That you do so wisely, with the understanding that money makes money.'

Josiah was already reeling through ideas, knowing that this portion of the gold delivery could mean a certain amount of independence.

'It is a beautiful day,' Josiah said now, standing beside his father, gripping the rails as the steamer navigated the treacherous routes through the massive coral reef.

'I guess you will be pleased to return home to your brother and sister, and back to school with your friends,' Ian said, gazing at the disappearing coastline.

'I am,' Josiah answered. 'What will become of Elise?'

Ian turned to look at his son. 'I will arrange for her to be placed in a good orphanage or with a suitable family when we return to Sydney,' he replied.

'Why can't she stay with us?' Josiah asked. 'We have a big home and servants who can look after her. She would not be a bother, and I am sure Becky would love to have a big sister.'

Ian frowned. He had noticed how Josiah was bonding with the Bavarian girl, but life was not so simple.

'I will consider it,' Ian said. 'But I make no promises.'

He felt Josiah grip his elbow and smiled to himself. Even on the edge of manhood, his son was still a boy in many ways. It was obvious that he had a growing affection for the young girl and Ian knew that could lead to complications at their age.

FIVE

All the gold and adventure of the Palmer could not equal the sheer happiness Ian experienced when he walked through the front door of his harbourside mansion in Sydney.

Two overjoyed children ran and clung to him in a display of unrestrained love for the man who was the centre of their universe. Rebecca squealed her delight and Samuel – a little more formally – hugged his father. Josiah received a similar welcome.

The smiling servants watched the scene before offering their greetings.

'Welcome home, Captain Steele,' their butler Henry said with genuine warmth. Henry had also once been a young soldier serving with Ian. There was a mutual respect between the two men who had shared in the hardships and dangers of serving the Queen on faraway battlefields.

'I hope they behaved themselves,' Ian said to the children's governess, Irene. She was in her late thirties and the widow of another soldier Ian had once commanded.

'They have been absolute angels,' Irene replied with just a touch of humorous sarcasm. Ian winked at her.

'What have you brought back for me, Father?' Rebecca asked, tugging at Ian's elbow.

'Me,' Ian said with a broad smile and Rebecca immediately looked disappointed. Then Ian produced a packet of boiled sweets from his pocket and gave them to his beloved daughter. She uttered a gasp of delight and kept them close to her body so that Samuel could not share in her windfall.

With the exuberant welcome over, the two young children looked with curiosity at the pretty blonde girl standing behind their father and brother. They were not alone in their interest, as Irene and Henry were also wondering who the stranger was.

'This is Elise,' Ian said. 'She does not speak English because she is from Bavaria. Her mother and father were killed in an accident, and the poor girl is now an orphan. Elise will be staying with us for a short while. I will make enquiries with the German Consulate to see if we can find her relatives.'

'I am sure she will be welcomed by the staff, Captain Steele,' Henry said. 'Poor young lady.'

'I am sure another in my fold will be no bother,' Irene added warmly.

'Josiah will assist you, Irene, as he has a relatively good grasp of the German language,' Ian said as Josiah turned to Elise to explain the situation. She listened and Ian was pleased to see the tension leave her face.

The following day, Ian travelled into the city to visit the German Consulate. He was able to speak with the consul, showing him the official documents they had retrieved from the wagon.

The consul recorded the information and promised that he would endeavour to write to the German government in an attempt to locate any living relatives. The consul retained the original documents and Ian left with the hope that the search for Elise's relatives in Bavaria would be successful.

Ian stepped out onto the busy street, dodging big wagons harnessed to draught horses and Hansom cabs carrying paying passengers to their offices and homes. Ian hailed down a Hansom cab and was conveyed to his office overlooking Circular Quay where he was warmly welcomed by his staff. There would be meetings with lawyers and accountants to ascertain the finances of the Steele Enterprises, as well as a visit to the Australia Club to catch up with Ian's network of wealthy bankers, business owners and aristocratic squatters with their vast landed estates.

But what was at the back of Ian's thoughts was the fate of Elise. He wondered what his beloved wife Ella would have thought of the girl. Knowing Ella as he had, he already knew the answer.

*

Before Josiah returned to his school, Ian warned that he was not to speak of the events that had occurred in the colony of Queensland. Ian was firm on his son swearing an oath to that effect, as their time away might cause a whiff of scandal to the family name. Josiah understood that the five hundred guineas he had earned for his participation in the venture sealed the promise. But to Josiah, the battle-axe he had kept from the dangerous encounter in the north was a valued trophy, reminding him of another world so far-flung from Sydney's relative civilisation.

It was one of former Corporal Will Bowden's daily tasks to deliver and pick up Josiah from the private school in the city. Ian had carefully chosen the educational establishment for his son's education. The school had written into its charter that any colonial student could enrol, and he wanted Josiah to be able to mix with the sons of the colony's elite, regardless of his Jewish religion. But Ian also carried out his late wife's wish for a reluctant Josiah to regularly attend the synagogue and receive religious instruction in the faith of his Jewish ancestors.

Josiah dismounted from the horse-drawn carriage his family owned, glancing around at the many faces he knew as they entered the esteemed portals of the double-storeyed sandstone building.

'Josiah, old chum. How was the term break?' The question came from the cheery-faced friend he had known for years, Douglas Wade, a thin boy with red hair and freckles. His father was an influential banker and a friend of Josiah's father.

Josiah greeted his old friend with a smile. 'Good,' he replied. 'I travelled to north Queensland with my father and saw a real-life crocodile at Cooktown.'

Douglas looked impressed before his expression turned gloomy at the parade of boys filing through the entrance. 'I was hoping that Anderson would not be coming back.'

Josiah saw the person Douglas referred to surrounded by minions laughing at his jokes as they strode with purpose back to a new year of schooling. Horace Anderson was the school bully, a handsome young man from a wealthy family of squatters with tentacles in colonial politics and the judiciary. Josiah had stepped forward to defend the new boy – his now close friend Douglas – when he had come across Anderson picking on him. Anderson had backed off that time, but for years a running battle of animosity had persisted between Josiah and Anderson, who had a strong following of younger boys who worshipped their best rugby player.

Anderson looked over his shoulder and saw Josiah gazing at him.

'Hey, Jew Boy. Why aren't you at the synagogue with all the other Yids?' Anderson called.

'Ignore him,' Douglas whispered.

'I will.' Josiah smiled. 'It is possible that one day I will be able to convince him to join me at my athletics club and put on gloves for a round in the ring.' Josiah knew that the school bully had heard of his prowess at boxing, and that this had always kept him wary of a physical confrontation. The break in the summer months had toughened Josiah even more, both in fitness and spirit, and although Anderson was a year older, as well as taller and heavier, Josiah did not fear him. He had faced opponents in the ring who were taller, older and heavier, and he had stepped out the victor.

When Josiah returned from school that day, he immediately sensed something was not right. It was just a bad feeling. When he asked his young brother, Samuel, where Elise was, the boy simply answered that she was gone.

Josiah ran up the steps to his father's study, where he found him poring over papers on his desk.

'Where is she, Father?' Josiah demanded.

'I have spoken with the German Consulate, and they have found a German family who is happy to take Elise in until we are able to locate any family she may have in Bavaria,' his father answered.

'But you promised she could stay with us,' Josiah pleaded.

Ian rose from behind his desk and walked to his son, placing a hand on his shoulder. 'It was not easy for me to agree to the accommodation, but the young lady needs to be with those who speak her language. I have been assured that the family are good Christians and of sound character. They will assist with her education, and I have also sponsored Elise with our financial support. You will be able to visit her anytime you wish. I know that you may not truly understand my decision now, but I hope one day you will.'

'But Father –'

'The decision is made, Josiah,' his father replied firmly. 'At the moment, you see me as some kind of unfeeling ogre, but I can assure you that I am also very fond of Elise. It was not a decision that I came to without a lot of soul-searching.'

Josiah knew further protest was futile and stormed away in a cold fury. Why would his father have done this? At least there was the consolation that he would be able to visit Elise.

Ian sighed as his eldest son left the room. He could see that Josiah was becoming too attached to the orphaned girl and he reflected again that this could prove troublesome as time went on. Josiah was at an intense age when emotions rather than logic ruled.

★

The German Consulate scribbled a report of the girl rescued on the Palmer River Goldfields, then placed it in the mailbag for posting to the newly established German Empire under the rule of Kaiser Wilhelm of Prussia. The appointment of a German Kaiser had been made after the French capitulated to Bismarck's army in the Franco–Prussian war of 1870. Finally, all the small and large German-speaking states were now one nation.

The consular official had briefly wondered where the letter should be sent: to Bavaria, or the new capital of Berlin?

As a Bavarian, he still held the belief that Bavarians were Bavarians – and not Germans – but ultimately decided to send it to the new capital of Berlin, where the civil servants could sort the matter out. It was a simple decision which would have long-reaching consequences for the Steele family of the colony of New South Wales – especially Josiah.

★

The clash was short and bloody.

Before dawn, soldiers of Zhu's Tong from Cooktown silently crept upon an enclosure set atop a rise overlooking the track between Maytown and Cooktown. It was cleverly camouflaged, but its existence was well known in the Chinese communities of the Palmer. Zhu's men fell upon the sleepy guards in the stone-walled encampment with knives, hatchets and a couple of ancient muzzle loaders. The attacking party of around a dozen men outnumbered the seven defenders. Wild and terrified screams in Mandarin and Cantonese echoed in the wilderness of Queensland's northern forests, far from outsiders. As the sun rose across the Great Divide, blood splashed the dry red earth. The slaughter was over in minutes with the loss of only one of Zhu's men from a musket ball fired by one of the Chinese defenders.

Zhu's men quickly rummaged through the supplies and equipment until they found what they sought: four leather bags filled with gold dust. The uneasy peace between the two opposing Tongs had been terminated. From now on, only one Tong would dominate the Palmer.

News of the slaughter of his men reached Wang in Maytown days later. He knew that this was a declaration of war. Wang knew that his enemy was diverting gold to a secret society bent on rising against the foreign powers in their homeland, ridding them of over a century of military subservience. To the deluded Zhu, gold could be converted into modern weapons, arming rebels to fight the imperial puppets of the despised foreign powers. Zhu was indeed a strange man, in Wang's opinion, and his aspirations were lunacy: the present was all that mattered, not the future of a free China.

★

Former Rifleman Ryan Walsh stumbled into the township of Cooktown in the late afternoon. In his late twenties, the former soldier of the British army had officially been declared a deserter, but his flight from his regiment in Hong Kong was not an unusual occurrence in a time when a fabulous fortune could be made in the Great South Land. Tall and solid, the scars on his face were evidence of all the brawls he'd been part of in taverns and back alleys in the places his regiment had been posted across the British Empire. More than once he had lost his corporal rank due to his misdemeanours. He had always been a good soldier, but his natural intelligence told him there was no future in soldiering for the Queen. Ryan had always dreamed of having a family and life away from the terrors of the battlefield and the dreariness of the barracks. Here, it was possible to make his fortune.

But it had not gone as planned; misfortune on the goldfields had left Ryan destitute. The only person he knew who could help owned a pub and had also served the Queen on foreign battlefields – Major Hamish MacDonald.

'The Chinese had a big barney up in the hills not far from Maytown,' Walsh said, holding a bottle of English beer in his hands. The bar was filling with patrons as the sun set and a fiddle screeched, accompanied by raucous voices attempting to sing a sentimental song of Ireland.

Hamish gripped a tumbler of gin and tonic as he listened to the former British soldier relate the events of the Tong war. Hamish was aware of the big man's past, but this did not deter the Scot from accepting Ryan, as the Irishman had a reputation for courage and loyalty to those who had earned it. More than that, he was a natural leader and Hamish needed such men to work for him.

'Do you know for sure that Zhu was behind the attack?' Hamish asked, leaning forward.

'Pretty sure, boss,' Hamish's other Irish employee, Frank McNeil, interjected. 'It's all the talk around the Chinese quarter of the town here.'

McNeil was also a valued employee because he had a passable knowledge of Cantonese and Mandarin from his time working in southern China with an English trading company. He was not fluent but able to get his message across when Hamish needed an interpreter.

Walsh nodded and Hamish leaned back to reflect on the situation. Why had Zhu made a pre-emptive strike against his rival? The answer seemed obvious; he was out to have complete control of the gold smuggling to China. So where did that leave himself in the equation? Hamish mused with some anxiety. In the past, a European face had been required to assist with the colonial civil servants who governed the flow of gold for tax reasons. At best, Hamish might be cut out of the lucrative dealings in the smuggling operation; at worst, he would be found in a back alley with his throat cut. Cooktown was a lawless place at the best of times and the murder of a local hotel owner would hardly be noticed by the overworked legal system.

Hamish took a good cigar from his pocket, lit it and blew the aromatic smoke into the still air of his hotel bar. 'If you need a job and a place to stay, I have both for you,

Mr Walsh,' Hamish said, considering that he might need extra qualified men as protection in the near future.

'I would be thanking you, Major,' Ryan said, extending his hand. 'You can be sure you have my total loyalty and diligent service.'

'I know, Mr Walsh,' Hamish said, accepting the firm handshake from his new employee. 'The boys will get you settled, and tomorrow, you start work.'

'What would you be having me do?' Ryan asked.

'I will be fitting you out with a couple of firearms. You are now my official escort wherever I go outside these premises,' Hamish said. 'I know that you are remarkably familiar with firearms and handling yourself in a rough spot.'

Ryan nodded. That he was.

Hamish watched as Ryan was taken away to his new quarters and considered the future. War between Zhu and Wang could impact the establishment of the gold-mining company registered for a promising field not far from Maytown. Ian Steele was the main financial backer, with rock-crushing machinery to be delivered. For the moment, though, that project was of a secondary concern to the Scot's nefarious dealings with gold smuggling.

Damn the bloody Chinese and their Tongs! Hamish cursed. He finished his gin and tonic and considered writing a letter to Captain Ian Steele. But what would he say about the current situation?

SIX

Elise had been placed with a former Prussian gunsmith and his wife in the city. Otto Schmidt and his wife Karla were middle-aged and childless, and Otto had made a good living in his gunsmithing trade over the last ten years in Sydney. The couple welcomed Elise into their home above the gun shop as if she were their natural daughter, and were appreciative of Ian's generous payments made to assist in Elise's support.

Josiah would visit each weekend and was also welcomed by the Prussian couple, who were impressed by his natural charm and the fact he spoke German. Josiah also endeared himself to Otto with his depth of knowledge about guns. During their first meeting, Josiah showed great interest in one of the repeating rifles Otto had imported from the USA, an 1866 model Winchester that fired a .44 calibre Henry rimfire cartridge. Josiah held the rifle, moving the lever action loader/ejector.

'We could have done with one of these when we were on the Palmer,' Josiah said.

'Ah, but it is only accurate up to two hundred yards, my young friend,' Otto said.

'That was within the range that we encountered the threats to our lives,' Josiah replied, reluctantly passing the rifle back to Otto.

'Did you encounter the black savages of the north?' Otto asked.

'We did – and others who would do us harm. I had my Snider and my father his Colts. We were fortunate in both clashes.'

Otto now gazed at the young man with new respect. 'Please, join me for coffee,' Otto said, and the two retired to the small but comfortable sitting room decorated with portraits of relatives on the multicoloured paper-lined walls.

'Elise is not of our Lutheran faith,' Otto said when Karla placed mugs of strong coffee on a small table. 'She is a Catholic. I feel that Elise should be granted access to her church for services.'

Josiah was surprised at this information, as it had not crossed his mind to ask. 'I could take Elise to the Catholic cathedral for Sunday services,' Josiah said. 'It is not far from here.'

Otto smiled. 'If I granted your wish, my wife should chaperone you both.'

Josiah understood the tradition for young ladies to be escorted in public ensuring no dishonour could be linked to their name. Now it was time for Josiah to smile. 'So, a good Lutheran woman attends a Catholic church in the company of a Catholic girl and Jewish boy,' he said with a wry smile.

'If that must be, it is God's will.' Otto sighed. 'Elise is a highly intelligent young woman whose knowledge of the English language is improving each day, just as your grasp of German has improved since we first met you.'

'We help each other,' Josiah said with a shrug. 'My father hopes that Elise will be able to attend one of the better private schools in the near future if she does not return to Bavaria.'

'It is as if your father views Elise as another daughter,' Otto said. 'He has shown a great interest in supporting her.'

'My father is very much involved in charitable causes,' Josiah replied. 'He is well known in the colony for such beneficial contributions. My mother was his inspiration.'

Elise entered the sitting room in the company of Karla. Both women were dressed in their finest Sunday dresses and Josiah could see a kind of serenity in Elise's expression.

'My husband has informed you of our small dilemma,' she said. 'Concerning Elise's spiritual needs.'

'He has, Frau Schmidt,' Josiah said, rising to greet the two women. 'We discussed escorting Elise to St Mary's Cathedral for Sunday services.'

Karla frowned but nodded her head. 'We will do that, Master Josiah.'

And so, the practice of taking Elise to Sunday mass became a fixture, where Josiah simply stood, knelt and sat during the service without intoning prayers or singing hymns. He at least understood the Latin service, as it was a language he was compelled to learn at his prestigious school, though he held little interest in the dead language. Mrs Schmidt had more trouble, as the icons displayed throughout the cathedral were contradictory to the austere Lutheran church she regularly attended with Otto. But for the sake of Elise, she also feigned compliance with the papist service.

Sundays also became a time when the four would take picnics, strolling in the sprawling Hyde Park, listening to the military bands playing popular tunes. On a couple of occasions, they took ferry rides to dock at the village of Manly on the northern side of the harbour, wandering the beaches barefooted.

Ian was aware that his son took an exceptional interest in Elise's welfare but was also assured by the Schmidts that he was the perfect gentleman.

Josiah was drawn to Elise because she was different from all the other girls he knew from contacts his school had with the privileged young ladies of colonial society from other private schools, the daughters of the colonial elite.

Elise told stories of a childhood spent in a castle with her parents, and Josiah was happy to indulge her in this fantasy. No doubt Elise had, for whatever reason, retreated to a make-believe world after the terrible accident, and Josiah accepted her imaginary stories as a means of avoiding the tragedy that had haunted her young life.

*

The night was moonless and the ground muddy from one of the rare winter downfalls in the official dry season at Maytown.

The German geologist, Gustaf von Kroth, staggered from the public house in his usual state of intoxication. He knew the path to his tent, drunk or sober, and reeled through the darkness of the night in that direction. He did not see Charlie Goodson step from behind a scrub tree, accompanied by two shadowy figures.

'Good eve'n, Dutchie,' Charlie greeted him, causing the German geologist to stop in his tracks, his alcohol-sodden mind recognising the voice.

'Vot do you vont?' he asked cautiously.

'To give you a message from Wang,' Charlie said, stepping forward.

Kroth did not see the knife but felt the sudden pain in his chest. He staggered back and collapsed in the mud, the knife hilt protruding from his chest. The German gasped once but his eyes rolled back in death as the blade had sliced through his heart.

'Even with one hand, I can still put a knife where it is meant to go,' Charlie said, leaning over the dead man and yanking the blade from Kroth's body. 'Drag the Dutchie into the scrub,' Charlie said, wiping the knife on the leg of his rain-soaked trousers. 'It won't matter if the traps find him. A lot of death around the Palmer and no one saw us.'

Charlie's two accomplices obeyed his order, dragging the dead man a hundred yards to a small gully where he was rolled down. They guessed that the aerial scavengers would find Kroth before his absence was noted by the publican of his favourite bar.

The war over gold smuggling had forged unusual alliances. But Charlie and his newly formed gang were not finished. There were others to be eliminated amongst the Europeans connected to Wang's now sworn enemy, Zhu.

News of the German geologist's murder reached Hamish within weeks, and he did not have to ponder on its meaning. It was already well known in the Chinese quarter of Cooktown that the two main Tongs were at war, and it confirmed Hamish's fear that he was caught in the crossfire. He knew that it would reach Cooktown and he had to be prepared with his tiny army of four.

Hamish sat at the desk in his office, wondering if now was the time to write that letter to his business partner in Sydney and alert him to the dire situation. But what could he write? That Hamish's illegal source of income had come to a bloody halt?

*

The dark clouds of impending danger were far from Captain Ian Steele's thoughts when he attended a tea party at a business friend's luxurious estate at the fringe of the village of Parramatta. Ian had chosen to travel by the steam train from central Sydney to the village, where a horse-drawn gig provided by his host took him to the estate. Sir Godfrey Pollard owned a two-storeyed sandstone house surrounded by neatly manicured gardens, a tennis court and riding stables.

Ian stepped down from the gig and was met by an elderly butler. 'Captain Steele,' he said. 'Sir Godfrey is with his guests in the garden. I will announce your arrival.'

Ian was dressed in a fine suit and wore a hat. He followed the butler to an area surrounded by rosebushes, imported exotic trees and shrubs, where a marquee had been erected with tables laid out with expensive food. Champagne and various wines were also in abundance, served in crystal goblets.

Ian would have preferred a cold beer but accepted a flute of champagne from one of the elegantly dressed waiters. He had hardly taken a sip when he was joined by a portly man.

'Sir Godfrey,' Ian greeted him. 'Thank you for the invitation to your grand soiree on this beautiful winter's day.'

'Captain Steele, it was good that you could join my excuse for a tea party, what.' Sir Godfrey Pollard extended his hand in a welcoming manner. 'I am sure that my guests prefer champagne to tea.'

Ian smiled. He was aware of the older man's reputation as an old goat with an eye for pretty young girls, and tea was not his preferred beverage.

'I presume Lady Pollard is here?' Ian asked, a sly hint at the older man's womanising reputation.

'Ah, yes,' Godfrey answered, shifting slightly in his embarrassment. 'A fine lady, my dear wife. I think I last saw her in conversation with our neighbour a short time ago. But I invited you here today to discuss your investment in a gold mine in Queensland. I hear that fortunes are being made on the Palmer.'

'Only by a handful of fortunate men,' Ian replied. 'The time has come for large-scale mining operations using heavy machinery.'

Sir Godfrey was about to ask further about Ian's latest venture when his butler, hovering nearby, signalled to the landed gent that he was required elsewhere. Sir Godfrey apologised to Ian and followed, leaving Ian alone with his flute of champagne. When Ian scanned the guests, he recognised many familiar faces of the colony's most notable personages. Amongst the guests were also prominent members of the judiciary and even the police commissioner.

His eyes fell on a lady who stood out for her beauty and long silk dress. Ian guessed that she was probably in her late forties. She was standing alone, as the man she had been in conversation with had left her with an empty crystal flute, seeking a refill. Ian was only ten paces from the striking woman with golden tresses piled under an expensive hat.

As if aware that she was under observation, she turned her head to stare back at Ian, who suddenly felt as if he had intruded on her privacy. Their eyes locked and an expression of puzzlement crossed her face, and Ian suddenly experienced the shock of realisation that he had seen her before. From what he could see, she felt the same.

It was Ian who made the first move and walked with almost shaky legs to where she stood. 'Please excuse my boldness but I feel that we have met before,' Ian said, frowning. 'You remind me of a young girl I once knew when I lived not far from here, many years ago.'

'You could not be the young blacksmith, Ian Steele?' the woman replied, and it all came rushing back to Ian.

'Isabel MacHugh!'

The woman looked flustered, and Ian hoped that she would not faint.

'You *are* Ian Steele!' she said. 'But I am no longer Isabel MacHugh,' she added, the little colour in her pale face waning even more. 'I was married to John Halpin, who you may remember. I still remember how you defended my honour at a picnic we had by the river. At the time, I did not condone your use of violence, but I never forgot it was you.'

Ian shook his head, a broad smile crossing his face. 'Mrs Halpin, it was so long ago.' For the moment, the world had shrunk to just two people in the garden of flowers and shrubs. He was in the company of the woman he had once had a great crush on but who had been outside his social circle; she, the daughter of landed gentry, and he, the son of a convict mother and a tradesman, wielding a hammer in the heat of a blacksmith's shop.

'I am a widow, so please call me Isabel,' she said. 'After all, we were once childhood friends. What should I call you, Captain Steele?'

'You know of me?' Ian countered in his surprise.

'Who has not heard of your mysterious and colourful past, Captain Steele?' Isabel replied with a warm, mischievous smile.

'As we were friends in our youth, I think the formality is not required. I am just Ian to you.'

'I could almost imagine that we were young again,'

Isabel said. 'But, alas, so much has occurred since those happier days.'

'Do you have children?' Ian asked, and saw the disappointment in Isabel's face. He regretted the awkward question, but Isabel replied. 'I do not. My deceased husband had a liking for young men.'

Ian sensed that Isabel would not have confessed her secret to just anyone and felt a strange bond with her. All he could do was bow his head and respond softly, 'I'm sorry.'

'It is not anyone's fault,' Isabel said. 'It is just the way some men are. I learned to be a good wife when we were together in public and wile away the years in charitable works. I heard that your wife sadly passed away and that you have three children.'

'Yes. Two boys and a would-be princess,' Ian said. 'I think that you would like them.'

'I am sure I would,' Isabel said with a smile. 'I would also like to hear of your life since that day you simply disappeared from our lives in the village. No one seemed to know where you were until you finally returned to New South Wales, and stories followed of the Queen's Captain who had fought in exotic places such as the Russian Crimea, along the banks of the Euphrates, in India and even in New Zealand.'

Ian was surprised to hear Isabel speak of his past life with so much knowledge. He was flattered. But the bubble of intimacy was burst when Isabel's companion returned with a full flute of champagne.

'Hello, old chap,' the man about Ian's age said. 'I don't think we have met.'

Ian felt just a touch of jealousy for this other man, who was tall and handsome with flecks of grey in his dark hair.

'This is the well-known Captain Steele,' Isabel said. 'You may have heard of him, Harold.'

'Ian Steele,' Ian said, offering his hand. The other man's grip was weak and clammy.

'Harold Skinner. I am a good friend of Sir Godfrey. I must say, I have not heard of you, old chap,' he replied.

Ian knew this was probably a lie if he was friends with Sir Godfrey, who often spoke about Ian to his friends. Ian suspected the man was not going to admit to knowing Ian's reputation in front of Isabel.

'I should mix with Sir Godfrey's friends,' Ian said. 'It has been a pleasure meeting you again, Isabel, after such a long time.'

'I feel that we should meet again and reminisce about the old days in the near future,' Isabel said, passing Ian her card.

'That would be grand,' Ian said, exchanging it for one of his own. 'Possibly a dinner in the city soon?'

Ian could see the dark expression on Harold's face when he departed. Ian's use of Isabel's first name had disturbed the pompous man. Worse still was Isabel's suggestion that she should meet Ian in the future.

As Ian strolled away, he experienced a mix of emotions. Guilt for allowing the memory of his beloved late wife to be forgotten for even a moment in time, yet a warmth for the strange connection he felt with Isabel, especially when he admitted to himself that he very much wanted to see her again. He could not fathom how Isabel MacHugh could stir these feelings he had thought were dead.

*

Harold Skinner glowered after the man departing. 'Damned rude of him to presume that he should make contact with you,' he growled. 'I should give him a thrashing for his impertinence.'

'Harold, dear man,' Isabel said sweetly. 'It was I who made the offer to meet again. He is, after all, a childhood friend from my village. And it may not be a good idea to attempt a confrontation with a man who has a reputation for killing many men in combat.'

Harold did not reply, knowing full well that the man walking away from them was indeed known for his personal bravery on the battlefield. However, there were other, subtler ways to eliminate a love rival.

★

Harold Skinner was never a man praised by his peers. Despite his charm and good looks and lofty position as a civil servant working for the colonial governor of New South Wales – a position that provided him with access to many secrets of the rich and powerful members of colonial aristocracy – he was known to be petty and vindictive.

He sat in his office of expensive wooden panelling, brooding. His rival for Isabel Halpin's favours, Captain Ian Steele, had apparently left Sydney, and Harold was determined to be rid of the man from his social circle permanently. Until the infamous Captain Steele had arrived, she had been enamoured of him. Skinner knew Isabel was the colony's best catch – a widow with a considerable fortune and a beauty to boot. So often had he dreamed of ravishing her body until she cried out in pain, as the others he had bedded had done.

Harold Skinner had the razor-sharp mind of a man who had spent his adult life formulating bureaucratic schemes and regulations governing the populace. He had connections to the influential members of the ruling class; it would be easy to launch a smear campaign to bring Captain Steele down. Bit by bit, he would bring that high and mighty soldier down to his knees, making him grovel in surrender.

Harold steepled his fingers and smiled, leaning back in his expensive office chair. For one thing, Captain Steele had once been married to a Jewess and it was known his children were being reared as Jews, despite the fact Steele was supposed to have been Christian born. Not anything of great consequence, but it would be the first building block in his rumour campaign.

SEVEN

Ian Steele gazed with admiration at the landscape painting of Apsley Falls. The artist's work was well known to him. Conrad Martens had shown his numerous landscapes of Sydney and of exotic places he had visited in previous exhibitions.

Ian stood in the Clarks Assembly Hall in Elizabeth Street with Isabel.

'It is beautiful,' she said beside him. 'It is well worth the fifty pounds we paid to gain it for our growing collection.'

Ian found he admired her all the more, as this was just one of the many public services she volunteered for. 'I have promised myself that one day I will purchase one of his watercolours.'

'Do you prefer watercolours to oils?' Isabel asked.

'I find them less sombre,' Ian replied.

'Captain Steele,' Isabel laughed softly. 'I would not take you for a man of such cultural sensitivity.'

Ian felt a rush of blood when he realised that she had impulsively slipped her gloved hand under his arm but then gently removed it. Neither commented on the intimate gesture.

'I feel that you and I should retire to a teahouse for refreshments,' Ian suggested. 'It is warm and the teahouse I know is a cool retreat.'

Isabel turned to Ian with a warm expression. 'I would like that,' she said, once again slipping her hand under his arm, but this time leaving it there.

Ian knew that this woman had entered his life from the past with a promise of a long friendship. *But could it be more?* he asked himself, hardly daring to think about the future. The memory of Ella still echoed daily in his thoughts. Was it possible that he could find love again at his age? The thought stayed with Ian as they made their way to the street where Ian's carriage, manned by Will Bowden, awaited.

'Where to, Cap'n Steele?' Will asked cheerily. Ian gave directions and assisted Isabel to step up into the single-horse carriage.

They sat in comfortable silence as their transport passed by the shoddy weatherboard buildings in need of repair on Market Street. But Ian could feel the tension like electricity between them on the short journey, an almost desperate desire to touch – but did she feel the same?

Talk resumed when they reached a small but pleasant teahouse that had a warm and welcoming ambience. Tea was ordered and Isabel removed her gloves. Ian suddenly realised how awkward he felt in her presence, taking this as a sign the woman opposite him had unsettled his life – but in a nice way.

They chatted about trivial matters, but Ian was impressed with Isabel's investments in real estate. She had farming land that was being sold in the Five Dock, Canterbury and Bankstown areas for residential subdivisions and Ian guessed that she was truly a woman of astute business sense. He also guessed that her wealth must be considerable, and that her late husband had been her benefactor, as she had inherited his financial resources. But her money did not matter to Ian. All he saw across the tiny table was a beautiful woman who, thirty years earlier, he had had a crush on. Now he was forced to confront that it was becoming something much more.

★

The letter posted in Cooktown by Hamish finally arrived at Ian's address in Sydney just as summer arrived again, and Ian pondered his decision after he read the contents. Sitting in his library, he could hear the shrill screams of his beloved daughter as she ran down the hallways, chased by her brother, followed by the chiding voice of their governess demanding that Samuel surrender the frog he was threatening his sister with. Ian smiled at the banter outside his door. Oh, if only Ella could be with him now to share all these moments.

The door to his study was flung open and Becky launched herself onto his lap. 'Daddy, save me!' she gasped breathlessly. Behind her in the doorway stood a grim-faced Irene holding Samuel by the ear, a squirming frog in her other hand.

'The situation is in hand, Captain Steele,' Irene said.

Ian nodded with a smile. 'I am sure it is, Irene,' he replied as Becky snuggled into her father's protective chest. 'I think that Samuel should be shown to his room until he is ready to apologise to his sister, and the frog returned to the garden.'

'Yes, Captain Steele,' the governess replied, gesturing to Becky to go with her, which she did, reluctantly.

With his solitude returned to him, Ian gazed at the letter lying on the table. He knew he would need to make a fast decision on whether he should return to the Palmer or remain in Sydney. The thought of his family urged him to stay but he also had to consider that an old comrade called for help in what Ian knew was a dangerous situation. He went to his whisky cabinet and poured himself a straight shot. This he drank in four gulps, letting the alcohol roll through his body.

He was reluctant to take time away from his children – although Josiah could no longer be called a child. He had well and truly proved himself on the trip they had shared to the Palmer the previous summer. Ian was torn between the old desire for dangerous missions and the need to be a good father.

Ian slid open the bottom drawer of his big desk and gazed down at the twin Colt revolvers lying next to the engraved metal powder container and box of cartridge primers. Strange, he thought with a wry smile, they were so much a part of his past and present life.

The former British army officer knew what his decision would be as there was still a small flame that he had been unable to put out since he had left the service of the Queen. Ian made his choice, knowing that he could not travel north until the wet season was over. He still had Christmas with his children – and with Isabel.

★

Ryan Walsh wiped away the sweat from his brow and entered Hamish's hotel in Cooktown. He had gone up the track to Maytown on horseback and had narrowly avoided a long spear hurled from the surrounding scrub early one morning. The Merkin warriors had dispersed when he had laid down six shots from one of the Tranter revolvers which Hamish had supplied for the journey. Shaken but still alive, Ryan had wended his way back down the track until he reached Hamish in Cooktown.

'It is bad,' Ryan said as Hamish passed him a bottle of English beer to slake his thirst. 'Wang has put Goodson and his men on his payroll. From what I heard around Maytown, you and Goodson have met before.'

Hamish took a swig from his own bottle as the two men sat in Hamish's cramped office, cluttered with papers and bound folders.

'I was with Captain Steele and his son Josiah when we were ambushed by that man and his cronies some months ago.'

'Apparently, Goodson lost his right hand when you were ambushed. He has sworn to kill the man who caused it.'

'It wasn't a man but the lad, Josiah Steele, who shot Goodson.'

'Goodson has already asked questions and worked out who shot him,' Ryan said. 'He has sworn to settle accounts if he ever comes across the lad.'

'That is not likely,' Hamish replied. 'After the first time the boy was here, I strongly doubt that Captain Steele will ever allow young Josiah to return to the Palmer. But what is the situation as far as you can ascertain?'

Ryan finished his bottle of beer and sighed with the pleasure of the brown ale. 'It appears that Wang has cut you out of any future dealings, Major,' Ryan replied.

'So has Zhu,' Hamish said bitterly. 'If that damned treacherous Chinaman Zhu had not broken our lucrative partnership in smuggled gold, I could have amassed a tidy sum in the bank. The local authorities have little interest in the goings-on of the Chinese here and leave them to their own devices. They have always kept to themselves and avoided us as much as possible. But the Tongs are a different story.'

'What are you going to do, boss?' Ryan asked.

'I have not received an answer to a letter I wrote some time ago to Captain Steele,' Hamish confided. 'But he will be steaming up to Cooktown soon enough to review the progress of the mining machinery. The only problem is that from the last report I had from the Yankee, the machinery has not reached Maytown and I don't know why, although I have my suspicions.'

'From what you have told me, boss,' Ryan said, 'the captain is an honest businessman. I doubt he would be interested in getting his hands dirty with your smuggling scheme.'

Hamish smiled. 'There is more to Captain Steele than you know,' he said. 'He was born a couple of centuries too late. In the past, he would have made a good captain on a privateer, cruising the Caribbean. He was never cut out to sit in an office, growing old. In the meantime, you and I will be travelling to Maytown to sort out the problems there with getting the crushing machinery going. We will have to leave very soon before the wet arrives and cuts us off from Maytown. Frank can remain here to look after any matters that might arise in our absence. Make arrangements and inform Mexican Jack that he will also be in our party and ensure that we carry the best firepower we have for the trek.'

Ryan glanced at his boss. 'Do you expect trouble?' he asked.

'Better to be prepared for any enemy – Merkin or Chinese.'

★

It was Josiah who noticed that his father was often absent from his office in the city and even on the occasional weekend leading up to Christmas. When he once asked his father where he was on those occasions, Ian was vague in his reply and Josiah did not push the matter. He spent his free weekends with Elise at the Schmidts'.

Josiah was sixteen now and the coming year would be his last year of school. He had topped his class in academic subjects and excelled at the school sports of athletics and swimming. He was also gaining a reputation as a boxer at the athletics club and had won more bouts in the ring than he had lost, and to more experienced fighters.

Josiah was hardly aware that he was a favourite with the colony's young ladies – and even their mothers! Invitations were regularly sent to the Steele residence to attend afternoon tea parties at influential gatherings, and Ian was surprised that his son always turned them down. For a fleeting moment, Ian wondered if his son was like his old friend Samuel Forbes, whose identity Ian had assumed so many years earlier to become a commissioned officer in the British army. Ian knew that Samuel had preferred the company of other men, though it was never mentioned in polite company. And then Ian remembered his son's friendship with Elise, who was thriving in the care of the Schmidt family. He was aware that the treasured friendship took up a lot of Josiah's free time.

Ian felt a cloud of guilt for the time he spent in Isabel's company, which was at every opportunity he could manufacture. Whenever they were together, it felt as though they had known each other for a lifetime, and the friendship tipped over into love one evening when Ian was invited to share a meal at her estate just outside the now sprawling city, creeping westward towards the Blue Mountains.

Ian held Isabel in his arms and they gave in to their mutual desire in the wonderful universe that was her bed. The little guilt Ian still held over the memory of Ella was washed away in the physical act of becoming one creature with the woman in his arms.

When the sun rose across the fields filled with spring flowers outside Isabel's bedroom, Ian recalled words of a poem by the Elizabethan poet, John Donne, and softly recited the first verse of 'The Good-Morrow' to the woman in his embrace.

> *I wonder, by my troth, what thou and I*
> *Did, till we loved? Were we not weaned till then?*
> *But sucked on country pleasures, childishly?*
> *Or snorted we in the Seven Sleepers' den?*
> *'Twas so; but this, all pleasures fancies be.*
> *If ever any beauty I did see,*
> *Which I desired, and got, 'twas but a dream of thee.*

Isabel touched Ian's face and he could see tiny tears at the corners of her eyes. 'I remember when, so long ago, you and Samuel were the only two men I knew who could appreciate the beauty of poetry,' she said. 'You are such an enigmatic man that I doubt a lifetime with you would reveal a fraction of the soul of Captain Ian Steele.'

'I was jealous of Sam when we were young and picnicked at the river. You seemed to be so enamoured of him,' Ian said with a smile. 'But later I would learn that my friend had no designs on you.'

'I was not enamoured of him,' Isabel said, pushing Ian playfully away from her. 'I was a confused young girl whose parents insisted that he would be a good husband because of his family wealth. You were a mere blacksmith and in my foolish snobbery, I was unable to entertain thoughts of any future between us.'

'And now?' Ian asked. 'I am no longer a *mere* blacksmith. In fact, the colony perceives me as a gentleman of means.'

Isabel laughed at this. 'I still remember how – even then – I felt an unnatural desire for you when you confronted those bullies with brute strength that day by the river. I must confess that I was disturbed by what could be called erotic dreams of you that same night. I often wonder how unbridled passion may have led me back to you.'

Ian gazed into Isabel's eyes and could not detect any deceit in her words. What might have become of his life if he had remained in the village in the shadow of the mighty hills to the west? But he had left, and ten years of his life had been a lie that had provided the basis of his current wealth.

★

Christmas Day at the Steele mansion was celebrated in the traditional style. It was a day when all the staff were treated to a feast and gifts from the master of the house. Ian ensured that everyone, from the stable boy to his head butler, was seated at the great dining table and that he and his family served them delicious courses of fresh fish, and roasted joints of lamb and beef as well as a turkey slow-roasted in the kitchen, which was a hellhole on the hot summer's day. Laughter and goodwill filled the hallways and rooms of the big house while sherry, gin and cold beer were served. Ian and his family joined the feast when all their work was done.

Will Bowden, fortified by one or two tots of gin, staggered to his feet and raised his glass. 'A toast to Captain Steele and his family,' he said, and this was followed by, 'Hear, hear!' from those seated.

Ian rose and thanked all at the table for the wonderful

service they had provided, then indicated it was time to pass out the presents, to squeals of delight from the women who received new dresses, and grunts of satisfaction from the men for new boots.

The afternoon saw the lunch party break up and the staff retire to sleep off the huge meal and alcohol, allowing Ian to share time with his children under the shade of the evergreen trees planted on the grounds of the estate. A couple of children of the staff about the age of Samuel and Becky played hide-and-seek while Josiah and Ian sat on a garden bench in the shade, sipping on cool lemonade. Ian was never a big drinker and the freshly squeezed lemon drink was refreshing.

It was Josiah who first noticed the expensive carriage on the gravel driveway to the house. He shaded his eyes and turned to his father. 'It appears that we have an unexpected guest, Father,' he said.

Ian rose from the bench. 'Not an unexpected guest, son,' he said, ignoring Josiah's puzzled expression and striding towards the carriage, with its single passenger holding a parasol against the sun.

'Isabel, I am so pleased that you could accept my invitation to be with us on this day,' Ian said, assisting Isabel from the carriage.

'I must admit, my love, that I am incredibly nervous about meeting your children,' Isabel said when she had alighted. 'But I brought gifts as a way of introducing myself to them.'

Ian directed the carriage man to take the horse and coach to the stables while he escorted Isabel back to the garden.

'Josiah, this is Mrs Isabel Halpin, an old friend of mine.'

Josiah nodded his acceptance of the introduction and mumbled that he was honoured to meet a friend of his father.

'Children,' Ian called. 'Please come over here and meet a special lady who might have brought you presents.' Ian knew the latter part of his statement would bring Sam and Becky running – which it did.

'I am very pleased to meet you both,' Isabel said with a warm smile at the two children gazing up at her with intense curiosity. 'My man will fetch the presents for you.'

Ian turned to Josiah. 'I think Mrs Halpin would enjoy a refreshing lemonade.'

'Yes, Father,' Josiah replied, snapping himself out of the stupor the appearance of the strange woman had brought on. Possibly the very pretty lady was the reason that his father had been absent on many occasions recently, Josiah mused as he went to the kitchen. He smiled as he poured the drink and was pleased to see the expression of happiness on his father's face when he returned with the glass for Isabel. Josiah knew how much pain the passing of his mother had caused and to now see his father almost boyish in the presence of this woman made him feel much older.

'Your father has informed me of your adventures earlier this year on the Palmer,' Isabel said, accepting the glass from Josiah. 'He told me of your extreme bravery under fire and how you saved his life.'

The statement by Isabel almost floored Josiah, as his father had said what happened in the north was not to be repeated to anyone. That this woman was obviously important to his father and should shower him with praise flattered Josiah.

'It was not a great matter,' Josiah said, almost spluttering in his surprise.

'Oh, no,' Isabel quickly interjected, touching him gently on the shoulder. 'Your father explained that on two occasions you had to fight for your survival. You are truly an extraordinary young man.'

Josiah blushed at the ongoing praise. He already knew that he would be giving his blessing to his father to be in the company of this beautiful, charming woman. It was just a matter of explaining to his siblings that the beautiful lady might have an important role in the future of the family.

It was the best Christmas Day both the Steele family and staff had experienced since the passing of Ella Steele *née* Solomon.

EIGHT

Ian broke the news to his children at the dinner table and his two youngest looked sorrowful.

Josiah simply said, 'I will be travelling with you, Father.'

Ian turned to his son. 'I am sorry, Josiah but your school-work is far more important.'

'I can take time off,' Josiah pleaded.

'I am sorry, son, but I will not permit you to neglect your studies when you are near the top of your class. It is far more important that you are grounded with a good education than travelling with me to the Palmer. The adventure is over for the moment.'

Josiah realised that he was not about to change his father's mind and returned to eating his roast beef. A tense silence followed and when the meal was over, the governess ushered Samuel and Becky off to bed. For a short time, Josiah and Ian remained at the table, sitting across from each other.

Josiah had come to know his father well enough to sense the strain in his face. It was obvious that danger lay ahead. Josiah was fully aware of how perilous the northern frontier was, and he also knew with the confidence of youth that he could take his father's side when the situation required action. Had he not proved his worth when they had been ambushed on the Palmer track?

'Elise would miss you,' Ian said, taking a sip of fine claret.

'The Schmidts are doing a grand job of looking after Elise. She is being schooled by Frau Schmidt who was once a teacher in Prussia,' Josiah replied, still hoping that his father might change his mind.

'That might be so,' Ian replied, 'but I hope that I will not be long gone from you all. It is simply a business trip to oversee the establishment of our gold-mining operations. Nothing more.'

'Yes, Father,' Josiah said, a dutiful son, but already his mind was scheming. One way or another, he would join his father on the Palmer.

★

The family had gone to Circular Quay to see off Ian Steele for his sea journey to the far north. There had been tears from Becky, who clung to her father's legs, and a solemn handshake from young Samuel. Josiah had also shaken his father's hand and wished him well.

'You are heir to our financial enterprises,' Ian had said, gripping his son's hand. 'I have great expectations of you.'

'Yes, Father,' Josiah answered dutifully. 'I wish you a safe voyage.'

The call to board resounded with the ship's bell and Ian walked up the gangplank.

They waited until the steam cargo ship pulled away into

the deep waters of the harbour and was out of sight before Josiah shepherded his brother and sister to the carriage with the assistance of the governess. He asked Will Bowden to drop him at the Schmidts' gun shop and residence before taking the others back to the Steele mansion.

Josiah had prepared for this moment and was welcomed inside by Herr Schmidt.

'You have come to visit with Elise?' he asked.

'I will also do that, but I have come to purchase the Winchester and one of your revolvers,' Josiah replied. 'Along with a good supply of Henry rounds and ammunition for the pistol.'

'They are expensive,' Otto said.

'I have the money,' Josiah answered, producing a wad of currency that caused Otto to look at the young man with surprise.

'It is legal, Herr Schmidt,' Josiah said, noting the expression on the German gunsmith's face. 'My father granted me the money after we returned from the Palmer.'

Otto nodded and went about retrieving the required items. 'It will take me some minutes to properly prepare your purchases,' Otto said. 'I am sure that Elise will be pleased to see you. She is with my wife in the kitchen.'

Josiah took Otto's advice and went to the kitchen, where he was greeted warmly by Frau Schmidt. Elise beamed from a face that was spotted with flour from the bread she and Karla were making together.

'I have come to say goodbye for a while,' Josiah said.

'Why is that?' Frau Schmidt asked, wiping her flour-covered hands on her apron. 'Where do you go?'

'I am travelling back to the Palmer to be with my father,' Josiah answered.

'Why do you have to go?' Elise asked with a frown.

'You are my best friend, and I would miss your visits and all the wonderful times we have shared.'

Josiah felt awkward. 'My father will need me,' was his simple explanation. His heart squeezed when he saw the tears welling in Elise's eyes.

'I fear I will never see you again,' she said, the tears now rolling down her cheeks, causing furrows in the traces of flour. 'I had a terrible dream that you left me and never returned.'

Josiah felt a stab of pain and wanted to reach out and hug Elise as a gesture of sympathy, but she turned on her heel and ran from the kitchen, sobbing.

'I will go to her, Master Josiah,' Karla said gently. 'She is at that age where young girls become very emotional. I am sure she will recover her composure.'

'Thank you, Frau Schmidt,' Josiah said. 'I wished to give this to Elise before I left,' he continued, producing a small golden cross with a tiny red ruby inlay. He passed it to Karla.

'I will ensure Elise receives your generous gift,' she said.

'I should return to Herr Schmidt and complete my business with him,' Josiah said with a note of sadness at not being able to present the gift himself. It had been his first purchase days earlier when he had made his decision to run away from home and travel north.

'Be safe in whatever lies ahead for you,' Karla said. Josiah nodded his head and left the kitchen to find that Otto had wrapped his rifle and revolver, along with cardboard boxes of the required ammunition for both weapons.

He stepped out into the street as the sun was setting and hailed a Hansom cab to return home. Will Bowden's son George met Josiah on the gravel carriageway that led to the Steele residence.

'Wotchya got there?' he asked with a friendly grin, seeing the wrapped rifle package.

'Nothing much of interest,' Josiah replied, not wanting to give away any part of his plan yet. 'I had better get inside and get ready for dinner,' he continued, quickly brushing past his childhood friend.

'Your business.' George shrugged, watching Josiah disappear into the big house.

Josiah went directly to his room and laid the wrapped rifle on his bed. He glanced at the wall where he had mounted the Merkin battle-axe and stared at it for a moment, reflecting that this time he was better prepared for any dangerous confrontations on the Palmer frontier.

Josiah unwrapped the rifle and picked up the .32 calibre revolver, slipping them into a large canvas bag that was part of his luggage. He knew that he could buy canned food supplies en route to Cooktown, and a couple of horses when he reached his destination. In all this would eat up most of the money he had but was well worth the investment if it meant protecting his beloved father.

The following day, Josiah was not to be found at the Steele residence, nor was he at his desk in the classroom of his expensive school. In the early hours, before sunrise, Josiah was standing at the stern of a steam-powered coastal ship, passing by the vessels that still relied on wind power to navigate the oceans. He watched the great cliffs of the harbour's entrance as the tough metal ship travelled outside the heads and ploughed into the great Pacific waves of the Tasman Sea. It was only then when the ship steered north that the full realisation of what lay ahead hit the young man. But he knew that he had chosen a course of action and it was too late to turn back. He felt from the little he knew of his father's past that such decisions were not unusual for the men in the family. Josiah's long-dead grandfather had fought at Waterloo against Napoleon Bonaparte and his mother's father had been a notorious businessman in London, where Josiah was born.

It was in his blood to risk all in pursuit of fame and fortune – and for family.

★

Josiah's ship anchored in the Brisbane River alongside the main settlement, the stone government buildings on the banks of the river giving a promise of permanence to the capital of the colony of Queensland. Josiah was able to purchase a crate of canned goods from a local manufacturer, including green turtle soup, canned fruit and the delicacy of dugong pate.

With the stores taken aboard, the steamer left the following day for its final leg to Cooktown. There were a few other passengers aboard – mostly would-be prospectors headed for the Palmer River Goldfields, where they dreamed of making their fortunes. Josiah hardly had the heart to tell his fellow passengers that the days of picking up nuggets along the river and creek beds were long over. Now it was the time for big companies and their heavy machinery to take over the gold seams in the quartz rock.

One morning, Josiah stood at the railings, gazing at the calm turquoise sea around the ship. Smoke from the ship's stack rose lazily into the clear blue sky above and a gentle breeze washed over the deck. Josiah was thinking about his friends at school – how unlucky they were not to be with him on this beautiful day at sea. He smiled to himself, but it quickly faded as he considered how his absence had most probably been noted by now. The good thing was that his father was not at home to receive news of his truancy.

Josiah was not alone when he glanced down the railings. Between he and a couple of bearded passengers was a young Chinese man wearing a clean white shirt and European-style trousers. He wore a cabbage tree hat and Josiah guessed him to be in his early twenties. When the Chinese passenger caught Josiah staring in his direction, he smiled and nodded to acknowledge Josiah's interest. Josiah returned the nod, listening to the two European passengers make derisive remarks about the Chinese man's presence.

'Not right that Chinks be allowed on deck,' was one remark Josiah heard muttered. 'They should be kept in cages below decks like the vermin they are.'

Josiah noticed something peculiar when he glanced back at the Chinese man a short distance away. Josiah could see from his expression that he seemed to understand the derogatory comments being made about him. There was a flash of anger in the eyes.

'Hey! You two!' Josiah called to the bearded men making the remarks. 'Why don't you push off down the deck to continue your conversation?' Josiah suddenly realised that he had put himself in a precarious position, as the two men turned to him with expressions of utter surprise. Some young yahoo had challenged them over a Chink! One of the men was a head taller than Josiah and shoved away from the guardrail to move towards him.

Josiah wrapped his hand around the butt of the small revolver in his trouser pocket. He prayed that the sight of it would cause the man moving towards him to back away. But the hammer on the pistol caught in the pocket and Josiah could not retrieve the gun. It was then that Josiah bitterly regretted his bravado.

Then . . . it happened so fast that Josiah could hardly remember the blur of action of feet and fists. One moment, the bigger man was approaching and suddenly, he lay on his back, groaning in pain as the Chinese man stood over him, facing the second bearded passenger, who was backing away.

'You alright?' the young Chinese stranger asked Josiah.

'Yes,' Josiah answered in shock. 'He did not have the chance to lay a hand on me.'

'I thank you for standing up for me,' the Chinese man said as the bearded man crawled a short distance away, holding his elbow. He was helped to his feet by his companion.

'The captain is going to be informed about this attack on my pal,' the man called. 'Mark my words, you will be arrested by the traps when we dock.' Then the two retreated from the deck, leaving Josiah and the mysterious Chinese man alone.

'Josiah Steele,' Josiah said, extending his hand towards the Chinese man who looked surprised at the gesture but tentatively took Josiah's hand.

'Ling Lee,' he responded.

'Where do you come from?' Josiah asked.

'Parramatta,' Lee replied. 'My family have a market garden there.'

Josiah was totally surprised to hear Lee speak with almost no accent, and Lee could see the puzzled look on his new friend's face. 'I was born in the new land,' he said. 'My parents came from China to the goldfields at Ballarat. My father and mother realised that more money could be made by feeding the miners than digging for gold. Then my family moved to Sydney and out to Parramatta. It seems that I have a good ear for languages.'

'Where are you intending to sail to?' Josiah asked.

'The Palmer River Goldfields,' Lee replied. 'I am hoping that my ability to speak Mandarin and Cantonese will help me get a job as an interpreter for one of the Tong leaders.'

'You know about the Tongs on the Palmer?' Josiah asked.

'All Chinese living in Sydney know about the Palmer Tongs,' Lee said. 'Are you going to the Palmer to prospect for gold?'

Josiah shook his head. 'No, I am going up to find my father and be with him.'

'Is your father a prospector?' Lee asked.

'A mine owner,' Josiah replied. 'Well, sort of.'

Lee looked at Josiah and smiled. 'So, your father has had no luck finding gold?'

'It's a long story,' Josiah sighed. 'All I know is that I have to be with him on the Palmer fields.'

'Maybe we stick together,' Lee suggested. Josiah was about to reject his offer – Europeans did not have Asian friends – but then again, private schoolboys did not run away to frontier colonies either. This was a trip for breaking rules.

'Maybe we will,' Josiah said, and an alliance was struck that would last for life.

*

The wet season was coming to an end in the north, and Ian Steele found that he was temporarily stranded in Cooktown without any sign of Hamish MacDonald, who Ian was told had left for Maytown months earlier.

Ian found a decent hotel but paid a high price for clean sheets and good food.

Outside the small room Ian occupied, the heavy rain belted down, keeping the main street a muddy quagmire. He chose to occupy his time talking with prospectors in the main bar, drinking little but listening a lot. There was little gossip concerning the Chinese population of the Palmer. Ian realised that the Europeans dismissed them as unimportant, but the existence of so many prosperous enterprises in Cooktown made the Chinese a significant player in the future of the colony's north. As a businessman, Ian commenced formulating possible future ventures with the populous Asian territories to the north of the Australian colonies. Ian had not established any concrete plan for future investment but was convinced future trade would assist the Steele and Sons Enterprises in the years ahead.

★

Josiah's ship arrived at the Cooktown wharf as the rain pelted down, drenching anyone and everything not under cover.

'We'll get shelter in the Chinese quarter,' Lee said. 'I have a cousin who has a shop there.'

Josiah pulled the cape over his head as he stood on the open deck. 'I appreciate your offer,' he replied. 'Just until I can get my own accommodation.'

'My cousin sent me the address of his shop,' Lee said, leaning into the rain. 'Let's go now. The government men seem to be staying out of the rain, and we have our chance to get ashore without interference.'

Josiah knew that he had nothing to hide from the government inspectors but felt it was silly to wait around for a break in the weather. Hoisting the two heavy canvas bags he carried as his personal luggage, Josiah followed Lee off the ship onto the shore. He would return the next day to fetch the rest of his luggage from the cargo hold.

With an uncanny sense of direction, Lee quickly found his cousin's shop off the main thoroughfare. It was a Chinese pharmacy where Josiah was assailed by the heavy scent of many herbs and spices from faraway places. The wall racks were jammed with mysterious jars and glass bottles, and dried herbs hung from the low ceiling.

Lee was greeted warmly by his cousin, a man in his thirties wearing a ponytail and a traditional silk tunic and trousers. 'My cousin does not speak English,' Lee said. 'I have told him who you are and how I consider you a friend.'

The Chinese herbalist bowed to Josiah, who felt that he should return the bow.

'My cousin is Hai Lee, and you can call him Hai so we are not confused,' Lee said with a grin. 'He welcomes you to his humble abode and has prepared a meal for us.'

Josiah sat down with his new friend and his cousin at the back of the store, where Lee explained how chopsticks are held and used in eating. Josiah learned quickly and received smiles and nods from Hai as they ate the delicious meal of pork and vegetables. It was the first time Josiah had eaten Asian food and he delighted in the new tastes on his tongue.

The rain continued to lash down outside the shop, and Hai showed Josiah and Lee where they could sleep, a cramped corner on top of bales of soft goods. A candle lantern cast a yellow glow in the corner and when the night came, Josiah felt at home, surrounded by the sights, smells and sounds of this tiny portion of China in the colony of Queensland.

NINE

The following day, Josiah and Lee awoke to a beautiful blue sky with just a few scudding clouds. Josiah reported to the Customs office to retrieve his luggage and was fortunate to find a boarding house that had accommodation available. He paid in advance for a week and stowed his possessions in a small, clean room that had the added advantage that it could be locked.

Josiah joined Lee on the street as he had promised Josiah a meal at his cousin's place. Josiah accepted because he was enjoying the journey into a new world of Asian cuisine but insisted that he pay.

'I have been curious about the incident on the boat when you were able to defeat the bigger man using a series of kicks and punches,' Josiah said as they strolled along the wooden boardwalk to avoid the mud of the street. 'I have never seen that kind of fighting before. Where did you learn it?'

'My father was a Shaolin monk before he came to this land,' Lee answered. 'He taught me the ways of martial arts from the day I could walk. He was a strict master.'

'It was very impressive,' Josiah said when they reached the Chinese pharmacy. 'I am a boxer, but we only fight with our fists. Is it possible that you might be able to teach me some of your arts of fighting with your feet?'

'If you are a boxer then you are part of the way to mastering the art of my fighting,' Lee said. He stopped outside Hai's abode and sniffed the air. 'I can smell that my cousin has been cooking.'

Josiah could also smell the food and it intrigued him. This was not the meat and potatoes he knew from life in Sydney.

Hai chatted with Lee in Chinese while Josiah enjoyed the bowl of pork pieces and vegetables. When they had finished the meal, Josiah had another question for his newly acquired friend.

'Now that we are here, what will you do next in your search for work?'

Lee placed his chopsticks aside and seemed to reflect on a matter better not divulged. 'I seek a man. A very special man.'

Josiah was intrigued. 'What man could be so special for you to travel so far?'

'The man I seek is known to even the Chinese people from where I lived near Sydney,' Lee replied. 'He will be our freedom from the foreigners who have invaded our lands.'

Lee's answer sent a chill through Josiah. 'May I ask who this man is?' Josiah prodded.

Lee turned to him with a frown. 'Maybe you will find out one day,' he answered. 'For now, I will have to leave you, but you know where I am if you wish to share a meal with my cousin and me.'

Josiah recognised that he should not ask any more questions. He thanked Hai, who nodded, not really understanding the English words but recognising the grateful tone in which they were delivered.

As Josiah returned to his lodgings, he could see a trickle of gaunt prospectors filing into Cooktown off the Palmer track, where they had been trapped by the swollen creeks and rivers during the wet season. Hotels and brothels opened their doors to welcome them back.

Josiah's thoughts went to his father. How could he find him and convince his father that he would need Josiah as his companion on the difficult and dangerous Palmer track to Maytown?

★

Lee found his special man after Hai sent a message to the cluster of buildings off the main street, and Lee was invited to meet with the man. Now he stood in the presence of the feared Tong leader Zhu, who eyed him with some curiosity.

'I have heard as far south as Sydney that you are a man who desires to overthrow the foreign enemies of our nation,' Lee said, nervous to be in the presence of this great man, and with another exceptionally large man standing only feet behind him.

'We cannot call ourselves a nation,' Zhu replied from behind a teak table. 'We are currently a land of warlords and an imperial family that has no real power, serving as puppets to the Europeans. We need armed rebellion by the people to take control of our destiny.'

These were the words Lee wanted to hear. From his earliest childhood, he had listened as his father spoke of the need to be a free people. Lee saw himself as a future warrior in the struggle against foreign oppression and felt that he may be able to contribute something important, as he had a foot in two worlds – and one of those feet was in the world of the enemy.

'I have come to dedicate my life to the future rebellion,' Lee said in a humble but strong voice.

'What skills do you bring to our struggle?' Zhu asked.

'I have lived amongst the Europeans all my life and speak their language. I can read and write English. I also speak Cantonese and Mandarin.'

Zhu lifted a fine porcelain cup and sipped his tea. 'It is true that you speak English very well,' he said, changing to English from the Cantonese they had been speaking. Lee was surprised that the Tong leader knew of his ability, and that he was equally fluent. 'Do you have a knowledge of firearms?' Zhu asked, catching Lee off guard for the moment.

'Yes, master,' Lee replied. 'I know how to operate a Snider rifle. I watched the European people of my district use them.'

'I was informed by your cousin that your father was once a Shaolin monk. Did he teach you the ways of fighting?'

'Yes, master.'

Zhu rose from behind his low desk and turned his back on Lee, who was starting to wonder if he had travelled so far for nothing.

'I have enemies amongst our own people,' Zhu finally said, turning to face Lee once more. 'Our movement needs cash to purchase modern weapons for the future of an armed uprising. So far, I have only had half of what is needed to progress the future rebellion in China. There is a man who has foiled my attempts to gain total control of the Palmer, a warlord who is now the leader of his Tong. He is at a place called Maytown and my informants have told me he has now recruited a gang of white outlaws to his cause. His name is Wang. If you are truly a warrior for our freedom, I want you to go to Maytown and kill him.'

Lee sucked in a deep breath. He had not expected to be called on to kill anyone. He thought that his knowledge of the European ways would be enough to give him a position in the Tong dedicated to furthering the cause for Chinese liberation.

Zhu returned to his table and sat down, continuing to drink his tea. 'Are you truly a man who can do that for our cause?' he asked calmly.

'Yes, master,' Lee replied, bowing to emphasise his commitment.

'That is all I need to know until I have been informed of Wang's death. Your cousin has told me that you have befriended a young white man who will be travelling to Maytown in search of his father. I suggest that you nurture this friendship and travel with him. That will make you less conspicuous. You may go now with my wishes for a successful mission.'

Lee had never killed a man before and this land to the north had little in common with the land he had travelled from. He departed, his head swimming. It was not murder if it was in the greater cause of arming a future rebellion, Lee justified to himself.

It was time to seek out the unsuspecting Josiah and offer his services for the trek to Maytown.

★

Hamish MacDonald stood outside his tent on the outskirts of Maytown, gazing at the blue skies. Finally, the big wet was retreating, allowing the dry to rule the Palmer once again. Trapped by the heavy monsoonal wet season, Hamish had learned a lot from the American gold dealer Beauregard Connors. Hamish had learned of the mysterious death of the German geologist, Gustaf von Kroth, and that all his surveys had disappeared after his death. The American had heard rumours that Kroth had been murdered by the Goodson gang on the orders of the Chinese Tong leader, Wang, but why he was killed was not so clear.

Hamish was informed that the heavy machinery required for ore crushing had been deserted somewhere down the Palmer track. The bullock-drawn wagon sat off the track, minus the big bullocks used to pull it. Whether they had fallen victim to the Merkin warriors or to some other nefarious hazard, Beauregard could not tell. Whatever the reason, the project was in serious trouble.

Mexican Jack joined Hamish and passed him an enamel mug of sweet black tea. 'Goddamned pleased to see the last of the wet,' Mexican Jack commented, sipping from his mug. 'I swear I have grown webs between my toes.'

'I think it is time we got out of here and make our way back to Cooktown. I am hoping that Captain Steele may be there.'

'We will still have to cross a few flooded creeks and rivers,' Jack cautioned.

'We will only take the rest of our supplies on horseback, which gives us a better chance,' Hamish replied. 'We keep our powder dry and remain vigilant. Tell Mr Walsh that we leave at first light tomorrow.'

Jack finished his drink and walked away to prepare for the long trek back to Cooktown. He was pleased at the boss's decision because the local drinking establishments had almost run out of alcoholic supplies. Cooktown would not have the same problem.

★

Josiah distributed his supply of rations and other essential goods for the trek and stay at Maytown between the saddlebags of the two horses he had purchased at a steep price. His own mount was not like the fine horses his father owned down south but it looked sturdy enough. He slipped the prized Winchester into the rifle bucket and the small revolver into a holster on his belt. Josiah had to admit to himself that he was scared. Travelling the Palmer track alone was fraught with danger – so many things could go wrong, from a Merkin ambush to simply having an accident.

'Josiah!'

Josiah recognised the voice and turned to see Lee striding towards him across the muddy main street of Cooktown. Josiah could see that the Chinese man had a swag over his shoulder and once again wore a European shirt and pair of trousers. He also had a wicked-looking sword strapped across his back.

'A good morning to you,' Josiah responded. 'You look like you are going somewhere.'

Lee caught up to Josiah. 'I am hoping that you would like company on the track to Maytown.'

'I only have the one riding mount,' Josiah said. 'If we leave some supplies, maybe –'

'I do not know how to ride. But I am happy to walk,' Lee said confidently.

Josiah experienced a rush of relief. Two travelling together provided better defence, and when Josiah glanced at the sword, he suspected strongly that his companion knew how to use it.

'Welcome aboard,' Josiah said with a grin. 'Sorry that you have to walk but I have enough supplies for us both.'

Lee removed the swag from his shoulder and strapped it to the packhorse. The two men and two horses departed the civilisation of Cooktown for the dangerous wilderness of the Palmer goldfields. Josiah was not to know that he was a mere day behind his father.

★

Ian Steele had gambled that the wet was near its end and departed on horseback, leading a packhorse. His gamble had paid off.

He knew truly little of the situation that lay ahead of him because communications had been cut by the wet season. All he did know from speaking with Frank McNeil at Hamish's hotel was that his boss was probably stuck in Maytown. Anything else about why the former British major had gone to Maytown with Mexican Jack and Walsh in the first place was a bit murky to McNeil.

Ian kicked his horse forward from the ridge where he sat and began the descent to the valley below, where he could see a small party of prospectors gathered around two bullock wagons. Even from a distance, Ian could see that the small party appeared to be in some distress.

When Ian reached the party, he scanned the men gathered about a large campfire and could see that they were on the point of starvation. He counted around a dozen men who stared at his arrival with sunken and rheumy eyes. Ian also noted that a handful were armed with a variety of rifles and pistols, and his sudden appearance had caught their attention.

'You come from Cooktown?' one of the bearded miners asked.

'A couple of days out of Cooktown,' Ian replied, alert to the situation around him. Desperate, starving men could be dangerous.

'You got any spare tucker in those saddlebags?' the miner asked again. 'We could surely do with some food.'

'Not enough for you all,' Ian said, covering one of his Colts with his hand. 'Just enough to give you all a mouthful at best.'

Ian became aware that some of the armed men had lifted their rifles, and wished he had remained outside the perimeter of their camp. He could see the scattered bones of the bullocks that had been used to haul the empty wagons and guessed that the trapped men had long ago used up any supplies the wagons had carried and the bullocks themselves had provided their last meals.

'I would recommend that no one attempts anything stupid,' Ian said, dropping the reins and drawing both his revolvers from their leather holsters. 'I have more than enough rounds to deal with you all.'

The bearded prospector who had first confronted Ian backed away and Ian could see that his statement had made an impression on most of the armed men, who were aware of the devastating firepower of the big Colts at close range. Their own rifles were single-shot weapons whereas Ian could pump out twelve lead balls in a noticeably short time.

'No one will do anything to you, mister,' the miner said wearily. 'You are welcome to share our campfire.'

Ian nodded, replacing one of the pistols to pick up the reins and continue his ride to the riverbank beyond the camp. He could not cross the river in the dark and would be forced to set up camp near the stranded prospectors. He was aware of the sullen demeanour of the men behind him and realised that he might not get much sleep that night as he would have to be prepared for a sneak attack by desperate men, attempting to seize his valuable supplies by force.

Ian removed the packs from his supply horse then hobbled both animals nearby. They grazed on the lush native grasses as Ian set up his small campfire, always keeping a wary eye on the party some hundred yards away.

He opened a tin of meat and a packet of hard biscuits, settling down to eat his evening meal. This he followed with a tin of peaches and a billy of tea. Ian felt for the starving miners but knew his stores were vital for his journey to Maytown. This was a land where only the prepared survived and he knew he had to harden his heart to their plight. They were only a couple of days from Cooktown and if they pushed on, they would survive.

Ian decided not to pitch his tent as it was a star-filled, moonless night. He settled with his back to a large log that had been washed down the river by the receding flood waters and plugged his pipe, ready to begin his solo sentry duty.

★

'Smell that!' one of the prospectors snarled. 'The bastard's got tobacco!'

'He's got enough food to feed us all,' a second man growled. 'Not right he keep it all to himself.'

'Would you share your supplies with anyone if you were going down the track?' a third man questioned calmly.

'He ain't starving,' the second man said. 'I say we wait until he's asleep and just go and take it.'

'He's got those pistols,' the first man cautioned. 'What if he's awake when we go for his supplies?'

'We have guns,' the second man answered. 'And there are a lot more of us than him.'

For a moment, the three men fell silent until the first piped up. 'We wait until the early hours of the morning, then we make our move.'

The other two nodded their agreement and the word

was passed to the others sitting in the circle around the flickering flames.

★

Ian fought the need for sleep, sitting back with a Colt in each hand, but his body had an overwhelming need for total rest. His body jerked awake at each strange nocturnal sound, the distant howling of dingoes waking him for a fraction of time before he dozed off again. His horses nearby remained silent but for the occasional snort and jangle of their hobbles.

Finally, Ian fell into a deep sleep, and the Colts slipped from his fingers.

Just after two in the morning, as the last embers of Ian's fire smouldered into ashes, five of the desperate prospectors quietly crept towards his campsite.

TEN

Ian was not sure if his old soldier's sense of danger or the snorting of his horses hobbled nearby snapped him awake. He opened his eyes, but his mind was muddled from the deep sleep he had been in. Ian wrapped his hands around the revolvers at his fingertips and sat up.

The night was pitch-black, but he could hear the movement around him and knew that the enemy was close. Ian fired a shot into the dark and heard a man swear mere yards away. Behind him, he could hear the scuffling of bodies and realised they were near his packed supplies.

A rifle shot cracked the night air and Ian heard it thump into the big log that he had been lying against.

'We got it!' a voice called out only yards away. Ian turned his attention to the sound of the voice, pistols levelled.

Then Ian heard the sound of men retreating, leaving him alone, and the noise of his two horses being led away. The inky blackness of the night had saved him from a bullet at such close range, and he was not about to risk the prospectors coming back to finish him off. All the same, he remained wide awake until the dawn came and, as he suspected, it brought the discovery that his supplies and mounts were gone. The rogue prospectors had also packed up and left before dawn and Ian guessed that they were not about to risk Ian confronting them with his considerable firepower.

Ian rose and stretched to take the stiffness from his limbs, which were cramped from huddling by the log, and surveyed the campsite of the departed prospectors turned bandits. He was at the least grateful that he was still alive and armed, but without the supplies, any thought of continuing his journey to Maytown was now impossible. He knew that he could reach Cooktown on foot and resigned himself to admitting his mission was over until he could once again renew his one-man expedition.

Ian went to the river, drew water in a billy that he'd had with him by the fire and boiled the water with the few tea leaves he still had in a can that had been missed by the looters.

His meagre breakfast of black tea complete, Ian turned his attention to the long walk to Cooktown.

★

Josiah and Lee pitched camp on their first night on the track and shared a meal of canned meat and biscuits around the small fire overlooked by tall trees. Around them, the sounds of the wildlife emerging from the big wet made an almost musical backdrop to their meal.

Josiah had told Lee of his experiences on the track to Maytown the previous year and explained that he always kept the Winchester close in case of a Merkin ambush.

'I suspect that the Merkin are cannibals because this land has little in the way of animals to sustain them as a people,' Josiah said sympathetically. 'I cannot blame them for their choice.'

'Much is strange to Europeans, and also to my people,' Lee commented. 'We abhor their choice but wonder if we were in the same situation, we would not be cannibals ourselves. I have heard stories of the Maori people resorting to cannibalism and yet the soldiers who have fought them consider the Maori a proud and worthy foe.'

The two men ceased discussing the subject when the howls of dingoes in the distant forest drifted to them.

'Have you ever travelled to China?' Josiah asked, sipping his hot tea.

'I have never visited China,' Lee replied, continuing to gaze up at the patch of stars above them. 'I only know about the homeland from stories told to me by my father and mother. They told me they left a land of warlords and foreigners who exploit my people.'

'Do you feel a part of this land where you were born?' Josiah asked.

For a moment, Lee remained silent. 'I will never be accepted by you Europeans despite the fact I was born here and speak your language,' he said finally. 'I continue my dreams that China will one day be free of warlords and foreign invaders. Then I could belong to a nation that accepts me.'

'I consider you a friend,' Josiah said. 'I am Jewish, and the Christians of this country do not consider me an equal either. I think I know something of what you feel.'

They retired for the evening and in the early-morning hours were awoken by a large party passing below on the track. From their hidden position, Josiah and Lee were not detected and once the noise had passed, they fell asleep again until the sound of the morning birds heralding the dawn awoke them.

After a quick breakfast of canned sardines and a billy of tea, the two young men broke camp and set off on the trek to Maytown, where Josiah hoped to eventually find his father.

He did so quicker than he could have imagined.

★

Ian Steele struggled up a ridge. He paused to swig water from his canteen and became aware that he could hear horses approaching. Instinctively, Ian rested his hand on one of his Colts. Then he saw a mounted man leading a packhorse with a Chinese man walking alongside the stirrup. Maybe the arduous trek on foot had caused him confusion but Ian swore the young man astride the horse looked very much like his son. But that was impossible.

When they were about twenty paces away, the man on the horse halted and leaned forward in the saddle.

'Father!' came the mounted man's shout, and Ian stumbled forward to stand before his son, who had dismounted. Without another word, the two men embraced in a crushing bear hug.

'What the devil are you doing here?' Ian asked when they broke apart.

'I came to find you,' Josiah simply said.

'And now you have found me,' Ian replied with a broad smile.

'This is Lee,' Josiah said, turning his attention to the man standing next to him. 'He is my friend and travelling companion. He speaks English better than I do,' Josiah added.

Ian nodded to Lee who returned the gesture.

'Pleased to meet a friend of my son,' Ian said, extending his hand.

'I have heard much about you, Captain Steele,' Lee responded, taking Ian's firm grip. 'Your son has spoken of your exploits as a soldier. It appears that you may have suffered some misfortune if we have met you afoot.'

'Some damned bandits stripped me of everything a couple of nights ago,' Ian said. 'I was on my way back to the coast to resupply.'

'We could do that,' Josiah said. 'But if we carefully ration the supplies I have, the three of us could push on to Maytown.'

Ian looked at his son with a new respect for what his and Ella's blood had produced. At sixteen, Josiah had developed a maturity beyond his years. Ian knew he should be angry – Josiah had disobeyed his order that he remain at home, attending school. But he decided that was a conversation for another time. He conceded that his son had arrived at a fortuitous moment. Ian carefully considered Josiah's offer, glancing at the boxed supplies on the packhorse and weighing the option of wasting maybe a week if they turned around.

'We continue to Maytown,' Ian finally said. 'I notice that you have a repeating rifle in your gun bucket and not your Snider. Why do I suspect that it was purchased from Herr Schmidt?'

'It was,' Josiah replied sheepishly. 'I also have a .32 revolver.'

'Good – wise purchases,' Ian said. 'Between us, we have enough firepower to defend ourselves.' Ian turned to Lee and noticed the deadly sword strapped across his back. 'That could come in handy at close quarters,' he said to Lee.

Josiah insisted that they eat before they continued to Maytown, knowing that his father had most probably not had a meal since he was robbed. Ian did not argue with his son, and they opened a couple of cans of fruit and washed it down with sweet black tea.

As they sat at the edge of the earthen track, Ian watched his son with fresh eyes. He had proved that he was no longer a mere boy but a man. That his son was the equal of any man Ian had commanded in battle swelled his heart with pride. He knew Ella would have been proud of the child she had produced, albeit not in agreement with the stunt he had pulled. But mothers were like that, Ian thought with a wry smile.

'Father, you will ride my mount,' Josiah commanded.

'Do you think that I am an old man who is unable to trudge the distance?' Ian asked with a warm smile.

'No, Father . . . well, yes,' Josiah answered sheepishly. 'Lee and I are younger and better suited to walking.'

Ian accepted the invitation to mount the horse and thought to himself how times had changed. It seemed like just yesterday he had marched through rugged country with his company of British infantry. When he looked at his son, he was so much reminded of himself as that same officer. How the passing of time had reversed roles.

★

Charlie Goodson surveyed the motley gang of desperate men he had recruited during the wet season in Maytown. He now counted seven, including himself, in his crew, ranging in age from a teen to men in their late thirties. They had been easy to recruit when food was short and Charlie was able to supply them from his stockpile of mostly stolen goods, taken before the big wet had arrived at the Palmer.

Not only was he able to feed them but also provide them with rum and gin in copious quantities. One vital asset each man had was his own firearm, and this boosted Charlie's firepower. One of his new recruits had military experience with the Austro–Hungarian Empire and another Charlie suspected was a murderer on the run from the legal system in the colony of Victoria. Tough and now dedicated to Charlie, they gathered around his tent on the outskirts of the small township still eagerly awaiting fresh supplies from the coast.

'You have lived off my generosity for the last few months and now it is time to earn your keep,' Charlie said to the men gathered in a semicircle with their assortment of firearms at hand. 'You know who I am and what I do to put food on the table and money in the pockets of those who follow me.' Charlie could see heads nod amongst the gathered men. 'If any of you want to quit, say so now.'

Charlie stood outside the flap of his tent, scanning their faces. He was good at reading other men's expressions and could see just a hint of doubt in a couple of the bearded faces before him.

'We're with you, Charlie,' one of the recruits piped up, and the rest mumbled their agreement. Even the doubting expressions on the couple of men disappeared as they decided it was safer to agree.

'Good,' Charlie grunted. 'Tonight, we will drink what's left at the pub and tomorrow you get your orders.' The men ambled away to the tents Charlie had provided for them.

Martin Donahue waited until they had all gone and turned to his boss. 'Has Wang told you what he wants?' he asked, scratching at his beard, which itched.

'He has and we owe him for the grog,' Charlie answered. 'We have heard that the Scotsman and his two offsiders are leaving Maytown for the coast. Wang wants them to disappear.'

'Why?' Martin asked.

'He has his reasons, but I think it concerns the ore-crushing machinery the major had organised to come up here.'

'Does it have something to do with us chasing off the bullocks back down the track just before the wet came?'

'I suspect it does. I think Wang wants to take over the ore-crushing business here so it don't bide any competition from the Scotsman and his crew,' Charlie mused.

Martin shrugged. It was so easy to kill travellers on the Palmer and make them disappear into unmarked graves in the wilderness, where they would be presumed to have been killed by Merkin ambush, or simply starvation or disease.

Charlie was extra keen to take out the major, having learned the identities of the men they had attempted to ambush months earlier. He was furious when he also discovered that he had lost his hand to a mere youth, the son of the former Captain Ian Steele. All Charlie could do was hope that the young man would return to the north and that he would have the opportunity to slit his throat in some dark alley.

★

Hamish sat outside his tent with Ryan and Mexican Jack, sharing a brew of strong tea as they sat on sections of logs as improvised chairs.

'Enjoy the tea,' Hamish said. 'Because we are going to have to ration it on the way back to Cooktown.'

'And we leave at first light?' Ryan asked.

'Yes, with everything we can scrounge for the journey,' Hamish answered. 'It appears that Wang has a monopoly on the meagre goods here and claims he has nothing to spare for us even when I made a generous offer for what we need.'

'That goddamned Chink is in cahoots with Goodson and his buddies,' Mexican Jack suggested. 'I heard from a few other prospectors that he has bought up a few good claims around here.'

'They won't be good to him if he doesn't have the ore-crushing machinery needed to extract the gold,' Ryan said.

'If all had gone well, we would be crushing ore right now,' Hamish said. 'It seems a bit queer that the machinery did not arrive in Maytown. At the time we arrived in the town, I was hoping to open talks with Wang to smuggle gold to the coast, but he told me he had no interest in our old arrangements. He said he did not trust me because of my business dealing with Zhu but I think there was more to it than that.'

'Well, a last drink tonight before we head off in the morning,' Mexican Jack said, rising from the log and spilling out the tea leaves at the bottom of his metal mug. 'I would give my goddamn soul for a good mug of coffee, and not this goddamn brew you Limeys drink.'

'Should I remind you, Jack, that I am a Scot and not a Sassenach,' Hamish said good-humouredly as the American frontiersman strode away.

★

On the third day after Ian was reunited with his son, they came down off a ridge and onto a rich river valley of lush pastures. As they descended, they could see a gathering of bullock drays and their teams as well as pitched tents, camp-fires and a variety of people – including women.

'Good place to let the horses graze,' Ian said.

He rode in with Josiah and Lee walking alongside him

and saw a woman standing on a bullock wagon, selling liquor to thirsty prospectors. She was probably in her thirties but her hair, drawn back in a bun, was streaked with grey. The scramble of men seeking her product clamoured at the back of the solid bullock wagon, waving currency and even small chamois bags of gold dust. If they used obscene or profane language, she refused to sell to them – there were plenty of customers who were more polite.

'That is where the real gold is,' Ian commented as they passed by. 'Having the essentials to provide life, not scrabbling around in the mud of the Palmer. When we pitch camp, we will do so away from the masses and always keep vigilant,' Ian continued, remembering his bitter experience a few days earlier at the hands of desperate men.

Josiah and Lee set up the small campsite, and Josiah deliberately displayed his repeating rifle as a warning to anyone who would consider robbing them. In the meantime, Ian wandered away to speak with some of the men in the camping grounds. He was gone for some time and returned just as Lee had established a small fire to cook their meal and boil tea.

'What were you doing, Father?' Josiah asked, stirring the tea leaves in the blackened billy suspended over the fire.

'I was doing what any good soldier would do.' Ian smiled, making a place by the fire. 'I was gathering intelligence on the track ahead. It seems, other than a few creeks and rivers still swollen by the wet season, the track is open to us.'

Josiah poured a mug of tea, sweetened by sugar. He already had flour roasting in the hot embers of the edge of the fire, which he poked with a stick to ensure it did not burn. He would use it to make a form of bread once it was ready.

In the distance, they could hear the raucous singing and laughter of drunken men and women while a fiddle screeched out a tune. 'I don't sense that this crowd is dangerous, as they appear to have adequate food supplies, but we still stand guard during the night,' Ian said, sipping his hot tea as the stars began to appear in the night sky. It was a time of tranquillity, shared with Ian's precious son and his new friend. Ian had questioned Lee on his purpose to travel to Maytown. Lee had been a little evasive but said he was going to meet a relative who worked the goldfields in the Maytown district. Ian did not press the young Chinese man any further on the matter, pleased that Josiah had not attempted to travel the dangerous road to Maytown alone. They took turns that night awake on guard duty but were relieved to experience nothing unusual.

The horses grazing in their hobbles were given another half day to fill their bellies before the trio once again set off for their destination. Now they turned south and knew that the dreaded terrain of the craggy hills and the infamous Hells Gate lay ahead. Their journey was far from over but each day bonded father and son in a way that could never be achieved in Sydney. They were passing landmarks they remembered from their journey the previous year, as well as the occasional grave, and the bleaching bones of those who had no one to bury them.

It was on the tenth day, around mid-morning, that they heard volleys of gunfire ahead.

ELEVEN

The pain was intense, and Ryan Walsh groaned as he held his thigh with both hands. Blood oozed into his trouser leg, staining it in a widening patch. He was only vaguely aware that he had been shot as he sheltered behind a large boulder next to Hamish, who was attempting to peer from the safety they had sought when they were ambushed.

'Do you see Jack?' Hamish asked, gripping his shotgun.

'Too bloody concerned with not bleeding to death,' Ryan replied through gritted teeth. From his position, he could see his horse lying dead on the grassy plain and his Snider too, still in the rifle bucket attached to the saddle.

'I'm here!' Mexican Jack shouted from the safety of another boulder about twenty yards away. 'It's that goddamned Goodson gang,' he added. 'It has to be them for sure.'

Hamish silently agreed. Only Europeans had the fire-power to be their ambushers, and Hamish guessed from the volume of shots splattering the rocks around them that they were outnumbered and outgunned. Hamish also knew that their chances of survival were not good and only a miracle could save them. His own shotgun did not have the range to outdistance the rifles of their would-be killers.

'What are we goin' to do?' Jack shouted to Hamish.

'Keep our bloody heads down. Maybe we have a checkmate situation. They have to stand off if they don't want to engage us at close range.' Hamish was reverting to his military experience, and the frightening thought nagged at him that their ambushers might have already attempted to outflank their dubious protection. His answer came quickly – a bullet ricocheted off the edge of the rock protecting them, and Hamish calculated it had come from the side. He shrank himself as well as he could, waiting for a fatal shot to impact. Next to him, Ryan was in obvious pain and bleeding badly, turning ashen under his tanned complexion. Hamish removed his shirt and tore a strip to make a bandage which he applied as another round slammed into the earth a foot away. It was only a matter of time before they were outflanked.

*

'Sniders,' Ian said, listening to the echo of rifle fire. All around them was a plain of lush, waist-high grass, with the sight of the craggy hills rising to the clear skies in the distance. It was mid-morning, and the day would soon turn hot as the sun bit into the earth below.

'Is it a fight against Merkin?' Josiah asked, retrieving his fully loaded Winchester from the saddle bucket.

'I don't think so. I can hear a Colt a distance from the

main source of rifle fire. More like some poor traveller is being robbed,' Ian answered. Years of battlefield experience had attuned Ian's situational senses and he noticed the scattered boulders half a mile ahead, calculating that this was the scene of the gunfight. His professional guess was confirmed when he could see puffs of gunpowder smoke and hear the report of the heavy-calibre rifles.

'What do we do?' Josiah asked nervously, and Ian realised that his son was awaiting orders.

'I suppose we are obliged to assist the poor blighters, whoever they are,' Ian replied. 'Before we do, we need to size up the situation. How many are we up against and where they are positioned. Hobble the horses and we will go in on foot.'

Josiah quickly did so and turned to Lee. 'Do you know how to handle a pistol?' he asked.

'You point it and pull the trigger.' Lee grinned.

'That's good enough,' Josiah said, handing Lee the small-calibre revolver and a handful of cartridges.

Ian looked to his son, holding his Winchester and a bandolier of ammunition across his chest. For a moment, he wanted to tell Josiah to remain with the horses, but he realised that on this frontier age was not a consideration and Ian was forced to acknowledge that his son was a true man. This did not dispel Ian's fear for Josiah's safety.

The three men set out towards the scattered boulders, armed as well as they could be, Ian holding a pistol in each hand while Josiah had his repeating rifle and Lee strode beside them with the revolver Josiah had given him. The tall grass tufts concealed their rapid approach towards the sound of gunfire.

★

'Hey, Scotsman! Give up while you still can,' Charlie called. 'We are just about to surround you and it will be all over when we do. But if you come out, we will let you go.'

'No goddamned way, Goodson!' Mexican Jack called back, recognising the voice that called to them. 'You are out to slay us.'

A fusillade of shots followed Jack's answer.

Hamish agreed with his employee as it was obvious that the ambush was meant to eliminate them. He felt aggrieved that he had survived so many battles, serving as an officer with Her Majesty's army, only to face the end of his life on this godforsaken piece of earth.

'I am proud to have served with you, Mexican Jack,' Hamish called softly across the short distance between them, then looked down at Ryan, who was no longer moaning in his pain, and swore. Hamish knew from experience that the young man had bled to death.

'Goddamned Alamo all over again,' Jack muttered, laying out his ammunition for the Snider just as another round smashed into the rock he was sheltering behind. This time, Jack knew the lead bullet had been fired from behind him. He swung around to see a head pop down behind another boulder only fifty yards out, the smoke from the shot lingering in the still, hot air of the Palmer track. Jack raised his rifle and took careful aim at where he had seen the smoke. 'Stick yer head up again,' Jack grunted under his breath, looking down his rifle sights.

★

Ian and his army of two were now only around fifty yards from the scattered boulders. Crouched down below the level of the pasture, he could peek above to see the figures of three men armed with rifles firing and bending down to reload their single-shot weapons. He noticed that a fourth man, who had only one hand in which he held a revolver, seemed to be directing the operation against the unknown travellers pinned down a short distance away.

Ian pointed to the four men and indicated to Josiah to open fire when he was ready. Josiah nodded his understanding and rose just above the tall grass, taking careful aim at the back of the ambusher nearest him. Breathing in and exhaling slowly, he squeezed the trigger. Almost instantly, his target threw up his arms, falling forward. Without waiting, Josiah levered another Henry round, ejecting the metal case and reloading a live cartridge. His second shot hit another of the riflemen, who fell and crawled into the long grass behind the ambush position. Ian, kneeling beside him, saw the utter confusion on the face of the one-handed man, who had now taken cover to one side of the boulder.

*

Hamish heard gunfire coming from a different direction and groaned. Charlie Goodson must have more men than he had first calculated.

'That's a goddamned Henry!' Jack swore. He too was confused at the entry of the new source of gunfire. It was not possible it was help, as miracles were something only good Christian folk believed in, and Jack was not good Christian folk.

*

'Advance!' Ian said as if he was once again back on the battlefield. They had used their element of surprise and had scattered the first group of shooters.

The three men rose from the long grass and swept cautiously forward; weapons pointed ahead in readiness for any threat they may encounter. Ian also realised that they were vulnerable until they reached the cover of the boulders. When they did, they found the first man Josiah had shot lying on the earth, staring with dead eyes at the blue sky above. The round had taken him in the head and already flies were gathering to feast on the blood from the wound the flat-nosed bullet had inflicted.

Lee picked up the dead man's rifle and ammunition. Their firepower had just incrementally increased with the addition of the Snider.

★

Charlie and the third member of his gang had already secured cover behind another boulder twenty yards away. He was shaking and confused at the intrusion of the strangers in his fight, and now realised that it was he and his men who were the prey.

'How many did you see?' Charlie hissed at his comrade.

'Didn't see anyone, boss,' the frightened man answered. 'All I know is we got bushwhacked.'

Charlie leaned against the rock, reassured that he still had the five men he had sent to surround the three men trapped in the rocks, not aware that one had already been killed. His instinct was to withdraw until he could ascertain what had gone wrong. Charlie always had an exit plan and he had left one of his men with their horses a half-mile away.

It was time to run. He shouted to his remaining men to pull back from their current positions and run like hell for the horses.

★

'Father!' Josiah shouted. 'I can see four men running away towards the hills!'

'No sense wasting ammunition on them, son,' Ian said. 'They are out of accurate range for your rifle. Time that we found the poor souls the ambushers were after – if they are still alive.'

'God almighty! Captain Steele!'

Ian was stunned to hear the familiar exclamation from his friend as he emerged from behind a boulder a short distance away. 'Major MacDonald! Hamish!' Ian responded in his shock. 'You seem to draw bad luck every time you travel this road.'

'Sadly, it has been thus for Mr Walsh,' Hamish said, indicating a man behind him. Ian approached Hamish and saw the body of Ryan lying propped up against the boulder.

'Ah, a sad sight,' Ian said with feeling. 'I suppose that we will have to bury him here and report the matter to the troopers.'

'It was Charlie Goodson and his son-of-a-bitch men,' Jack said when he joined them. 'The yellow dogs ran like the gutless cowards they are when you arrived. I swore we were only seconds from being dead men until you came upon Charlie and his men. I never made any promises to God until I thought I was a few seconds from dyin' but now I believe in miracles and will keep my promise to stay away from strong liquor and loose women.'

Hamish pulled a face at Jack's statement, knowing his promise would only last until the first jug of rum or loose woman crossed his path.

'Father!' Josiah shouted. 'Over here!'

Immediately, Ian turned his attention away from the body of Ryan Walsh and walked quickly to where Josiah and Lee stood staring down at a wounded man in the long grass. From the bloodstain, it appeared he had been shot high in the shoulder and the bullet had exited through his throat. Ian knew it had been a bullet from his son's Winchester that had inflicted the fatal wound; the man was barely alive.

Ian was joined by Hamish and Jack. 'That's one of Charlie's boys,' Jack said, gazing down at the almost dead bandit. 'See'd him drinking with Goodson an' his gang back in Maytown. Don't look like he's gonna live long with that wound.' With his final words, Mexican Jack fired a shot into the dying man's head. Ian and Hamish hardly flinched at his act of frontier mercy. Josiah cried out in shock but Lee remained silent.

Ryan was buried while the two men of Charlie's gang were left in the open for scavenging animals and nature to turn to bleaching bones.

They set up camp a short distance away and Hamish informed Ian of how he and his party had stumbled on the mining machinery and wagon on the other side of Hells Gate. The bullet holes in the wagons told their story.

Over mugs of rum by a campfire, they discussed the future.

'We have to organise more teams of bullocks to get the machinery to Maytown,' Ian said. 'It is costing more than I first signed on for.'

'I am also losing money,' Hamish sighed, taking another mouthful of the black liquor. 'Our lucrative sideline of transporting gold to the coast has dried up – thanks to an ongoing war between the Maytown and Cooktown Tongs. It appears Zhu is vying to be master of all the Chinese enterprises on the Palmer.'

'Your sideline,' Ian reminded. 'I thought that you and Zhu were firm business acquaintances?'

'I thought so,' Hamish answered. 'You can never figure what goes through a Chinaman's mind.' Hamish realised that Lee was sitting to one side of the fire and quickly added, 'Present company excepted.'

Lee just shook his head and took another swig of rum.

Josiah wandered a short distance away from the fire to gaze up at the brilliance of the night sky as dingoes howled in the distant hills. The events of the day swirled through his thoughts; the terrible wound to the man he had shot, and the deaths of Ryan and even the two bandits. It had all been so fast and almost casual to his father and the others. Death was just like life to them, he pondered, gazing at the stars above and recognising the distinctive constellation of the Southern Cross. He so much desired to be an officer in the British army, and at the age of sixteen he had conclusively killed his first man and critically wounded another. But as he gazed at the starry constellations, he was beginning to justify death. Those men would have killed him and his father, given the chance. Josiah remembered the gut-wrenching fear he'd felt as they had advanced on the rocks and the sudden calm when he had fired his first shot. Was this what his father had experienced as a soldier for the Queen those many years earlier?

At least now he was certain where his future lay.

*

Over a breakfast fire, the decision was made to return to the coast. It was here that Ian had access to money to payroll the bullock teams they would need to recover the mining machinery for conveyance to Maytown. As it was, they had just enough in the way of rations for their small party. Hamish was able to round up his packhorse with his supplies and one other of his mounts which he rode, using the excuse that he and Ian were older and might slow down the return trip if they were on foot. Ian did not agree but said he would take turns with his son and Mexican Jack to ride, while Lee politely turned down the offer. He explained that he preferred to walk as he had never learned to ride a horse.

The party set off to retrace their steps.

TWELVE

Ian's party returned to the coast without further incidents and Cooktown almost felt like home when they straggled into Charlotte Street. Ian was grateful beyond words that his son had survived the treacherous trail and clash with Charlie Goodson's gang.

Their first stop was Hamish's pub and Hamish ordered drinks all round for the few patrons in the bar. When the bleary-eyed prospectors had their glasses filled, Hamish raised his own.

'Here's to the passing of a man twice as good as any of you scurvy diggers. Raise a glass to Ryan Walsh.'

'Hear, hear!' rang out from the mouths of men who had no clue who Ryan Walsh was, but a free drink was reason enough to toast the dead man.

'Do we report Ryan's death to the Cooktown troopers?' Ian asked Hamish, settling into a corner with glasses of ale.

'No,' Hamish replied. 'I intend to settle the matter with Goodson and his crew myself in the future. Ryan was a good lad with promise and his death deserves the old biblical eye-for-an-eye justice.'

Ian understood his friend's anger and knew that when the final confrontation came, it would be bloody and final. 'I will go to the bank tomorrow morning and arrange for funds to finance bullock teams and crews to get our machinery to Maytown.'

'That would be appreciated, old chap. My own finances have been severely depleted since I lost the contract with the Tongs to smuggle gold,' Hamish said, finishing the last of his beer. 'I will draw up papers to recognise my half share in the loan. So, will you be staying on the Palmer to supervise the carriage of our mining machinery to Maytown?'

Ian shook his head. 'I have a business to run down south, and I think it is time to take Josiah home.'

'Or is Josiah taking his old man home?' Hamish countered with a grin. 'That boy of yours has a bright future.'

'I wish I could be as certain,' Ian replied gloomily. 'I fear he still desires to gain his commission with a British regiment.'

'Like his father if I remember rightly,' Hamish gently reminded him. 'I think that you should allow him a bit of his own life of derring-do. After all, from what I have seen of Josiah, he is more than competent to take on any challenge.'

'Has my son been talking to you?' Ian asked suspiciously, and Hamish winced.

'We might have discussed the matter of Josiah joining my old regiment,' Hamish said.

'You mean those damned mad Scots you commanded,'

Ian said. 'The way they throw themselves into a battle, Josiah can expect a very short, if courageous, career.'

'It is up to you, old chap,' Hamish said. 'He is your flesh and blood, but I am also very fond of the lad and can guarantee that a letter or two from me can assure him a commission.'

'I want to see my son inherit the enterprises I have established, not die in some faraway place in an unmarked grave,' Ian said. 'His life did not have an easy beginning.'

'Josiah is a grown man,' Hamish said. 'We had boys his age in the ranks of our infantry.'

Ian knew this was true. So many desperate young men attempting to escape poverty or a hopeless future lied about their ages to enlist, and the army looked the other way. But Ian had seen those same boys dead on battlefields, their bodies smashed and broken.

'I know that my son is obstinate and would probably find a way to travel to England to be commissioned,' Ian reluctantly acknowledged. 'All I can really do is support him until he learns the same lesson that we did.'

The two men fell silent on the subject and Hamish ordered another round of beers.

*

Lee stood before the much-feared Tong leader, whose ever-present personal bodyguard hovered close by in the store used as Zhu's headquarters.

'We were unable to continue to Maytown,' Lee said, feeling the sweat of fear trickle down his neck.

'My informants have already told me that you were confronted by the white men Wang employs,' Zhu said. 'You failed to complete the important mission I assigned you for the sake of China's future.'

Lee felt the knot in his stomach tighten as he tried not to stare at the Tong leader but looked down at the wooden floor. Was death mere moments away?

Zhu rose from behind his table and turned his back on the helpless young Chinese man. 'It was an unforeseen setback, but you will be given a chance to redeem yourself. I have a party of workers arriving soon who will go up the track. You will join them.'

At least I will walk out of here alive! Lee thought, realising that he had been holding his breath.

'Thank you, Master Zhu,' he gasped.

Zhu raised his hand to dismiss Lee, who bolted from the room. On the street, Lee quickly weighed up his options and concluded that Zhu was not a man to disappoint nor try to escape from. Lee realised that he had little choice but to complete the mission, one way or another, and wished he had not been so patriotic. To do so would require more than the sword he carried – he needed firepower.

★

'I am giving Lee my revolver before we leave for Sydney,' Josiah said to his father in the small room of Hamish's hotel as they packed.

'Why would you do that?' Ian questioned, carefully placing his Colts on top of his clothing in the bag.

'Lee has proven his loyalty to us,' Josiah answered. 'He could have been killed when we were confronted by Goodson and his gang, but he chose to join us in the fight.'

Ian nodded. He was impressed by Lee's intelligence and loyalty to their cause. 'It is your pistol to give,' Ian said, returning to his packing.

When Lee was informed, his face lit up with pleasure. 'I will return the cost of the gun,' he said.

'Call it a payment for the service you provided on the track,' Josiah replied. 'You do not owe me anything.'

But Lee silently disagreed. This was the first European who had ever respected him for who he was, and Lee was determined to show his gratitude in whatever way he could in the future.

Lee was at the wharf the following day to bid his new friends farewell before returning to his cousin's shop. As he walked back along Charlotte Street, he heard a voice call his name and turned to see Hamish striding towards him.

'I hope the Captain and Josiah were able to get away without any problems,' Hamish said when he caught up to Lee.

'They have sailed,' Lee answered.

'You know,' Hamish said, removing his hat and wiping his brow with the back of his hand, 'if you want a job, I have an opening for a bright and resourceful Chinese man.'

Lee quickly thought through his options. He could use the friendship of the Scot to achieve his mission, and hopefully impress Master Zhu with his efforts.

'I would be pleased to work for you, Major,' Lee replied, and was surprised to see the European man extend his hand in public to him.

'Jolly good,' Hamish said, gripping Lee's hand. 'You can move into my hotel today. Mexican Jack will settle you in.'

Hamish replaced his hat and walked away, leaving Lee to reflect on the fact that after Josiah, the Scot was only the second European who had ever shaken his hand.

*

The news that an undersea telegraphic cable had been laid between Botany Bay and New Zealand was trumpeted in the Sydney newspapers. This would allow the colony to be in contact with the world. Harold Skinner read the head-lines as he sipped tea in his office. It was a place of quietness, apart from a clock on a highly polished cabinet containing the leather-bound books of colonial parliamentary reports, which loudly ticked the seconds away.

A young man knocked tentatively at his open door and Harold glanced up.

'Enter,' he said, and the young man placed a folder on Harold's desk. This done, the secretary hastily retreated from Harold's presence. His boss had a bad temper, and no one knew when it might explode over the slightest mistake.

Harold opened the folder and saw the letters from England. He smiled; it had been months since he had contacted friends in high places amongst the army and aris-tocracy, inquiring about a former British officer known at the time as Samuel Forbes. There had been rumours around Ian Steele for some years and he was almost a legend to those who knew him as a captain with an infantry regiment.

Harold was not going to allow Isabel to slip through his fingers when – until Ian Steele came into her life – they had virtually been engaged. It had been a forgone conclu-sion that they would marry, and her estates would be joined with his own. As he gazed at the unopened letters on his desk, Harold reflected that when his and Isabel's paths had crossed recently, she had remained aloof to his fawning compliments. It was obviously a result of the influence of that man, born a common blacksmith outside Sydney in a tiny village, the progeny of a former convict mother and equally common British soldier. How dare he attempt to join the ranks of the colonial aristocracy, Harold fumed, let alone interfere with his ambitions towards Isabel?

Harold slipped open the first letter with an ornate letter opener and read a report from a high-ranking officer in the British War Department in London. He confirmed that the officer Harold enquired after had been exposed as an imposter and the real Samuel Forbes had died under an assumed name in the recent civil war in the American states. The matter had embarrassed the British army, but the uppers had discreetly decided to turn a blind eye to protect the well-known Forbes family.

So, Harold mused, the man has proven to be deceitful and a fraud.

The second letter he opened was a report from a private investigator that stated that Ian Steele's late wife was the daughter of an infamous Jewish criminal who had amassed a considerable fortune from ill-gotten money. Harold smiled. It was just getting better. He had already known that Ian was raising his children in the devious Jewish religion, which he and many of his associates eyed with contempt. Had they not crucified the Lord? Harold's twisted dislike of all Jewish people extended to the business world, where he and many other highly placed men in colonial society viewed the enter-prising and hardworking Jewish community as avaricious and dishonest money-makers bent on dominating the world and destroying two thousand years of Christian advancement.

Harold leaned back in his chair and rubbed his hands together. Such an ignominious background would be gold for the right newspaperman, and it would be a public service to expose the criminal amongst them.

What would Isabel Halpin think of her Captain Steele when they next met? he wondered with malicious glee.

*

Josiah stood on deck, watching Circular Quay coming into sight, and wondered how the two worlds to which he belonged could be so different. He had left a land of rugged hills, rainforest, swamps and raging rivers to return to this place of stone and timber, bustling street traffic of horse-drawn drays and carriages of all types. Men and woman in their fine clothes filled the footpaths, children in their wake. It was a world so divorced from the Palmer that he could have been on the moon.

'We will take a cab directly home,' Ian said, standing beside him. 'I believe that Sam and Becky will be pleased to see us.'

'I know Becky will be the first to greet you, Father,' Josiah said with a smile. 'And want to know what you have brought home for her.'

'I will need to make a stop and purchase a couple of bags of boiled sweets,' Ian said.

A cab took father and son to their mansion on the harbour where a surprised butler opened the door to them.

'Captain Steele, welcome home,' Henry greeted them with genuine warmth. 'Master Josiah, we were so worried! We had not heard anything while you were away and feared for your safety in the savage lands.'

'As you can see, we are both well,' Ian replied, stepping inside his house to be quickly rushed by Sam and Becky, who had recognised the voice at the front door. A time of squealing, hugging and demands of what presents Becky could expect from her wayward father followed. Josiah greeted his brother with an uncharacteristic hug, which then extended to his little sister, and when the fuss was over, Irene herded the two excited children away with promises that they would all be together at dinnertime.

It was Ian who first noticed the tension in Henry's face when he returned from taking the luggage to their rooms. Ian was good at reading and understanding such an expression from his days as a soldier.

'You do not appear yourself, Henry,' Ian stated when they were alone in Ian's study.

Henry looked uncomfortable. 'Just before you came home, the newspapers have written about you, Captain,' Henry said, pointing to the desk, where papers had been arranged for Ian's scrutiny. Amongst the formal business reports, Ian could see two folded newspapers and he walked over to his desk, picked up one and flipped it open to the second page, where he recognised his name in large print with the headline: *Does a fraudster walk amongst the colonial gentry? Evidence has come to our attention that Captain Ian Steele . . .*

Ian scanned the page, reading the sensational article accusing him of amassing his wealth through criminal activity traced back to his time as an imposter in the British army, and stating that the so-called hero of the Crimea, Persia, India and New Zealand campaigns was little else than a secret Jewish sympathiser supporting their nefarious acts of criminality.

'Damned lies!' Ian snarled. 'The only part that is true in the article is that I served the Queen in the places they mentioned.'

'We were all upset when the paper came out with the scandalous article,' Henry said sympathetically. 'No one could honestly believe that you are a criminal.'

'Sadly, Henry, once it has been written, it cannot be forgotten,' Ian said, tossing the paper back on his desk. 'I'm damned well going to track down the author of such lies and thrash it out of him as to who is the source of his so-called facts.'

'Sir, please believe that all the staff are soundly behind you to a man – and woman,' Henry said. 'If there is nothing else, I will attend to my duties.'

'Yes, thank you, Henry,' Ian replied, still reeling from what he had read. He knew there was an actual basis in some of the matters reported; that his deceased wife was the daughter of an infamous Jewish underworld figure Ikey Solomon, and that she had inherited his financial empire in England. It was also true Ian had assumed the identity of Samuel Forbes, but papers discovered a few years past had explained the swapping of lives. It had been a mutual contract, albeit involving deceit with Samuel's aristocratic family. However, Ian had not exploited the situation to make any financial gain from the Forbes estates. Well, he did force Charles Forbes to purchase his captaincy, but that was the extent of the financial gain. Ian had ensured that Samuel's sister, Alice Campbell *née* Forbes, had inherited the Forbes wealth after the deaths of all the Forbes men.

Ian walked to his liquor cabinet and retrieved a bottle of his best scotch. Pouring himself a generous drink, he slumped down at his desk, hardly noticing all the business reports and papers requiring his signature. His thoughts were for his children. Maybe he should send Sam and Becky away to one of his country properties until this all died down. But having them hide away could only embolden the people trying to ruin his good name and reputation for charitable causes in the colony.

And what would Isabel think, presupposing she had read the article or, just as likely, caught the gossip from her circle of well-heeled friends? It was Isabel's opinion that mattered more than what the public read about his past life.

Then again, he had not disclosed a lot of what was written in the article to Josiah. What would his firstborn son think of his father if he knew a lot more about him?

THIRTEEN

Ian was determined to track down the source of the damaging story that had appeared in the Sydney newspaper and at the same time attempt to make contact with Isabel to ascertain her reaction. But he had a more pressing duty, which was to travel to his offices in the city and review the current status of his many business enterprises.

He was welcomed by his staff but also felt that the welcome was a little reserved and guessed they had heard about or read the article. His chief bookkeeper seemed even more standoffish than usual but did not mention the content of the paper. Was Ian imagining it? He pondered whether he should gather his staff and refute the claims or simply ignore it.

He left the office and walked to the newspaper offices. The strong smell of ink from the presses and the clatter of them being run dominated the building. The chief editor was a middle-aged overweight man who was bald and wore spectacles. Ian vaguely knew him from when his staff covered social events and charities.

'Captain Steele,' he said without offering his hand. 'I presume you are here concerning the story we released about your colourful past.'

'Damned right!' Ian answered angrily. 'It is libel in its existence and without factual basis.'

The editor took off his spectacles and wiped them on the sleeve of his shirt. 'I am afraid, Captain Steele, that we have the facts from a reliable government source, and you are aware we have the right to publish anything that has the interest of the public.'

'Who is your supposed source?' Ian scoffed, knowing that it was not in the interest of the colonial government to pursue the story of his wealth and smear his name in the press.

'I am not at liberty to reveal who has supplied us the information, but I am convinced it is totally reliable. If you are not happy, I can personally interview you and you may attempt to refute any matters raised by the story.'

Ian glared at the man, sensing the smugness in his offer. Whoever had provided the information must have had some influence on the colonial government, he thought, and knew that short of threatening the editor's life with extreme violence, which would then probably be published, he was not about to reveal the name of the person who had initiated the damaging newspaper story.

'Do you wish to respond to the story, Captain Steele?' the editor asked, replacing the spectacles on his nose.

Ian stormed out of the building without replying. Fuming, he strode back to his office, where he found Josiah loitering out the front.

'Were you responsible for Elise being taken?' Josiah asked, barely containing his own fury as he stood eye to eye with his confused father.

'Elise? Taken where?' Ian replied.

'I have just returned from the Schmidts', and Herr Schmidt said a couple of days before we returned, a man and woman came to their shop with papers from the German Consulate. Otto was shown the papers that gave the two people the authority to take Elise with them. He said the papers appeared legal and he was not even given an answer to any of his questions concerning who they were or where they were taking Elise. Was this your doing, Father?'

Ian shook his head. It was bad enough that he was engaged in a battle to clear his name, but now he was being blamed for something he had had no hand in. 'Did Otto say what nationality the two were?' he asked, attempting to calm his agitated son.

'He said they had Bavarian accents and claimed to be relatives and that Elise seemed to be comfortable in their presence. Elise thanked Otto and his wife for their hospitality but said she had to go with the man and woman. She said nothing else concerning the matter.'

'I swear on your mother's name that I was not aware of these matters,' Ian said, placing his hands on his son's shoulders and staring directly into his eyes. For a moment, Josiah stared back, and then Ian could feel the tension evaporate between them.

'I believe you, Father,' Josiah finally said. 'What are we to do?'

'I will go directly to the consulate – and you should come with me in case I need an interpreter.'

Josiah nodded his agreement. Ian accepted that the girl they had rescued was special to his son, and after all they had experienced together in the past year on the Palmer, he deserved Ian's support. Between them, they would seek an explanation from the Germans and find Elise.

But they received extraordinarily little help from an evasive consulate official, who explained that the matter was of great importance to his government. When Ian questioned the man as to where Elise was, he apologised and said he honestly did not know. When Ian asked the man who the man and woman were, he said he was not authorised to disclose their identities, except to say they had authorisation directly from Berlin to take the girl into their custody.

Frustrated by his visit to the newspaper and now the German Consulate, Ian considered finding a pub and ordering a stiff drink. But he was with his son.

It was time to go directly to their home and reflect on his – and Josiah's – problems.

★

Hamish had organised bullock teams to recover the mining machinery to be relayed to Maytown but knew he would have to supervise its construction on the land that he and Ian Steele had purchased at the first signing of contracts for the mining company. He was hoping to wait until the Danish engineer he had hired arrived from Brisbane, but he might not be able to delay. He knew there were vested interests trying to sabotage the operation at Maytown, and strongly suspected that Wang was behind the conspiracy. Lee had related stories of violence between opposing Tong forces on the Palmer track. Lee seemed to understand that one of the reasons he had been hired was to eavesdrop on the events in the secretive world of the Tongs, although Hamish had noticed that Lee seemed to avoid Zhu and his men around the town.

Hamish was also impressed that Lee carried Josiah's pistol under his jacket and thought that if Ian Steele's son had given it to the Chinese man, he must have respected him a lot.

Hamish stood in the bar of a more refined hotel than his own where a pretty young woman was singing a ballad popular amongst the miners, accompanied by a fiddler with a long beard. Hamish took a swig of his gin, listening to the words and the raucous cheers of the patrons of the bar when it was time to join in the chorus.

The wind is fair and free, my boys, the wind is fair and free

The steamer's course is north, my boys, and the Palmer we will see

The Palmer we will see, my boys, and Cooktown's muddy shore

Where I have been told there's lots of gold, so stay down south no more

So, blow ye winds, heigh-ho

A-digging we will go

I'll stay no more down south, my boys

So let the music play

In spite of what I'm told

I'm off in search of gold

I'll make a push for that new rush

A thousand miles away

They say the blacks are troublesome, and spear both horse and man

The rivers are wide and deep, no bridges them do span . . .

'Major.' Hamish turned as the singer continued the ballad.

'Jack. How are things progressing with the packers and bullockies?'

'We got a good team, but they will cost. They are sayin' they won't go up the track unless we provide protection.'

'Then we will have to go back on the track to ensure all goes well,' Hamish replied, finishing the last of his gin just as the drunken patrons raised their drinks and joined in the chorus.

So, blow ye winds, heigh-ho . . .

★

Lee was summoned to Zhu's shop, where the scent of joss sticks burning reminded Lee of his parents' home down south near Sydney.

'Why are you working for the Scot?' the feared Tong leader demanded.

'He has financial interests in Maytown and is planning a trip there very soon. I am going to volunteer to travel with him.'

Lee thought he saw the flicker of interest in the man sitting opposite of where he stood in the shop packed with crates and parcels of imported Chinese goods. Lee was also aware that Zhu distributed opium to those in the Asian community and a few trusted Europeans.

'So, you are confident that you will carry out the mission for our patriotic cause,' Zhu said. 'Time is a precious commodity, and it is running out.'

'I am prepared for the moment I am able to get close to Wang,' Lee replied. 'I am in possession of a pistol and know how to use it.'

'Good,' Zhu said. 'If you die in the attempt, then your countrymen will remember you with great honour.'

Lee had no intention of dying and felt that the revolver gave him the edge in a close fight. But the assignation would need to be under conditions that did not draw the attention of the police.

'I do this for a free China,' Lee dutifully said before he was dismissed by the Tong leader.

When Lee found Hamish and put forward his offer, it was immediately accepted. Lee was even more surprised when Hamish said he would issue him a further firearm – a Snider rifle.

★

Ian Steele could see that the sudden disappearance of Elise had upset his son. The pompous position the German Consulate had taken in refusing to provide further information on who had taken the girl and why still annoyed Ian. The consulate refused to say where she had been spirited away to, as well, and Otto and his wife were as much in the dark.

Ian's worry had been tinged with guilty relief that the young girl was gone from their lives. He had hoped that maybe Josiah would start spending his free time with chums from school. However, no sooner had they given up hope of finding out what had happened to Elise than Josiah reminded his father that Hamish would be able to secure him a commission in his old Scottish regiment.

Ian despaired of ever changing Josiah's aspiration to serve the Queen. Although he had warned his son against it, he knew he was wasting his breath, and that Josiah had to learn from firsthand experience that his decision to serve would come at a high physical and mental cost to the rest of his life. A compromise was finally reached; Josiah would go with Hamish's recommendation and Ian's blessing to serve for no more than three years before resigning his commission. He would then return to the colony of New South Wales and assume his mantle as Ian's successor.

Josiah's joy at his father's approval was painted across the young man's face.

'Thank you, Father,' Josiah said, extending his hand.

'You also have to promise me that you will not try to be a hero.'

'I will do my duty,' Josiah answered, and Ian guessed that his son really wanted the recognition from his father, as sons often do.

'I may not understand your choice to risk your life, but I think I understand why you have elected to chase your dream of adventure and glory,' Ian said sadly. 'You will have to find out for yourself that there is no adventure – nor glory – in war.'

*

It was the greyhound of the sea, a sleek and fast clipper with a mass of sails already south of Adelaide and plunging forward as it sailed west.

Elise stood at the bow, snuggled in a fur coat against the biting cold, a thick scarf around her neck. She wore fine clothes befitting a young woman of her age and status, and an older man stood behind her like a watchdog.

'You should go downstairs, my angel,' he said firmly. 'Dinner with the captain will be served soon and I know he would like to meet his special passenger.'

Elise could feel the crusting of salt on her face from the fine spray of seawater misting in the air. It was overcast but she had been informed the southern seas were relatively peaceful for the moment.

'Yes, Uncle,' Elise replied and turned to join the tall man, who took her hand to steady her on the rolling deck.

'Your aunt will meet us at dinner,' the man said, desperately holding on to his top hat as they crossed the finely polished deck.

For a moment, Elise was reminded of how she had originally come to this strange land with her parents, what seemed a lifetime ago. It had not been as fancy as the way she was now travelling. The steam and sail ship had conveyed them from Europe, packed in with so many other immigrants searching for a better life away from the politics and poverty of the Old World. Now she travelled in style, enjoying the privileges of a first-class passenger with her aunt and uncle.

A memory of a voyage from the savage north of the continent came to Elise, when she had travelled with a true knight of the fairy stories that she had read. She felt guilty that her memory of Josiah was already fading as she looked forward to her life in Bavaria, in the castle she still remembered.

When they reached the small dining room set aside for the captain, he rose at her entrance and bowed his head.

'I am pleased to make your acquaintance, Duchess.'

FOURTEEN

On the third day of their journey to Maytown, Hamish and his party of Mexican Jack and Lee passed a column of Chinese porters walking in single file with baskets and pots swaying on bamboo poles slung across their shoulders. Most wore only loincloths and sweated under the tropical sun, while others wore European-style trousers with smocks. They were obviously the supervisors striding ahead of the column.

Lee walked beside Hamish and Jack, who were mounted, trailing three packhorses. But Lee carried his rifle and as they passed, he received curious looks from some of the Chinese porters. The sight of such a modern firearm in the hands of one of their countrymen was unusual, as the only guns they carried were usually ancient muskets, and these were in the hands of their supervisors as protection for the men they oversaw.

That night, Hamish pitched camp by one of the rivers they would cross in the morning, and the Chinese workers caught up to also pitch camp not far from Hamish's tents. On their nights around the campfires, Lee had come to like and respect the two men he travelled with, and they seemed to accept him as an equal. Hamish was duly impressed by the fact that Lee spoke excellent English with a colonial accent and was also proficient in both Cantonese and Mandarin. Furthermore, Lee could read and write English, Cantonese and Mandarin.

'How is it that you are literate in three languages?' Hamish asked that night as they boiled water for their tea.

'My father was a monk and is a learned man,' Lee replied, stirring the tea leaves into the boiling water. 'He made me learn and go to a little school near our garden plot. The teacher was a good man who had once been a Methodist missionary in China and believed even we Chinese should learn like the other kids of the district. But the parents of the other pupils protested my presence amongst their own children, so he would have to teach me when school was over. I was forced to learn fast. And after I had done my work in my family's garden, I would learn of my Chinese traditions.'

Hamish rummaged for his pipe and tobacco, lighting the bowl with a twig from the fire. 'Despite the fact you are from China –'

'No, I'm from New South Wales,' Lee interrupted. 'Maybe I have a foot in each world.'

'Maybe. But while you are in this one, I want you to know that you have a permanent place in my employ if you want it. I will raise your pay to equal that of Jack and Frank. I could do with someone who is able to read and write in three languages.'

Lee experienced a strange feeling of acceptance into the European world that he had never been afforded before.

'How old are you?' Hamish asked, puffing on the pipe.

'Eighteen, but soon to be nineteen,' he replied.

'Good age for a young man to seek adventure and his fortune. You may not know Zhu in Cooktown, but he is skilled in finance and speaks English well. He is, I believe, what you call a Tong leader.'

'I have heard of him from my cousin,' Lee answered carefully, not wishing to reveal that he knew the dreaded Tong leader. 'Maybe I will meet him when we return from Maytown.'

'I will attempt to arrange a meeting,' Hamish said, gazing at the full moon. 'You have made it a long way by yourself, Lee. I admire that.'

An hour or so after the evening meal, Hamish and Jack retired to the tent and Lee was left to stand his guard shift in a position just outside the light of the now dying fire. It was a pleasant night and Lee had to force himself from slipping into a deep sleep as he held the loaded rifle close to his chest.

Lee came wide awake when he felt the razor-sharp steel of a knife at his throat and a voice hissed in Cantonese, 'I will not harm you, Ling Lee. I recognised you today on the track as the Chinese man that Zhu spoke of.'

The knife came away and Lee cautiously turned to see the face of one of the men he vaguely recognised from earlier that day, an overseer of the column. He was possibly in his mid-thirties, and, like Lee, his head was shaved.

'What do you want of me?' Lee replied, struggling through his surprise to use the language he rarely spoke, as he and his father normally conversed in Mandarin.

'We are on the same mission,' the man answered. 'I am Kwong. I work for the freedom of China from the shackles of the Qing dynasty and the Dowager Empress. Then we shall confront the European invaders and free our glorious country to rule itself, free of foreign intervention.'

Lee could hear the passionate fervour in the man's voice and realised that he was truly dedicated to the cause of the future revolution.

'What do you know of my mission from Zhu?' Lee asked.

'That you are to kill Wang,' Kwong answered. 'The men I am taking to Maytown have been assigned to assist you.'

'Zhu could have told me that when we last met,' Lee replied, annoyance in his voice.

'He decided the day after you were supposed to have left Cooktown,' Kwong said. 'It was too important a mission for just one man of untested skills. You did not tell Zhu you were leaving later than expected.'

'The major's horse threw a shoe. We were delayed.'

'It has been good fortune you overtook us when you did.'

'So, what happens now?' Lee asked.

'We continue separately on our journey and meet in Maytown,' Kwong said. 'There, we will complete our mission and Zhu will control the whole Palmer goldfield. We will need much money to purchase the European's military hardware to succeed. This is our opportunity to swell our war chests so that we are ready for the day when we find the man to lead us to our republic. Now, I must return to my men.'

With these words, Kwong disappeared into the scrub under the waning moon, leaving Lee with greater confidence in achieving his mission.

★

Captain Ian Steele noticed a change in attitude from business acquaintances. They were more aloof in their dealings with him. Even at the Australia Club, he felt that he was being shunned, no doubt a reaction to the article concerning his supposed links with the Jewish community and the underworld in London. Voices whispered and heads turned in his direction as he sat alone nursing a tumbler of scotch.

Josiah was also being shunned by those with whom he had attended school, except for his close friend, Douglas Wade, and George Bowden, the handyman's son. No longer was the eligible handsome young man being invited to tea parties, tennis matches and colonial balls.

Occasional anonymous letters arrived at the Steele home, expressing a hatred for Jews, which were disposed of in the flames of the wood combustion stove in the kitchen. The ironic part was that Ian was not Jewish but baptised a Catholic. However, he held to Ella's wishes that her children be raised in the Jewish faith. As it was, Ian had long lost his faith in any god on the battlefields. He knew well that men did not cry out to God when they were dying, but for their mothers.

But the part that affected him most was the silence from Isabel. He had written seeking time with her without any reply. No doubt the press articles had influenced her opinion of him.

One invitation Ian did receive was from Sir Godfrey Pollard. In his letter, he had expressed a continuing interest in Ian's gold venture on the Palmer as a future investor. Ian decided that he should visit the colonial aristocrat, and when he did so was met warmly by Sir Godfrey himself when he stepped from the carriage sent to meet him at the railway station.

'Ah, Captain Steele,' the colonial knight said, extending his hand. 'So good that you were able to accept my invitation for dinner. I have a few other guests attending.'

'I must say, I was surprised to see that there was anyone left in the colony who was on speaking terms with me,' Ian replied, accepting the gesture.

'I don't put any stock in what those damned newspapers say,' Sir Godfrey replied cheerfully. 'Besides, better they write about you than me! We all have a few skeletons in the closet. Anyway, that you are a Jew is not a bar to us working together to advance our fortunes.'

'I am not Jewish,' Ian said. 'My children are.'

'Oh, the newspapers no doubt got most of your story wrong,' Sir Godfrey said. 'Come inside and mix with my guests before we sit for dinner. A few sherries before a meal whets the appetite, what?'

Ian followed Sir Godfrey inside his country mansion to a large room where men and women stood sipping pre-dinner drinks, the men in dinner suits and ladies wearing their best jewellery. Candles flickered shadows as Ian was offered a sweet sherry in a small crystal goblet. He had hardly sipped from it when he was aware of a tiny hush in the conversation and many eyes looking in his direction.

He was startled to see that Isabel was one of the guests, and beside her stood Harold Skinner. Isabel locked eyes with Ian, and he was not able to read her reaction to him. Skinner leaned over and whispered something in her ear and Ian saw a flash of annoyance in her eyes. She broke away and made her way to Ian.

'Good evening, Mrs Halpin,' Ian greeted formally. 'A surprise to meet you here at Sir Godfrey's where we first made our reacquaintance.'

'I suppose you are wondering why I have not responded to your correspondence,' Isabel said promptly. 'I read the newspaper articles.'

'Isabel, I can —'

'Why on earth had you not spoken of these things in your past to me?'

'Many were not true,' Ian retorted, but added, 'and the rest were things of the past with no bearing on the present. I did not think they were important to our friendship.'

'Friendship!' Isabel snorted. 'I feel that our friendship ended when you bedded me.'

Ian was confused. He could read a battlefield easily, but the person standing before him was a complete mystery.

'Isabel, my love for you is not in doubt,' Ian said quietly, wondering if his declaration was of any use. He saw a slight change in her cold expression. 'The future has always been my main concern. I am not a man who dwells on the past. I am sorry if mine so horrifies you.'

'Ian, I am only angry that you did not tell me of your past yourself,' Isabel said. 'You could have distinguished what was true and what was not. I lived with a man who held a secret that all knew about – except me. Complete honesty is the basis of the future for a man and woman who love each other.'

'So, you still love me?' Ian asked, snatching this tiny opening in the conversation.

'Yes,' she said tartly. 'And as much as I wish I could remain angry, there has not been a night past that I have not desired your body next to mine.' Isabel reached up and touched Ian's cheek with her gloved hand. 'Just promise me that there is nothing else that I should know of.'

'The essential facts are correct,' Ian replied with a slight shrug of the shoulders. 'I served as the Queen's soldier in all those places across the world that the article mentioned. Ella's father was a well-known Jewish entrepreneur in England who left her and now my children a considerable fortune. And my children are being raised in the Jewish faith, as I promised Ella they would be.'

'She would be proud of them.'

'As am I,' Ian replied. 'But I see you are here in the company of that Harold Skinner. You should know that I have traced the articles in the press back to him. He and I are due for a chat.'

'Harold just happened to be here alone when he approached me,' Isabel said, glancing back at the man glowering at Ian. 'He appears to be annoyed that I am speaking with you.'

A dinner bell tinkled, and a servant announced that all guests were to make their way into the large dining room, where Isabel ensured that she was seated next to Ian while Harold Skinner sat on the opposite side, glaring at them. Ian simply stared back until the weak-willed public servant looked away.

For the first time in weeks, Ian felt a warm glow spread through him. He had regained what was a most important part of his life – the love of a woman he desired.

The first course was served, kangaroo tail soup, and Skinner waved it off, instead demanding a flute of champagne.

'Damn you, Steele!' Skinner suddenly yelled, standing and tossing his champagne into Ian's face. Shocked, the whole room of guests at the table abruptly fell into silence.

Ian wiped the liquid from his face with a napkin, pushed out his chair and stood, leaning across the table.

'We will leave the table and settle this matter outside,' he growled. 'That is, if you are man enough.'

Skinner pulled back his shoulders. 'I do not think a Jew lover would be man enough to face me,' Skinner said, aware all eyes were on him. Skinner's bravado was assisted with the alcohol he had consumed, and when he stared at Ian opposite him, a head shorter than he, he had no doubt that he was more of a man than the overrated hero of the Empire. He would be able to give the pretend hero a good thrashing that would show Isabel who was the real man in the room.

Both men departed from the table to the silent stares of Sir Godfrey's guests.

'Capital!' Sir Godfrey exclaimed. 'Would anyone like to make a wager on who will be the last man standing?' With that, Sir Godfrey lit a big cigar and waited for the scramble of elegantly dressed men and women out to the garden adjacent the mansion.

Isabel watched the procession in shock, feeling sick to the stomach as she blamed herself for this possibly violent clash. Sir Godfrey sauntered to her chair. 'My dear,' he said, offering his arm. 'Can't have a fight for a lady's favour without the lady bearing witness.'

Excitement filled the air for this totally unexpected entertainment as lanterns were fetched by servants to illuminate the ground selected for the bout.

'Too bad duelling has been outlawed,' one of Sir Godfrey's guests muttered as Sir Godfrey guided a horrified Isabel to the makeshift ring.

Both men had removed their jackets and stood facing each other. Already an enterprising guest was taking bets on the side. Harold Skinner was the favourite as he was the larger man, but Sir Godfrey placed a hefty bet on Ian.

'No hitting below the belt or eye-gouging,' Sir Godfrey explained to the contestants while he puffed on his cigar. 'May the better man win.' He stepped back, signalling the commencement of the duel.

Ian and Skinner first circled each other in the straight-backed style of bare-knuckle fighters and Ian could see the glazed expression of hatred in his opponent's eyes. He did not underestimate Skinner, but he had never forgotten all he had learned growing up amongst the tough Irish boys of his village, who had never heard of the Marquess of Queensbury or his rules.

Skinner threw the first punch, which came a lot faster than Ian had anticipated. It caught Ian above the eye, opening a wound from a ring Skinner was wearing.

Ian stepped back as Skinner threw another punch, which missed, then Ian closed in, delivering a vicious headbutt to his opponent, which caused him to stagger back and almost fall. Some in the crowd moaned at the lack of sportsmanship displayed by the Jew lover, urging Skinner on. Ian took advantage of Skinner's grogginess from the broken nose he had suffered and released a barrage of short, hard blows into Skinner's face and stomach, drawing more blood. Skinner was hardly able to keep his hands up to defend himself. He continued to reel back from Ian's unrelenting punches. Ian felt as if he was back in the terrible hand-to-hand fighting he had once known on the battlefield, and the man before him was an enemy he must kill. The pent-up anger of having his family's name smeared in the newspapers at the behest of the man in front of him gave Ian the adrenaline-fuelled strength to make each blow count.

The fight was over in short minutes as Skinner slumped to the grass, moaning in his pain and shame. The crowd was silent; Ian's victory was not applauded. Money changed hands as they ambled back to the house, leaving Skinner on the ground. Ian knelt by his defeated foe and whispered into his ear, 'If you continue to persecute my family, next time, I will kill you.'

Ian took in deep breaths, then stood alone until Isabel joined him, gently examining the deep cut above his eye.

'I will need to bandage that wound,' she said just as Sir Godfrey stepped forward, a grin on his face.

'You have made me a nice windfall tonight, Captain Steele,' he said, extending his hand. 'I gambled that the killer spirit of a soldier would win out over the bravado of a civilian. Congratulations on your undisputed win.'

Ian nodded to acknowledge Sir Godfrey's faith in him.

'This is the second time we have meant to meet to discuss your gold venture, but I think Isabel has plans to take you home to tend to your wound,' the colonial knight said with a wink, causing Isabel to blush.

Ian shook his head with a smile. The old knight was wiser than most knew him to be. He might be a womaniser, drunk and a gambler, but he was also very perceptive.

That night Isabel washed and bandaged the cut above Ian's eye before they fell into bed in a night of passionate lovemaking.

FIFTEEN

Hamish's party continued travelling to Maytown along the track and eventually through Hells Gate. Lee continued to walk beside the mounted men, carrying his rifle and concealed revolver. Each night, they camped out and Lee found himself very much accepted by Mexican Jack and Hamish. There was easy banter around the campfire and Lee's nationality did not come between any in the party.

At one stage, they passed the site of the skirmish where Ryan had been killed and paused to stand by his grave before pressing on.

When Maytown finally came into sight the weary men sought out the American Beauregard Connors, who welcomed them with his last bottle of rum.

'You can set up camp next to me,' the American said, leaning on his cane. 'The town has grown a fair bit since your last time here.'

Hamish could see that the introduction of the heavy ore-crushing machinery by other entrepreneurs had swelled the population with workers. 'We are still waiting for our bullock teams to retrieve our machinery, which we passed this side of Hells Gate.'

'Must have been hell getting the machinery over the range,' Beauregard said, knowing it could not be transported via the walking trail. He turned to Lee, who had remained silent during the meeting. 'I see you got a Chinaman, Major.'

Hamish bristled at the off-handed reference to Lee. 'His name is Lee and he is as good a man as I have known,' he replied.

Beauregard eased his weight onto the cane and extended his hand to Lee. 'Pleased to make your acquaintance,' he said. 'Any man the major speaks highly of deserves my welcome. You could come in handy with our dealings with Wang.'

'Where is Wang?' Hamish asked.

'Gone bush with his men,' the American answered. 'From what I've heard, seems he is building an armed base somewhere out in the scrub. I heard a rumour about some of Zhu's men coming up from the coast.'

'Charlie Goodson and his gang. What of them?' Hamish asked.

'They are still around, and I also heard a rumour they are working for Wang, who pays them for protection. Fancy that, white men working for a Chinese boss.'

'Strange times,' Hamish replied. 'What's the situation with the local troopers?'

'We rarely see them in force around here,' Beauregard replied. 'They are occupied with gold escorts and patrolling the fields against attacks from the darkies.'

'Is there a good supply of drink in the pubs, Colonel?'

Mexican Jack asked. He had also served in the past civil war with a Texan brigade and the two men had a lot in common – except Jack had been a non-commissioned sergeant during the war between north and south.

'Enough, if you desire to pay the high prices the thieving sons of bitches demand.'

'We have the money,' Hamish said with a wry grin, tapping the money belt around his waist.

'Well, you have been heaven sent.' Beauregard grinned. 'This is my last bottle.'

Hamish, Jack and Lee pitched tents, hobbled horses and spread out their essential cooking supplies for a long stay. They would await the arrival of the mining machinery and establish the ore-crushing plant. In the meantime, Hamish was particularly good at organising men and he would use the time to recruit workers.

Lee listened carefully to the conversations between the Europeans and spent his leisure time cleaning his rifle and revolver. These were to be his tools when the Chinese column they had left behind eventually reached Maytown, and the mission to hunt down Wang and his Tong followers was implemented. His role was now to mix with the considerable local Chinese population of the mining town and collect intelligence.

★

'Your brother Paul was a fool,' Karl von Mann said to his wife Karin as they strolled the decks of the clipper bound for Europe. 'A careless adventurer. It cost he and Anna their lives in that barbaric country, leaving Elise an orphan.'

The seas were relatively calm in the central southern section of the Indian Ocean and it was a fine day to be above deck as Elise played with a couple of young girls her age at the stern railings, observing the pod of dolphins swimming in the wake of the clipper.

'An orphan who has inherited the Bavarian estates,' Karin said bitterly. 'A mere child who is deemed a duchess.'

'It is the way of things,' Karl said calmly.

'We are a family of fools. One brother dead in a hunting accident, the other in a godforsaken place halfway across the world,' Karin said, pulling her shawl tighter around her shoulders.

'Yet they were still family, and we must see to the care of our young niece,' Karl said. 'As her nearest living relative and next in line for the title, it is our duty to guide Elise until her majority.'

'And then it is we who can dictate the finances and run the estates,' added Karin with cold calculation. Perhaps this situation was not so bad after all. Of course, much could happen before the little girl playing on deck turned twenty-one.

*

Josiah had been forced to settle a couple of insults with his fists. A former classmate and ally of his archenemy David Anderson had spat on him in a Sydney Street, which had had a conveniently located dingy alleyway nearby, where Josiah dragged the frightened teen and gave him a thrashing. That news spread, and only one other fight was necessary to convince them that the young man they had named Jew Boy was a lot tougher than they were. Little did Josiah know that he was carrying on a family tradition from Ikey Solomon's own youth on the mean streets of London.

Josiah still mourned the sudden disappearance of Elise but felt that the bond was not broken. In discussions with his father, they both deduced that relatives had been informed of her survival, travelled to Australia and taken her home to Germany. Both had to acknowledge that they'd always said they would find any living family she might have, so they had done as promised.

Still, Josiah missed her company. He prayed she was safe and well in her imaginary castle but was realistic enough to know he would never see her again.

★

Charlie Goodson knew that Hamish and his small party were in town and wondered if he and his men had been recognised during the abortive attempt to kill Hamish months earlier. Not that it mattered now. A message had been delivered to his hideout in the bush near Maytown that said it was essential that the ore-crushing machinery did not complete its journey. It was obvious that Wang had a plan to dominate the Palmer with his own ore-crushing plant.

Charlie sat outside his bark hut, smoking a pipe under a pleasant sky of scudding, fluffy clouds and was joined by his second-in-command, Martin Donahue.

'What are we goin' to do?' Martin asked, sitting down beside his boss. 'We only have a couple of the boys left.'

'Wang has promised us a bonus if we can stop the Scot's bullock teams reaching Maytown. We have enough guns to do that.'

'What about the troopers?' Martin asked.

'The traps are too scattered to interfere,' Charlie replied. 'That is, if we think hard enough as to how we can stop the Scot and his men.'

Martin did not say anything else. He had faith in his boss's ability to come up with a plan, hopefully one better than their last, though Martin grudgingly admitted it would have worked if it had not been for the unexpected intervention of another party, who they now knew was Hamish's business partner in the mining venture. This time, luck would be on their side.

★

Lee had few duties to perform other than to stand guard when required. Hamish knew Goodson and his gang were still in the district from reports by locals. Mexican Jack spent a good amount of time in the local drinking establishments, listening to the gossip around the miners' tables. He was smart enough to limit his normal quaffing of raw spirits and only feigned inebriation. When he returned to Hamish's camp, though, he allowed himself to indulge in an excess of rum and gin.

'Charlie's got a hut about a mile outside of town, in the scrub,' Jack said, swigging from a bottle of gin. 'His goddamn men hang around with him there.'

'How many?' Hamish asked, leaning forward to poke their campfire with a stick, stirring embers into the clear night sky.

'Dunno, maybe three or four,' Jack replied.

'Two,' Lee said quietly from the opposite side of the fire, and Hamish turned towards him in surprise.

'How do you know?' he asked.

'I have made friends with some of the Chinese here who were originally from my father's village. One even remembered him as a Shaolin monk. They told me that they knew Charlie was working for Wang and that only four men have been sighted at Charlie's hut. They also warned me to be careful because there was talk that Wang knows who we are.'

'Goddamn! Well done, Lee,' Jack said, passing the bottle of clear alcohol to him.

'Thank you, Jack, but I do not drink,' Lee politely declined.

'Not even sake?' Jack said frowning.

'Sake is a Japanese drink, and we Chinese have no love for the Japanese.'

'Might explain why we don't see any Japanese on the Palmer,' Jack chuckled, withdrawing the bottle and swigging from it. 'What do we do, Major?'

'My military experience tells me that we launch a strike against Charlie with the element of surprise on our side,' Hamish mused, staring into the glowing coals of the fire.

'Their hut is too close to Maytown,' Lee said. 'It would attract attention from the people here.'

'Wise man,' Hamish said. 'You may be right. We could find ourselves hanging for murder if we are caught. Do either of you have any ideas?'

Lee was pleasantly surprised to be acknowledged for his input into the scheme. He had a secret and felt that this was the time to confess something of vital interest to both he and the Major. 'Major, we have help.'

Hamish glanced up at Lee. 'What help?'

Lee explained how he had been approached on the track many days earlier by Kwong acting for Zhu, and that it was Zhu's intention to send a party of handpicked men to wipe out Wang and his men. Both Jack and Hamish listened intently until Hamish broke in.

'What is your role in all this?' he asked suspiciously.

Lee did not want to look the former British army officer in the eye and partially regretted revealing what he knew. 'I am supposed to kill Wang,' he replied.

Hamish stood up, almost scattering the small fire at their feet. 'Damnation! Is that the only reason you asked to come with us to Maytown?'

'No, Major,' Lee answered honestly. 'I need the wages. But you have a saying: I was killing two birds with one stone and my mission is the same as yours. Wang will be coming for you, one way or another. This I have learned from my friends in the Chinese community.'

Hamish was annoyed but he had too much respect for the young man to lose his temper. He resumed his seat, rubbing his brow at the same time. 'You could have told me all this before we left the coast.'

'I was not sure if you would let me travel with you,' Lee said. 'I was not then aware of Wang's intentions towards you and Jack.'

'Well, if this Kwong is on our side, our odds are now a lot better,' Mexican Jack said, raising his bottle in a toast.

Hamish considered the new option and granted it had merit. This was a dirty secret war, fought for absolute control of the Palmer and its gold. No matter what Zhu's motivation, there was more of a guarantee of establishing the Steele MacDonald mining enterprise without serious opposition from a powerful Tong leader and his European mercenaries.

The following day, Lee arranged a meeting between the major and Kwong outside Maytown, at a location in the thick scrub.

Kwong arrived with four of his men armed with swords and a couple of ancient muskets. He was suspicious, and angrily berated Lee for revealing their existence to the white man.

'What did he say?' Hamish asked.

'He said it is good to meet you, Major,' Lee lied.

Hamish suppressed a smile at the young man's diplomacy. 'Tell Mr Kwong that it is also a pleasure to meet an ally.'

Lee translated what Hamish had said and some of the

anger left Kwong's face. He spoke again and this time Lee interpreted what he said correctly. 'Kwong has expressed that his party are impressed by the weapons we have and will work with us in a mission to destroy Wang's Tong. He has news that Wang intends to prevent your wagon teams reaching Maytown.'

'That I already strongly suspected,' Hamish said to Lee. 'But express my thanks for his information anyway.' Hamish appraised Kwong and his men with the eye of a soldier; they were tough men with a killer look. They would be good back-up in any armed confrontation with the larger numbers of Wang's Tong.

'Ask Kwong if he has any ideas about how we can confront Wang and his men without much fuss?'

Lee did so and Kwong nodded and began to speak. 'Kwong says that they know where Wang's men have built a new fortress in the bush, well away from here. He says that they are well prepared but with our guns, we could make the difference in an attack on it.'

Hamish turned to face Kwong and nodded. They would work to the Chinese warrior's plan. If it did not work, then they would all find themselves as food for the scavenging goannas, dingoes and crows. But Hamish had faced worse odds, as had Mexican Jack. The only question was how Lee would perform in such a premeditated mission to kill.

SIXTEEN

This was a dilemma Captain Ian Steele had never encountered before. Around him, in the many rooms of his offices, his staff went about managing the many company interests Ian had developed over the years, from agriculture to manufacturing. But this situation was beyond bookkeeping and speculative investment. What was he going to do about Isabel, their strengthening relationship, and his children?

The memory of his beloved Ella would always be with him, but Ian was also a man of practical values. There was nothing he could do about the past, but he could change the future. Deep within himself, he had finally admitted that he would like to spend the rest of his life with Isabel. But there was the matter of his responsibility to his children.

On her many visits to Ian's house on the harbour, Isabel's sense of fun and genuine warmth had won Becky's affections and even those of young Samuel. However, Josiah had never shown any response to Isabel other than politeness.

Ian had requested that Josiah join him at his office so that he could speak with his eldest son concerning the future with Isabel.

How ironic, Ian thought, that he would require his son's acceptance of the delicate situation, when he was the father and responsible for the futures of his own children.

'Master Josiah is here, Captain,' a secretary said, knocking lightly and poking his head around the door.

'Send him in,' Ian replied, rising to greet his son.

'Hello, Father,' Josiah said, walking to a large window overlooking the busy harbour of steam and sail. 'I presume that you have something to discuss, as I am rarely summoned to your office.'

'Nothing of any trouble,' Ian answered half-heartedly. Maybe he could postpone the talk till another time, Ian thought, and simply take Josiah to lunch?

'Is it about me travelling to England to commence my training to be an officer in the army?' Josiah asked.

'No, no,' Ian replied, and decided that he might as well bite the bullet. 'Take a seat. It is about another matter closer to home for you and I.'

'You have information about Elise?' Josiah asked eagerly.

'Not as yet. It is something I think I should discuss with you, concerning Mrs Halpin,' Ian said, walking to the window over the harbour to gaze out. The weather was fine, and the sun shimmered on the water.

'I know our governess is jealous of her,' Josiah said, taking a chair in front of Ian's big, polished teak desk. 'It appears that Sam and Becky have a strong liking for Mrs Halpin.'

'What are your thoughts about Mrs Halpin?' Ian asked, almost holding his breath in anticipation of his son's opinion.

'I think she is a fine lady,' Josiah answered. 'I strongly suspect that you and she have spent a lot of time together since we returned from Cooktown a few months ago.'

Ian was not sure how to answer his son's incriminating question but decided to be honest. 'I have, and we have become very fond of each other.' That part was a lie as both had expressed their love for each other as they had lain side by side in her bed.

'Would you object if I asked for Isabel's hand in marriage?' Ian blurted.

Josiah broke into a laugh that filled the room, confusing Ian. 'I think you deserve love – even if you are an old man,' Josiah said. 'I have seen the way you look at each other, even if you think I am too young to know what love is.'

'How did you get so wise for such a young man?' Ian answered with a smile and shake of his head.

'I have had you in my life to show me,' Josiah replied. Ian felt their very special bond was strengthened. Josiah rose from his chair and pushed out his hand to his father. 'You have my blessing, and I am sure that of Sam and Becky,' Josiah said with a smile.

'Love is not exclusive to the young, you know,' Ian replied with his own firm handshake. What had been a dilemma was now a victory, and Ian was prouder than ever to have this man as his son.

Ian announced to his staff that he was going to lunch and took his son to the best restaurant he knew to celebrate.

*

For two days, Hamish waited for intelligence to be collected on Wang's fortress. He spent most of his time talking to Lee, asking the young man about his childhood in Parramatta and what he planned to do with his future. Lee had so much potential for greatness, Hamish hated to see it wasted out on the Palmer.

Eventually, one of Kwong's men returned to report. From all signs, it seemed Wang was expecting an attack.

'Around fifteen men, half of them armed with muskets,' Lee said, while Hamish and Jack knelt by the tiny map Lee had made from earth, twigs and stones. 'Kwong is impatient and wants to launch an attack in a couple of days' time. He has twenty men but fewer muskets and needs us to provide the extra firepower in an attack.'

'What are the fortifications like, what kind of structure is it?' Hamish asked with a military man's eye.

'According to Kwong's man, just a loose stone wall about waist high surrounding bark lean-tos and cooking fires.'

Hamish stood up to stretch his back. 'Does Kwong intend to attack at first light or at last light?' he asked.

'First light,' Lee replied, also standing with his twig pointer in hand.

'So, we have to move in the scrub without being detected and be in position for the assault,' Hamish said. 'A lot easier said than done.'

Hamish's comment did not lift the morale of Jack or Lee, but they did not express any concerns, trusting Hamish would guide them on the day. Lee reported back to Kwong to coordinate the operation, and returned with instructions a few hours later. It was near nightfall and the sounds of merriment drifted from the nearby hotels and other less salubrious drinking establishments.

'You have done well, lad,' Hamish responded. 'How do you feel about what might happen within the next forty-eight hours?'

Lee had to admit that he was sick with fear and Hamish nodded. 'It is always the same before any military campaign battle,' Hamish reassured the younger man. 'But once the action is joined, the fear becomes secondary to your need to survive, and that might keep you alive. You know, I am proud to have you in my tiny army of three, Lee. You have proved to be a highly intelligent, brave and resourceful young man.'

Lee was stunned by the Scot's professed respect, almost bordering on affection. 'Thank you, Major,' Lee said with a lump in his throat. 'I will follow you anywhere you command.'

Hamish stood with a warm smile and extended his hand to Lee. 'Time to open a bottle of my best rum, and I invite you to join me in a toast, if you would not mind making an exception.'

Lee nodded, reflecting that an exception was appropriate under the current emotional times. Hamish poured the dark liquid into two enamel mugs, handing one to Lee.

'To a successful campaign – and to you, Ling Lee, with a promise of a bright future. *Slainte mhath!*'

Lee did not know what Hamish had said as he did not speak Gaelic but repeated the words as best as he could.

'*Slainte mhath!*'

*

Ian was not sure if he should be angry, depressed or just emotionally numb.

He had hinted at a marriage proposal. A reconnaissance. He had lain beside Isabel in her bed, listening to the melodic sound of currawong birds outside the window of her house, and raised the subject only to be met with a short silence.

Eventually, Isabel responded with her answer. 'If you are considering a formal proposal of marriage, my love, I am unable to accept at this time in our lives.'

'I feel that we would be a suitable match,' Ian said.

Isabel turned to Ian with a sad expression. 'You are not settled. I fear that you are still a man who yearns for danger in your life rather than wanting to settle for the quiet life of a businessman. I have heard rumours that when you travelled north to the Palmer, you were involved in violent confrontations where you risked your life. I fear that I might once again become a widow if I accepted your possible proposal of marriage.'

'What happened up north was an exception,' Ian feebly attempted to defend his actions. 'It is not likely to happen again.'

With a sad smile, Isabel touched Ian's face with her fingers. 'I love you, Captain Ian Steele, but I need to know that you will always be with not only me but your children in the years ahead.'

Ian felt a twinge of guilt at Isabel's reminder of his frequent absences from his home in Sydney. Any excuse to travel to his far-flung enterprises would do, and he grudgingly had to confront the fact he had neglected his domestic responsibilities.

'Does this mean that we will no longer meet with each other?' Ian asked.

'No,' Isabel replied quickly. 'Nothing will change between us. I love you, but I need a guarantee that you are prepared to settle down.' Then Isabel sat up, letting the sheet fall from her breasts. 'I think that we should have breakfast, and if you are not busy today, visit the gallery. We have acquired some particularly good oil paintings,' she said cheerily.

Ian sighed. It had been at the back of his mind to travel to Cooktown once more to ascertain firsthand how his latest enterprise was progressing. He knew that Hamish was a competent partner, so his yearning to be outdoors under the Southern Cross was exactly what Isabel had intimated: a selfish personal choice.

★

Lee had carefully cleaned his rifle and revolver, even examining each cartridge to ensure they had no apparent faults. He had twenty-five Snider rounds and eighteen revolver cartridges. Lee knew that every round had to count in the upcoming battle.

Hamish had his shotgun and a large Tranter revolver while Jack was equipped with a Colt revolver and Snider rifle. He only bemoaned that he did not have one of the fancy new Winchesters that Josiah owned, the kind of repeating rifle that had emerged during the American Civil War that could be loaded on Sunday and shot without reloading until the following Saturday, as he had heard many of Jack's Texans say in jest.

The sun was going down over the distant ridges and Hamish lit a cigar, passing out another to Jack; Lee politely refused the offer. His stomach was a mess and his hands just a little unsteady as he thought of what was ahead.

'Well, boys, time to move out,' Hamish said.

Lee strapped his sword across his shoulders and took point position while Hamish and Jack mounted their horses. He knew the place where they planned to rendezvous with Kwong and his men, and they set out just as the sun disappeared below the distant scrubby hills.

After a final briefing where Lee acted as interpreter, the plan was cemented and the two parties separated and set out towards the fortified encampment of Wang and his men.

Hamish was impressed by how silently the body of Kwong's men moved in the dark night, with the half-moon

182

above casting only a feeble light. Eventually, Kwong moved to one side of the route, leaving Lee and his friends alone. It had been decided that they were to establish a position where they might pour withering fire into the encampment from a right-angle, support Kwong's assault while ensuring that they did not cause casualties to the attackers.

Eventually, Hamish called a halt and dismounted. He and Jack hobbled the horses when Lee whispered that the enemy camp was not far from them. His keen hearing had picked up the sound of distant voices and he guessed it to be Wang's men. It was reassuring that from what he could deduce the enemy was confident they were safe and not expecting any armed assault against their encampment. Lee felt the knot in his stomach tighten.

★

Hamish, Lee and Jack manoeuvred through the gloom, using the sound of the distant voices drifting to them from the Tong camp to navigate in the dark. According to the plan, Kwong's men would be crawling through the long, dry grasses bordering the stone enclosure just before first light. Hamish, Lee and Jack were also creeping forward, ever alert to any sentries, until they could view the glow of campfires and see the silhouette of a few men obviously posted to keep a lookout from within the enclosure.

'Don't see any forward guard posts,' Hamish whispered. 'And I can just make out a small rise to our left, maybe a hundred yards from the camp. We will make that our position for covering fire when Kwong attacks.'

They crawled to the small rise, Lee wriggling to the top to check it had a relatively good sight of the camp. He could see many Tong members moving about, preparing for the day. Lee rested the rifle on the mound and took a sight on one of the Chinese standing beside a fire he was stoking. The thought that he could very soon kill this stranger caused Lee to have second thoughts but he quickly reminded himself that he was motivated by Zhu's dream of financing a future revolution in Lee's father's country. This was war, Lee told himself as he continued to follow the Wang Tong member's movements. Beside him, Jack took up a position and also selected a target, adjusting his sights to one hundred yards.

Then, the sun barely a sliver above the tropical horizon, a blood-curdling cry rang out and Lee saw Kwong's men rise and charge the encampment, waving swords and spears. One or two musket shots rang out and Lee readjusted his sights on his original target, who had frozen in his surprise at the sudden death streaming towards the stone enclosure. Lee took a breath and let it out slowly while squeezing the trigger. The rifle bit into his shoulder and the man he had been aiming at dropped.

Lee rolled the Snider to the right to discharge the spent cartridge and reached for another lying near his hand. He loaded and quickly found a Tong member with a musket raised. Lee fired, and his second man also flung up his arms and fell. Beside him, Jack was doing the same in a calm, calculated manner, while Hamish observed the action with a small telescope.

'Take out any you think might be trying to rally the defenders,' he said to Lee and Jack. On this tiny battlefield in the middle of nowhere, Hamish was once again in command. He could see that Kwong's attacking force was already over the wall and engaged in vicious hand-to-hand fighting with knives, swords and spears. The screams of dying men and clash of steel against steel came to the three of them as Lee reloaded.

It was then that Hamish yelled out in shocked pain, and when Lee turned to him, he could see Hamish lying on his back, gripping his shotgun. The blood from a chest wound spread quickly across the shirt Hamish wore just as dirt spouted up next to Lee's foot.

Something had gone terribly wrong.

SEVENTEEN

'I'm done,' Hamish gasped, blood welling from his mouth. Lee watched in horror as the life went from the Scot's eyes. The flurry of shots from the four mounted men Lee could vaguely discern a short distance away with the rising sun at their backs caused the dry earth to fly up around Lee and Mexican Jack. The Texan was firing his big Colt towards the men at a desperate rate to scatter them.

Lee withdrew his small revolver and joined Jack, knowing the small pistol was probably ineffective at what he calculated as fifty yards distant. When the revolver was empty, he scooped up Hamish's loaded shotgun. Behind them, the battle for the encampment sounded as if it had reached a finality, but their small war continued at the edge of the mound.

*

Charlie Goodson had the luck to ride onto the two hobbled horses, grazing a hundred yards from Hamish, Lee and Jack's position, and as the sun rose, he saw the attack on the Wang Tong. Almost at the same time, he could see the three men firing at the encampment, providing a crossfire on the unfortunate defenders. Charlie immediately recognised that damned Scot and gave the order to his men to approach on horseback and surprise the small party. A volley of shots from their rifles struck the Scot, but Charlie realised that the small party had fangs when they returned fire and a shot hit him in the lower leg, leaving him in excruciating pain. He also saw that the Wang Tong defenders were being overrun and slaughtered. His order from Wang to ride out in defence of the Tong leader's base was now a lost cause. That he had been wounded added to the fact their presence was a waste of time.

'You been hit?' Martin asked in alarm when he saw the agonised expression on his boss's face as he slumped in the saddle.

'C'mon boys!' Charlie yelled through gritted teeth. 'We're gettin' out of here!'

The bandit gang galloped away, each hoofbeat sending a surge of agony through Charlie's body.

★

A weird silence fell on the early-morning scrub, with only the moans and cries of wounded men drifting to Lee and Jack, who were reloading their weapons in case Charlie's gang returned.

Jack crawled to Hamish's body in the dry grass and propped his head in his lap. 'Ah, Hamish, they slew you,' he said sadly. 'But you died a soldier's death.'

'What do we do?' Lee asked, joining Jack just as Kwong appeared at the position on the low mound.

'You did well,' Kwong said in his language to Lee. 'Your shooting disoriented the enemy, and we were able to subdue them. Zhu will be pleased when we next meet and I report our victory.'

'Did you find Wang?' Lee asked wearily. The adrenaline was leaving his body and the long night march had brought on exhaustion.

'Wang is dead,' Kwong said. 'For a man who lives in two worlds, you have made your ancestors and father proud. Our cause will profit from this morning's events.'

'I am not sure which world I belong in,' Lee sighed quietly in English. The man who had acted almost as a father to him since they had met was dead, with the only consolation that he had unwittingly died fighting for the freedom of China. Maybe it was better that Hamish did not know the real reason for the small war between the Tongs, Lee thought as he gazed at the dead Scot.

'What did Kwong say?' Jack asked suspiciously when the other Chinese man had gone back to his men.

'Our mission is over, and we can return to Maytown,' Lee replied.

'We will have to bury Hamish out here. If we take him back, the troopers will start askin' what happened here and things might just get a bit sticky for us.'

Lee agreed and went to the horses to retrieve a shovel they carried on Hamish's insistence, in case they had to dig a small trench. Now it was being used to bury him in the vast landscape of dry, arid scrub, far from the misty glens and deep lochs of his native land.

By mid-morning, the shallow grave was dug, and Hamish was placed in the earth.

'What do Christians do in funeral rites?' Lee asked as he and Jack stood beside the freshly buried body.

'I don't think Hamish was much of a Christian,' Jack said. 'Some folks say a prayer over the body, but I ran out of prayers during the war between the states.'

'My people leave gifts for the dead at their graves,' Lee said.

'Hamish had a bottle of gin in his saddlebags,' Jack said. 'Maybe we leave that at his grave for a drink in the hereafter.'

This seeming fitting, the tribute was made to the tough Scot who died so far from home.

With the assistance of Jack, Lee mounted Hamish's horse and they rode away from the slaughter, leaving just a rough homemade cross at the head of the grave.

When Lee and Jack reached Maytown, Jack asked around the pubs whether anyone had seen Charlie and his boys. He was told that they were no longer at the bark hut and their whereabouts was unknown. This did not reassure Jack as he knew their existence in the Palmer would always be a threat to him and Lee.

The machinery for ore-crushing finally arrived, and Jack did his best to have it set up on the land the company had purchased. Jack was competent but mining procedures on such a scale were beyond his experience. He despaired that he would do Hamish right, until a Danish engineer arrived with a letter from Hamish to say he would take over management of the project. Mexican Jack breathed a sigh of relief as the engineer went about organising the crews to operate the heavy machinery. Within days, its steady thump-thump was heard in the bush as rock ore was brought in. The engineer had access to an account to pay the workers and all was working smoothly.

Jack met Lee at their tent campsite one evening and commenced packing his kit.

'My work here is done,' he informed Lee. 'I'm goin' back to the coast to help with the pub. Hamish said that if anything happened to him, me and Frank were to keep the business goin' and take our pay from the profits. Better than being up here listening to that goddamned rock crusher goin' day an' night. You are welcome to travel with me back to Cooktown. Better two than one on the trail if Charlie an' his boys are still out there.'

Lee pondered the offer. His mission for Zhu was completed and Lee suspected that news of their success would already be on the track back to Zhu, whose attitude to Lee was no doubt much improved. It was possible that he might even have a paid job with the Tong leader of Cooktown. 'I will travel with you,' Lee said. 'There is nothing here for me anymore.'

'Glad to hear it,' Jack replied, extending his hand. 'Hamish was right about you. You are a man going somewhere in this life.'

Lee accepted the firm handshake. They would spend one last night in their tent and ride out in the morning. Although Lee was still a novice when it came to horses, he was a fast learner. That night, under a cloudless sky filled with the brilliance of countless stars, Lee allowed himself an enamel mug of rum as a toast to Hamish.

The next day, the two rode out, leading two packhorses.

★

Charlie Goodson lay on a table in the tent of the goldfields doctor they had been able to reach after a couple of days riding. The bottom half of his right leg was swollen and turning black. The stench of putrefaction was already evident.

190

The doctor was a tough man who was known to personally confront patients who did not pay their bill for his services and had never lost a fistfight recovering medical costs.

'How much to get the bullet out?' Martin asked, standing alongside the table, gazing down at his boss and his wound.

The doctor did not bother to probe the wound. 'Nothing to get the bullet out,' he said, 'because he is going to die from gangrene poisoning unless his leg comes off. That will cost you. I charge extra for ether.'

The matter of the fee was negotiated as Charlie lay semi-conscious, occasionally moaning as sweat ran down his pallid face into his bushy beard.

As promised, ether was applied to knock the patient out and the surgeon cut away the leg below the knee, leaving Charlie now minus one hand and one leg.

Extra costs were incurred for pain relief medicine and the changing of bandages for the next couple of weeks. Charlie's two other men deserted him, but Martin remained with his boss and only friend.

When Charlie was sufficiently recovered, he realised that he and Martin no longer had a career robbing travellers or working for Wang, who he had confirmed was dead. But as Charlie rode away, he was bitter and swore to avenge himself on the rest of Hamish's crew, and especially the kid who had caused him to lose his hand.

★

When Mexican Jack and Lee eventually reached Cooktown, the monsoonal wet season was upon the north of Australia, slowing or closing most mining operations as the rivers swelled and low ground flooded.

Frank was pleased to see both weary men, and they sat down in the bar busy with would-be miners waiting out the wet before pursuing their dreams of gold on the Palmer. Frank was shocked and genuinely saddened by Hamish's death. Jack informed him that Hamish had requested he and Frank continue operating the pub in his name.

'What about Lee?' Frank asked.

'I will find work here with the Chinese community,' Lee said. 'I have a cousin here and I think a new friend in Zhu.' Lee knew that any work around the pub would be menial without Hamish.

'Well, partner,' Jack said. 'If you need help, remember old Jack and Frank. I will report the boss's death as an accident to the troopers and tell them where he is buried. You will be able to support the story and I doubt that with all the deaths on the Palmer they will send a patrol out to dig him up.'

On a handshake, Lee took his kit and made his way to his cousin's shop, where he knew he could get a decent meal and a place to sleep. It was time to remove one foot from the world of Europeans and stop straddling the two worlds.

A great thunderstorm rolled in, and the rain fell as if the clouds had ruptured.

★

It was November and Ian had made the choice to be home with his children for Christmas. That was a good thing, but he wondered why he had not received any correspondence from Hamish on the Palmer with reference to their joint enterprise until a thick battered envelope arrived at his office in the city.

Ian recognised that it was from Hamish and opened it with anticipation for a situation report. The first paper out was a letter explaining that if Ian had the envelope, then he, Hamish, was dead.

Stunned, Ian could hardly believe the letter's contents. The next file of papers was a will naming Ian as executor. It had been legally drawn up in Maytown and laid out the disbursement of all Hamish's goods and chattels. His shotgun he willed to Josiah and his hotel to his friends Mexican Jack and Frank.

It was the next item that caused Ian to gasp: Hamish had bequeathed his half-share of their mining operation on the Palmer to the young man Ling Lee!

Ian read the papers twice to ascertain if what he read was correct. So, now the Steele Enterprises had a Chinese partner in its ranks! Ian had the greatest respect for Lee and the more he considered him as a joint owner, the more he was able to see that Lee could prove to be the right man for the northern operations.

A smile slowly creased Ian's face as he leaned back in his chair. It would be interesting to watch the expressions on the faces of his staff when he declared the mining operation was also part-owned by a young Chinese man, albeit a man born under the Southern Cross.

Josiah was just as stunned as his father when Ian explained the beneficiaries of Hamish's will. 'I should travel to Cooktown and locate Lee, as well as Frank and Mexican Jack,' Josiah immediately responded.

The two men stood in Ian's study as the sun sank over Sydney. Ian looked at his son and noticed that he was now taller than he had been and developing the physique of an adult. Josiah was much more mature than his friends and Ian had come to trust his son's decisions.

'I will allow that,' he said, and noticed the expression of happiness in Josiah's face.

'Thank you, Father,' Josiah replied, barely able to hide his enthusiasm for the responsibility his father had bestowed upon him. 'I will make preparations to go north tomorrow on the first ship steaming to Cooktown.'

'Remember, it is the wet season up there and your travel will be restricted to Cooktown only.'

'Yes, Father,' Josiah answered. 'I am sure that I will be able to find accommodation at Hamish's hotel and I know I might find Lee at his cousin's shop.'

'Good lad,' Ian said. 'Inform Lee that he is a welcome member of our enterprises and I offer him all the help he may require to manage the mining operations at Maytown. From what I have seen of your friend, he seems an intelligent and capable young man. Be very careful up north and may luck be on your side.'

Josiah held out his hand to his beloved father. 'I will not let you down,' he said.

'I know you will do the family proud,' Ian responded with his own firm handshake. 'I will provide the finances you need, as you are working in the interests of our companies. By the way, the major also included a glowing reference to his old regiment on your behalf.'

Josiah left the study as if floating on a soft cloud. That his father had treated him as a full partner in this venture meant everything to him.

Josiah went to his room, where the Merkin battle-axe adorned the wall next to his Winchester rifle on a rack. He gazed at both as symbols of the parts of his life in which he had proved himself a man. Josiah took down the rifle for packing and included a couple of boxes of cartridges. Not that he anticipated he would have to use the rifle; it was simply an insurance policy.

Josiah also looked forward to catching up with his friend Lee and the frontiersmen who had become a part of his life.

EIGHTEEN

There had been a break in the rain when Josiah stepped ashore at Cooktown.

The main street had been churned to mud by the traffic of bullock wagons and horse-drawn carts. It was obvious that the brothels and drinking establishments were doing a roaring trade as hopeful miners and prospectors were forced to take shelter from the weather of the monsoonal wet season.

Josiah hefted his canvas bag over his shoulder. It contained the barest of essentials and his Winchester. He had grown several inches in height since he was last in Cooktown and he was a commanding figure in the street as he strode towards Hamish's hotel.

He stepped inside and was assailed by the stench of tobacco smoke and sweat and the raucous noise of drunken patrons. Behind the bar was a harassed young lady Josiah had not seen before. Her face reflected a sheen of sweat as she fought to keep up with the orders and the occasional lewd comments.

'I am looking for either Mexican Jack or Frank,' Josiah asked, pushing his way to the bar.

'Out the back,' she replied with hardly a glance.

Josiah knew where Hamish had his office and made his way to it. The door was open, and he saw Frank sitting behind the desk while Jack leaned against a wall. He could see that they were deep in conversation.

'Goddamn!' Jack said when he saw Josiah standing in the doorway. 'If my old eyes don't deceive me, it's young Josiah!'

Frank stood up and offered his hand. 'What in hell are you doin' here? Is Cap'n Steele with you?'

Josiah put down his kitbag and grinned at the two frontiersmen. 'No, just me, and I bring tidings I think you will be surprised to hear.' He produced slightly crumpled papers which he held out to Frank, who retrieved a pair of spectacles from his pocket.

'What is this all about?' Frank asked with a frown, glancing up at Josiah.

'In short, the major posted down his last will and testament to my father and stated that you and Jack are now legal owners of his establishment. You are now bona fide partners in the pub with the title transferred to you.'

Jack shook his head in amazement. 'That goddamned son of a bitch had a heart bigger than Texas,' he said in a tone of awe.

'I was hoping to find accommodation here for a short while,' Josiah continued, knowing that such a thing was at a premium in the wet season.

'Young Josiah, I can fix that right now,' Jack said.

Frank turned to his new business partner. 'All the rooms are full.'

'One of our rooms has a goddamned Yankee in it who I have heard boasting in the bar about how he was with Sherman's March to the Sea,' Jack growled. 'About time he vacated the room for a real gentleman.'

And so, Josiah had a roof over his head and a bed for his stay in Cooktown. Now he could go in search of Lee and deliver the good news of his involvement with the Steele Enterprises. His first stop was Hai's shop in the Chinese quarter of the booming town, where he found Lee assisting his cousin, unpacking wooden cases of imported Asian goods.

When Josiah walked in, Lee broke into a broad, welcoming smile.

'What are you doing here?' Lee asked, wiping his hands on his trousers before extending his hand.

Josiah accepted the handshake and felt the firmness of genuine pleasure from his friend. 'I am here representing my father and, in a way, Major MacDonald,' Josiah replied.

'Hamish.' Lee frowned. 'Hamish is dead.'

'I know,' Josiah answered. 'He is the main reason I have travelled to see you, to welcome you to the Steele Enterprises.'

Lee's frown turned to an expression of puzzlement and Josiah once again produced a ream of papers from his trouser pocket, handing them to Lee. 'The major left you his half-share of the Maytown ore-crushing project. He wrote about how highly he thought of you and said that a man with your intelligence and talents deserved every opportunity. Congratulations on stepping into the barbarian world of Europeans.'

For a moment, all Lee could do was stare at the papers in his hands. 'Is this really true?'

'It certainly is. I have further papers signed by my father for you to take over the management of the Maytown operation.' Josiah passed the formal deeds to Lee, who appeared overwhelmed. His cousin hovering in the background said something to Lee in Chinese and Lee responded. Josiah heard the cousin gasp and did not need an interpreter to know what Lee had just told him. The cousin approached respectfully, chattering with tears in his eyes, taking Josiah's hand with both of his own.

'My cousin says that you bring great honour to the family,' Lee said.

'Now that you are in our world, my father expects great things of you,' Josiah said.

'I promise on my ancestors that I will not let you or Captain Steele down,' Lee replied.

'I know you won't,' Josiah said. 'I have always sensed that you were born for great things.'

'I have some Chinese rice wine. I don't usually partake, as you know, but I feel that we should raise a toast to this wonderful change in destiny for me, and to the major. I hope that his spirit is free to join his ancestors,' Lee said, and Josiah had his first taste of the traditional drink of China as they raised their glasses in the musty confines of the herbalist's shop.

Josiah's mission was over, and his return journey was booked on the first steamer leaving the port for the south. That would be in two days and all he had to do was fill in time until he boarded. He quickly put away any thought of visiting the house of ill repute next to the pub where he was staying. Josiah decided that he would be in safer company with Lee, Frank and Mexican Jack.

★

'I seen 'em!' Martin Donahue exploded. 'The Chink and the kid who shot you, Charlie!'

Charlie Goodson lay on a filthy blanket in a bark hut on the outskirts of Cooktown. Fever racked his body and the stump of his amputated leg throbbed. At least he had avoided infection but he still had a fever common to the tropics. Times had been hard since his wounding and the desertion of his two other gang members.

'Where?' Charlie asked, attempting to prop himself up on his elbows.

'On the street in the Chinese quarter. They were together, almost hand in hand. I followed the kid to the Scot's pub where he seems to be stayin' with the other two who worked for the Scot.'

The rain continued steadily outside, pouring in torrents through the flimsy roof of the hastily made hut and drenching the earthen floor.

'Those bastards are going to pay for this,' Charlie snarled. 'I swear, so long as I can hold a pistol or knife in my hand, there will be a reckoning.'

Martin was not sure if his boss could carry out any promised revenge in his current condition, but he also saw the fire burning in Charlie's eyes. 'How do we do it?' Martin asked.

'I strap on that wooden leg in the corner and get on my feet for a start,' Charlie answered through gritted teeth. Missing a hand and a leg had finished his life as he had known it as a bushranger, but at least he could wreak revenge on those responsible for his drastic misfortunes.

'You got to take it easy, Charlie,' Martin pleaded lamely, knowing that he would be ignored.

'Fetch the leg,' Charlie said, ignoring his fever. 'We are goin' to find the bastards and kill 'em.'

★

Josiah was looking forward to the evening meal with Lee and Hai as he had acquired a taste for the exotic foods they prepared, so different from the traditional meat and vegetable European menu. He wondered if the Chinese influence on cuisine would ever take a hold amongst his friends and others in the country.

The rain had ceased, and darkness was falling over the coastal town as Josiah stepped onto Charlotte Street to walk the short distance to the Asian shop of herbs. This would be his last night dining with his friend before he joined the ship to take him south to Sydney the following morning.

Josiah was not aware that he was being watched by two pairs of eyes.

*

'I knew he would come out of the pub,' Martin said as he and Charlie stood in the shadows of a brothel opposite Hamish's pub. Charlie fought the terrible pain the raw stump caused from the weight of his body on the wooden leg that supported him with the help of the two crutches. Shoved in his belt was a fully loaded Tranter revolver and a Bowie knife, which he would use to mutilate the bodies. Charlie still had enough sense not to confront Josiah in a public place and had learned from Martin how the target of his obsession had visited the herbalist's shop in the Chinese section of town where the opium dens were also located.

Charlie had deduced the herbalist would have a supply of the much-sought opium flower, as the laudanum he was taking for the pain was not working. 'We kill two birds with one stone,' Charlie muttered, launching himself forward on the crutches.

Martin gripped the small derringer in his pocket and followed Charlie into the maze of alleyways where bearded men sat smoking long pipes in the doorways of their shops and small, flimsy houses strung with colourful paper lanterns.

★

Josiah was enthusiastically welcomed by Hai, with much smiling and bowing upon entrance. His greeting was accompanied by the delicious aroma of cooking food.

'My cousin thinks that you are like what Christians call angels,' Lee said, now practised in the European custom of handshaking. 'He has prepared a banquet for your last night in Cooktown.'

'It smells like nothing else I have eaten before,' Josiah said as Lee's cousin moved away to prepare the bowls and chopsticks for the meal. He was only a few feet away when the entrance door was flung open and Martin appeared, the derringer pistol in his hand. Behind him was Charlie on his crutches, gripping his Tranter.

'No one do anything stupid,' Martin shouted, barging into the shop with Charlie following close behind.

Both Josiah and Lee froze in shock at the sight of the apparitions from the past. Neither was armed and they were at the mercy of the two vicious killers.

'Where's the old Chink keep his opium?' Charlie growled, his eyes glittering with fever. 'You, John China, get it fast.'

Lee instinctively understood that it was not only the opium the two men were after as he could sense the hatred in Charlie. As soon as they had the opium his cousin stocked, they would be killed.

'I have to ask my cousin,' Lee said, desperately considering their options. The only one he could think of was to fight; fleeing was not possible. Lee still had the pistol Josiah had given him, but it was stowed away in a chest. The only weapon at hand was his sword, stashed on a shelf a few feet away. Lee was acutely aware that he might have a small chance to reach it and even take out one of the two armed men, but the second man would be able to open fire and kill them.

Hai shuffled forward with a metal pot, smiling as if he was a simpleton. Martin frowned at the approaching man and raised his derringer as a gesture of caution. Suddenly, Hai lifted the container and flung boiling soup into Martin's face, causing him to scream out in pain and fire off both barrels of the tiny pistol. One of the bullets hit Josiah, who spun away from the impact to his head.

Taken by surprise, Charlie had trouble aiming his pistol, but Lee did not hesitate. In a second, the sword was in his hand and as Charlie fired once, he had no chance to pull the trigger a second time. The sword flashed in the light of a lantern and caught Charlie in the side of the neck. Blood spurted from the severed artery, splashing Lee and the close walls. Charlie dropped the pistol, desperately clutching at his neck. His crutches fell away as he slumped to the floor. Lee's sword came down on Charlie's head, smashing through the skull with its razor-sharp edge.

Lee swung around and, with the sword, slashed at the back of Martin's neck, cutting the spine and almost decapitating him. Martin fell to the wooden floor, dead.

For a few seconds, silence echoed in the shop until Lee saw the blood running down the side of his friend's face as Josiah stood, holding his hand over the wound.

'Let me see,' Lee said, pulling away Josiah's hand from his head. Lee could see the graze mark the small projectile had made above the ear on Josiah's scalp and let out a breath of relief. 'The bullet did not penetrate your thick skull,' he said in his examination. 'You will only need a bandage to stop the bleeding, but you will have a scar.'

Josiah's head ached from the minor wound, but he gratefully accepted Lee's diagnosis. He gazed at the two dead men and the copious amount of blood seeping across the floor. 'We have to report what happened to the troopers,' Josiah said as Hai applied a bandage around his head to stem the bleeding.

'Not a good idea,' Lee replied. 'A couple of dead white men in a Chinese shop? No, there is another way.'

'What else can be done?' Josiah asked.

'They were never here,' Lee replied. 'After all, the troopers are not interested in searching for a couple of men well known on the Palmer for being bandits. There is someone who owes me a favour.'

In the early hours of the morning, four shadowy figures of Zhu's Tong slipped dismembered human parts into the river at a place known for large congregations of the great saltwater crocodiles. Before they departed the scene, they could hear the chilling sound of thrashing as the chunks of human flesh were devoured by the descendants of the dinosaurs.

Josiah did not mention the incident to either Jack or Frank when he returned later that night and in the morning. Neither questioned him about the wound to his head and Josiah had not offered to explain. This was, after all, a frontier town.

As the rain returned, Josiah boarded the ship that would take him south and into a new future.

★

Elise huddled in the fancy closed carriage drawn by four thoroughbred horses. Snow was falling and the expensive furs she wore were so different from what she had known only months earlier living in Sydney.

Her aunt and uncle sat opposite, silently watching her. Elise experienced apprehension when she was in their company and missed her parents more than she would admit.

The carriage wound its way along a road between great evergreen forests covered in crowns of snow as the flurries continued in the overcast midday sky. They passed through small villages with deserted streets as the residents sought warmth beside their hearths until eventually, they were on a hillside road overlooking a sprawling valley below.

Elise stared out the glass window frosted by the cold and rubbed it when her aunt proclaimed that they were almost at their destination.

Through the window, she could see the castle atop the hill and memories flooded back of a time when she had played in its grounds.

Part Two

London

1878–1880

NINETEEN

Although Josiah Steele had been born in London, his memories of the city were all too vague. As he was transported from the docks by a Hansom cab through the streets, he was awed by the sheer size and bustling activity of the centre of the island nation and of the modern world. A steady stream of horse-drawn carriages and carts filled the narrow streets bordered by tall buildings. It was a place of grey, and the colourful flowers in a basket carried by a very thin young girl selling her wares to passing traffic stood out like a flash. For his arrival, the weather was bleak and tinged with cold and drizzling rain.

Josiah could occasionally smell the rotting waste of discarded rubbish when his cab took him past the rundown tenements of the poverty-stricken masses who worked in the odious factories producing leather and other products. London was a stark contrast of rich and poor, and for a brief moment, Josiah experienced a twinge of guilt for having so much wealth. Before departing for England, Josiah had read newspaper stories about some Irish bushranger, Ned Kelly, and his gang rampaging through the colony of Victoria, driven to crime by poverty.

At least he had attended the consecration of the Great Synagogue in Elizabeth Street, where he had been promptly chided by his rabbi for being absent from so many services. Josiah had felt shame as he realised that, like his father, he was not deeply religious, although Josiah clung to the Jewish roots of his mother's family. He had at least adhered to the rites of passage as a young boy growing to manhood, at the insistence of his mother while she was alive, but since the tragic passing, he had wavered in his religious obligations. Not that he ever conceived of converting to Christianity even though his father had been baptised a Catholic. He did not follow the religious doctrine as devoutly as his Catholic friends either. Well, like father, like son, Josiah reminded himself.

In preparation for his journey to England, his father had written to his mother's lawyers in London to announce that Josiah would be visiting them. Armed with letters of introduction, Josiah was prepared to meet them and explore the extent of his mother's estate, of which he, Samuel and Becky were also the beneficiaries.

However, his first stop was not to his lawyers but to an address he had been given, to meet with a man his father had told him was special. In fact, the man had been awarded the prestigious Victoria Cross and had served with Ian throughout their time together in the British army.

The horse came to a stop and the driver on the seat above Josiah's small cabin called down to him. 'This is where you said, master.'

Josiah glanced up and down the street and saw the rows of tenement houses wall to wall in the quieter and obviously more affluent London suburb. The people on the street were impeccably dressed as they strolled along avenues devoid of the inner-city traffic of rich and poor rubbing shoulders. Here, it seemed only the rich rubbed shoulders.

Josiah dismounted with a small bag containing essential items, as his main luggage would be delivered later to this address until he found more permanent lodgings. He paid the driver with the English currency he had carried from Sydney and, as the drizzle began to turn to rain, Josiah quickly made his way up a set of stone steps to stand before a door with a large bronze knocker. He pulled up the collar of his coat and tapped the knocker.

Within a short time, the door opened and a young woman wearing a white cap and apron stood in the doorway.

'Yes?' she asked the tall stranger. 'May I help you?'

'Is this the residence of Sergeant Major Curry?' Josiah asked.

'Who may I ask wishes to know?' the young maid asked, eyeing Josiah with interest.

'Josiah Steele, son of Captain Ian Steele,' Josiah replied. The maid turned to return inside and was almost knocked over when a big, burly man sporting a thick black beard shot with grey filled the doorway. His face beamed and he grabbed Josiah by the collar, pulling him out of the rain and almost crushing the startled maid.

'Mildred, this is the son of the greatest officer I ever had the honour to serve with,' Conan Curry said. 'We don't leave him out in the rain to catch his death of cold.'

Josiah was taken aback by the lurch he experienced as the big man hauled him inside to a clean, dry hallway adorned with bric-a-brac and pot plants.

'Molly!' Conan shouted down the hallway. 'Young Josiah has just arrived.'

A plump lady suddenly appeared behind the burly man. Josiah could see that she had a warm expression and beamed her happiness at his presence. Before he could recover from the shock of being hauled into the house, he felt her arms wrap around him in a hug.

'Come in, lad,' Conan said after Josiah had disentangled himself from Molly Curry.

'Mildred, go and make a pot of tea for our guest, if you please,' Molly commanded, and the confused maid disappeared to obey her mistress's command.

Josiah was surprised at the enthusiastic welcome from people he had never met before, but obviously they knew about him. He suspected his father had sent many letters to his former sergeant major.

Conan and Molly bustled Josiah into a comfortable sitting room with expensive furniture and paintings of landscapes on the walls. He was ushered to a divan and Conan sat opposite on a lounge with Molly beside him.

'You have your mother's eyes,' she said, reminding Josiah of his links to England.

'You are much more robust than your father,' Conan added. 'You must have got that from your mother's family. But first, we must get you settled into the guest room upstairs before we have a chance to chat about life back in New South Wales and my dearest friend, your father. He says very little about his life back home in his letters to us.'

A young woman appeared in the room and Josiah was immediately struck by her beauty. She had flaming red hair and the deepest green eyes Josiah had ever seen. He rose and the slightest of smiles appeared on her milky white face.

'Our daughter, Marian. Meet Josiah Steele, son of the man I have often told you about.'

'It is a pleasure meeting you, Mr Steele,' Marian said, turning to Josiah with a wide smile. 'My father has regaled me with the stories of how he and your father served together.'

Josiah was just a little lost for words in Marian's presence, awestruck by her beauty. He remembered that his father had once told him his old friend had a daughter, and Josiah knew that she must be a year or so younger than he.

After a pause, she continued, 'Well, it has been a pleasure meeting you, Mr Steele, but I must excuse myself as I have a social engagement and my chaperone will be waiting.'

'The pleasure has been all mine,' Josiah replied and remained standing as Marian departed the room, leaving him in the state of a shy schoolboy.

*

Josiah was shown his room. It was clean and comfortable with a sloping ceiling, and when Josiah had settled in and laid out a change of clothes, he joined Conan and Molly in the sitting room. Over tea and an assortment of cakes and scones, Josiah exchanged stories about his family's life in the colonies and learned that Molly was the reason the Currys had acquired a respectable wealth, through her confectionery shops around London and now a small factory producing her much-sought Turkish Delight. Molly had also invested her profits in Welsh railways and the shares paid an excellent dividend. Thanks to his beloved wife's investment, Conan owned a public house named 'The Crimea' in a growing middle-class suburb. Conan was proud of his public house, and many of the patrons were former soldiers who knew the owner had earned the Victoria Cross.

They exchanged stories all throughout the day with only a break for a lunch of cold sheep's tongue and bread. Josiah was aware that Conan had been born in the same village at the bottom of the Blue Mountains outside of Sydney as his own father. In discussions about that period, Josiah's father always remained vague, only saying that he had been a blacksmith. He never spoke of knowing Conan before being commissioned into the British army except to say they had met by chance before the Crimean campaign.

'So, do you know anyone else in London?' Conan asked.

'I do,' Josiah replied, placing his teacup on its fine china saucer. 'A school friend of mine, Douglas Wade, is attending Cambridge. His family have the means to support him as he studies the classics.'

'I happen to know the solicitor you are to visit,' Conan said. 'He also handles my legal matters. A good and honest man – for a lawyer,' Conan added. 'We should let you retire for the evening and be ready for a big day tomorrow,' Conan said, rising from his chair and tapping his tobacco pipe in an ashtray. Molly bid Josiah a good night and the young man made his way up the stairs to his little room overlooking the street below, realising that this was his first day on English soil after almost fifteen years.

★

The following morning, Josiah was served kippers, eggs and a cup of strong tea with milk for breakfast. He and Conan were alone in the dining room as Molly had risen early to travel to one of her prosperous shops in the city centre.

'I believe that you will be attending the officer training college at Sandhurst for a commission into a Scottish regiment,' Conan said, sipping his tea across the table from Josiah.

'I have been accepted for entry,' Josiah said. 'It helped that my birth certificate mentions I was born here and that my father and the late Major MacDonald provided references. It seems that coming from wealth still counts for entry into the officer class – even if the wealth is in the colonies.'

'I suspect that your academic record also helped.' Conan smiled. 'Your father wrote to me of how you excelled at school in your studies.'

Josiah was not surprised to learn of Conan's knowledge of his past. 'I just pray that I make my father proud,' Josiah replied.

'I know that he is already proud. He wrote of your adventures on the Palmer River and how you acquitted yourself like the best of his former soldiers under fire.'

Josiah glanced at Conan. 'He wrote to you about the Palmer?' he asked in surprise, as it was meant to be a secret. But then he considered how close this Irishman was to his father; they were more like brothers than friends.

'Yes. He was against you becoming a soldier of the Queen but after the Palmer venture, he felt that you were ready to experience what your dad and I saw in our young years. As it is, you might find yourself back in the Crimea where Captain Steele first made a name for himself. It is being reported that Disraeli, our prime minister, has sent the Royal Navy to the Dardanelles to prevent the Russkies from occupying Constantinople and has mobilised our reserves in readiness for a showdown with our old enemy. We are stretched a bit thin with the army over in Afghanistan under Sir Samuel Browne, advancing to Kabul to capture an important fort. The way things are going, who knows where those mad Scotties will end up serving.'

Josiah ate a mouthful of the kippers and realised that he would, one way or the other, most probably be in action when he graduated from the military academy. The thought both excited and scared him. Josiah was old enough to know that on the battlefield, luck was everything.

Conan excused himself, saying that he had to travel to his public house to oversee his new manager, but that Josiah should consider his house was also Josiah's house for his visit. Josiah thanked him and watched as the big man exited the dining room. Josiah took an orange from a sideboard basket containing exotic fruits such as bananas and plums. It was a sign of how London was linked to the wider world, with its imports from so far away.

He was not alone for long. Marian appeared from the kitchen, greeting him before sitting down at the table with a plate of fruit and slice of toast prepared by the cook.

'What are your plans for your stay in London?' Marian asked, selecting a plum from the platter.

'I have meetings with my mother's solicitors regarding her estate,' Josiah answered.

'I believe that your mother left a considerable fortune behind in London before she travelled to the colonies,' Marian said, taking a dainty bite.

Josiah sensed a little snobbery in her tone. 'That's what I'm here to ascertain,' he said. He wanted to ask Marian questions but was just a little intimidated by her, so instead he said, 'I am grateful for your wonderful hospitality.'

She glanced at him. 'According to my dear papa, he and my mother consider you a part of the family. I think it is one of those things soldiers have for life,' she said airily.

Mildred appeared in the doorway. 'Mr Steele, your luggage has been delivered.'

'Well, I must attend to matters,' Josiah said. 'Good day, Miss Curry.'

'Good day, Mr Steele.'

Josiah was grateful for an excuse to break off the moment with Marian and gather his wits. Soon, he was able to open the chest containing his more formal wear, including a top hat worn by gentlemen. As winter was almost upon Europe, the clothing was suitable for the weather.

Josiah changed into a formal outfit of mid-length coat, trousers, shirt and tie. He winced as he was not fond of looking the dandy but understood that it was necessary to appear as such in a society very conscious of class.

He left the Curry residence carrying an umbrella and hailed a Hansom cab to convey him to London's commercial centre, to the address he had for his mother's legal representatives.

Josiah alighted and stepped through the single doorway into a gloomy narrow hallway at the bottom of a flight of wooden stairs. He walked up and found the sign of *Sharon & Sons, Solicitors at Law* on a brass plaque.

Josiah knocked a couple of times and, without being asked, stepped inside to see a dark wood-panelled room with a single desk behind which sat a striking young woman with jet-black hair secured in a bun and the darkest of brown eyes. Her olive skin indicated that she was not of Anglo–Saxon heritage but perhaps Mediterranean. He guessed she was about his own age. She glanced up at him.

'Yes, may I assist you?' she asked politely, appraising him.

'My name is Josiah Steele and although I do not have an appointment, I have just travelled all the way from New South Wales to meet with Mr Sharon. Mr Sharon was once my mother's legal representative when her father, Ikey Solomon, passed.'

The pretty girl's eyes widened at the mention of Ikey Solomon. 'Your mother must have been Ella, who I believe married a gentile with the same name as you.'

Josiah nodded and the girl pushed away her chair to go to a door into another office. She knocked once and opened the door, closing it behind her, leaving Josiah feeling just a little bit nervous. He was not sure what to expect at this meeting with David Sharon.

The door opened and the girl gave Josiah the slightest smile.

'It appears that you do not need an appointment, Mr Steele, as my father has been expecting you for some time.'

Josiah nodded his thanks and stepped into an office adorned with shelves of leather-bound books with the musty smell of old cigars. A balding man of medium height and slim waist rose from his desk, stepping across the room to meet Josiah.

'David Sharon, Mr Steele,' he said, offering his hand, which Josiah accepted. 'It has been many years, but I can see your grandfather Ikey in your demeanour. I received correspondence from your father some weeks ago, advising that you would visit me. Please, take a seat as there is much to cover.'

Josiah found a comfortable leather chair with a high back and sat down opposite the expensive wooden desk of the London solicitor, who was already rummaging in his files.

'Ah, here it is!' he exclaimed, holding a thick ream of papers in a leather folder. 'A concise record of the investments left by your mother to you and your siblings, Samuel and Rebecca. I believe you intend to train as an officer in the army and that will be costly. Fortunately, there will be no problem in that matter. You are an exceptionally wealthy young man, which will endear you to the gentry of our fair London society. The first item is the house you own in Kensington, which is a place where you will encounter some of our wealthier members of society. The second item

216

is that you have a bank account that will fund any lifestyle you should choose, but I must warn you to stay away from the habit of gambling your means away. Drinking when you have time on your hands is also a problem with young gentlemen of means.'

'I neither gamble nor drink, Mr Sharon,' Josiah said. 'I envisage that I will not have time to take up either before I enter my military studies.'

'That is good to hear,' Sharon said. 'While you are in London, I will always be here for you, as I was for your mother's father and your mother. If you have any questions, please ask and I will attempt to assist in any way I can. I will give you your bank details and the current amount available to you.'

The lawyer passed Josiah a small, finely bound leather folder and Josiah opened it. The first thing he saw was a bank balance that almost made him faint. It was money beyond his wildest dreams, and he had not had to work for it as he had done risking his life on the Palmer track.

'Thank you, Mr Sharon,' Josiah finally replied, gripping the precious folder.

'If that is all for the moment, I would be pleased if you would visit my residence outside London for the Sabbath,' David said, and Josiah experienced the old guilt of not being a devout Jew, as he hardly recognised the Sabbath at home unless his mostly absent father reminded him. 'My daughter Avigail, who you met in the reception, will be able to assist with any administrative matters concerning your mother's estates and enterprises here in England in the future. I have delegated the Solomon file to her.'

Josiah rose from the big leather chair and extended his hand. 'Thank you, Mr Sharon,' he said, and departed the office to step back into the reception area.

'We were not formally introduced, Miss Sharon,' Josiah said in the most mature way he could for a young man. 'My name is Josiah and your father informed me that I might call on your knowledge of my mother's estate in the days ahead.'

'I will be of as much assistance as I can, Mr Steele,' Avigail replied with a warm smile. 'Shall we meet tomorrow so I can show you your Kensington property?'

Josiah left the reception area as if walking on clouds. He had an opportunity of meeting the beautiful young woman again. It seemed the long and sometimes treacherous sea voyage to England had been worth it in more ways than one.

Now all he had to do was catch up with his old friend Douglas Wade to complete his warm welcome to the other side of the world.

TWENTY

Josiah was pleasantly surprised to find that his tenement house was only a short distance from the one owned by Conan and Molly. He stood in the kitchen, looking at the fully equipped house with its furniture and kitchen utensils.

'You may require servants,' Avigail said. 'At least someone to cook, unless you intend to dine out every day.'

'I think that you are right,' Josiah replied. 'My knowledge of cooking is restricted to what can be prepared around a campfire.'

'I can find someone for employment almost immediately,' Avigail suggested. 'I know of an elderly widow in dire circumstances. She can cook and clean. She is an Irishwoman, Mrs O'Brian, and you have a small room she can live in.'

'If you feel that she will be able to look after my digs then employ her,' Josiah said, walking to a sitting room with a large rug in the centre of the floor. 'I already feel at home.'

'Good,' Avigail said. 'I must return to my father's office and prepare a brief for one of his clients for a forthcoming court matter.'

Josiah turned to Avigail. 'I am surprised that you did not follow your father into law as a solicitor,' he said, which brought a slight frown to the young woman's face.

'My father and brothers all agree that the law is not a profession for women,' she replied. 'I disagree. After all, my mother wins all the arguments at home.'

Josiah laughed at her logic. 'I think that you have a point,' he replied, which caused Avigail to smile.

'At least I may have won that argument for women to read law.'

'I hope that I may require your assistance in the future,' Josiah said as he escorted Avigail to the front entrance, where her personal one-horse carriage awaited. Josiah assisted her into the carriage, and she smiled a goodbye to him.

Josiah watched her depart, pondering how he might get closer to the beautiful woman. For the moment, though, he had an old friend to locate.

★

When Josiah saw Douglas coming down a flight of stone steps with his books tucked under his arm, he broke into a broad smile. Douglas spotted the lone figure gazing up the stairs and almost leapt from the steps.

'Josiah! Is it really you?' he exclaimed when they met at the bottom of the stairs, with Douglas's fellow undergradu-ates brushing past on their way to lectures.

'It is good to find a fellow colonial in this place of smog, snow and ever grey skies,' Josiah said, gripping his old school friend by the hand. 'How have you fared?'

'The studies are intense, but I achieved high marks last

year. My professors inform me that I may have a future as an academic if I continue to progress. But perhaps we can discuss this over tea?' Christmas was not far away, and the first flurries of light snow fell as Josiah walked with Douglas Wade along the hallowed archways of the university.

Josiah accompanied Douglas off the prestigious university grounds to a small but warm tea shop already crowded with other Cambridge students. They were able to find a table and order tea with fruit tarts. Settled in, they swapped story for story.

'Before I left home, I heard a rumour that your trips to the Palmer entailed some violence,' Douglas said, sipping his tea. 'Is it true that you fought off the blacks and shot it out with bandits?'

Josiah was not surprised to be asked the question as it was almost impossible to hide a secret with so many people involved. 'Yes, we were forced to defend ourselves with gunfire.'

'You are a true renaissance man,' Douglas said with awe in his voice. 'You are a scholar and adventurer and soon to be one of the Queen's officers on some far-flung frontier defending the Empire. Such a noble cause.'

Josiah did not know how to respond to his friend's flattery and diverted the conversation. 'Have you met any other colonials while you have been here?' he asked and saw a dark cloud cross his friend's face.

'That cad David Anderson is living in London. He has a position with his father's English office for trade. I ran into him a month ago at a party at a mutual friend's country residence.'

Josiah was surprised at the news. Of all the people to be on this side of the world, it would have to be his old, bitter enemy from school. 'Well, I hope that I do not have the misfortune to meet with him. You will have to come and spend a weekend at my residence in Kensington, old chap.'

'I would like that. I heard that a Scot, Alexander Bell, demonstrated a device to the Queen that can transmit voices through a metal line a long distance. He called it a telephone, and I believe one can view the device in London. I feel that such an invention might change the world if we are able to communicate across long distances without being in sight of each other. Just imagine in your military world how it would be possible for the commander of the battle to be able to speak with his subordinates at the front.'

'We already have telegraph,' Josiah replied dismissively. 'I doubt that voice communication is necessary.'

The two men sat, ordering more tea and tarts until the night drew close and they had to part with promises of meeting again soon. They left the cosy tea house and Josiah hunched against the bitter cold, drawing the collar of his warm coat up around his face. In a matter of minutes, he was able to hail a Hansom cab to catch his train back to London.

He was met at his front door by a formidable, large woman with grey hair tied into a tight bun who questioned his identity and politely ushered him in when he proved that he was Master Josiah Steele. Mrs O'Brian had come to rule the household of two with an iron fist in a velvet glove, and Josiah came to appreciate how much she cared for the handsome young man she considered her responsibility.

★

Josiah did not celebrate the Yuletide season as his Christian friends did. However, he did enjoy the festive season for its merriment and goodwill. Conan and Molly had invited him to attend a Christmas Eve dinner at their house. It was a short walk as the cold snow fell and a warm welcome when Josiah stepped into the Curry residence.

A fine meal was served and after dinner, Conan and Josiah sat around a fire, sipping sherry and reminiscing about the Christmas season back home in the colony, with its sunny, hot days. Josiah could see that the tough old soldier had a tear in his eye at the memories of his youth, when he and his gang of friends would swim in the river after a lunch of lamb and roasted vegetables. If they were fortunate, a roasted chicken would also be on the menu. The men of his clan would retire to drink themselves into oblivion and sleep off the generous Christmas lunch. But Conan also remembered other Christmases, spent in the snow of battlefields. Josiah could see his growing melancholy and Molly rescued Josiah with an invitation to return the following day to join them at the Christmas luncheon.

Josiah bid good night to Conan, who had already slipped into a troubled sleep after bemoaning the fact that his dearest friend, Captain Ian Steele, was not with them to celebrate this special time of year.

Josiah returned to an empty house and sought out a bottle of whisky. He normally did not drink but his head was fuzzy from the sherry and port, inducing him to seek further inner warmth. He sat in his living room in front of his coal fire with the bottle in his hand, feeling the loneliness of not sharing the season with his family so far away. What would they be doing? Would they go to the beach after Christmas lunch and paddle in the ocean? Josiah slipped into a deep sleep in front of the fire, the bottle slipping from his hand.

★

Over ten thousand miles away from the snow of London, summer was at its peak in the southern hemisphere. Once green pastures were desiccated white, and the heat shimmered across the plains outside Sydney. Despite the sweltering heat, Christmas would be celebrated with roasted turkey and goose served with a mix of seasonal vegetables. Plum puddings and assorted sweet pastries would follow as people sweated under the summer sun.

One man sat at his desk in a government office in the city staring at the wall. His staff had departed and there were signs brewing outside that bore the promise of relief from the heat by way of a southerly buster. The temperature would drop, and there was the possibility that a short sharp storm would follow.

Harold Skinner brooded on his lonely life, reflecting again on how Captain Ian Steele had publicly humiliated him and, just as bad, taken the love of his life from him. Harold obsessed about Isabel, dreaming that she loved him and was being fooled by the unscrupulous man who had fought for the Queen. He knew that Isabel could never love another from the day they had met, and he knew that he was the only man to remain in her life.

But Isabel shunned him, and this was not right when he considered Ian Steele had turned his back on his working class background as a blacksmith and dared enter the ranks of the colonial elite, an imposter.

Something drastic had to be done about the situation to set the world right, and Skinner knew what that had to be. He would go to Isabel and profess his love for her. Surely, knowing Steele's background, she had to see sense and come back to him. His obsession with Isabel was stronger than any rational thoughts of consequences.

*

Ian had counted the days to Christmas because it meant three days of Isabel sharing his house on the harbour. He had arranged to take a gig from the railway station to her residence to collect her, and then return to the railway station for the journey back to Sydney.

Ian knew that his younger children were looking forward to Isabel's visit, as she had endeared herself to both of them, and despite the heat of summer, it would be a grand time, with a visit to the beach to splash in the cooling waters. They would laze around the gardens in the shade of the trees and Ian hoped that Isabel could see that he was settled and might reconsider his proposal of marriage.

★

A crow cawed in the distance as Isabel finished packing the items she would require for her three-day holiday with Ian's family.

She had given her staff of cook/housekeeper and gardener/handyman three days off to be with their loved ones over Christmas, so only the cawing of the crow broke the silence until she heard horse hooves on the gravel driveway.

Isabel paused, wondering why Ian was on horseback instead of bringing a carriage to convey her to the railway station as he must have known she would have luggage.

She paused and then walked down the hallway to the front entrance. For a second, her heart felt as if it had stopped as she saw Harold Skinner dismount from his horse and walk towards her.

'Harold, what are you doing here?' she asked from the front entrance.

Harold stepped onto the front veranda and Isabel could smell alcohol on his breath.

'I have come to convince you of your foolishness,' he said, pushing Isabel back into the hallway. Frightened by the distant look in his eyes, Isabel backed away. 'You have no future with that man,' he said.

'Harold, I would rather you leave now,' Isabel commanded, but he ignored her, swaying slightly and glaring at her.

'You know your future is with me, not him. I have just as much to offer as Steele. You would have a life with me in polite colonial society. I have always loved you, Isabel, and cannot live without you sharing my life.'

His last statement was a plea and Isabel felt a rising terror. Harold was a big man and she felt physically helpless with him towering over her.

'Harold, I can see that you have been drinking and would rather you depart now. Captain Steele will be here any moment,' Isabel said as calmly as she could.

'Let the bastard come,' Skinner hissed, his mood changing dangerously at the mention of the man he loathed. 'He can have what's left over.' His voice was a snarl now as he lunged forward and pushed Isabel to the floor of the hallway. Isabel attempted to scream but he hit her in the face, causing Isabel to see a shower of red stars. The last words she heard as she started to lose consciousness were, 'If I can't have you, no one will.'

★

Ian could see the figure approaching on horseback as he drove the gig towards Isabel's cottage. When he came closer, Ian saw that it was Harold Skinner. It was obvious that Skinner also recognised Ian as he passed with a scowl of pure hatred on his face. But there was something else there too, an expression Ian couldn't read. Ian noticed that his enemy looked dishevelled, causing Ian to feel a rising concern when he realised Skinner was riding from the direction of Isabel's house.

Skinner urged his mount into a gallop, leaving puffs of dust in his wake. Ian knew that it was fruitless turning around and attempting to intercept the man. Instead, Ian urged his carriage horse into a trot and within minutes could see Isabel's house, surrounded by its green gardens watered by the nearby creek.

He flung himself from the gig and ran to the open door and was horrified when he saw Isabel lying motionless in the hallway, her clothes torn and in disarray.

'Isabel!' Ian cried out, flinging himself through the door to go to her. He could see blood beneath her head as he knelt beside her body.

TWENTY-ONE

Ian gently rolled Isabel onto her back. He was relieved to hear her moan, and then she opened her eyes. He could see that she had a gash on her forehead, which bled profusely.

'My love, I am here,' he said, fighting back the fear. 'I will fetch you to a doctor.'

He lifted her in his arms, carrying her to the carriage where he placed her gently on the seat beside him. She had not spoken, and Ian guessed she was suffering shock as he had often seen in soldiers on the battlefield. This was little different as Ian instinctively knew from his past.

Ian drove to a little cottage not far from Sir Godfrey's estate where he knew the local physician. Fortunately for Ian, the doctor was at home and his wife answered the door as Ian held Isabel in his arms.

The doctor's wife wore an apron covered in flour.

'Captain Steele,' she said, and a concerned frown appeared on her face when her gaze fell on Isabel in his arms. 'I will call my husband. Bring Isabel in immediately to his surgery.'

'Thank you, Elizabeth,' Ian said, following the woman and placing Isabel on a padded table in a room of medicine vials, books and cupboards containing medical equipment. Isabel attempted to sit up, but Ian gently convinced her to remain until the doctor was fetched. Within a couple of minutes, Dr Gillespie appeared wearing a vest over his shirt. He glanced at Ian and at Isabel lying on his padded table.

'What has happened, old chap?' he asked Ian as his gaze moved back to Isabel.

'I think Isabel took a bad fall,' Ian lied. 'As you can see, she has a wound to her head.'

Dr Gillespie immediately examined the bleeding wound to Isabel's forehead and turned to his wife who was hovering in the doorway. 'I will need clean water, antiseptic and a roll of bandages,' he said, and she hurried away.

'When did this happen, Captain Steele?' the doctor asked as he leaned over to examine Isabel's eyes.

'About three-quarters of an hour ago,' Ian replied. 'I had intended to provide Mrs Halpin transport to the railway station and found her in this condition on her hallway floor.'

Elizabeth returned with the items requested and the doctor had Isabel sit up on the bench, where he rinsed the wound with clean, previously boiled water before applying an antiseptic. He then wrapped Isabel's head with a swathe of bandages to suppress the bleeding. He asked her questions concerning her health while Ian stood aside, considering what he was going to do.

It was obvious that if Isabel reported the matter the police would probably weigh up the case with her word against that of a well-known and respected civil servant, and justice would not be served.

Ian fumed at the probable outcome of reporting the matter to the police. He knew there was the law and then there was justice, and the two often did not coincide. But justice was justice, and it came in other forms. Had he not dispensed justice outside the bounds of legal niceties before? Ian knew there was only one way to find Isabel justice.

After Dr Gillespie was satisfied Isabel was well enough to be released from his immediate care, he cautioned Ian that his patient required rest until he saw her again. He agreed that with someone beside her, she would be able to travel to Sydney, and gave Ian a bottle of laudanum for any pain she may be suffering. Ian thanked him and paid the fee for his medical service, leaving with Isabel to travel to his home on the harbour.

★

When Ian and Isabel finally walked through the entrance to his house, they were met by shocked expressions from Ian's staff and children. Becky immediately expressed her concern but was told by Ian that Mrs Halpin had taken a fall, causing her head wound.

That evening, Ian and Isabel sat in the garden on a stone bench side by side as the sun disappeared over the harbour. Twinkling boat lights appeared and the evening cooled to a balmy warmth.

'Thank you for not telling anyone what really happened,' she said quietly.

'I felt that you wanted the privacy and that it would be your choice in how you wanted this matter to be dealt with,' Ian said, taking her hand in his own.

'I know how the law works in these matters,' Isabel

sighed. 'It would be my word against his, and a public scandal in the courts which the newspapers would relish. I do not want that.'

'I felt that it had to be something you could reflect on when your physical wounds were dealt with,' Ian said gently. 'But I can promise you Skinner will face another kind of justice.'

Isabel turned to look at Ian. 'Please do not do anything foolish,' she pleaded. 'I suspect that as you are a man who has seen so much violence in your life that you may feel ready to resort to doing so to avenge me. I beg you to let this matter be put in the past. If you do something foolish, I might lose you, and that is something I could not bear. Remember, you have your children to consider.'

Ian did not reply but stared ahead at the twinkling lights, listening to the sounds of the clanging of buoys on the harbour. He had made up his mind and now only had to formulate a way of killing Skinner without being caught by the law. This was not murder; this was real justice. After all, a proven case of rape was a hanging offence in the colony.

*

Christmas was a subdued affair at Ian's residence. Isabel was confined to rest in a guest room where Ian had hired a doctor to check her medical condition every day, although Isabel said he was making too much of a fuss over her.

She was able to be in the large living room when presents were handed out to Ian's children and the staff, but the planned trip to the beach to wade in the surf was cancelled. Instead, the staff and Ian's family enjoyed an afternoon playing cricket in the expansive gardens.

Josiah's presence was sorely missed by all, and Ian raised a toast to his eldest son's future in England. They had not received any letters and Ian explained to Sam and Becky that it took time for mail to cross the Indian Ocean and eventually travel to the east coast of the continent.

Ian had his doubts that Isabel should return to her home. However, she assured him that her staff had returned, and she would be safe.

Ian was not sure she was right and before he took her back to her house, he presented her with a small derringer pistol that held two rounds.

'Promise me that you will always keep this close,' he said, and she promised. Satisfied after leaving Isabel with her staff, Ian returned to Sydney. The new year meant his enterprises were back in motion and the eternal promise of better times ahead kept him busy.

But when he sat at his desk in the city office, he stared at the walls, pondering how he would wreak revenge on Harold Skinner. His military training made him consider the element of surprise. He knew it would be best to choose his ground and carry out the attack swiftly, while concealing any trace of the reprisal. Despite his promises to Isabel, Ian was consumed by his plans to confront Skinner and kill him. It was not merely for revenge but Ian's way of removing a future threat to the woman he loved with his heart and soul.

★

Josiah met Douglas and his university friends at the entrance to the Lyceum Theatre, and he was impressed by the majestic architecture of the building with its Greco-Roman columns. It was early evening, and the snow was no longer falling on the city, but the night was still bitter cold.

'I have the tickets, old chap,' Douglas said when he spotted Josiah lingering on the steps crowded with elegantly dressed members of London's high society; ladies wearing the finest fur coats and gentlemen in dinner suits wearing top hats shining in the reflected light from inside the tall building.

The carriages disgorged their wealthy occupants and moved on as Josiah and Douglas waited for Douglas's friends to join them. It was obvious that Douglas's fellow students came from wealthy families, enabling them to attend such a gala affair, and Josiah easily had the financial means to be a part of Douglas's circle.

A carriage drawn by four matching black horses stopped about twenty paces from where the two stood in the cold evening air and Josiah idly admired its fine ironwork. The carriage was adorned with gilded artwork indicating that it belonged to European royalty.

Josiah noticed that an older couple stepped down first with the assistance of a fancily dressed servant. The older couple had severe expressions, and Josiah was about to turn away when a younger woman was helped to disembark, followed by a tall and handsome German army officer, resplendent in his uniform. For a moment, Josiah stared at the young woman as a distant memory stirred.

It cannot be! Josiah thought. Time had passed but Josiah had never forgotten her face, and when his eyes fell a little lower, he saw the tiny cross at the woman's breast that he had purchased in Sydney all those years earlier.

'Elise!' he gasped.

'What, old chap?' Douglas queried. 'Why are you staring at the future duchess of some obscure state in Bavaria?'

'Do you know her?' Josiah asked, turning to Douglas.

'Not personally,' Douglas replied. 'But I have a friend who does. She and her aunt and uncle have been visiting London for the last month. The future duchess has broken the hearts of many an aspiring suitor at all the aristocratic socials she has attended. If I remember rightly, she will be the Duchess von Meyer when she reaches twenty-one years of age.'

Listening to his friend, Josiah could almost hear his heart beating as he gazed at the pretty young girl who had blossomed into a beautiful young woman. Her golden hair was piled on top of her head in the fashion of the day and golden ringlets fell on either side of her face.

It was Douglas who blanched as he watched the young woman walk up the steps and disappear into the building on the arm of the dashing young German officer.

'Good God!' Douglas exclaimed. 'She looks like that young girl you brought back to Sydney after a trip to the Palmer. I remember seeing you with her one Sunday at Hyde Park. But surely it could not be her.'

'Her name is Elise, and I am sure it is her,' Josiah replied. 'I have to meet her again.'

'That will not be easy,' Douglas cautioned. 'She is accompanied by a special bodyguard of former Bavarian soldiers who keep everyone away unless they have permission. She is some kind of German royalty, with links to the Kaiser.'

'There has to be a way,' Josiah said just as Douglas's friends joined them. It was obvious they had consumed a good amount of alcohol before attending the premiere.

They entered the majestic theatre and were seated in the cheaper seats on the bottom floor, surrounded by the boxes of the much wealthier patrons. Josiah scanned each box until he saw Elise in one of the grander viewing boxes. She was seated next to the German officer, and Josiah could see her smiling as they chatted before the curtain was raised. She appeared happy but Josiah was still determined that they should meet again.

TWENTY-TWO

Josiah hardly watched the play as his attention was on the young woman in the side stalls beside the German army officer. He planned to leave the theatre early so that he could position himself at the exit and intercept the woman he was now a hundred per cent sure was Elise. Even the family name of von Meyer convinced him that he was right.

With the last act being played out, Josiah slipped from his seat and made his way to the street where he stood waiting in the cold air.

The applause and shouts of 'Bravo, encore' alerted Josiah that the crowds would soon spill out to the waiting carriages. The first patrons to appear through the doorway were those not wearing the finery of the upper-class attendees, and they milled around chatting, planning visits to parties.

The crowd grew larger, and Josiah waited impatiently

for the rest of the playgoers to appear as he found himself pushed back by the jostling crowd.

Suddenly, she emerged, and a couple of burly men forced a pathway for her and the rest of the Bavarian party to the waiting carriage as Josiah used all his strength to force a passage towards her. She was a mere ten feet away but already a wall of curious spectators had amassed to view the visiting Bavarian royalty. Josiah realised that he would not be able to reach her before she climbed into the carriage and instead called out her name, 'Elise!' His voice must have reached her as she suddenly paused with one foot on the carriage step, glancing around the crowd of onlookers. Josiah could see a hint of confusion in her expression, but she was bundled into the carriage and it drove away, leaving Josiah frustrated. He had been so close and yet she may as well have been on the moon for all his efforts to reach her.

Standing forlornly, Josiah was joined by Douglas, who said sympathetically, 'I gather from your face you were unable to make contact with the future duchess.'

Josiah turned to him. 'I called out her name and saw that she reacted to my voice,' he sighed. 'I will need to find another way of meeting her.'

'I have some bad news,' Douglas said. 'One of my friends at the play informed me that she is due to return to Bavaria tomorrow. I do not think you will have enough time to arrange a meeting before she leaves.'

'Does your friend know which ship she will be leaving on – and from where?' Josiah asked, a spark of hope ignited.

'I can find out,' Douglas said. 'He is just over there,' he said, pointing to a young man with a large scarf laughing with a huddle of friends. Douglas went to him as Josiah watched and then returned with his news.

'Well?' Josiah asked and Douglas informed his friend of

the details of Elise's departure the following day. The ship was a private and luxurious steam-driven yacht moored at the Thames docks.

That night, Josiah made his way to the dock area to wait outside the gates. He hardly felt the cold anymore and fought off the need to sleep as he stood like a sentry in the dark chill of early morning.

Dawn came and the docks were soon swarming with wharf labourers preparing to load the yacht. The day was still cold with dreary clouds moving across the smoggy sky. Josiah rubbed his eyes and could feel the effects of sleep deprivation. He slipped through the gates when they were opened to the public and stood with his back to the brick wall of a three-storey shipping office. His presence hardly raised any interest among the workers and Josiah was rewarded when, over the hooting of ship horns, he heard the distinctive clatter of a carriage approaching the dock.

It was driven by four fine black horses and appeared in the yard bustling with dock hands. Behind it was another smaller, less conspicuous covered carriage, from which alighted the same two burly men Josiah recognised from the evening before.

Elise's carriage was only fifty paces away and Josiah strode towards it. From the corner of his eye, he could see that his approach had been spotted by the two civilian guards, who rapidly caught up to him. Josiah attempted to ignore them as the door to the regal carriage was opened and the first to appear was the uniformed German officer.

A strong hand rested on Josiah's shoulder and a growl in German asked, 'What are you doing? Who are you?'

Josiah knew he would not be able to resist the body-guards, who were most probably armed with concealed pistols. 'I am a British citizen and demand that you take your hands off me,' Josiah replied in his relatively fluent German which took the two bodyguards by surprise. He felt the hand on his shoulder relax slightly.

'What do you want?' one of the guards asked, still suspicious of Josiah's move towards the carriage.

'I am a friend of the duchess,' Josiah responded. 'I am not here to harm her.'

The German officer was striding towards the three men and when he was within a couple of paces, the two bodyguards stiffened to attention.

Josiah could see that the handsome German officer stood ramrod straight and that his German army rank insignia identified him as a major in a brigade of Hussars. 'Who is this man?' the officer demanded calmly.

'He says that he is a friend of the duchess, sir,' one of the guards answered, still with his hand on Josiah's shoulder. 'He speaks German.'

The German cavalry officer turned to Josiah. 'How do you know Fräulein von Meyer?' he asked. The lack of reference to her title made Josiah think that he had a very personal relationship to her. He guessed the man was in his mid-twenties, and he could see the trace of a duelling scar on his cheek. Josiah knew about the tradition of such scars in the German army as they were considered a badge of honour.

'I met Fräulein von Meyer when she was in the Australian colonies,' Josiah replied. He was not about to disclose how to this stranger. 'Please inform Elise that an old friend from Sydney would like to speak to her before she embarks.'

'You speak her name too familiarly,' the German said with a frown. 'I am Major Maximillian von Kellermann of the Kaiser's Hussars, and I am her fiancé. She has said very little about the deaths of her parents in that godforsaken land of Queensland, or what followed before she was returned to Bavaria. Remove yourself before my men use force.'

Josiah could see beyond the tall German Hussar and saw Elise alight from the carriage, followed by the stern-looking man and woman who he had seen her with the evening before. Elise gazed across at the huddle of four men then directly at Josiah. For a moment, she stared before suddenly breaking away from the older couple hovering near her.

'Josiah!' she shouted, hurrying towards him.

The three men surrounding Josiah looked both confused and shocked at this reaction. 'Maximillian, it is all right, this is the man who saved my life. I wish to speak with him.'

'Elise, are you sure?' Kellermann asked, reluctant to allow this stranger to contact such an important personage as his fiancée.

'I am sure,' Elise said. 'It was Josiah who gave me this little cross, to protect me.' Elise touched the religious item on her breast. 'I heard a voice last night at the theatre and for a moment I thought it was you,' she said, her eyes glistening with tears.

'It *was* me,' Josiah said, noticing that the guard's hand had been removed from his shoulder. 'I just wanted to contact you. I could hardly believe that this would ever happen again after you left Sydney, and now you are home, in your castle.'

'I would like to speak with Josiah alone,' Elise said in a commanding voice. The three men reluctantly backed off.

'I met your fiancé,' Josiah said. 'Albeit under unusual circumstances.' At his statement, he saw a troubled expression cross Elise's face.

'Yes, we are to be married next year in June,' she replied. 'He will share my duchy with me.'

'Do you love him?' Josiah asked.

'Love is not relevant,' Elise replied. 'Though when I was much younger, I used to dream that I would be old enough one day for you to take notice of me as a woman,' Elise confessed. 'But those were the dreams of a young, infatuated girl far from home.'

'I looked for you. I never forgot you,' Josiah said. 'I always hoped that we would meet again one day.'

'And so we have,' Elise said with a sweet smile.

'Come, girl,' a woman's harsh voice called. 'We are about to depart on the change of tide.'

'My aunt,' Elise explained. 'I must go. But I feel that we may meet again in the future, as friends.'

Elise suddenly leaned up and kissed Josiah on the cheek before turning away, escorted by her fiancé and the two bodyguards. She did not look back, but her fiancé did shoot Josiah a coolly appraising look.

Josiah stood watching Elise board the impressive steam yacht emblazoned with the Kaiser's coat of arms on its bow. He remained on the wharf, the kiss lingering on his cheek and a thousand confused thoughts running through his mind, as the yacht slipped the wharf and steamed into the great river's main channel.

*

Over ten thousand miles away, Ian Steele only had a single, clear-cut thought: justified – if not legal – vengeance for the terrible crime committed against the woman he loved.

While Isabel insisted all was well, she had declined almost all Ian's invitations since Christmas. It was as if she had withdrawn from the world. Why should his beloved be forced to hide while the monster who hurt her roamed free? Ian well knew that Isabel would have no hope in the legal system, so there was only one way to find justice and give her peace of mind. Killing did not concern him – only getting caught.

He stood in his garden on a hot, sunny day going over every scenario he could think of to get Skinner alone and in a place where he could wreak his bloody revenge. Even now, Skinner was spreading false rumours that there was proof that the once respected colonial soldier was linked to the Jewish bankers of Europe and that he supported their Zionist cause for Palestine occupation. It was not true, but rumours are always more interesting than facts. Ian was feeling the pinch of business acquaintances and even a few friends avoiding him as if he had the plague. It was yet another reason for Skinner to be eliminated.

Ian gazed at his gardener, former Corporal Will Bowden, who was watering flowers with a can. If he could rely on any man, he knew that it had to be Will Bowden. Ian remembered the times that the man in his command had followed him into the hell of shot and shell. The shared experience was something that no man could put asunder.

Will glanced up from watering the flowers and smiled. 'Mornin' Cap'n,' he said with a wave.

'Good morning, Will,' Ian replied with a wave of his own. 'Would it be possible to have a word with you?'

'Of course, Cap'n,' Will replied, straightening his back. 'Anytime.'

Ian gestured for him to sit on a wooden bench under the shade of an imported English tree and they sat together.

'Will, do you ever remember those days we served the Queen under fire?' Ian asked.

Will looked puzzled. 'I surely do, Cap'n Steele. Every night when I close my eyes. Me missus says I do a lot of yellin' in my sleep.'

'I know what you mean,' Ian said, nodding. 'I too have

trouble sleeping on some nights when the ghosts of our friends return. It is not something that those who have never experienced what we have could ever understand. But reminiscences of the past are not what I wish to speak to you about. I have a proposition that promises a grand financial return for you and the family.'

Will turned to Ian with interest in his expression. 'What would that be, Cap'n Steele?' he asked.

'A matter with just a slight margin of risk but a promise of a hundred guineas cash in return,' Ian said quietly. He saw the shocked expression on his former corporal's face. The sum was a fortune to the gardener.

'For that money, I would risk the hangman's noose,' Will replied.

'Hopefully it won't come to that. But it will mean killing a man,' Ian said. 'A man who has attempted to destroy me and those I love.'

'You mean that Harold Skinner who's been tellin' lies about you through the newspapers,' Will said with passion. 'He deserves to die.'

Ian was impressed by the fact his former corporal had identified the target. 'It goes even beyond his lies about me and my family. He is guilty of a horrific act for which he will never face the legal system.'

'You know that me and the family owe you everything, Cap'n,' Will said. 'Knowin' how smart you are, I trust any plan you might come up with.'

Ian smiled. 'Maybe a couple of dangerous bushrangers would do the job.'

Will sank back against the bench. 'Where would we find such fellas?' he sighed. 'Most are out in the bush and not aroun' Sydney anymore. That Kelly fella is down Victoria way an' a bit hard to contact.'

'You are in the company of the bushrangers. You and me,' Ian said with an evil grin. 'All we need is to ambush our man on a lonely stretch of track and do away with him.'

Will almost gasped. 'You an' me,' he echoed and for a moment, Ian thought his gardener might wish to withdraw from the pact. 'When and where?' Will asked.

'The when and where I have yet to discover,' Ian said. 'But when I do, we will plan our ambush. You and I will carry it out as if we were once again on the battlefield.'

Will looked up at the blue sky and nodded.

Ian felt a rush of adrenaline. Death would surely come for Harold Skinner.

TWENTY-THREE

Josiah was on the verge of beginning his officer military training at the Royal Military Academy Sandhurst and was a constant visitor to the Curry residence for meals and even outings. At those times, he came to learn more about Marian, who still treated him with aloofness. Her father had commented to Josiah over sherry that he feared his daughter had become very much like the upper-class snobs he had encountered in the army when he served with Josiah's father. Although she was still only fifteen, she mixed in the best social circles of London, and Conan knew her beauty had attracted attention from many young men from wealthy families.

'I believe that you will commence your military studies soon,' Marian said across the table during the traditional Sunday roast lunch. 'I personally do not believe we should be attempting to dominate the poor savages of other lands.'

Josiah looked up from his meal in surprise. 'I will be, but I am not to become an officer of the Queen to dominate other people I do not know. I will simply obey the orders passed to me from my superiors. That is what a soldier does.'

'Please, no talk of politics at the table,' Molly pleaded. 'We are looking forward to an afternoon at Hyde Park to view the trooping of the colours and enjoy the music afterwards.'

'My daughter has strong opinions on many matters,' Conan chuckled. 'She even believes that women should be granted the vote.'

'That could be a good idea,' Josiah said unexpectedly, which caught Marian's attention.

'You surprise me, Mr Steele,' Marian said. 'I would not think a colonial would have such modern ideas.'

'My mother was one of the most competent people I ever knew. She left a financial empire behind in England for the sake of her love for my father. But in New South Wales, she was able to organise and manage many charities. My father would say that she was the equal of any man he knew.'

Conan frowned, aware of the source of Ella's fortune, but did not comment. 'I think that we should ensure we are suitably clothed for our foray to the park,' he said to disrupt any further political talk as Mildred cleared the table.

They took an open carriage to Hyde Park and alighted to stroll towards the gathering of soldiers in the park. Bands played and a festive ambience was apparent as crowds in their Sunday best milled and red-coated soldiers marched in step. It was a rare sunny day with a chill in the air at the end of winter.

Marian fell into step beside Josiah, surprising him. 'Do you really believe that women should be allowed to vote?' she asked.

'I do,' Josiah replied. 'I believe that men and women are equal, but different.'

'That is a very wise observation, Mr Steele,' Marian said warmly and for a second, their hands touched accidentally.

Josiah felt a thrill of sudden excitement course through his body. 'Sorry,' he said as he pulled away.

Marian turned to him with a mysterious smile. 'You need not apologise,' she said. 'I know it was an accident.'

Josiah was a little deflated by her response and continued to walk on. 'I would like it if you would call me Josiah,' he said.

'Then you may call me Marian,' she responded. 'After all, you are like a member of my own family. Almost like a big brother.' That answer did not please Josiah either, but he was forced to accept it.

'Oh, I almost forgot to mention that I have met another young colonial man recently at a tea party I was invited to by my friend, Gwen: Horace Anderson. I must mention your name when we next meet, I am sure he would love to meet a fellow colonial.'

Josiah could hardly believe his ears. 'I thank you but there is no need. We were at school together in Sydney,' he said stiffly. 'We are not friends.'

'Oh! I was not aware,' Marian said. 'I found him to be quite charming.'

Josiah did not wish to hear her compliment the man with whom he had unresolved matters to settle for his past ridicule of Josiah's Jewish faith. 'Is he a close friend?' Josiah asked with a touch of jealousy.

'Not at this time,' Marian answered with a mischievous twinkle in her eye. 'It may be possible for you two to meet and settle your differences like gentlemen. After all, the past is in the past.'

Ten thousand miles and several years made little difference, Josiah was certain. 'I think that would not be a good idea,' Josiah said. 'Our mutual dislike cannot be changed with a handshake.'

'That is a pity,' Marian said with a pout. 'I believe all matters can be resolved with a respect for each other.'

Conan and his family all knew that Josiah was of the Jewish faith, and it had not made any difference in their attitude to the youth, who they accepted as family. Josiah could not begin to explain to this pretty, popular young lady the basis of his hatred for the man she praised.

*

'It's like the old days, Cap'n Steele,' Will Bowden said as the two men rode side by side along the hard-packed earthen road leading to the crest of a hill from where they could view the blue haze above the trees below. 'Goin' into action again.'

Ian noted his companion's observation and silently agreed with him. 'We bivouac at the summit of the hill off the road,' Ian said. 'According to my calculations, we have a day's lead on Skinner and his coach.'

Ian had discovered that Skinner sometimes travelled across the Great Divide to inspect government projects and that he was due to travel on the Great Western Road. Ian had travelled the road on many occasions to visit his sheep properties around Bathurst and Goulburn. It was bordered by thick bush and traversed a rugged terrain of hills and valley before descending to the Hartley Valley and onto the plains of western New South Wales.

The two men rode to a section of the crest which Ian felt had a good view back down the winding road, and there they hobbled their horses. Ian had packed camping equipment on the packhorse Will led and concealed all firearms in saddlebags. Ian was armed with his two Colts, and Will a short, double-barrelled shotgun.

Passing through the first tollgate on the road, they had given false names when Ian paid the fee. The tollgate keeper barely glanced at the two men as all he was interested in was the toll collection. So far, so good. Both men were dressed in working men's garb and blended into the traffic they passed on the highway across the Great Dividing Range from Sydney.

It was a fine day with a chill in the air from the approaching winter, and they soon set up a small tent in the bush.

Ian noticed that Will appeared calm and relaxed; he would follow his former officer into hell for no payment. For a hundred guineas, he would also face the very devil himself.

When the camp was established, both men sat around a small fire burning in a ring of rocks Ian had scrounged in the bush, as he was aware how deadly any stray fire could be in the eucalyptus forests. They sipped freshly brewed tea and bit into hardtack biscuits covered in jam.

'Tomorrow morning before first light, you will wait in a concealed position about a hundred yards down the road,' Ian said, taking a sip of his tea from an enamel mug. 'From what I observed on the way here, you should have a grand view down the road to anyone coming up. You should have at least five minutes to warn me when you see a carriage that you think might be Skinner's. When it reaches the top just adjacent to where we are, we will ambush him. The driver is not to be harmed. It will be your task to ensure that he can continue without Skinner on his way to the valley below. I will look after Skinner. In the morning, we strike camp, pack the equipment away and be prepared to return to Sydney as soon as the mission is over. Do you have any questions, Will?'

'None, Cap'n.'

'Good,' Ian replied. 'Tonight, we get a good sleep so as to be up before dawn.'

For the rest of the afternoon, they reminisced on past battles they had shared on the campaigns, recollecting the names of good men who had not survived and the funny incidents that had occurred in the regiment. It was as if Ian was back on those campaigns, but the scent of eucalyptus reminded him that this battle was on the soil of his home ground.

Before dawn, they arose and ate a hot breakfast of damper bread cooked in the coals of the refreshed fire with a generous helping of tinned beef. The tent was struck and their excess kit packed on the horse carrying their supplies. The fire was extinguished, and Will hefted his shotgun onto his shoulder, taking one of the water canteens to his post a hundred yards down the road.

After unhobbling and saddling the horses, Ian tethered them to a tree close to the road and took up a concealed position to observe the traffic passing by.

Mid-morning, Ian saw a big bullock wagon hauling bales of wool struggle by, the bullockies walking beside the big dray with whips cracking to spur on the oxen, whilst a man on a horse travelling up the hill also passed. When Ian glanced up at the sky, he groaned. Rising in vast columns, dark clouds in the west promised a big electrical storm.

'He's comin',' Will Bowden called out as he stumbled up the road. Ian retrieved his small telescope while Will pulled a bandana over his face and tugged his broad-brimmed hat down over his eyes. The bullock team was gone and no other travellers were to be seen on the road. Within minutes the coach appeared, and Ian could see the face of his hated enemy sitting beside the driver. He pulled on his own face covering under the floppy bushman's hat.

Overhead, a flash of lightning followed almost immediately by a clap of thunder startled the horse drawing the gig. It was ten paces from Ian and Will's position when they stepped out on the road.

'Stand and deliver!' Ian roared the traditional robbery demand of the bushranger. The driver immediately dropped the reins and threw up his arms in terror at the sight.

Ian levelled both the pistols at Skinner as Will moved in on the gig. 'Get down!' he ordered the driver, who immediately complied.

While Ian continued to cover Skinner, Will led the driver off into the bush adjacent to the road. The driver was begging Will not to kill him, and Will attempted to reassure the man that if he obeyed orders, he would be spared. Will secured the man to a tree just out of sight of the road, placing a full water canteen close by, knowing that the knots he used would allow the driver to eventually untie himself.

'Get down,' Ian ordered Skinner, who alighted from the carriage with shaking legs, his hands in the air. 'Walk to that clearing over there,' Ian continued, pointing the barrel of his Colt at an area devoid of trees on the opposite side of the road to where the driver was.

'If you want money, I have money in my luggage,' Skinner pleaded. 'I beg that you do me no harm.'

When they reached the clearing out of view of the road, Ian removed his bandana.

'You!' Skinner spluttered, his face darkening with fury. 'Have you gone stark raving mad?'

'Possibly,' Ian replied. 'But you can be assured that I do not want your money – only justice.'

'I don't know what you are talking about,' Skinner answered defiantly. 'I am a man highly regarded by the governor. It will be you brought to justice when I report this incident.'

'What if you are unable to report the incident?' Ian asked. 'I just want you to explain and apologise for the terrible pain you caused to Isabel before Christmas.'

'I do not know what you mean,' Skinner lied, and it was obvious that he believed he would be able to talk his way out of his current situation. After all, Captain Ian Steele was known as a rational man, if not one who could be considered honourable by Skinner's few friends.

'I know that Isabel suffered a grievous assault at your hands,' Ian said.

'She has played you for a fool. She would have reported me to the constabulary if such a matter had occurred,' Skinner sneered. 'She is well known as a woman of loose morals.'

'By whom?' Ian asked calmly even as his rage was rising at Skinner's last statement.

'By all my acquaintances,' Skinner answered.

'Is that because that is what you have told them?' Ian snarled.

Skinner seemed to finally comprehend the danger he was in, and for a moment, they both stood silently as the first fat drops of rain fell ahead of a rising wind.

Ian placed one of his Colts carefully on the ground and walked a few paces away, turning to see Skinner still watching him with an expression of fear.

'Pick it up,' Ian said. 'I will not attempt to stop you.'

For a moment, Skinner stood petrified, but then stumbled forward to stoop down and raise the heavy revolver.

'You now have a chance to defend yourself, although you do not deserve it,' Ian called out over the sound of the rain now splattering hard into the dry forest. Ian held his pistol at his side with his finger on the trigger of the cocked revolver.

'This is not a civilised way to settle matters,' Skinner spluttered, his hands clearly shaking. 'I refuse to indulge in this ridiculous duel.'

'You are lauded as a great man of government, but it is men like you who order others to go off to war,' Ian said bitterly. 'You stay safely at home while the blood of young men is spilled to make you and your wealthy friends even greater fortunes, to bring you even more power. You must feel invincible, believing you can do whatever you want, have whatever you want, never being called to account. But the time has come to pay your debt, Skinner. You now have the great honour of knowing what it is like to face imminent death.'

Ian raised his Colt to shoulder level aimed directly at Skinner, whose face reflected sheer terror. Lightning flashed and the crack of nearby thunder was echoed by two almost simultaneous shots.

*

Ian was surprised at the speed with which Skinner raised his pistol and was spun around as the heavy-calibre shot struck him. He stumbled, falling to the wet earth.

'Cap'n! Cap'n!'

Ian could hear the concerned voice of Will Bowden drift to him through a haze of pain. Ian groaned, opening his eyes to see his man kneeling beside him with a concerned expression on his face.

'Cap'n Steele! The bugger clipped yer head.'

Ian sat up with some difficulty, his head throbbing. He touched his head above his ear and felt the warm blood matted in his hair. Probing with his fingers, he could feel the indentation caused by the heavy lead ball. A fraction of an inch further and it would have killed him. As it was, it had proved to be a grazing shot.

'Skinner?' Ian asked through gritted teeth, blinking at the rain pouring onto his face as lightning flashed around them to the accompaniment of violent thunderclaps.

'You blew the top of 'is 'ead off,' Will replied matter-of-factly. 'The bugger is well an' truly dead.'

With Will's assistance, Ian stood but felt nauseous. His head ached and the blood continued to run down the side of his face, diluted by the rain. Will had recovered Ian's two revolvers and helped Ian back to their horses, tethered to the trees a short distance away.

'I think we should let the coachman free in this weather,' Ian said as he mounted his horse with some difficulty. Both men were drenched to the skin and a real chill was setting in.

Will replaced his bandana around his face and went to where he had secured the driver. He released him with a warning to keep his mouth shut but was fully aware this would not happen. It was only a matter of time before the man would contact the police to explain how his employer was missing at the hands of two bushrangers.

TWENTY-FOUR

Marian's flaming red hair was accentuated by the flicker of the candles and Josiah felt just a little bit uncomfortable in her almost regal presence. The playing cards were spread on the varnished table between them in Conan's sitting room. Conan and Molly had shared the evening game of whist but had now retired, leaving the young people to sit up and continue the game, and Josiah was acutely aware that he was trusted to be alone with Marian, her parents knowing that as a gentleman he would not do anything to cause her shame. For a moment a silence followed as Marian dealt the cards.

'Have you ever read Mr Marx's work *The Communist Manifesto*?' Marian asked, breaking the awkward silence. 'Mr Marx actually lives in London.'

'My apologies, but who is Mr Marx?' Josiah asked, hating to appear an ignorant colonial.

'Mr Karl Marx, who I believe is a fellow Jew,' Marian replied. 'I thought that you may have known about him as you are also Jewish.'

Josiah was a little surprised at her bluntness regarding his religious background. 'I am afraid my rabbi in Sydney would chide me for my lack of devotion,' Josiah answered. 'My father is a Christian but in our religion a child inherits our beliefs through the mother.'

'I did not know,' Marian said. 'I suppose I must excuse you for not knowing about Mr Marx.'

'Why is he so important?' Josiah asked, and Marian was quick to explain his socialist ideas. Josiah did not interrupt except to ask pertinent questions which Marian was happy to answer.

'My thanks for allowing me to further my knowledge, learning how to be a communist,' Josiah said with a twisted smile.

Marian also smiled at his statement. 'Do I hear a note of sarcasm in your gratitude?' she asked. 'I do not wish to be a communist, but I do lean towards socialism. I think that Marx does not fully understand the primeval need of individuals to struggle for personal wealth. But I believe we who are fortunate are compelled to improve the lot of the poor and desist from enslaving native peoples in our colonies.'

'Well, I agree with you concerning the impoverished, but it is the British rule that brings civilisation to the savages of those colonies. Is that not also improving the lot of those less fortunate?'

Marian looked thoughtful at his reply, sipping a glass of aerated water. Josiah was beginning to have a small understanding of who she was now and was impressed that for a young woman of her age she was far more intellectually advanced than any other young woman he had ever met during his days at school. 'I'm not sure the people themselves see it that way,' she said eventually.

'I see,' Josiah said.

Marian shook her head. 'I don't think you do. Take my situation, for example. It is not easy for a girl from a family who have made their wealth from their own hard work and wise business management. I am not accepted by the upper classes of London society, but I have good friends who do accept me for myself and have opened doors for me in the past and will do so into the future. Now you may understand why I believe in many of the principles of Mr Marx's writings. I strive for a society where all men and women are equal and how we are perceived is not based on being born into the right family or the wealth of our estates.'

Josiah broke into a grin. 'I can see that you cannot take the colonial Irish or Welsh out of your own birthright,' he said and noticed a flicker in Marian's expression. She was not smiling and there was a sadness in her eyes.

'Oh, if we could simply live in a society where we are judged for our contribution towards our fellow man,' she said. At that moment, Josiah felt a strong bond with the daughter of Conan and Molly Curry. He too understood the many prejudices of English society.

'It has been a grand evening, Josiah,' she said. 'I hope that we are able to meet again before you leave for the Royal Military Academy.'

'I hope so too. But now I feel that the evening has grown long, and I must return to my own place and prepare to leave. Please thank your mother and father for such an enchanting and pleasant evening.'

Josiah rose from the table with mixed emotions. He knew that only time would confirm how he felt towards the daughter of Conan and Molly Curry. He was wise enough to know his feelings towards her could only be those of a brother because of her tender years.

★

Within a couple of days, Ian and Will had returned to Sydney. When questioned by his manager at his office in the city as to his journey to Bathurst, Ian replied that he had been forced to turn back due to a fall from his horse. Ian's wound was obvious, and his explanation made sense. Ian had not mentioned that he had been accompanied by Will Bowden.

Ian visited Dr Parkins, who carefully examined the injury and concluded that the skull had not been cracked and the wound was healing. When Ian told him it was the result of a fall from his horse, the doctor frowned but did not question the explanation.

At his home on the harbour, Ian was visited by Isabel, who informed Ian that she had sold her rural property, choosing to buy a comfortable cottage not far from Ian's own residence. She had hired a maid and gardener and said that she had always considered retiring in Sydney, where she was closer to lifelong friends. Ian was pleased to have her so close but realised that her assault by Skinner still haunted her. Ian hoped that once Isabel knew Skinner would never hurt her again, she would find some peace.

A week later, it was blasted across the Sydney papers that the well-known and respected senior civil servant had been murdered by two bushrangers on the Great Western Road. The coachman had been able to get to a police station to report the ambush, and a troop of mounted police had found Skinner in the bush. The dingoes and crows had scavenged on his bloated and decomposing body, and he was no longer recognisable. A reward was immediately posted for information as to the identities of the two men who had ambushed and killed Skinner.

Ian read the newspaper report at the breakfast table and was not concerned. He had known Skinner's death would eventually be reported but had selected his ground away from any witnesses – other than Skinner's driver, who had not seen their faces and was thus unable to identify them. His head wound was healing well and soon would be a mere scar, a memento of dispensing justice.

Will had returned to his duties around the house and Ian trusted him to remain silent about the events. Soon, Skinner's murder would be filed away in some police cabinet to collect dust as an unsolved case. All would be well.

However, Ian had underestimated the furore the death of Harold Skinner would stir up in the higher echelons of the government. The governor himself issued a demand to the Police Inspector General to allocate his best detective to investigate the death in the newly formed Criminal Investigation Branch located at 109 Phillip Street. The two-storey building also housed the Inspector General, and when Detective Third Class Andrew Paull was summoned to his office, he firstly wondered why this should be so as his record for solving criminal matters was exemplary and such an order from the top police officer's room often meant a disciplinary matter.

Andrew Paull was in his late thirties and married with two children. He had been a mounted officer and had received a prize for his work hunting down bushrangers before transferring to Sydney and the detective branch.

Andrew stepped into the large office and noticed a man wearing civilian dress standing beside the Inspector General, seated at his desk.

'Ah, Detective Paull. I have a need to assign you to a

very important case,' the Inspector General said. 'This is Mr Preston from the governor's office.'

Andrew shook the gaunt man's hand.

'Mr Preston represents the governor in this matter and may be of some assistance to you in investigating the case of one Harold Skinner, who worked for the governor.'

Relieved, Andrew relaxed and realised that he had been selected for a high-profile case. He had read that the victim had been cold-bloodedly murdered by a couple of bush-rangers weeks before. 'I can promise that I will do my best, sir,' Andrew replied.

'Your best means bringing the men responsible to the gallows, Detective,' Preston said. 'We cannot have Harold's death go unpunished. It is not a good look for law and order.'

Andrew was a little annoyed at the civil servant's demand as he knew from experience it would not be an easy matter. The crime had occurred without witnesses, except for the carriage driver, who had admitted he did not actually see the killing. Andrew needed more. Luckily, the civil servant was about to provide a list of suspects with just one name on it.

'We know of some animosity towards Harold from a former British army captain, Ian Steele,' he offered. 'It seems that the man had a motive to kill Harold because Harold had exposed Steele as a Jew lover. They were seen to get into fisticuffs at Sir Godfrey Pollard's residence outside of Sydney before Christmas.'

'Who won the matter?' Andrew asked.

'I believe that Captain Steele gave Harold a good thrashing,' Preston replied.

'So why do you think Captain Steele might have been behind the killing if he had already settled the matter?' Andrew asked. 'Is it possible that unknown bushrangers committed the crime?'

'I concede that that might be possible, but from what I have learned, such men usually just rob their victims, not kill them,' Preston replied. 'The carriage driver informed your colleagues at the scene that no money or valuables were taken.'

'Then I will enquire into Captain Steele with all due thoroughness,' Andrew said.

'You will have any assistance you require from my office,' the Inspector General said to Preston and turned to Andrew. 'I have informed your superior of your assignment and directed him to fully support your investigation, Detective Paull.'

'Thank you, sir,' Andrew responded. 'I will commence my investigation immediately.'

'Good,' the top policeman said. 'You are dismissed to your duties.'

Andrew nodded to the civil servant and walked out of the office, his head reeling with thoughts of how he would approach the prominent citizen. Andrew had read about Captain Steele's distinguished service for the Queen and was just a little intimidated by his task. But he reminded himself that no one was above the law.

Detective Andrew Paull had earned his illustrious reputation as a police officer who could solve difficult cases because he was meticulous. He could blend in with all classes of people and elicit information without them knowing that they were giving away bits and pieces that Andrew could use to reveal the truth.

As such, he stood at the bar of a hotel close to the offices of the Steele Enterprises on a Friday afternoon as workers from the city gathered to celebrate pay day. Andrew wore his cheapest suit and bowler hat, and to all intents and purposes could pass as just another office clerk. He was quick to pick up who worked for Captain Ian Steele and was able to infiltrate a small party of Ian's staff. He introduced himself as an admirer of the prominent Sydney figure with a story of how he once met a man who had served with their boss in New Zealand. This part of the story was true, as the man he referred to had been a fellow mounted trooper who had sung Ian's praises.

As the beer and ale flowed, tongues were loosened, and Andrew learned that their boss had recently travelled up the Great Western Road at about the same time that Skinner had been killed. Andrew latched onto the innocent remark and, with further clever questions in the haze of alcohol, also learned that their boss had been forced to return early as a result of a fall from his horse during a fierce thunderstorm. Andrew remembered the case notes he had read mentioned that Skinner had been shot dead during a fierce storm. Coincidence? There was no such thing as coincidence in the astute detective's experience. However, one of the now drunken employees mentioned that his boss had reported to his office with a bandaged head covering a nasty gash. This additional information gave a small amount of credibility to his suspect's alibi for returning to Sydney and not continuing his journey across the Great Divide to the Western Plains.

The detective was also concerned that his background questioning of government officials had yielded that Skinner was not held in high regard by those who he had worked with. It was only the newspapers lauding the dead man, and Andrew well knew how their only interest was making money from lurid stories to inflame the public. Those he spoke to overwhelmingly cast Skinner as an arrogant, cold and vexatious man.

On the Monday morning when Andrew Paull reported to the Phillip Street police CIB, he sat at his desk, pondering the notes he had put together. While the detective still considered the murder may have been the result of a robbery gone wrong by bushrangers, he felt that he had enough intelligence to finally approach the suspect that Preston had served up to him.

★

Ian had arrived early for his day at the office near Circular Quay. Very few of his employees had arrived, providing Ian with an opportunity to read through the business reports and financial statements and review his responses for the meeting at ten o'clock with the bookkeepers and managers of his various company enterprises. Only his secretary, Tom Porter, was at his desk in the room adjoining Ian's office. Tom was preparing the boss's morning cup of tea. Ian and Tom had a close relationship as Ian respected the young man's ambition, intelligence and ability to organise a smooth-running schedule.

'Morning, Captain Steele,' Tom said, placing a teacup and saucer on Ian's desk. 'I am not sure how to say this, but you have a couple of policemen waiting in the reception to see you. Needless to say, they do not have an appointment.'

Ian felt a stab of fear. It could only be about one thing. 'Please show them in, Mr Porter, and prepare another couple of cups of tea,' Ian responded calmly.

Tom ushered the men inside Ian's office. Ian rose from behind his desk to meet the two men, both dressed in cheap suits and wearing bowler hats. One of the detectives was around his late twenties and the other in his late thirties.

Ian extended his hand to the older man. 'Ian Steele,' he said, and the detective responded by shaking his hand and introducing himself as Detective Andrew Paull of the Phillip Street CIB. The man had an aura of intelligence and conviction. Paull introduced his partner and Ian gestured to a couple of chairs in front of his desk. Tom had already returned with a pot of tea on a silver tray with two cups, milk in a small jug and a container of sugar, which he placed on the desk in front of the two policemen.

'If there is nothing else, Captain Steele?' Tom asked, eyeing the two detectives with suspicion.

'No, thank you, Mr Porter,' Ian said and resumed his chair behind his desk. Tom reluctantly returned to his own desk outside Ian's office.

'Well, gentlemen, I doubt that you are here for a cup of tea. How can I assist you?' Ian asked, knowing full well why they had turned up without an appointment.

'Captain Steele,' Andrew said, pouring tea into his cup and milk from the jug. 'I must apologise for not making an appointment to speak with you but due to the nature of our work, we prefer to act immediately and dispense with such niceties. My first question is, did you know Mr Harold Skinner?'

'I did, and I can tell you that I did not like the man.'

'That seems to answer my second question,' Andrew said, scribbling in his notebook. 'Is it true that you and he came to a physical altercation before Christmas at Sir Godfrey Pollard's residence west of Sydney?'

'We did,' Ian replied calmly. 'We settled the matter over a serious slight to my name, and as far as I was concerned, that closed our difference of opinion.'

'Have you had any other contact with Mr Skinner since?' Andrew asked.

Ian shook his head. 'Not since that evening at Sir Godfrey's estate.'

'I have been reliably informed that you travelled on horseback on the Great Western Road about the same time

Mr Skinner was also travelling west in a carriage with a government driver. Surely you must have seen him on the road?'

Ian frowned, leaning forward slightly. 'No, I did not,' Ian lied. 'A rather large storm came up over the hills and I was thrown from my horse. As you can see,' Ian continued, pointing to the wound healing on the side of his head, 'I sustained an injury that forced me to turn around and receive medical treatment. If Mr Skinner was on the road, I did not have any contact with him.'

'Were you alone on your journey west?' Andrew persisted.

'I was,' Ian lied again. He and Will had ensured their stories were compatible with the help of Will's wife, who would swear her husband had been sick in bed for a couple of days in the caretaker's cottage at Ian's harbour residence. 'I can understand why you might investigate me as it was well known that Skinner and I did not like each other, but despite my dislike for the man, I would still have felt obliged to defend him if I had come across the two bushrangers I read about on the road.'

Paull swallowed the last of his tea and placed his notebook in his coat pocket, rising, as did his silent partner. 'Captain Steele, thank you for your time.'

Ian rose as well, extending his hand. 'I understand why you should be here today,' he said. 'You would be remiss in your sworn duty if you did not question me.'

Paull nodded and Ian ushered them out of his office, closing his door when they were gone and slumping in his chair with a heavy sigh. He had half expected the police to be knocking on his door when they learned of his dislike of the civil servant and knowing he had been in the vicinity of the crime. But they needed evidence and not simply speculation. Hopefully the detectives would be satisfied with his simple explanation.

★

On the busy street outside Ian's office, Andrew walked with his collar up, hunched against the bitter breeze between the canyon of multi-storey office blocks and shops.

'What do you think?' Andrew's fellow detective asked.

'I think he was involved in the murder,' Andrew replied. 'But he has a lifetime of coolness under fire behind him, so proving his involvement will be a gargantuan task. A man has to have a stronger reason to kill an enemy than a fistfight.'

TWENTY-FIVE

Josiah Steele had sat the army exams and was duly notified that he was to report as a Gentleman Cadet to the Royal Military College at Sandhurst. The college was originally structured as an alternative school for boys as young as thirteen who aspired to a career in the military. Now, it trained young men to fill the officer ranks.

Josiah was taken by his private carriage to the entrance of the imposing main college building. He dismounted while his carriage driver waited to be dismissed to return to London.

Josiah wore a fine civilian suit and top hat as he walked smartly to the entrance, where a tough and almost menacing senior NCO sporting a big moustache met him.

'Sir, I have your name listed to report to the commandant upon your arrival,' the warrant officer said when Josiah provided his name. Josiah knew from his military studies that the rank of warrant officer for a sergeant major had been introduced earlier that year. 'You can proceed to his office immediately. I will escort you.'

Josiah did not realise the request was unusual, as he expected each new arrival to be met by the man in charge of the college.

The warrant officer tapped on the door with his pace stick and a voice called out from within. 'Enter.'

He stepped inside the office and Josiah heard him say, 'Sir, I have Mr Josiah Steele with me.'

'Bid him enter, Sarn't Major,' the commandant said, and Josiah also stepped into the office. 'That will be all, Sarn't Major,' the commandant said from behind his desk.

Josiah felt some nervousness standing at the centre of the office with its walls furnished with books. After all, he was in the presence of a high-ranking military officer who held his future in his hands. For a moment, the older man behind the desk shuffled through a ream of papers, then finally retrieved a thin folder, which he flipped open to peruse for a short time. He looked up at Josiah.

'Mr Steele, I had the honour of serving with your father during the Anglo–Persian campaign. Your father was a fine man and great officer although, at the time, we knew him as Captain Samuel Forbes. I believe that deception was eventually explained, and your father left our army honourably after his service.'

'Thank you, sir,' Josiah replied, still standing to attention.

'You may stand at ease, Mr Steele. I should add congratulations on your commission to Major MacDonald's Scots regiment.'

For a moment, Josiah was totally confused at the senior officer's statement. 'Sir, I am here to train to be an officer in Her Majesty's army.'

The commandant smiled. 'You will be gazetted very soon as a second lieutenant in Major MacDonald's Scottish regiment as you were first amongst all the applicants in the last round of examinations in every subject, from tactics to languages. Not only that but we have always had a tradition of taking in the sons of serving and former officers of Her Majesty. This has been made even easier by the fact that while you may be a colonial, you were actually born in England. I am in receipt of reports of your past exploits under fire when you were a mere lad of fifteen years of age in the colony of Queensland. According to your father's letters, it appears that you have already demonstrated leadership characteristics.'

Josiah was astonished that his father would so enthusiastically support his desire for service in the army.

'No doubt you read of the disaster we suffered in the campaign against the Zulus in Africa earlier this year. The Empire is under siege at the moment and badly in need of junior officers to lead the ranks. Personally, knowing your father's outstanding leadership under fire, I have also endorsed your commission. Like father, like son, what? I expect great things of you, Mr Steele.'

Stunned, Josiah stood staring at the portrait of a young Queen Victoria affixed to the wall above the commandant's head. 'Yes, sir,' Josiah replied.

'You will need to make arrangements to purchase the necessary uniforms for the regiment and all other bits of kit they require you to have for service overseas. I will have a movement order drawn up and you can take it with you. If you have any questions, the regiment has an office in London. I am sure you will do well with those mad Scots.'

'Thank you, sir,' Josiah answered, still in a euphoric

state, knowing that within a matter of days, he would be officially a commissioned officer of the Queen's army.

'One word of advice, Mr Steele. When you are with the regiment, listen to the advice of your senior non-commissioned officers. They are very experienced soldiers who have often faced the Queen's enemies on the battlefield. Other than that, I think you will do well, if your father is any example of what a colonial is able to do.'

Josiah was dismissed then stopped off at the orderly room to pick up his official papers. He strode out of the main building just as a couple of carriages pulled up to discharge young men who would have to complete their military training before being commissioned.

★

When Josiah eventually returned to London's bright lights later that evening, he did not go directly to his residence but had the carriage take him to Conan's tenement.

It was around nine o'clock, and Conan and the family were still up. Josiah was bid to enter when Conan answered the door.

'Josiah, what brings you to my abode this time of night?' Conan asked. 'I expected you would be commencing your time at Sandhurst.'

'I have news!' Josiah answered, stepping inside the warm residence. 'I have just learned that I do not have to attend the Royal Military Academy but will have my name gazetted as a second lieutenant within the week, into a Scottish regiment.'

'Bloody hell!' Conan exclaimed, gripping Josiah's hand and drawing him in for a great hug. 'I am – and I know your father will be – immensely proud of you. Come through so we can share this joyous news with Molly and Marian.'

Josiah followed the big Irishman into the parlour, where he saw Marian sitting at the piano and Molly knitting gloves on the sofa. Both women broke into smiles when they saw the young man.

'I thought that you would be at the academy this evening,' Molly said, placing down her knitting.

'Josiah does not need to be at the academy,' Conan said, his chest puffed out with pride. 'The damned English recognised his colonial prowess, and he is to receive his commission within the week. Then he will travel to join his regiment as a second lieutenant. I expect that you will be on the first ship to Africa or to India,' he said. 'I suspect that you will see action within the month with your regiment in either location.'

At Conan's statement, Molly's smile evaporated and Marian closed the lid of the piano and rushed out of the room. Both men were confused at the women's dark reactions to the wonderful news.

Molly rose from the sofa and reached out to Josiah. 'I must congratulate you, Josiah, on achieving your dream. Please excuse me,' she said sadly, and left the parlour.

'What happened?' Josiah asked, still confused.

Conan shook his head. 'It is the way of women,' he replied. 'They fear for us when we serve in foreign wars. I suppose I can understand why. It is harder on those who wait.'

Josiah reflected on Conan's sage words and only had one question in his mind: why had Marian reacted so strongly to the news that he might be facing a war somewhere in the Empire in the next few weeks? Was it that the recent disaster the British army had suffered in Africa against the Zulus influenced her perceptions of a soldier's life?

★

Molly had gone to her daughter's room after observing her distress at the announcement of Josiah's acceptance as an army officer. She entered the room to see Marian lying on her bed, crying softly.

'My darling, what has upset you?' Molly asked, already knowing the answer.

Marian turned around to sit up and wipe away tears from her eyes with a lace handkerchief. 'Josiah had such a future ahead of him,' Marian said, resuming her composure. 'He could have entered any of our academic institutes. He is one of the most intelligent men I have ever met.'

'Is that the only reason you are sad?' Molly gently prompted when she sat at the end of the bed. 'Or do you have feelings for him?'

Marian looked up sharply. 'I don't understand your meaning, Mother,' she replied.

'I have seen the way you look at Josiah whenever you are in his company, and it reminds me of how I was when I met your father. I knew better than to fall in love with a soldier, but I did anyway.'

'You have told me stories of how you constantly spent life wondering if you would ever see Father again. You told me of the nightmares you had, dreaming of my father being killed in some faraway land.'

'But I loved him,' Molly sighed. 'That is a bond that only grows with time. I always thought that you might meet a rich young man who was not a soldier and find love. You are so bright and your education was always meant to be a means to access those circles.'

'I am in those circles, Mother,' Marian replied. 'I could go to a party tomorrow and find a rich young man who isn't determined to get himself killed.'

'I know, my dear, but you are still so young.'

'Fifteen is not so young.'

Molly smiled. 'You have been blessed with intelligence, passion and beauty. You can have and be whatever you want, my dear.'

Marian thought about what her mother was saying. 'What if . . . I do have some feelings for Josiah?' she asked slowly. 'He has never expressed any feelings towards me other than that of a good friend.'

Molly laughed. 'You are so intelligent, my girl, but you are not as perceptive as you think you are,' she said, taking her daughter's hand. 'Your father and I can both see the way he looks at you with adoring eyes. Almost like a puppy following his master.'

'Well, why is he not brave enough to express his honest feelings for me?' Marian countered angrily. 'I think he is a coward.'

Molly shook her head. 'He is a man, and you are a young lady. Men are simple creatures driven by foolish considerations. They think the ultimate test of their manhood is on the battlefield and ignore the possibility of being maimed or killed. It is almost a deadly game of ultimate courage for men like your father and Josiah and his father.'

'What do I do?' Marian almost pleaded with her mother for an answer.

'Alas, it will be you alone who will find that answer in the years ahead, but if you wish to protect yourself from future heartbreak, I would consider a future with someone other than Josiah. I hate myself for suggesting that, but my main concern is for your happiness. Deep down, I feel that a life with Josiah is not one you would wish to live. I know that from my own experience with your father.'

'But you still married him,' Marian quizzed.

'Only when I was sure that he would no longer have the

Queen as his mistress,' Molly replied. 'I would not marry him until he had left the army.'

Marian pondered her mother's advice, which rang with an element of truth. Marian knew how eligible she was. Perhaps Josiah was simply a dear friend who had chosen a foolish future. She slid from the bed and was prepared to return to the parlour and display her friendship towards Josiah, as a sister might a brother. But when she did, she was informed by her father that he had already left the house. Deep within her soul Marian was glad that she did not have to face Josiah again or she might experience the pain of seeing him for the last time in her life.

★

Detective Andrew Paull was frustrated. He sat at a desk in the CIB, staring at the wall through a cloud of cigarette and pipe smoke, ignoring the banter of his colleagues around him. He had reported to his inspector that he had interviewed a suspect, Captain Ian Steele, and that he felt there was a strong reason to believe that the man was involved in the slaying of the prominent civil servant on the road west across the mountains. But other than the carriage driver's statement, there was no positive evidence that one of the two bushrangers was Paull's prime suspect.

Andrew leaned back in his chair and removed his pipe from his suit coat. After plugging it with cheap tobacco, he lit the pipe and puffed smoke into the already cloudy air. There had to be another reason for Steele to execute Skinner, Andrew mused as he puffed on the pipe. From all that he had learned of Ian Steele from friends and business acquaintances, the man would have left any matters of contention between he and Skinner at Sir Godfrey's residence.

'So why go out of his way to hunt down and kill Skinner?' Andrew asked himself. If only he could find a reason strong enough to explain why an honourable man such as Steele would put his life and reputation on the line. If he did, Andrew knew he might have a motive. From his years of being a police officer, the detective reviewed the reasons people killed. Hatred . . . no, the feud had already been settled. Greed . . . Steele had ten times the fortune of Skinner, and this had not been a robbery. Lust . . .?

That is it! Andrew thought. He would need to enquire as to any personal relationship the former British officer might have. Andrew tapped his pipe into an ashtray and stood up. It was time to hit the streets again and ask discreet questions as to if Ian Steele was known to be stepping out with a lady.

'C'mon Frank,' Andrew said to his partner, who was eating a sandwich at the desk not far from his own. 'We need to go back to work.'

TWENTY-SIX

Josiah announced the news to his housekeeper that he would be closing his townhouse for a period of time but that it would remain her home while he was away. Her wages would still be paid, along with an allowance for food and coal. The elderly lady broke into tears of gratitude and impulsively hugged Josiah. 'God bless you, Master Steele,' she said, wiping her eyes with her cooking apron. 'Where would you be going?'

'It appears from my papers that my regiment will be travelling to Afghanistan,' Josiah replied. 'I am not sure for how long.'

'I have some mail I collected while you were away these past days,' Mrs O'Brian said, turning to a small hallway table and handing him a pile of letters. Josiah thanked her as she returned to the kitchen to finish cooking for the evening. Josiah flipped through the usual business letters until he came upon one letter on heavy paper embossed with a very German motif. Josiah placed the business letters aside and walked to his parlour.

He realised that his hand was trembling slightly as he unfolded the expensive sheet of paper. He knew immediately that it was from Elise, and she had written it in English for him.

Josiah sat down in a leather chair and slowly read the words, taking in each one.

She was back in her castle in Bavaria, and she was well. Elise wrote further that her aunt and uncle managed her affairs and had introduced her to her fiancé as a suitable match because of his familial links to the Kaiser. Elise went on to say that she knew it was her duty to marry him and bear him a son. At this statement, Josiah snorted his disgust. Were not the Germans a modern people? Then he considered that such customs still existed in England.

As Josiah read on, he sensed a terrible sadness in her carefully chosen words. Elise signed off the letter with the English words, *Sincerely, your Elise*. But she was *not* his Elise and Josiah knew the bridge between them was not just geographical but a division of culture and duty. It was easier for him to be shipped out to Afghanistan than to travel to Bavaria. His commission had been gazetted and he was now an officer in Her Majesty's army. He also had a duty.

Josiah carefully folded the letter and placed it in a desk drawer, and with the passion of a young man, swore an oath to himself that he would one day travel to Bavaria to meet with Elise once again – whether she was married or not.

Josiah spent his last night in London dining with Conan and his family. Although Conan attempted to make it a celebratory and jovial evening, Marian's sombre mood caused Josiah's spirits to plummet. He stared across the table at her, but she seemed to avoid his eyes, picking absent-mindedly at her vegetables.

When dinner was finished, it was Molly who suggested that Josiah and Marian should retire to their parlour. 'Conan, I think we should allow the two young people to share a moment together to make their farewells,' she said.

Conan agreed and Josiah followed Marian to the parlour, where tea was served by the housemaid. They sat opposite each other, sipping tea without speaking until Josiah broke the silence between them.

'I will miss your company and conversation,' he said lamely.

'Then why go to the other side of the world into such a volatile and dangerous situation?' Marian countered angrily. 'You have so much to give to the world, but you choose to throw it all away on a stupid venture.'

'I am an officer of the Queen, and I must go where I am told,' Josiah answered rigidly. 'It is my duty.'

'When I was a little girl, my father would drink too much and retire to sleep. I would hear him calling out a name in his nightmares, a place called Umbeyla Pass. He would thrash about and cry out for your father to be careful. My mother would wake him and soothe him with her words. One day, I asked my father about Umbeyla Pass and he dropped his head. He spoke quietly and told me it was a place of death to the British army. He had not expected to survive, except that your father saved his company with his wise leadership.' Marian paused then shook her head. 'It is no secret that trouble is brewing in that part of the world again. My father said that the warriors there are called Pashtuns and amongst the fiercest enemy he ever faced. Now you will be going to face the sons of the men your father and mine fought and barely survived.'

Josiah listened to Marian's words but reassured himself that he would not be in the list of dead if they came up against the Afghan warriors again. After all, the British army was no longer equipped with the old Enfield powder and ball rifle of his father's generation, but with better weapons, such as the single-shot Martini Henry rifle with its lethal .577 calibre bullet.

'If we have to face the Pashtuns, I know I will survive,' Josiah said.

'How can you say that?' Marian asked angrily. 'You are merely a foolish boy who believes in the sanctity of British imperialism. It is not even our land we are fighting for.'

'There are many times I have questioned my desire to serve but it must be in my blood. My father and your father did their duty and now it is my time to do so. I am no more or less foolish than any other man who wishes to serve.'

Marian stood up and glared at Josiah. 'Then go to your death to the sound of drums and bugles. Do not expect me to mourn a man as thoughtless as you.' Marian rushed from the room so that Josiah would not see her tears.

Josiah was alone in the parlour until Conan gingerly joined the son of his best friend.

'I gather that you and my daughter had a tiff,' he said, sitting down opposite Josiah, whose forlorn expression said everything. 'Not to worry, these things happen. You must understand that women are emotional creatures and do not think like us men.'

Conan's words did not help but Josiah smiled weakly, thanking Conan for his advice. It was time to return to his tenement, sleep and prepare for his journey to a distant shore.

★

Josiah looked every bit a young army officer in his new red-coated uniform, the walking out dress for officers. Packed in his gear was his khaki field dress for service in Afghanistan. He had also purchased an American Colt army 1873 model six-shot revolver with a metal cartridge weapon in a .44 calibre. This would be his personal side arm, and from what Josiah had learned, it had a deadly effect at close range.

The ship destined for India, where Josiah would join his regiment, was to leave on the evening tide. He had met two other junior officers who would be joining their infantry regiments in India before departing for the rugged hills of Afghanistan. The three soon bonded as they supervised their kits to be taken aboard the steam ship. They watched as military supplies were also loaded, and a few uniformed private soldiers arrived under the command of a couple of warrant officers and a sergeant. Josiah could see from the many medals on the senior NCOs' chests that they were battle-hardened men, and the sergeant made his way through the throng of dock workers and civilians, bidding goodbye to soldier sons. He was tall and solidly built with a bushy moustache and short, greying hair. His faded eyes seemed to reflect the arid places in which he had seen service with the British army. Josiah guessed he was in his forties.

'Mr Steele, I presume,' the sergeant said with a Scottish accent as he came to a stop and saluted Josiah, who returned the salute.

'Good morning, sergeant,' Josiah replied, curious to know how the Scot could have singled him out from his two officer colleagues.

'Thought so,' the sergeant said. 'You look just like Captain Steele when I knew him in India.'

'You served with my father?' Josiah asked in surprise.

'I was with his damned Sassenach regiment when we were at the Umbeyla Pass. Your father saved our necks on more than one occasion. We used to call him the Colonial. Maybe you might earn the right to be called the Colonial by the troops you command someday.'

Josiah felt a swell of pride. So far, all he heard from experienced soldiers who had served with his father was how good a soldier he had been. But in the Scots sergeant's last words, Josiah sensed a cautionary warning that the highest levels of leadership were expected of him in the future.

'I have been informed that I am assigned as your sergeant when we join the regiment in India,' the sergeant said. 'I am Sergeant Peene.'

'Well, I am pleased to have you as my sergeant,' Josiah said, extending his hand, startling the sergeant, who was not used to gentlemen officers accepting those socially beneath them as equals. 'I believe there is much I can learn from your experiences.'

'Yes, sir,' the Scot said, accepting the firm handshake. 'My job is to keep you alive long enough for you to become a captain.'

*

Conan Curry did not go to his job managing the public house he and Molly owned. Instead, he remained at home, swigging good scotch from his liquor cabinet in the parlour as he knew Josiah would be preparing for departure at the docks.

Conan stared at the wall and lifted his tumbler of scotch in a toast. 'To you, dear lad. May you return to us from those terrible lands.' As proud as he was of Josiah's commission and service to the Empire, he also knew the dreadful cost to the sons of Britain in those faraway places where he had once served.

Conan had accepted Josiah under his roof as a long-lost son and now he felt the deep depression of one who knew the possible result of the young man steaming to war. But how can you warn the young of such things? A soldier must believe that death would only come to the man next to him and that he would survive.

Conan knew he would be very drunk when Molly returned home, and she would know why. How many times had she stood on the dock to bid him farewell and welcome him when he returned? How much pain had that caused her? At least Josiah would not have to feel the ache he always experienced waving to Molly as the troop ships pulled away from the shore.

'Father.' Conan turned to see his daughter standing in the doorway to the parlour. 'Are you unwell?' Marian asked.

'I . . .' Conan did not provide an explanation but took a swig of the drink.

Marian walked over to him and placed her hand on his shoulder. 'Does this have something to do with Josiah sailing tonight?' she asked gently. When her father looked up at her standing over him, she could see tears in his eyes. She had never seen her father cry before and was taken by surprise. Marian sat down beside her father and took one of his hands in her own. What could she say?

'The poor boy does not know what lies ahead of him,' Conan said. 'All I can do is sit helplessly by while he goes off to war.'

'Josiah will come back to us,' Marian said, realising how feeble her hope was. The recent massacre of a regiment of British soldiers against the Zulu warriors was still a raw wound to the public in England. Admittedly the British army had eventually overcome the Zulu warriors, but it was at great cost.

'I do not have the heart to go to the docks to farewell him because I feel that he is a soldier because of his father and me.'

Marian was fortunate that all her friends were civilians with comfortable lives, but she also knew they cared little for the fates of the men serving in the Empire's wars. Their fates were simply printed words in the morning newspapers that did not personally touch them. Marian was against the deployment of troops to the war brewing in Afghanistan and had been vocal about the issue. Marx had taught that these were the means greedy imperialists used to make themselves even wealthier. Josiah was throwing away a life of wealth and good fortune. How could she go against her principles and support his involvement in this war?

After a short time in his daughter's company, Conan ceased drinking. He knew no matter how drunk he made himself, he could not help Second Lieutenant Josiah Steele. His thoughts were now with his dearest friend thousands of miles away in the place of his birth – the colony of New South Wales. How much must he be suffering knowing that his son was travelling to a country they had both sworn they would never return to?

*

The sun was creeping behind the tall brick buildings and chimney stacks of London when the order came for all to board. Rushed kisses and hugs followed the call and Josiah stepped onto the deck of the ship as a band played 'Auld Lang Syne'. He was in the company of a fellow junior officer, Second Lieutenant Cameron Maclean, a young Scot from Glasgow who Josiah had learned came from a middle-class family of moderately wealthy shopkeepers. He was a year younger than Josiah and had the pale clear skin of a man raised in the north of Britain. Josiah had taken a liking to him and felt a brotherly protectiveness as the young officer did not have the demeanour of a soldier. He would look more at home in a university library rather than amongst the tough, hard-drinking Scots soldiers he was to lead in war. His family had travelled to London to bid their second son bon voyage and were waving from the dock.

Josiah sighed as the ship separated from the dock. How fortunate he was that there was no one to farewell him, he tried to convince himself.

He was about to turn away from the railing when he glanced one last time at the crowd of people farewelling the troop ship and saw her; red hair and a wan face looking up at him. Even at this distance, their eyes locked, and he saw the sad smile of Marian mouthing words he could not hear. She waved a tiny silk handkerchief. Josiah waved back, but the ship slewed around, blocking his last view of Marian on the wharf.

Part Three

Kandahar to Majuba Hill

1880

TWENTY-SEVEN

It was hot.

For Second Lieutenant Josiah Steele, this arid land of jagged mountain peaks and deep gorges reminded him that God had forgotten to finish moulding the earth into a Garden of Eden and had apparently left the unused dirt and rocks in this country. Even the earthen houses and compounds scattered across the country seemed to have grown out of the very earth itself. Afghanistan had certainly earned the title of 'godforsaken' to the British soldiers posted to this frontier.

Josiah marched with his regiment. The heat was searing, but as he had lived in the southern hemisphere most of his life, he was able to tolerate the weather on the journey from Kabul to Kandahar. It was approximately three hundred and twenty miles to the besieged British garrison, and British honour was at stake. Josiah was but a tiny speck in a vast force of the Anglo–Indian army that had set out on the mammoth trek that relied as much on logistics as it did on the fighting prowess of its soldiers.

Josiah cared little for the complex politics behind the expeditionary force's motivation. He was just pleased that he and his fellow junior officers had passed the regimental duties training required to be included in the army now travelling south-west through the majestic mountain passes. He and the other new officers had been drilled by steely-eyed senior NCOs on their foot drill, sword drill for ceremonial parades, customs of the regiment, and use of the Martini Henry single-shot rifle, where Josiah had impressed the instructors with his deadly accuracy with the rifle. Josiah was rated the second-best marksmen in the regiment after one of the new private soldiers who was a member of Josiah's platoon.

As a junior officer, all that Josiah was concerned with was his role to lead his men into battle and keep as many alive as possible. The command to arms had been simple: General Sir Frederick Roberts had issued the order on 8 August.

It has been decided by the Government of India that a force shall proceed with all possible dispatch from Cabul towards Khelat-i-Ghilzai and Candahar for the relief of the British garrison in those places now threatened by a large Afghan army under the leadership of Ghazi Mohammad Ayub Khan.

A British force under the command of General Burrows at a place called Maiwand had been decimated by the advancing Afghan army under the command of Ayub, which had outnumbered the British force by ten to one. The survivors had retreated to Kandahar and were now besieged. This was a rescue mission and time was of the essence to save the survivors.

Orders had been issued to all regiments that they were to travel light, with each soldier to carry twenty to thirty pounds. Roberts's force was a polyglot, with Indian and Sikh troops as well the tough, small Nepalese soldiers known as Gurkhas.

The bugles had sounded before dawn and Josiah had ensured his men were assembled with the rest of the army before the walls of Bala Hissar fortress in Kabul. They had marched down the willow-lined avenue towards the river. Josiah did not regret leaving the city behind, with its sullen and hostile residents, filth and disease.

Josiah was initially welcomed with the natural suspicion of soldiers for junior officers commanding them. But the fact he proved very competent with their issued rifle impressed the men who had been enlisted from the poverty-stricken Highlands and overcrowded cities.

Josiah remembered much that his father had taught him about leadership of men whose lives he was responsible for. He had quietly researched the military records of every man he was in command of and written down in a field notebook every detail he could glean as to the names of wives, children and boot sizes. He even discovered that the first name of Sergeant Peene was Matthew. As a professional and experienced senior NCO, Josiah knew he must always refer to him by rank and surname, a strict custom of the British army. But it was still good to know more about the man he knew he would rely on for sage advice if he was to demonstrate competent leadership.

His father had also advised him to carry the standard weapon of the private soldier so as not to mark him as an officer to the enemy. They would know an officer by the pistol and sword he carried and attempt to eliminate him as a priority in battle.

After a few weeks under Josiah's command, the soldiers of his platoon soon came to accept him as their leader. He was firm but fair and even friendly to an extent. They learned that he really did care about them as individuals and the tough Scots soon accepted their Colonial as the man to take them into war.

As Josiah marched with his men, he differed in dress, wearing khaki trousers whereas they wore kilts and sporrans. All wore the khaki jacket criss-crossed with white belts and a white pith helmet, with puttees wrapped around the lower legs to protect them from cuts and insect bites.

Senior officers sat astride fine mounts, but Josiah chose to march alongside his thirty men. The platoon behind Josiah's was led by his friend, Second Lieutenant Cameron Maclean, and they averaged fourteen miles per day, with the marching men stopping every hour for a ten-minute break. The soldiers were stirred from sleep at 4 am and halted around 8 am for a breakfast of tinned bacon between unleavened Indian bread and washed down with cold tea. A tot of rum was also issued to the column of troops stretching for seven miles in the evening. The rationing of water kept the thoughts of the marching men on dreams of ice-cold cider and cool, clear water. So far, Josiah noted that his men's morale was good and so too was their health.

On the seventh day, they reached Ghazni in the Logar Valley of scattered cornfields, palm groves and poplar trees adjoining craggy ridges and torrents of water flowing down the mountainsides. But there would not be a break to enjoy the rare natural beauty; the force of arms had to move on. Josiah had started to wonder why he had not sought a commission with the men on horses, the cavalry and lancers. At night, he would lie on the hard ground in the bitter chill, staring up at the stars above, and fondly remember his days with his father on the Palmer track.

*

Even as Josiah slept under the constellations of the northern hemisphere, Detective Third Class Andrew Paull had finally tracked down the woman he had found in common with his suspect, Captain Ian Steele, and his murder victim, Harold Skinner.

When he questioned Mrs Isabel Halpin, she denied that Harold was anything but an acquaintance and insisted that there had never been any romantic relationship between them. As a matter of fact, Mrs Halpin said she had strongly disliked the man and had avoided him at every possible opportunity.

Andrew left, deflated. His theory of a love triangle seemed to have no substance. He still believed that the former British officer was involved directly in the prominent civil servant's death but was coming to accept that, short of a miracle, he would never be able to find evidence to substantiate a charge of murder.

When Andrew returned to the CIB in Phillip Street, he wrote his report and submitted it to his inspector with the conclusion that he had no other leads to follow. The inspector read the report and scribbled his comment that he concurred with Paull's conclusion and walked over to a big wooden cabinet, filing the case as unsolved. When he closed the cabinet door, he also closed the case, although he knew there would be a furore from the governor's office.

Ian Steele was unaware that he was no longer being investigated but was to remain a person of extreme interest in the death of Harold Skinner for the rest of his life.

*

The ground that Roberts's army now crossed was stony, sandy desert. They advanced under a blistering sun by day and passed bone-chilling nights under the northern stars. The army was able to use the mirror-like heliograph to keep contact with the rearguard trailing seven miles behind the vanguard, whilst the camp followers straggling at the rear of the column suffered fearfully from night attacks from marauding tribesmen.

Thirst was a constant companion, aggravated by the late summer heat and the dust raised by the movement of over ten thousand men and horses. Even when tents were pitched, little sleep was possible with sentry duties and early mornings of striking camp before sunrise.

General Roberts would ride out early after breakfast to move ahead, selecting the next night's bivouac, and his example of leadership inspired Josiah and his fellow officers. The general would take some hard-boiled eggs, cooked chicken and tea to eat and then return to his army.

On 23 August, Roberts's column reached Khelat-i-Ghilzai, where an abundance of forage for the animals and a plentiful supply of water for all was provided. Roberts had intelligence that the besieged force was still holding Kandahar and decided to rest his force before the final leg of the march. Finally, his men could expect more than three hours' sleep.

Josiah made his way to his friend Cameron Maclean's tent to pass time with him, sharing a precious tot of rum in their hot tea. Both young men sat beside a small camp-fire, swapping stories of their respective small commands. A meteorite flashed through the crystal-like display of stars in the dark night around them. The regimental band played a medley of tunes in the distance and to all intents and purposes, this night felt as if they were simply on a summer holiday, albeit a rather crude and rough one.

'I have heard that we will reach Kandahar before very long,' Cameron said, sipping his tea and pulling a warm greatcoat tighter around his body to ward off the chill. 'I must confess that as much as I fear death, I fear even more that I will be too afraid to lead my men.'

Josiah smiled as he gazed at the flickering flames dancing in the tiny fire. Timber was extremely hard to acquire in this arid land but could be purchased from the village people they encountered. 'If it is any consolation, I think all of us who have not yet faced the enemy have the same fear, that we will let down the men who rely on us.'

'I thought that I was the only one,' Cameron said. 'I never really wanted to be in the army, but my family insisted I join as my older brother will inherit our business in Glasgow, and I did not have the talent to attend university.'

'It could have been worse,' Josiah said with a grin. 'You could have been in the navy.'

They both chuckled at the old, mostly good-natured rivalry between the two services, but both still harboured the fear of failing the men they commanded. It was a fear as old as the first young commander of the first army in history.

The mournful sound of a bugler trumpeting 'The Last Post' drifted to the two junior officers, and they knew it was time to confirm that their men were seeking sleep before a rigorous march the next day.

★

It was Isabel's birthday and Ian was able to convince her that they should celebrate together with a picnic on a beautiful, balmy spring day in the well-tended gardens of his house. A luncheon was set up in the garden with courses of oysters on ice, fish baked with oyster sauce and a medley of salad vegetables and freshly baked bread. Cakes and tarts were also on the menu and the meal was shared with Becky and Sam, who still adored Isabel.

Champagne was served when the table was cleared under the marquee that had been erected to provide shade, leaving Isabel and Ian to stroll through the gardens to view the busy harbour below. Over lunch, Ian had noticed Isabel laugh for the first time in months and felt gladness in his heart.

Now they sat side by side on a stone bench with a panoramic view of the twinkling blue waters of the harbour and the white wakes of the ships and boats. A comfortable silence existed between them as they sat side by side, holding the crystal champagne flutes.

'I have had a wonderful birthday,' Isabel sighed, taking a sip.

'It has been wonderful to hear you laugh again,' Ian said.

'It has been hard trying to forget that day,' Isabel said sadly. 'It all came back when a police detective came to my house and asked me about Harold. I told them the truth, that he and I were not in any relationship. They asked me about you, too. It was as if the police suspected you, but I can never believe that you would have had anything to do with his death. It had to be the two bushrangers I read about in the newspapers.'

'I think you are right,' Ian replied noncommittally, staring at a yacht on the harbour manoeuvring its sails to catch the wind.

Isabel turned to Ian and took his hand in her own. 'I don't think I could be with a man who did such a deed out of anger or revenge,' she said firmly.

'What about out of love and justice?' Ian questioned. 'What if it was because a man has a duty to protect those he loves more than himself?'

For a moment, Isabel's grip tightened almost to the point of pain. Ian remained still.

'I am glad he is dead,' she said, venom replacing sadness. 'I hope he died painfully.'

Ian nodded. 'You sound a bit like me,' he said.

That brought a smile to Isabel's face. 'Perhaps you're a bad influence, my love.'

'I hope it's a good influence,' he replied. 'And I would hope that you might someday accept my proposal of marriage. I know that you said I had to prove myself as a man who has given up his adventure-seeking ways. I have had a lifetime of adventure, but my fondest desire is to spend the rest of my life living comfortably with you and the children.'

'I think that you mean that,' Isabel said with wonder in her eyes. 'And the best birthday gift I could ever have is your proposal of marriage.'

So, it was on Isabel's birthday that Captain Ian Steele bent his knee and asked Isabel to be his wife for a second time. And this time, she said 'yes' and flung her arms around his neck.

TWENTY-EIGHT

After weeks of suffering, the harsh march to Kandahar was finally over, with the city in sight on the last day of August. Josiah was so weary that he was hardly impressed by its massive walls. The column was given orders to halt while General Roberts rose from his sickbed, where he had been laid out with a severe fever, to mount his horse, Vonolel, for a dignified meeting with the besieged senior officers, General Primrose and Brigadier Burrows. The Union Jack fluttered on the walls of the city but there was no sound of welcoming bands. Nor was there any sign of the besieging Afghan army.

Cameron had briefly joined Josiah as they waited to enter the city.

'Not what we expected,' Cameron said. 'I thought that we would be forced to fight our way into the city through Afghan lines. It looks as if we missed out on our first battle.'

'I would not be so sure,' Josiah said, gazing at the surrounding countryside through his binoculars. He could see hills to the north, and something told him that is where the enemy lurked.

'What do you think will happen now?' Cameron asked, wiping sweat from his face with the back of his sleeve. 'Will we be tasked with garrison duties here? I do hope that will not be so.'

Josiah replaced his binoculars in the leather case attached to his belt and reached for his water canteen. 'I don't think that Bobs has come this far to simply use us as garrison troops. I strongly suggest that he will send out scouting parties to locate the Afghans and mount an assault.'

'Do you think that the Afghans are in the hills?' he asked.

'I would bet on it,' Josiah replied. 'We may be in for a hot time going after the buggers. They have modern artillery and rifles.'

Cameron did not ask any more questions. He had hoped that they might rest up and return to Kabul then back to their Indian bases.

Josiah was pleased that he had written letters to his father before embarking on this expedition to Kandahar. They had been filled with optimism, as if he were simply having a military holiday. Now, he had a sick feeling of fear from being so close to the dreaded Afghan warriors and tried to dismiss any outward signs of it, glancing at his men, who had been given the order to rest. Each face was now as familiar as if they were members of his family. He had come to learn so much about the men as individuals and the responsibility of keeping them alive weighed heavily on him. How would he perform his duties when the time came to confront the artillery shells, rifle fire and swords of men willing to die in their *jihad* against the infidel, when all he wanted to do was live? Josiah knew he was not far from finding that answer and, for a moment, regretted his choice to be a soldier. Maybe he should have listened to Marian and his friends in London when they had attempted to persuade him to not follow his dream. But he was a soldier, and he followed orders, clinging to the memories of how he had not let down his father years earlier when they faced danger on Australia's northern frontier.

Josiah had been correct in his calculations of the strategic situation. The following morning, he would find himself in a desperate battle to stay alive against a fierce and well-armed enemy in the hills.

★

It was almost a religious ritual each morning when *The Times* was delivered to Conan's house. He would retrieve the paper and flip through it until he found any section reporting on the situation in Afghanistan. Conan would carefully read the articles with a furrowed brow as he sipped his tea. From the latest edition, he learned that General Frederick Roberts VC was advancing on Kandahar, but the news was at least five days old. Conan placed the newspaper on the table just as his daughter entered the room with her own cup of tea.

'Good morning, Papa,' she greeted him warmly. 'What is the news from the Afghanistan front?'

'I will not really know until the reports concerning Bobs's advance to Kandahar are published,' Conan replied as Marian sat opposite him at the polished wooden table. For a second, he thought that he could see a slight trace of worry on his daughter's face. 'Do you share my worry for Josiah?' he asked.

'No, not really,' Marian replied. 'Josiah made his choice to serve, and I believe he can take care of himself. Horace has informed me that Josiah was considered a rough and ready boy when they were at school together in Sydney.'

'Horace Anderson?' Conan queried. The little he had learned from Josiah about the man caused Conan to strongly dislike this Horace Anderson.

'Yes, we have seen each other a few times at functions,' Marian said. 'I have found him to be a very charming and attractive man with a fine future in his family enterprises ahead of him. My friends inform me that he has a great desire to step out with me one day.'

'Would you?' Conan asked almost belligerently.

'I would consider it,' Marian replied defiantly.

'What about Josiah?' Conan asked.

Marian placed her cup on the table. 'My feelings towards Josiah are simply those of a friend,' she replied. 'I pray that he returns to London safe and well. If you will excuse me, Papa, I have matters to attend to.' She stood up and walked quickly out of the dining room, leaving her father puzzled. He had sensed a concern for Josiah, but she was obviously trying to hide it. But what did he know about the mind of a woman? He would have to ask Molly.

Conan snorted, picking up the paper to peruse other news, reading that Greenwich Mean Time was now adopted as the standard for all of the UK. 'About bloody time,' Conan growled. It would mean adjusting all railway timetables but at least it was a modern approach towards some sanity, instead of every little town working in their own time zone.

★

The orders had come down the evening Roberts occupied Kandahar. Scouts had reported the Afghan army was entrenched in the hills and, from observations, waiting for the British force to throw itself at the army that had withdrawn from the siege of the city. This was the same army that had bloodied the British army at Maiwand weeks earlier, forcing the British to fall back in defeat to Kandahar in the first place.

When Josiah received his orders from his company commander, he relayed what he knew to his assembled platoon late at night. In the morning, they would advance towards the hills to their north to engage the enemy. They now had the support of the artillery batteries at Kandahar which was reassuring and that was about all his men had to know for the moment. Josiah dismissed them with advice to ensure all their weapons were in good order and to get as much sleep as they could.

Josiah retired to his small tent to lay out his weapons on the camp cot. Under the dim light of a lamp, he cleaned his Martini Henry, made sure the bayonet fitted, and turned to his pistol. He had dragged his sword with him for the long trek and pondered whether he should carry it into battle the next day, possibly marking him out as an officer to the enemy snipers.

Josiah removed a writing pad and pen from a small wooden case that was part of his kit and sat on the cot, balancing the pad on the back of a map board. He dipped his pen in the ink bottle and poised it over the paper. He knew he had a desperate need to reach out to someone and decided that it would not be his father – not before a battle.

Then Josiah began to write:

My dear Marian,

I just desired to tell you how much I miss your wonderful smile, your company and our many conversations. I must apologise that I am not a particularly good correspondent, but I hope this letter dispatched from Kandahar to Kensington reaches you in good health . . .

Josiah did not get further with his letter to Marian as an orderly snapped to attention outside his tent flap and saluted.

'Sir, begging forgiveness for the interruption, but the company commander wishes to speak with all his subalterns at his tent.'

Josiah placed the writing pad, pen and ink back in the small wooden case. Duty called.

★

Josiah had hardly closed his eyes when the sound of bugles calling 'Reveille' brought him out of his world of dreams just before dawn. The great encampment stirred into action for the day and Josiah staggered to his feet. He glanced at the sword in the corner of his tent and made a final decision to wear it into battle.

Josiah stumbled to where his unit was forming up and Sergeant Peene took a roll call, reporting to Josiah that all were present and correct. Josiah dismissed his men to breakfast parade and joined the company officers for their own breakfast at the regimental mess tent where their commanding officer, a colonel, was last to enter. All officers stood and he gestured for them to sit.

Josiah was sitting next to Cameron, who looked paler than usual.

'Today we face the enemy in battle,' Cameron mumbled.

'Victory will be ours,' Josiah dutifully replied as the rest of the regimental officers chatted amongst themselves. Occasionally, quiet laughter filled the tent as men attempted to make light of what lay ahead. The colonel made a short speech, as if they were off to a grand cricket match, and breakfast was over.

Josiah and Cameron returned to their men, now under the bark of the company sergeant major, who was chiding them for deficiencies in their equipment. When the CSM came to Josiah's men, he found little fault. Josiah breathed again after he moved on. Although the CSM was junior in rank to Josiah, he had the company commander's ear and was a man to be feared by mere subalterns.

Josiah turned to his sergeant. 'Well done, Sergeant Peene,' he said, knowing the experienced soldier had been one step ahead of his senior warrant officer.

The sun was rising on another hot late summer day. Josiah had his orders as to where his men would be positioned in the mass of infantry, cavalry and artillery. It was a colourful display of many diverse uniforms of British and Indian troops on foot and on horseback. Josiah made way for a regiment of Bengal Lancers to pass through their ranks. The Indian cavalrymen rode with straight backs, holding their long lances erect with pennants fluttering in the slight breeze of the hot day dawning.

The grand spectacle of the army manoeuvring into position was a sight that filled Josiah with awe as dust rose and the heat of the sun was becoming apparent. Josiah stood in front of his small formation of thirty men dressed in similar khaki but wearing trousers where his men wore kilts below their khaki jackets and pith helmets. Josiah carried a rifle as well as his pistol and sword. Adjacent to his formation was that of Cameron's platoon. The two young officers glanced at each other and smiled. Cameron was less pale from fear and the exchanged looks reassured each man. Before them was a range of serrated ridges where the enemy were entrenched with artillery and relatively modern rifles waiting for them with shot and shell.

Horses galloped between formations carrying messages, ensuring that each commander was informed of last-minute orders. Like all young officers, Josiah was not aware of the overall strategy planned at the highest levels between the various generals under Roberts. He only knew that his understanding of battlefield tactics was all that mattered once the fighting commenced. As he stood in front of his men, Josiah found his thoughts sweeping a panorama of those he held dear. What were Conan and his family doing at this moment? How had his father felt in the past as a company commander facing battle? One question he did not want to entertain was would he be killed or maimed this day.

What Josiah did know was that his regiment was in the very vanguard of the army. He noticed that the Bombay troops on their flank had suddenly broken the formation to lead away from the army. Josiah wondered why they had done so and guessed they were under special orders known only to the brigade and higher HQ. To a soldier of any rank, all that mattered was the ground around and before them, for it would be control of the immediate ground they could see that mattered to their lives.

A haze of dust now filled the air from the ground disturbed by so many boots and hooves. When Josiah glanced at his brother officer, he saw that Cameron was resting his hand on the hilt of his sword and swore he could see him deep in prayer. It was the waiting that frayed nerves, when the mind had time to go to the deep and dark places of the imagination, unleashing the greatest fears of death. Josiah knew that he had to find a way to get his men's minds off their personal dark thoughts.

'Mr Maclean,' he called to Cameron. 'I believe my Highland boys can best your Glasgow lads in a game of football. I am prepared to wager a case of fine scotch whisky on the victory of my lads.'

Josiah's announcement caught the attention of both Josiah's soldiers and Cameron's men.

'I am afraid my lads will be sharing the whisky prize, Mr Steele,' Cameron replied, and Josiah could sense both platoons stir with excitement at the suggestion. It was taking their minds off the forthcoming battle, and a case of scotch could go a long way between a small unit. 'When do we play?'

'As soon as we defeat the Afghan army, I will arrange a game,' Josiah called back, and a cheer arose from both platoons, with one soldier from Josiah's platoon calling out, 'Good for the Colonial.' Josiah remembered how his own father had been referred to as the Colonial and swelled with pride.

Sergeant Peene moved to Josiah and quietly said with a faint smile, 'Well done, sir. I think the lads will follow you into hell when they know there is a crate of scotch waiting for them there.' Already Josiah could hear the murmur of voices from his men in their ranks behind him, discussing who would play the different positions on the field. They were interrupted when the sound of bugles trumpeting the advance drifted across the front of the army. Drums beat a cadence and Josiah drew his sword and raised it to his shoulder.

'Advance!'

Hell lay ahead and Josiah knew many would not get the chance to drink the scotch reward after the battle.

Kilts swirled and the sun shone off the fixed bayonets of Josiah's men as they marched in three ranks across the plain.

Josiah marched in front of his men with his sword resting on his shoulder, acutely aware that he stood out as an officer to any enemy snipers. He unobtrusively fell back to join the first rank of his section, his rifle slung over his shoulder.

Already, the mixed fire of Snider rifles, Martini Henry rounds and ancient musket balls cracked through the air around the advancing Scots, but they held their fire as the British poured explosive rounds into the high ground from the supporting artillery guns. One lucky enemy round smashed Josiah's sword, snapping it near the hilt. The impact temporarily numbed Josiah's arm and he dropped the useless hilt and immediately unslung his rifle and continued the march with his men. At least without his sword he looked a little less like an officer.

Roberts had planned that his infantry would not take a direct route into the entrenched Afghan army in the hills, and Josiah knew that they were carrying out a flank attack. Roberts relied on his infantry to take the enemy positions on the high ground. Not far from the advancing line of the Scots regiments were the men from Nepal, the Gurkhas, wound up for action against the long-robed men trying to kill them.

Josiah's men were already feeling the extreme heat of the day but had little time to take a quick swig from water canteens as they were now within range of volley fire from the fortress-like houses with their enclosed orchards of almond trees.

'Follow me, lads!' Josiah roared, swinging his unit into a bayonet charge against one of the stone-walled houses, as Josiah had seen smoke erupt from loopholes in the walls and knew that he must clear this small compound. His men were screaming words in Gaelic, as their ancestors had on the battlefields against the English years before. A wooden gate to the compound had been blown down and Josiah was first through the opening to confront a swirling mass of white-robed Afghans wielding swords and small shields and shouting, 'Allah Akbar!'

A bearded Afghan warrior rushed at Josiah, swinging a curved sword. Josiah instinctively thrust his bayonet at the man and the long knife slid into the enemy's chest. He fell but the bayonet was lodged in his body and Josiah stood on his chest, jerking the long blade free. The white robe of the Pashtun warrior was now stained red, but Josiah had no time to reflect on the split-second action to stay alive as his men were fighting a vicious hand-to-hand battle in the small enclosure.

Acrid smoke, dust and the coppery smell of blood filled the air, accompanied by the sounds of men screaming in pain, calling to their mothers and cursing their enemy in two languages.

Josiah was vaguely aware of his sergeant punching and kicking at one of the enemies against a wall and realised that Sergeant Peene had been disarmed in the melee. The Afghan had been able to retrieve a long dagger and was getting the better of Sergeant Peene, who now had both hands around the man's neck and did not see the dagger in his enemy's hand, ready to stab upwards into the sergeant's stomach.

Josiah immediately closed the short distance between them and thrust his bloodied bayonet into the warrior's throat, pinning him to the mud wall. Blood sprayed out, splashing both Josiah and Sergeant Peene. The Afghan slid down the wall and Sergeant Peene still did not let go until Josiah retrieved his bayonet. It was then that Josiah felt the heavy thud of a sword blade slice through his jacket sleeve, shearing away skin from his left arm. Josiah staggered from

the blow and spun to see his attacker fall from a bayonet
to his back from one of his private soldiers. Josiah tripped
on the body of a downed man and when he went to stand
up saw that it was one of his own men who had suffered a
terrible sword wound to the head, almost cleaving off the
dead soldier's skull.

'We made 'em run!' someone yelled as the sound of
close-quarter fighting subsided, leaving the compound
littered with dead and injured men. Josiah could see that
one of the wounded was a man of his platoon. He had a
stomach wound inflicted by a sword and lay holding his
hand over his bloody uniform jacket. When Josiah glanced
around the compound to appraise the situation, he saw one
of his men bayonet a mortally wounded Afghan through
the chest, an act of mercy rather than rage.

'Sergeant, take count,' Josiah said, blood dripping down
his left arm from the slash by the scimitar. He still had full
use of his arm and could see through the ripped sleeve that
the wound was only a long shallow laceration.

Sergeant Peene ascertained the dead and wounded of the
platoon. 'One dead, three wounded, sir,' he said, pencilling
in the names in the roll call book he carried.

Their small battle in the tiny village of mud-bricked
walls was just one of many others being fought along the
front and Josiah knew it was his duty to continue the assault
in support of the bigger battle.

'I will bandage your arm, sir,' Sergeant Peene said.
A bandage was produced and in very quick time, Sergeant
Peene had wrapped it around the wound while his men
gulped down water from their canteens and looked to their
commander.

'We rally, lads,' Josiah said when the bandaging had been
completed. 'We have more of these houses to clear.'

A group of bandsmen carrying litters found Josiah's wounded soldiers and took them away. When they were not members of the regimental band, the bandsmen acted as stretcher bearers and were appreciated for their role on the battlefield. The dead soldier's body would be recovered after the fighting ceased and buried in the earth of this far-flung battlefield.

A written message was delivered to Josiah by a runner from company HQ, directing him to continue clearing the fortified village. When Josiah had assembled his men, he saw Cameron's platoon close by.

'You have been wounded, old chap,' Cameron said when he saw the blood-soaked bandage around Josiah's arm.

'Nothing serious.' Josiah shrugged. 'Our bloody work is not yet over.'

Josiah continued with his task of clearing the houses and compounds of the village whose name he did not know. Nor did he know if they were winning. Amongst the craggy hills and heat came the never-ending sound of rifle fire and men screaming shouts of pain and death. All Josiah knew was that in their tiny section of the battle in the Arghandab Valley, bordered by the river of the same name on their left flank, they were killing more of the enemy than he was of them.

*

Josiah crouched, pistol in one hand and rifle in the other, then led his men forward through the rubble of some of the houses and compounds that had been destroyed by British artillery fire earlier that morning. The artillery had done its grim task as Josiah could see from the smashed bodies, this time mostly in traditional tribal dress. Dismembered bodies lay in the rubble and Josiah used its cover to good effect, bringing forward his best marksmen to snipe at any enemy who exposed himself from a shattered compound. The big, heavy Martini Henry rounds were devastating when they smashed into the soft targets. Returning fire found its mark, with another of Josiah's men wounded in the shoulder. Dust rose in the hot air and when Josiah was satisfied that his covering fire had decimated the Afghan tribesmen, he turned to the men crouching behind him.

'Bayonet charge. Charge!' he yelled, and his men followed him over the rubble to the broken wall of the fortified compound and into the ruins littered with bodies of the enemy. Defiantly, wounded and able Afghan warriors stood their ground with swords and shields and a couple of Snider rifles.

Josiah fired his revolver at one of the rifle-armed men, who fell, hit by three of the heavy revolver bullets. Josiah could hear his men screaming their Scottish war cries in Gaelic as they thrust bayonets, warded off swords and grappled in life and death struggles, biting, punching and cursing each other. Josiah emptied his last three rounds into an Afghan who was astride one of his men, attempting to stab the young man whose face reflected sheer terror. The Afghan pitched sideways, and Josiah immediately offered his hand to the Scottish private, hauling him to his feet.

'Thank you, sir,' the soldier said, reaching down to pick up the rifle he had lost in the vicious fighting.

It was midday before the regiment eventually cleared the village and saw those enemy who had survived fleeing to the next.

Emotionally and physically exhausted, Josiah wanted only to sit down and let the fighting pass him and his men by, but a runner from company HQ brought the message that they were to immediately advance on the next village. He once again saw Cameron and his men sitting amongst the rubble. Like Josiah, Cameron was now covered in blood from the fighting. They waved to each other and then it was time to advance.

As they advanced in formation, Josiah sensed that they had the enemy on the run, retreating from the Anglo–Indian army they had boasted they would destroy.

Sergeant Peene was already chiding one young soldier for losing his pith helmet, with threats that the unfortunate man would be made to pay for the loss of Her Majesty's property. Josiah smiled at the dressing down because it reminded the weary men they were still soldiers and not simply killers.

Sergeant Peene joined Josiah and gave his usual report as to the condition of Josiah's men. When he'd finished, Josiah said, 'When we first engaged the Afghans, they were wearing white robes, but since then I have not seen any others we have encountered in the same garb.'

'From my time here before, I know they were religious warriors,' Peene answered. 'We did well to defeat them as they have sworn to die rather than surrender. Hope we don't meet their like at the next village.'

'I don't even know the names of these places where we fight,' Josiah said as they moved forward in an extended line, always wary of the rocks and ravines around them that could conceal a sniper.

'Pir Paimal is the name of the village we are now tasked to clear,' Sergeant Peene answered. 'I remember it from my first time here.'

'Pir Paimal,' Josiah echoed, wondering if that was where he might be killed if his luck ran out. His men marched in silence and Josiah wondered if they were experiencing the same feelings, that kind of numbness to all they had seen and done since breakfast. Had that really been today? When he looked into the soldiers' faces, he noticed the reflection of fear and dread he also felt when the firing stopped. Most of his young soldiers had never been in battle before and Josiah noticed that his sergeant showed no emotion, and this gave Josiah some reassurance. He tried not to think about the casualties his command had suffered so far. Josiah was aware that no war was bloodless but the dead and wounded he commanded haunted him even as they approached the next fortified village.

Puffs of smoke appeared from the loopholes in the mud walls, followed by the crack of bullets passing through the ranks of advancing Scots. A man yelped in surprise and pain as a lead round tore through his upper leg. Stretcher bearers rushed forward to retrieve the wounded man and Josiah was relieved to see it was not one of his soldiers.

Along the line, a volley of returning fire at the village compounds rang out and then the shouted command came from the officers. 'Charge!'

Josiah echoed the same command to his men, waving his revolver over his head, his rifle slung over his shoulder. They stumbled across the short distance and when they reached the outer walls and penetrated the openings, they were dumbfounded to find that the defenders had fled.

Through his binoculars, Josiah could see the enemy running in small groups towards the road that led to Herat.

'I think we might have won the day,' Sergeant Peene said to Josiah when he joined him. 'I can also report that we lost none of our men on our last advance.'

'Good show,' Josiah said, replacing his binoculars in the leather case on his belt. 'Have the men fall out and rest until we get further orders, Sergeant Peene.'

The sergeant passed on the order and the men collapsed on the dry earth to immediately swig the last drops of water from their canteens. Josiah could see the river on their left flank and wished that they were down there to gulp the cold and refreshing water. He wondered how Cameron and his men had fared. Josiah walked across to the soldiers he recognised from Cameron's platoon lying about smoking pipes and cheroots. Like his own men, their faces were filthy from gunpowder, spilled blood and dust.

'Is Mr Maclean here?' Josiah asked a corporal, who stood to salute him.

'Sorry, suh, but Mr Maclean got hit just outside the walls,' the tall corporal answered. 'His body is still out there to be fetched.'

Josiah heard the words, but they did not initially register. 'Has he been wounded?'

The corporal glanced at Josiah with an expression of puzzlement. 'No, suh. He's dead.'

Josiah nodded his understanding, turned on his heel and walked back to his men with the selfish, bitter thought that thank God it was Cameron and not he who had fallen in the battle for Arghandab Valley.

Already, Josiah and his men could see the cavalry and lancers galloping across the valley floor in pursuit of the defeated Afghan army. The infantry had dislodged the enemy from the high ground with rifle fire and bayonets supported by artillery. Now it was a war for the men on horses to finish off any last resistance.

The Afghan army had been totally defeated and the dreams of self-rule gone for a long time. For the Russian Tsar, it was a disaster that also destroyed his mission to dominate India with the assistance of the Afghan rulers. But none of the geopolitical machinations meant much to

Second Lieutenant Josiah Steele, who had tasted war and now knew why his father had resisted his eldest son's desire to engage in one.

TWENTY-NINE

General Roberts's victory at Kandahar was being celebrated in the pubs and inns across Britain even as Josiah reflected sadly on the loss of men from his command.

Conan stood behind the bar of his pub, crowded with singing, drinking men of all classes congratulating themselves on the defeat of the Afghan army. Conan wondered at these same people who normally looked down on the soldiers who fought the bloody battles for the Empire. He frowned when he remembered those times in the past when the public hardly gave him a second look when he walked the streets of London in his uniform, wearing his Victoria Cross.

Conan had read the reports in *The Times* and remembered similar terrain to that in Afghanistan, with its small villages of mud brick and stone, rugged mountains soaring to the sky and, in places, heavily timbered slopes. The searing hot summer sun and the bitterly cold winters. But mostly he remembered the warriors of that harsh land who died bravely in the face of modern British artillery, rifles and cavalry. What would these drunken revellers know of the harsh life a soldier lived and lost so that they could push out their chests to boast of British prowess?

But they were drinking, and Conan smiled as the money crossed the bar to fill his tills.

That morning, the casualty lists had been posted in the newspapers and Conan had anxiously peered at the small print with a magnifying glass searching for one name. Twice he read the list of those soldiers who had fallen in the battle and sighed with relief.

'Thank God Josiah's name is not amongst the dead and wounded,' Marian said from behind her father as he sat in the dining room with the paper in front of him on the table.

'So, I was not the first to read my morning paper,' Conan said. 'You have never read the paper before me.'

'I will admit that I was concerned for Josiah,' Marian said. 'I was informed by friends with contacts in the know that Josiah was with General Roberts on the march from Kabul to Kandahar.'

'I know, Josiah is like a brother to you,' Conan said with a hint of sarcasm. 'Well, it is not likely that junior officers will return to England with Bobs's entourage to accept the glory from the public. He will probably be returned to the regimental barracks in India.'

'All that matters is that Josiah is safe,' Marian said.

★

Almost four and half thousand miles away, a young man recently graduated from Cambridge University sat at his desk in the grand British government building in Bombay.

A fan turned slowly, stirring the humid air, and Douglas Wade carefully read the dispatch recently arrived in the mail from London. He was a very junior member of the administrative staff of the Presidency of Bombay but had heeded his father's advice to join the Indian Civil Service as it presented great opportunities for any smart young man who wished to accumulate wealth.

Douglas had fallen in love with the subcontinent, with its completely alien sights, sounds and smells. It was a place in which he saw the magnificent architecture of an old empire alongside the poverty all around; a land he desired to learn more about. It was so vast that diverse cultures existed side by side in relative peace, although he was aware of the religious animosities that occasionally led to violence.

Already he had obtained a small bungalow not far from the office and had been able to employ a maid to clean and cook for him, but not on his meagre civil service salary as he had drawn on his father's generous allowance for such luxuries.

The report he now perused included his name personally for attention because of a previous contact with a fellow colonial. Douglas knew that his inclusion in the subject of the report would raise his status with his superiors; he would not simply be one of the many overlooked young men who scurried along the vast corridors of the building.

It was time to set in motion the network that would reach out to another young man soon to arrive in India – Second Lieutenant Josiah Steele.

★

The football game went ahead in front of the great walls of Kandahar and the men of the deceased commander, Second Lieutenant Cameron Maclean, won three goals to one.

Sergeant Peene had been able to obtain a case of scotch through his many dubious contacts, though it came at a huge financial cost to Josiah.

Josiah had visited the body of his friend and had seen that a bullet had pierced his throat. The young man lay under a cloud of flies, staring with sightless eyes at the Afghan sky, and was buried nearby with other British and Indian soldiers in graves carved out of the hard earth baked by the late summer sun.

That evening, Josiah returned to his tent and sat on his camp bed, staring at the empty ammunition crate that served as his desk in the dim light of the lantern. Although the men celebrated that night, there was also a sombre mood for the comrades who had fallen only hours earlier. But they also reminded themselves that they were a professional army of volunteers, and violent and sudden death was a risk they took in accepting the pay and conditions of the army.

Josiah's regiment remained in Kandahar for the next few weeks and Josiah found himself back in the routine of regimental duties for young officers. There were the matters of dealing with the usual charges of drinking, brawling and theft. Fortunately, none of his men appeared on the charge sheets and Josiah spent more time with his fellow officers in the officers' mess.

He now had a room for his quarters in one of the better buildings in the city which housed officers of the British army, and the echoes of battle faded – except when he slept at night and the memories of the violent fighting returned to haunt him.

There had been many times when he had retrieved the letter he had commenced writing to Marian on the eve of battle. He would stare at the few words written and carefully fold it without adding anything further. It made no

PETER WATT

sense to express his thoughts to the young woman with the passion for the rights of the colonial people he had helped put down in Afghanistan. Besides, she had never expressed any romantic interest in him other than the fondness of a friend.

Then one day, Josiah was summoned to the regimental commander's HQ. This was intimidating because the commanding officer of the regiment sat at the right hand of God in the view of all ranks below captain. He reported and was ushered into an airy office with fans and marbled floors. It had been the home of a local dignitary and now acted as regimental HQ.

Josiah marched across the floor in his best uniform, came to attention ten paces from the colonel's desk and smartly saluted. Josiah could see the brigade major standing beside the colonel's desk. Both men greeted him with impassive expressions.

'Mr Steele, you may stand at ease,' the colonel said.

Josiah found it hard to under the circumstances. Junior officers were usually summoned by the commanding officer to be admonished on the advice of company commanders, but Josiah could not think of anything he had done – or not done – that would require his attendance.

'Don't look so glum, Mr Steele,' the colonel said with just the hint of a smile. 'I have had you report to me to congratulate you on your promotion to full lieutenant. I have had time to review after battle reports and your company commander, Major Davidson, provided a glowing reference of your leadership under fire. You have earned the promotion.'

'Thank you, sir,' Josiah replied, stunned that he was not in trouble but being recognised for his leadership. Josiah could hardly wait to write to his father and Conan to inform them of his promotion.

'However, the BM wishes to tell you something that has come to his attention regarding your future.'

The brigade major was an impressive man with short grey hair and a colourful assortment of campaign ribbands on his jacket. 'I have received a dispatch from our civil masters in Bombay that you are required to report to them posthaste. The dispatch was signed at the highest levels, and we are to arrange for you to journey to Bombay. You will be travelling with a squadron of Bengal Lancers, who will deliver you to the coast. A navy frigate will then take you to Bombay. Whatever our government desires of your services must be of the utmost importance for all the organisation they are providing. I can only answer any questions you may have on your travel requirements as it seems that you will be briefed when you report to the government administration in Bombay.'

Josiah was stunned and completely mystified by the mission he had been designated by the British government.

'If there is nothing more, Mr Steele, you are dismissed to prepare for your journey,' the colonel said. 'All the movement details will be sent to your company orderly room, and you have my personal wishes of good luck in whatever our government has sought to task you with.'

'Thank you, sir,' Josiah replied, snapped a smart salute, then he turned and marched out of the office.

★

The good news of his promotion was tempered by the fact that Josiah would be forced to leave his platoon behind. He informed Sergeant Peene that he had been ordered to Bombay but was unable to say why this was so. A parade of his men assembled, and Josiah thanked them for their service.

'Three cheers for Mr Steele,' Sergeant Peene ordered, and the response was a heartfelt one as his sergeant saluted.

Josiah returned the salute and marched away to pack his kit. He was visited by a few fellow officers, who slapped him on the back, congratulating him on his promotion. They knew that the newly promoted officer was bound for Bombay and presumed that he was being sent there for staff duties. Many envied him as the sprawling city held many delights compared to what faced a soldier posted on this harsh frontier.

Josiah reported to the British captain in command of the lancer squadron he was to join for their long-range reconnaissance south to the coast. The captain introduced himself as Captain Kevin Jones, a Welshman.

'Are you able to ride a horse?' Jones asked with a smile. 'Being with the infantry, I presumed you may have a fear of such creatures.' The cavalry captain well knew that Josiah would be able to ride a horse, as it was a required skill by all British army officers, but could not help having a friendly jibe.

'What do you think? I'm a bloody colonial,' Josiah replied with his own smile. 'I grew up on the back of a horse.'

'Well then, I will ensure you get one of our better mounts. Welcome to the patrol.'

Within hours, the lancer squadron set out from Kandahar on a course south. Josiah eyed off the shortened version of the Martini Henry known as a carbine that the lancers carried as a secondary weapon. He rode beside Captain Jones and they chatted about many subjects as they passed through the arid lands and tiny villages. So far, no enemy activity was to be seen but Jones explained they were in bandit territory and his Bengali troopers were always aware of the places an ambush might be launched against them. Josiah was impressed by the professionalism of Captain Jones's men.

By a campfire one night, Josiah mentioned that he knew a Welsh lady who owned prosperous confectionery shops in London.

'Ah, that would be Molly Curry,' Jones said, puffing on a big cigar. 'Her husband is Sarn't Major Curry who won a VC in the Crimea and has a pub in the city.'

Josiah was taken by surprise that the cavalry captain should know the Curry name.

'They are personal friends of my family,' Josiah replied. 'Sarn't Major Curry served with my father, who recommended him for his VC.'

Jones looked hard at Josiah. 'Steele,' he said. 'There was an officer by the name of Samuel Forbes – a captain – who was legendary amongst the men who served with him. But you have a different surname.'

'Long story.' Josiah grinned. 'My father, Captain Steele, was also known as Samuel Forbes.'

'You damned colonials cannot be trusted,' Jones laughed. 'Is your father still alive?'

'He is and living as a gentleman in New South Wales,' Josiah replied. 'He is partly the reason I now hold a commission. I suppose you could call it a family tradition.'

'Well, Mr Steele, from what I have heard of you, the family tradition is strong.'

After a couple of uneventful weeks trekking south, they reached the ocean where a Royal Navy frigate sat anchored off the coast. It was signalled by the officer of the lancers with the heliograph and a boat rowed ashore to land on a small, muddy beach lapped by equally muddy waves.

Before Josiah was helped aboard the rowboat, he shook hands with the man he had come to like and respect very much. The hours of riding the arid lands together and the conversations around the nightly bivouacs had been almost a holiday. The wound to Josiah's arm had healed without any signs of infection but had left a distinctive long scar.

Josiah looked back at the beach as he was rowed towards the waiting naval frigate. From what he could calculate, he was only a day late, but the gruff ship's captain who greeted him as he clambered onto the deck of the naval warship clearly did not appreciate being held up.

'You must be someone very important for us to sit out here on our arses,' the captain said after Josiah had saluted him. Josiah wondered himself at the secrecy and the importance of him reaching Bombay.

The anchors clattered up and the ship sailed south, although it also had a steam engine intended to be used when the ship was in action as sail was still cheaper than a limited supply of coal when navigating the vast oceans the Royal Navy patrolled.

Josiah was quartered with the young naval officers, who were keen to hear Josiah's personal account of the already famous battle against the Afghan army, and from what Josiah was told by his naval compatriots, the whole of Europe knew about the victory.

Josiah was pleased to finally see the city of Bombay from the deck of the frigate as it manoeuvred to a wharf. Now he would learn of the reasons for all the mystery surrounding his dispatch to Bombay.

When the ship docked, Josiah was stunned to see a very familiar face amongst the crowds of dock workers and European travellers on the wharf. The man looked up, saw Josiah standing on the deck and smiled.

'Bloody hell!' Josiah muttered. 'Of all the people in the world!'

There was no mistaking the mess of red hair and thin face peering up at Josiah from the wharf. When Douglas Wade saw Josiah in his khaki field dress, he waved up at him. Josiah waved back and soon the two school friends were greeting each other on the busy wharf.

'Josiah, old chap, it is so pleasing to see you survived the rigours of Afghanistan,' Douglas said, gripping Josiah's hand as if never to let it go.

'I say, this is the last place on earth that I ever expected to see your face,' Josiah replied. 'What the devil are you doing here?'

'You are looking at a rising star in Her Majesty's Indian administration, albeit one that is rising a bit slowly.'

'I thought that you would have settled for the hallowed halls of academia at Cambridge,' Josiah said. 'But here you are, and why do I suspect it is not an accident that it should be you standing here to greet me?'

'It is not a coincidence,' Douglas said. 'But before I explain, we will arrange to have your kit conveyed to my bungalow where you will be my guest for a few days. We have an appointment at Government House first thing tomorrow with some very impressive people. I am not at liberty to tell you very much as I am sworn to secrecy. Tonight, we dine at my bungalow and share sherbets prepared by the best domestic cook in Bombay, who happens to be on my staff. You can recount your experiences at Kandahar, and I can relate the gossip from London from whence I've just returned.'

Josiah realised that his journey to Bombay was still wrapped in mystery, and no matter how he tried to find a reason for it, he always came up blank. All he could do was be swept along with his good friend and enjoy the delights of the expatriate class in a country of peacocks and poverty.

As promised, the curried lentils served with fresh chapattis followed by cooling sherbet drinks were delightful. Then

Douglas produced a bottle of gin and a box of good cigars which they indulged in on a small patio veranda overlooking the other European bungalows provided for civil servants and military officers in the Indian administration.

Settled back on wicker chairs, they watched as a huge yellow moon rose over the tops of the silhouetted buildings. Despite the late hour, the city was still noisy with markets and the mass of people going about their business in the bustling streets and alleyways below.

'What are you allowed to tell me of why I was posted from my regiment, provided with an armed escort to the coast, and picked up by a Royal Navy warship and an irate naval captain to be brought to Bombay?' Josiah asked.

'I can tell you that you will attend a meeting with former Brigadier General Sir Neil Thompson and another chap who even I do not know. I do know that Sir Neil is close to the Queen and her staff and that they will have a proposal for you which I am not privy to, but I must confess I had a hand in arranging it while I was in London.'

'That rings of disaster,' Josiah chuckled as he downed his tumbler of gin and puffed on his cigar, the smoke curling in the balmy evening air around their heads. 'What news of London?'

'Well, the whole of Europe has been fascinated by Bobs and his army's defeat of the Afghan army. It appears your trek from Kabul to confront the Afghans will be written into military study books. From what I could glean in the corridors, that is part of the reason for you being here. But all will be revealed on the morrow.'

Josiah was curious but acknowledged that he must remain patient and not push his friend. Douglas worked in a world of political secrets, as Josiah did in a world of military confidences.

With the bottle half empty, the two men chose to retire for the night. When Josiah entered his room, he stopped and stared at the uniform laid out on his bed. It was a dress uniform reserved for formal occasions and displayed his rank as a captain. Such a uniform cost an officer money and he had not ordered one – especially one that displayed his rank incorrectly.

'Oh, I forgot to mention,' Douglas said, standing in the doorway. 'That is a gift from Brigadier General Sir Neil Thompson. It came today. Good night, old chap, and sweet dreams.'

Josiah stared at the red jacket, trousers and military braiding on the sleeves denoting his rank. The mystery deepened.

That night, Josiah did not sleep well. His dreams were a confused set of images of bloody hand-to-hand combat, dead men mutilated by artillery that tore bodies apart and the face of Marian amongst the carnage of dead and dying. No one heard his moans as he tossed and turned under the mosquito net until the sun rose.

THIRTY

The room was vast, and Josiah's boots echoed on the marbled floor as he marched smartly towards the two men standing beside the desk at the end. Josiah was wearing his new ceremonial dress of red coat, and when he was within ten paces, he halted and saluted.

One of the men was tall and broad shouldered and Josiah guessed that he was in his late seventies with his greying beard and matching hair. He had the bearing of a former soldier and Josiah guessed that he was Sir Neil Thompson. His civilian suit was obviously from a good tailor and he grasped a silver-topped walking cane.

The second man appeared to be in his mid-forties and wore spectacles. Josiah had the impression that he was more like a businessman. He was shorter and what little hair he had left was also grey.

'Lieutenant Josiah Steele reporting, sir,' Josiah said. 'My

apologies, but there appears to be an error with the captain's rank on my jacket.'

'Be at ease, Mr Steele,' Thompson said. 'You are not on the parade ground here. I am Sir Neil Thompson, and I once had the pleasure of commanding your father in India, back when he was known as Samuel Forbes.'

'Sir,' Josiah answered.

'The gentleman accompanying me is a representative of the Rothschild banking institutions. You do not need to know his name.'

'Sir.'

'We have a proposition to put to you, Mr Steele, that is rather unusual but of great national interest to Britain. Your name came up when I was searching for the right man for a delicate mission to Germany. We became aware that some years ago, you rescued the soon-to-be Duchess Elise von Meyer when she was in the Australian colonies.'

'Yes, sir,' Josiah replied. This was somehow about Elise? he thought.

Sir Neil continued. 'Your military record shows you are fluent in German, and having just come from the battle for Kandahar, you would be something of a minor celebrity to the Europeans. If you are half the man your father was under my command, I strongly suspect you are also loyal to the Queen and her Empire.'

'Sir. My sworn oath to Her Majesty is unbreakable.'

'Good,' Thompson said with a smile. 'I believe that you are also a Jew.'

Josiah was surprised at the extent of the man's knowledge of him and suspected that Douglas had had a hand in supplying the background. But the declaration as to his religion surprised Josiah all the more and made him feel uneasy.

'I don't suppose you know that I wanted to recommend your father for the award of the Victoria Cross on two occasions while he was under my command,' Thompson said.

Josiah did not know of this. 'No sir, my father made no mention of the matter.'

'No, he would not have; your father is not the type to brag. On both occasions, it was rejected. It was not until later that I learned your father had enemies close to parliament. At least Sergeant Major Curry was recognised, and I know that he and his family have been good friends to you while you were in London.'

'Yes, sir.'

'A good man.' Thompson nodded. 'I have even partaken of an ale in his public house. The pies he serves are the best that I have had.'

Josiah relaxed a little as the former senior army officer drew him onto familiar ground.

The mysterious man took a seat on a divan a few feet away and remained silent but listened to every word as he leaned on his silver-topped walking stick.

'Sir, is my religion of some concern?' Josiah asked boldly.

'No, Mr Steele. It is just that you are not only a Jew but also a colonial. There are people who surround Her Majesty who have a view that both aspects of your background make you inferior to a true English gentleman officer. But I do not share that opinion and have informed Her Majesty that I feel you are the best choice for our mission considering the very close link you share with the Kaiser and his family.'

Josiah was confused. 'I don't know the Kaiser's family, sir.'

Sir Neil nodded thoughtfully. 'You will, Mr Steele. When we post you to our embassy in Berlin, you are to renew your friendship with Elise von Meyer. Naturally, you will also get to know her fiancé, Major Maximillian von Kellermann.'

'Sir?' The major had not been fond of Josiah when they had met in London, to say the least.

'The major grew up with the Crown Prince Friedrich Wilhelm Viktor Albert. He is the grandson of the Kaiser, and the son of our own Princess Royal, Victoria. We have heard rumblings that the Prussian old guard are starting to influence the prince, and we must learn of his attitudes towards England. We have a particularly good relationship with Bismarck and the German Empire. There is even talk of signing a treaty, but our government prefers to pursue the policy of splendid isolation. It is in the interests of the British Empire that we learn as much as we can about any of the royal family who may one day be in a position to become the German Kaiser. The crown prince is one such person.'

Josiah kept his expression neutral but felt a whirl of confusion. What did all this have to do with him and Elise?

Sir Neil continued, his tone softening. 'Naturally, Her Majesty has an interest in her daughter, and in her grandson. She considers Prussians barbaric and is concerned, both as a monarch and as a grandmother. It will be up to you, Mr Steele, to befriend the fiancé of the future duchess and learn as much as you can about the prince and his attitudes. There will be a series of social events in Bavaria before Christmas that you will attend as the military attaché to our embassy in Berlin. You will report to the Palais Strousberg with the rank of captain. That is why we made no mistake in displaying your current rank on your jacket.'

'Captain, sir?' Josiah queried. 'I have just been promoted to full lieutenant.'

'Let us say that your temporary promotion has been approved by people close to Her Majesty,' Thompson said with a wry smile. 'A lieutenant as a military attaché would be conspicuous to any learned observer from the German diplomatic staff.'

Josiah's mind was reeling. A secretive mission to the new Germany with the rank of captain directly connected to Her Majesty . . . and contact with Elise. 'Thank you, sir,' Josiah dutifully replied.

'Ah, the intrigues of the royal families in Europe,' Thompson sighed. 'God help Europe if the time ever comes that they fall out. The Tsar, the Kaiser and our royal family, and not to forget the damned French. Never trust the French, Captain Steele.'

'Yes, sir. What happens next, sir, if I may ask?'

'You will take passage on a ship from here to Hamburg, where you will be met by a member of our embassy staff. The ambassador will command you in Berlin and from there, you will be directed to the social events, representing your Queen. I need not have to explain how important your discretion is in all matters of your life.'

Josiah nodded sharply. 'Will my ship be going via England?'

'I am afraid it will not as time is of the essence and we need to have you in situ as soon as possible. You go directly to Hamburg.'

'Yes, sir.' So there would be no possibility of seeing Marian.

'If there is nothing else, Captain Steele, I suggest that you prepare to depart immediately as your ship sails on the early tide tomorrow morning. Mr Wade has made the arrangements for your travel. I bid you good luck with your contacts in Germany. If there are no other questions, I will excuse myself as I have another appointment.'

Josiah saluted the former senior soldier before he strode

out of the room, leaving Josiah with the second, silent man. When the mysterious Sir Neil Thompson was gone, the silent man stood from his seat and glanced around before addressing Josiah.

'I am afraid I cannot identify myself, but you already know I work for the Rothschilds. Like you, I am a Jew, and it has never been easy for me to find a place in the upper echelons of European society. My current realm of influence is England and Paris, and I am pleased that Sir Neil set aside his bias against we of the Jewish faith to entrust you with this vital mission. Your father must be a truly great man for him to do so.'

'My father is a Christian,' Josiah replied. 'My mother was of our faith.'

'I also know a considerable amount about your mother's father,' the man said. 'He was a colourful man of considerable influence. On occasions, we had fruitful contact with him.'

'Sir, if I may ask, why are you here?'

Before answering, the unidentified man removed his spectacles and polished them with a handkerchief. 'The history of peace is based on trade between nations,' he replied. 'It is in the interests of business that peace flourishes. The Rothschild family know this and have an interest in gathering knowledge of future German imperialism. So far, we can glean that Bismarck has no great interest in expanding the German Reich, but we must look to secure the future. As far as we know, the Kaiser's son has no aspirations for expansion and you may be in a position to learn more about the aspirations of his grandson.'

'I feel as if I will be what you might call a spy.'

'That you will be, my young friend,' the man said with a smile. 'But for the right reasons. Knowledge is power, and in the interests of peace in Europe, we need to know of the future ambitions of German rulers.'

'I am an officer of the Queen,' Josiah said. 'Not a spy.'

'You are both.' The man sighed. 'The future peace of Europe may depend on all that you learn at this early stage. *B'hatzlacha*, my young friend.'

And with that Hebrew wish for success, the grey man walked away.

THIRTY-ONE

Light snow was falling as the ship docked in Hamburg.
Josiah was wearing his ceremonial dress and a warm
greatcoat. He went ashore and was approached by an officer
whose uniform Josiah recognised as that of the Royal
Marine Light Infantry.

'Captain Steele, I presume,' the royal marine said,
extending his hand. 'I am Captain Bruce Forsyth of Her
Majesty's Royal Marine Light Infantry.'

'Josiah Steele,' Josiah replied. 'Of Her Majesty's Scottish
Infantry.'

Both men smiled and Josiah instantly took a liking to his
naval counterpart.

'Welcome to Germany. We have your quarters organised in Berlin,' the officer said. As he spoke, Josiah noticed
something in his upper-class accent.

'You are originally a New Zealander!' Josiah exclaimed, and Bruce turned to him.

'Very observant, Captain Steele,' he said. 'But a long time ago. I suppose it is an interesting coincidence that two colonials should be assigned to the British embassy. As you and I will be working closely, I suspect that if anything goes wrong, the English will blame it on amateur colonials.'

Josiah was not sure if the man was joking or not.

Bruce continued. 'You will have to relate your experiences with General Roberts in your march to Kandahar and subsequent victory. Bobs is all the fashion in London at the moment, and I know one or two of the Kaiser's officers would love to hear of the expedition – especially the Prussian officers.'

Both men laughed, but again, Josiah wondered.

The two British officers went to Berlin by rail, then by a grand coach to the embassy. Josiah was greeted by one of the embassy secretaries, who informed him that he would be quartered at a fine hotel not far from the embassy. When all administrative matters were squared away, Bruce invited Josiah to join him upstairs, where a coal fire provided warmth against the German winter. The only furniture was a couple of big leather chairs and a richly carved table, the only adornment a portrait of a young Queen Victoria. On the table was a decanter of a dark liquid and a couple of glass tumblers.

'Rum, old chap?' Bruce asked, walking to the table and taking out the decanter's stopper. 'I also have cigars.'

'Rum and a cigar will be welcome after the trip from Hamburg,' Josiah said, taking a seat facing the fireplace. Bruce produced a large cigar and passed Josiah a glass of rum.

'I would have pegged you to be a gin drinker after your service in Afghanistan,' Bruce said, lighting Josiah's cigar.

'But the embassy has a leaning towards the senior service and rum is freely available to the staff. By the way, this is the room set aside for you and I to carry out mission briefings as the ambassador does not wish to know what we are up to. He is a very competent man with a strong rapport with Bismarck, as both men are very conservative and agree on many matters of policy. That has put him in conflict with the crown prince and princess, Her Majesty's daughter and her husband, who have more liberal views. German politics is as messy as it is at home. For now, you and I are the eyes and ears of those in London who decide on foreign policy. In my opinion, Germany will become the dominant power on the continent as they have already defeated every European nation they have confronted, including the French. It was only the influence of the Rothschild family that allowed the French to rule themselves after their defeat by Bismarck.'

Josiah immediately thought of the mysterious Jewish man he had encountered in Bombay who was associated with the banking family. 'I gather that we are officially spies,' Josiah said, sipping his rum.

Bruce pulled a face. 'No. We are like our scouts. We simply collect information to be converted to intelligence so as to give our side the advantage.'

'Spies,' Josiah repeated, puffing thoughtfully. After a pause, he said, 'Spies are executed if they are caught.'

'I have faith that a New Zealander with a New South Welshman can prove our worth and succeed.'

Josiah raised his glass. 'To our colonial partnership,' he said.

'Hear, hear,' Bruce echoed. 'Alas, down to business.' He sighed. 'On the morrow, you will meet many of the embassy staff and hopefully the ambassador. You will also prepare to travel to Bavaria, where you have been invited to a pre-Christmas ball as our Queen's representative. Also invited is your old friend, Elise von Meyer – the future duchess – and her fiancé, Major von Kellermann. Your focus will be the major, and your skills as a diplomat will be tested – if it is possible for any officer commanding those mad Scots to be diplomatic.'

Josiah grinned. 'Anyone who can get a Scot to obey orders must have some diplomatic skills.'

'Touché, old chap.' Bruce smiled back. 'You will be departing Berlin tomorrow afternoon and will be met in Munich by your host's staff, who will take you to your destination in the Bavarian Alps. If there are no further questions, I suggest that you get a good night's sleep. We will meet for breakfast here, six-thirty sharp.'

Josiah finished his rum and cigar before being led to the front entrance, where an embassy carriage awaited him for transport to his hotel a block away.

Josiah signed into the hotel, which was comfortable but oozed a sombre Gothic ambience. His room was clean and tidy although a little chilly, but the great eiderdown blankets would ensure a warm night in the bed.

A gas lantern provided a sickly yellow light and Josiah also had a small desk in his room.

He sat down at the desk and took in a private moment to reflect on the last twelve months of his turbulent life. From second lieutenant, he had shot to captain. From London to Afghanistan and now Germany. Nothing was normal in his life. His thoughts drifted to Marian, who he had had no contact with since leaving London. Letters from his father and Conan had eventually caught up with him and acknowledged that his letters had reached them. Those letters always expressed the great pride they felt for Josiah and always ended with a request to him to take great care. Josiah wondered if they knew about his recent promotion and posting to the British embassy in Berlin. He still had the unfinished letter to Marian and drew out the crumpled, worn page from his personal kit. For a moment, he stared at the page before putting it away with a sigh.

*

After a rail journey from Berlin to Munich, then a carriage drawn by four fine horses through the dark forests of Bavaria, Josiah found himself stepping out onto the cobble-stoned entrance of a castle straight out of a picture book. He half expected to see knights in armour trotting through the great gates, over the drawbridge and into the surrounding forest of tall trees.

Snow was falling gently in the dim light of the overcast sky and Josiah wore his greatcoat over his red-jacketed ceremonial uniform to keep warm. An elderly man wearing a top hat and suit met Josiah and addressed him politely in German with a Bavarian accent. He led Josiah inside and Josiah smiled when he remembered the stories the young Elise had told him in Sydney years earlier of living in a castle. Josiah had never imagined that they could be true.

Josiah was led to a bedroom furnished with tapestries depicting boar hunts and a huge wood fireplace where logs burned with a gentle heat. To Josiah, it seemed he had stepped back in time to a medieval age.

'Sir, you will have time to refresh as the ball does not officially commence until eight o'clock. We are expecting late guests from other embassies,' the staff member said. 'I pray that you enjoy your brief stay with us. If you require any services, pull the cord near your bed and a servant will respond. I must congratulate you on your grasp of our language. Most Englishmen are not as fluent as you are, sir.'

'Thank you. I had a good teacher,' Josiah responded but did not tell the man that it was the future duchess.

Josiah thanked the man again and removed his greatcoat. There was a mirror in the room and Josiah stared at the reflection of himself, wondering if Elise would recognise him even after a few months. He could see that war had changed him in ways that were hard to explain.

Hours later, when Josiah's name was announced, he entered the ballroom. The room was spectacular, with its multitude of sparkling candles, chandeliers and uniformed men from many countries representing their embassies. Civilian guests wore expensive dark suits, and their wives' jewellery reflected the candlelight with the sparkle of wealth.

A band of men wearing the uniform of a German infantry regiment played traditional songs as the guests mingled, drank champagne from crystal flutes and showed off their status. This was not simply some grand affair to provide entertainment before Christmas but an opportunity to establish diplomatic and political connections, and Josiah was aware that he must be diplomatic as he was on a mission important to the British Empire.

It was then that he saw Elise standing by the German officer Josiah knew to be her fiancé, and her beauty stood out amongst the crowd of women in attendance. She saw Josiah and broke into a warm smile, turning to her uniformed fiancé and saying something. He immediately walked over to Josiah.

Von Kellermann clicked his heels and nodded his head to Josiah. 'Captain Steele,' he said by way of greeting, 'I must apologise for my churlish behaviour when we first met in

London. I have been informed by Elise how you saved her life and that she would not be by my side if you had not acted when you did. I have also been informed that you are recently returned from the battlefield in Afghanistan under the command of your impressive General Roberts. As one who saw action in the Franco–Prussian war, I feel that we could be brothers in arms.'

'Your apology is accepted, and I also feel that we could exchange stories of battle,' Josiah replied. 'I must thank you for the invitation extended to the British embassy that has brought me here.'

'If I had known you were the military attaché, I would have personally made the invitation. I know Elise would have insisted.'

Josiah sensed sincerity in the Prussian officer's words and his feelings towards the man thawed.

'I feel that I should make my greetings to the future duchess,' he said.

'Of course,' Kellermann said. 'It would be rude not to. I shall escort you.'

Josiah followed the major to Elise, who wore a long flowing white dress of silk, her golden hair drawn up in a bun and topped with a tiara of precious stones.

'Josiah, what a delight to have you as one of our guests!' she exclaimed, extending a gloved hand to him. Josiah bent to press his lips to her hand in the continental way he had learned years earlier from his mother. 'I trust Max would have apologised for his rude treatment of you in London.'

'Major von Kellermann has done so, and I fully understand why he might have met me with suspicion at the time.'

'I will make amends tomorrow,' Max said. 'Captain Steele and I will drive out to the forest for some shooting, if that would suit you, Captain? I am sure you would be enthusiastic to try our new Mauser rifle, which I feel will be the outstanding infantry weapon in the future.'

'I was informed that you no longer use the Dreyse needle-gun after your experiences against the French Chassepot rifle,' Josiah said.

'Ah, yes, but we still defeated the French,' Max responded. 'Both rifles provide the infantry the option to be in the prone position when engaged. That has dramatically changed tactics.'

'It appears that I am unable to contribute to this conversation,' Elise said with a smile, touching Max's hand affectionately. Josiah could see from the way Elise and her fiancé interacted that there was a strong bond between the couple. 'I fear that I may lose two important men in my life to such military talk.'

'I must apologise, my dear,' Max said contritely. 'It is not often that I have the opportunity to meet with an Englishman and converse on the subject of modern military tactics. By the way, your German is excellent, Captain.'

'I will join you both on your silly shooting expedition if the weather is good,' Elise said. 'I will inform my aunt and uncle of the arrangement.' Elise walked away, leaving the two men alone. Josiah noticed the scowl on Max's face.

'You appear somewhat annoyed, Major,' Josiah commented.

'It is Elise's aunt and uncle,' he replied. 'They have a great dislike for me, and I believe they have great animosity towards Elise. I think they have convinced themselves that they should inherit the duchy. I sometimes think of myself as Elise's personal protector against them as much as her fiancé.'

'I would consider that Elise could have no better man to protect her,' Josiah said. He wanted to ingratiate himself with the crown prince's childhood friend, but his opinion also happened to be true.

Max glanced at him with an expression of gratitude. 'Elise has always expressed her respect for you, so much so that I sometimes grew jealous,' Max confessed.

'My friendship towards Elise is that of a brother for a sister,' Josiah said.

'I respect that,' Max said. 'Then I would consider you a brother also – albeit English.'

Josiah experienced the beginnings of a genuine if strange friendship with this foreign officer.

'Tonight, we eat and dance the night away. Tomorrow, my valet will fetch you for a sleigh ride to the castle's shooting range, Captain Steele.'

As the night progressed, Josiah was singled out by the daughters of the aristocracy for his dashing uniform and handsome looks. He danced and ate until two o'clock in the morning, careful not to consume too much champagne so as to keep his wits about him.

The next morning came too soon but a beautiful, cloudless sky reigned over the once sombre mountains of Bavaria.

A grand breakfast spread had been set out for guests able to overcome the dulling effects of the copious quantities of wine and spirits consumed at the ball.

Josiah ate a hearty meal alone, as very few guests were awake at this hour. He could see a couple of smartly dressed military attachés from the French government as well as some smaller European countries sitting for the morning meal. He nodded to his attaché counterparts politely and they returned the gesture. It seemed the military men were more accustomed to the early hours than the aristocrats.

Josiah stepped into the courtyard, which was covered in a thick blanket of snow, to see a sleigh harnessed to two snorting black horses stamping their hooves against the icy chill of the early morning despite the pale blue sky overhead. There was no wind and the day promised to be pleasant if chilly. Josiah wore his ceremonial uniform with his greatcoat, but he still felt the chill.

'Good morning, Captain Steele,' Max greeted him, crossing the courtyard holding two Mauser rifles. Beside him was Elise, whose pixie-like face poked out from a complete covering of expensive fur.

'Good morning, Josiah.' Elise smiled. Josiah could see that she was by far the best dressed against the cold, whereas Max also wore his field uniform with a greatcoat.

Josiah returned the greetings and Max indicated that they would mount the sleigh. Josiah sat in a front seat beside Max while Elise took the rear seat. The sleigh was open and when it commenced its drive through the gates of the castle Josiah felt the cool breeze around his head. He immediately retrieved a balaclava from his pocket and placed it on his head and face, but the leather gloves he wore did not effectively stop the biting chill.

The sleigh moved slowly on the hard-packed snow between tall timbers until five minutes later when it reached a cleared space, where it stopped.

Josiah could see painted stumps of timber spaced out at different distances, from about one hundred to three hundred yards away.

'My private shooting range.' Max dismounted from the sleigh and passed Josiah a silver hipflask. 'Schnapps,' he said. 'It will warm you up.'

Josiah took a swig of the fiery liquid, then handed the flask back to the German officer. 'It certainly does,' he gasped.

Max laughed. 'Not like your weak English whisky.'

Josiah stamped his feet. His long leather boots let the cold creep through but at least he was not going to suffer frostbite with the thick socks he wore.

The driver of the sleigh and his offsider quickly moved down the range to place empty champagne bottles on the flat tops of the stumps.

Max removed the two Mauser rifles along with a couple of boxes of cartridges. He passed one of the rifles to Josiah, who had an immediate interest in the weapon. He marvelled at the bolt mechanism for loading live rounds and ejecting spent cartridge cases. Josiah gripped the bolt and pulled it back. The action was smooth.

'I hope that you gentlemen are not long at your manly games,' Elise shouted from the sleigh, where she remained snuggled against the cold.

'It will not take long to impress Captain Steele with the superiority of German industry,' Max called back. 'Or of the superior marksmanship of the German army.'

Josiah grinned and tore open the cardboard box, removing one of the lethal-looking rounds. He placed it in the chamber of the rifle and slid the bolt forward. The rifle had a good balance and Josiah brought it to his shoulder, peering down the iron sights to a bottle at three hundred yards.

'I think today we shall not adopt the prone position. Standing or kneeling will suffice. Our first target will be at one hundred yards,' Max said, loading his own rifle. He stepped forward to stand beside Josiah. Josiah raised his rifle before he heard the distant boom of a rifle being fired and the thud of a bullet hitting the sleigh. Elise cried out in terror and for a second Josiah was confused. He looked to Max, who also looked perplexed, but the battlefield experience of both men immediately registered that they were under fire.

'The woods over there,' Josiah yelled, swinging his loaded weapon towards the line of tall fir trees covered in snow where he could vaguely discern a wisp of smoke. Max followed Josiah's direction and immediately went down to one knee. A spurt of snow erupted inches from where Josiah stood, and he threw himself onto the snow before glancing back at the sleigh. Elise was cowering down under the sleigh's rim while the two staff huddled behind it.

The shot that had almost hit Josiah had come from a different direction, and Josiah realised there must be more than one marksman.

'Can you see him?' Max called, swinging his rifle in the direction of what he felt was where the first shot had come from.

'There are at least two of them,' Josiah yelled back, feeling extremely vulnerable as a third shot slammed into the side of the sleigh and Josiah grasped who the true target was – Elise!

Josiah rose and struggled forward through the snow towards the tree line, rifle ready. The snow slowed him down, as did his heavy greatcoat, now sodden with melted snow, and his breath came out as steamy exhalations. He was aware of something ripping at the sleeve of his coat but also saw the puff of smoke from the edge of the forest. His enemy had revealed his position only fifty paces away. Josiah flung himself to the snow, raised his rifle to his shoulder and aimed at where he had seen the shooter fire from. He took a quick aim, calculating the position, and fired. He was rewarded with a yelp, and as he drew back the bolt to reload a round from the pocket of his greatcoat, he saw a shadowy figure scurry deeper into the forest. Josiah was on his feet again and became aware that Max had joined him.

'I think you have wounded the man,' Max said. 'We must go after him.' Josiah had almost forgotten that there was a second marksman in the trees, until Max cried out as a bullet hit his leg.

'I have been hit!' Max gasped. 'Keep going, Captain Steele. It is not serious.'

Josiah knew that they were still easy targets in the open and if they failed to eliminate the threat, Elise was surely dead.

Josiah plunged into the tree line, where the world was gloomy under the foliage. His dull khaki greatcoat concealed the brilliant red of his regimental jacket, and the carpet of snow provided a series of boot prints to follow. Red blood spots stood out against the white snow as Josiah quickly glanced as far ahead as he could and noticed, thirty paces away, a fallen log. That was where the wounded man would be if he were partially incapacitated, Josiah calculated, and waiting for any pursuer to ambush. Josiah backed his hunch by turning off the trail of prints in the snow and moving through the forest to a position that would outflank any ambusher. He moved cautiously forward in a crouch, rifle extended, and from the corner of his eye, he could see a man lying on his stomach behind the log. At the same time, the man became aware of Josiah and attempted to swing around. Josiah was faster and flung the butt of his rifle to his shoulder, firing a rapid but precisely aimed shot at the prone man. The ambusher's body jerked as the heavy bullet struck him. Josiah quickly reloaded the single-shot rifle before he approached the man and saw that he wore a dark cloak over the peasant civilian clothing of a farmer. Blood soaked the would-be assassin's chest and he stared with dead eyes at the snow. His identity was a mystery, but the rifle still clutched in his hands was an expensive hunting rifle which made Josiah consider that this was no simple peasant.

Not far away, Josiah heard the cracking of low-level branches and guessed that the second shooter was making a hasty retreat deeper into the forest. At least it appeared that he would not be an immediate threat.

Josiah made his way out of the forest to Max, who was sitting up with his Mauser across his legs.

'How bad?' Josiah asked as he knelt beside the German officer.

'The bullet merely grazed my leg. I will be able to reach the sleigh.'

Josiah helped him up and, with an arm under his shoulder, helped Max reach the sleigh, where the two servants peered over the top at their approach.

'Elise!' Max cried out, and both men sighed with relief when she struggled to sit up from a bundle of blankets.

'I am not injured,' she said in a shaky voice. 'The bullets missed me.'

'Thank God!' Max said, hobbling towards Elise, who dismounted to embrace him.

'But you are hurt, my love,' Elise exclaimed when she noticed the blood and how her fiancé was barely able to stand. 'We must fetch a doctor to attend to your wound.'

Josiah and the two servants assisted the wounded man into the sleigh and they hastily covered the short distance back to the castle. Once inside, the injury finally caught up with the major, and Elise insisted he lie down, cradling his head in her lap as he dozed in the warmth of the room and its log fire. The laudanum medicine also helped ease any pain and, after examining the minor wound, the village doctor declared that it would only require bandaging.

'Thank you, Josiah,' Elise said. 'I saw how you bravely

charged into the forest and distracted the assassin. If you had not been by my beloved Max's side, he or I may have been slain.'

'Max saved you,' Josiah modestly replied, attempting to deflect the praise. It was then that Josiah noticed the hole in the sleeve of his greatcoat and realised he had come close to being shot himself in his charge across the snow. 'Do you have any idea of who might wish you harm?' Josiah asked.

Max stirred from his stupor to answer. 'I strongly suspect the von Manns, Elise's aunt and uncle,' Max said. 'Under the stipulations of inheritance, Elise would inherit her title as soon as she marries me, as we plan to do in the spring. Should something untoward happen to Elise before we marry, they would have a claim on the duchy.'

'Do you plan to arrest them?' Josiah asked.

'I was informed that they left for Vienna late last night and I do not have enough proof to convince the police that they were behind the assassination attempt. I will still have our police investigate but, other than identify the man you were able to shoot, I doubt there is anything they can do. The best I can do is have Elise confront and banish these relatives from Bavaria if they return. I agree with my beloved that you not only saved her life but mine as well. We will always be eternally grateful for your God-granted intervention on this day.' He reached up and clasped Josiah's hand in his own. 'We will always be brothers.'

Josiah was invited to remain a guest of Elise and Max for Christmas, and a telegram to Berlin granted him the extra leave.

The events of the past days had cemented the bond between the two soldiers and on many evenings, Max trusted Josiah enough to answer questions concerning the German officer's childhood friend, Prince Wilhelm.

Josiah came to learn that the future Kaiser was vastly different from his parents, who harboured dreams of Germany becoming a true democracy. However, Willie – as Max referred to the prince – was heavily influenced by the martial philosophy of his Prussian generals.

'Willie has sided with the generals who are secretly sympathetic to the Dutch farmers of South Africa,' Max once commented. 'I have read reports that a couple of weeks ago, your army was soundly defeated at Bronkhorstspruit by the Boers armed with our Mauser rifles. I have also been informed that you will be joining your regiment of Scots in Natal after your attaché posting is complete. You must be careful, my friend.'

Josiah had read of the report of the clash between the Boers and the British army in Africa and was disturbed to read how the one hundred and twenty Irish Connaught Rangers had been slaughtered in the battle between the British and the Boers.

Josiah had just settled into an easy-paced life at the castle, treated more like a member of the family than a guest, and had come to learn over a sumptuous dinner one night that Elise's aunt and uncle had decided to take up permanent residence in Vienna.

The local Bavarian police had retrieved the body of their attacker and he was identified as an Austrian citizen with a shady criminal background. Max took credit for killing the man as he did not want Josiah to be tangled in police matters. The police took a dim view of foreigners – especially English army officers – with the current attitude in Germany sympathetic to the rebellious Dutch farmers in Africa.

Josiah was surprised when one day Captain Bruce Forsyth arrived at the castle.

'A fellow countryman of yours has come to meet with

you, Captain Steele,' Max said, leaning on his walking stick.

Josiah stood up and greeted Bruce with a firm hand-shake. 'What the devil are you doing here?' Josiah asked in surprise.

'I have come to fetch you back to Berlin, old chap,' Bruce replied in English. 'It seems you are needed there before we post you back to London.'

Josiah could see from the frown on the royal marine's face that something was amiss.

'Very well, orders are orders,' Josiah replied. 'When do we return?'

'As soon as you are able to gather your kit,' Bruce said. 'I have a carriage outside that will take us to the nearest railway station.'

'Is all well?' Max questioned in German, although his grasp of English was particularly good.

'It seems my government requires me back in Berlin,' Josiah answered. 'I am to leave immediately.'

'Ah, it is a shame,' Max said with genuine concern in his voice. 'But you will always be a welcome guest with Elise and myself here, at any time. I hope you will come for our wedding, if not before.'

'Thank you, Major,' Josiah said in response. 'I will make my apologies to Elise and express my thanks for your wonderful and warm hospitality.'

'It was our pleasure to share time with a true friend who we owe unspoken gratitude to,' Max said, stepping forward and extending his hand.

As Josiah was in uniform, the two men spoke as profes-sionals – officer to officer. But the handshake went beyond the formality of officers from two different armies.

When Josiah had completed his farewells, he had his kit taken to the waiting carriage. Snow was falling gently as he entered the closed carriage. Elise and Max, standing side by side at the front entrance to the castle, waved to Josiah as the carriage departed, and when it was through the great fortress gateway and across the moat, Josiah finally turned to Bruce.

'What has happened?' he asked. 'As tasked, I have come to learn about the future Kaiser and other matters that may be of interest to our military.'

'News has trickled back to the embassy that you were involved in the death of a man before Christmas.'

'The news is correct, although Major von Kellermann told the police that he killed the man who had attempted to assassinate the future duchess.'

'It seems that a second eyewitness has let it be known that a British officer was responsible,' Bruce said. 'The news has reached the German government and they are not especially sympathetic to us at the moment, what with the current matters in Africa with the Boers in revolt. We cannot risk an international incident, so you will be shipped out of Germany as soon as we get to Berlin.'

'But it was a matter of saving a German citizen's life!' Josiah protested.

'Such matters carry little weight at a political level,' Bruce sighed. 'You did the right thing, old chap, but politics trumps reality. We need to get you out of Germany before the police can hold you for questioning.'

Josiah slumped back against the padded seat and stared out the window at the scene of snow falling gently, providing a cap on the tall trees and turning the landscape into a canvas of white.

By nightfall they were in Berlin and had retired to the room set aside for their missions. There, Bruce produced a bottle of rum and a couple of cigars. Josiah gave a brief verbal report on what he had learned about the possible future Kaiser.

'I think that the British government will not be pleased to hear of the prince's attitudes towards us,' Bruce said. 'This Boer business in Africa is bringing out the real attitude of the Prussian military towards us, and from what you have told me, the prince has aspirations towards expanding his Empire in Africa and the Pacific. Those kinds of things can lead to confrontation and war. But I am a simple soldier and the intelligence you have will assist the higher ups to decide on future foreign policy.'

'What happens now?' Josiah asked, puffing on his cigar.

'I'm afraid that you will be travelling to Hamburg first thing in the morning to ship out to London,' Bruce said. 'The ambassador has decided that the quicker you disappear from here, the better. You will need to report immediately upon your return to an office in London. I will give you the paperwork before you depart tomorrow. In my opinion, you have done very well in the mission, and your friendship with the German major may assist us in the future as our intelligence informs us that he is slated for high rank in the German army.' The marine officer raised his glass. 'Here's to returning to the life of a simple soldier.'

Josiah nodded and raised his own glass in the toast. Based on the past year, Josiah had to wonder what lay ahead in his life.

THIRTY-TWO

Josiah's steamer arrived in London in the early hours of the morning. It was a bitterly cold day, and the falling snow had helped clear some of the smog from the city streets. He disembarked, huddled against the icy wind, and found a Hansom cab which took him immediately to the address he had been provided before he left Berlin. The building was one in a row of other insignificant tenement structures located not far from Westminster.

When Josiah rapped on the big brass door knocker, he was ushered into the foyer by a man wearing a cheap civilian suit. 'Captain Steele, we have been expecting you,' the man said, guiding Josiah along a hall to an office. Josiah went inside and was pleased to feel the warmth of a coal-burning fire in the corner, where two men stood warming their hands with their backs to Josiah, though they turned when the door opened.

'Ah, Captain Steele. Warm yourself before we proceed to the matters you have brought back from Bavaria.' Josiah recognised the man who had addressed him as the Jewish Rothschild banker from his briefing in Bombay. 'I believe you have some insights into the character of the crown prince.'

Josiah did not recognise the second man. He was tall with a bushy beard streaked with grey, and Josiah calculated him to be in his mid to late sixties.

'I have ordered breakfast for you,' the Jewish man said. 'But first, we would like a verbal summary of your findings. Tell us what you have gleaned about the prince.'

Josiah gave a brief summary of all he had learned from Major Max von Kellermann as the two unidentified men listened, rubbing their hands in front of the coal-burning heater. At the end of his briefing, the tall man spoke.

'You have done well, and I believe made a solid contact with the future duke. From what we know of Major von Kellermann, he has been singled out to be rapidly promoted in the ranks of the German army and I am sure that you will be assigned to visit he and his future wife again. Your unexpected friendship with the future duke and duchess may have favourable returns for us in Britain. We will naturally require a full and precise written report from you before you are reassigned to your regiment in Africa. Sadly, your temporary rank of captain has now expired. You will re-join your Scots with the rank of substantive lieutenant.'

Josiah nodded. 'Yes, I fully understand,' he replied. At least he would once again be with his men.

'Those damned Dutch farmer rebels are causing us a lot of concern and I am sure that it will be men such as yourself who will teach them a lesson. I am sure you will be glad to have some leave before steaming to Cape Town to reunite with friends. Thank you, Mr Steele.'

With the last statement, the men left Josiah alone in the room just as the man who had answered the door brought Josiah a breakfast of kippers and a pot of tea on a tray, placing it on the table. Josiah was hungry and ate the breakfast alone. When he was finished, he was ushered to the door of the nondescript building, where a cab was waiting.

Josiah gave directions to his residence, where a startled Mrs O'Brian met him with an expression of great pleasure. 'I did not expect you,' she said with a broad smile. 'Welcome home, Master Steele.'

With that, she immediately shuffled off to the kitchen to make him a second breakfast of bacon, eggs and fresh mushrooms. It was so good to be surrounded by the warmth of the house and Mrs O'Brian that Josiah did not have the heart to tell the motherly woman he had already eaten.

*

That same afternoon, Josiah stood at the entrance to the Curry residence wearing his best civilian suit with his heavy overcoat.

The door opened to the maid, who recognised Josiah. 'Mr Steele, you should come inside. Mrs Curry and the master will be pleased to see you.'

Josiah thanked her as he stepped inside, where Conan stood at the end of the hallway, grasping a newspaper.

'Josiah! Molly! Josiah is here!' Conan cried, striding forward to grasp Josiah in a great bear hug. 'It is so good to see you safe and well, my boy,' he said, releasing the young officer. 'We feared you may have succumbed to one of those terrible foreign diseases when we hadn't heard from you.'

'I was temporarily posted to our embassy in Berlin,' Josiah replied with a weak smile.

Molly appeared and rushed to hug Josiah, tears of joy streaming down her face. 'Josiah, you stopped corresponding with us,' she chided gently. 'We all feared that something may have happened to you.'

'I must apologise,' Josiah said. 'Circumstances gave me little opportunity to write.'

'Come through to the parlour and sit down,' Molly said. 'I will arrange for tea to be served and you can tell us all of your adventures with General Roberts. His defeat of the Afghans has been all the talk in England. Conan heard through old soldiers he knows that you were wounded in the fighting. I hope your wounds were not severe?'

'Just a bit of a cut down my arm,' Josiah said, shrugging off the long scar he would carry for life. 'It was stitched at the time, and I was fortunate to avoid infection.'

'Thank God!' Molly exclaimed and pushed Josiah towards the warm parlour.

The maid took Josiah's heavy overcoat and the young man seated himself not far from the hearth. Conan immediately went to a liquor cabinet and withdrew a bottle of whisky. 'Tea is nice, but this is better, my boy,' he said, pouring liberal shots into a couple of glasses. When he had done that, he immediately raised his glass. 'To your safe return to those who hold you dear.'

The tea came but went cold in the pot as the men exchanged military talk. Molly withdrew, informing Josiah she insisted that he remain to share dinner that evening. Josiah was happy to accept.

'Your father and I have corresponded on a weekly basis,' Conan said. 'He expresses his concern for you in every letter. I suppose he does not know you have returned to

London, and I feel that a telegram should be sent to him to say you are safe at home.'

'I had little opportunity to write,' Josiah said again with a guilty conscience. 'I may have written more to you and Mrs Curry than I did to my father.'

'Then you may not know that your father was married just before Christmas,' Conan said. 'He expressed that his only regret was that you were not able to attend the wedding they held at the family house in Sydney. He has also written that young Sam and Becky are well although they miss their big brother.'

'I am truly pleased that my father finally married Isabel. She is a wonderful woman who I know will make my father happy,' Josiah said. 'I thank you for the news that you have of my family.'

Conan related more news from Sydney and the afternoon soon became the early evening. At one stage, Josiah casually asked about Marian and Conan frowned. 'She has been going to meetings at friends' houses to discuss organising a movement by women for equal rights. For one so young Marian is deeply passionate about the issue, and I worry that all this rot about socialism is taking her away from us.'

'I am sure that she will always be close to her family,' Josiah responded. 'She is the most intelligent young lady I have ever had the honour to meet.'

Just as the sun set behind a bleak sky, Marian arrived home.

'Oh my God!' she exclaimed, seeing Josiah rising from the leather chair. 'Josiah!' In a couple of steps, she crossed to him and flung her arms around his neck, kissing him on the lips. 'When you stopped writing, we feared that you might be dead.'

Josiah was reluctant to let Marian out of his arms but did so in deference to Conan.

'Well, despite your fears, here I am,' he said. 'I have a few days' leave before I join my regiment in Africa.'

'Where in Africa?' Marian asked, releasing her arms from his neck.

'The Transvaal, I believe,' Josiah answered.

'That is where all the trouble is,' Conan piped up. 'You will have to be careful. We are to find ourselves against an intelligent and skilful enemy.' Marian glared at her father, so he added quickly, 'I think I need to speak with Molly.'

Josiah turned to Marian when her father left the room. 'I saw you on the wharf when I left for India,' he said. 'I tried to write to you the night before the battle but was at a loss for words. But I have carried the unwritten letter with me into action and it has become a kind of talisman for me.'

'I would have loved to have received that letter so that I could write back to you,' Marian said softly. 'I always wondered why you did not write to me.'

'I thought that you would not be interested in hearing from me,' Josiah replied.

'Do you still have the letter you did not finish to me?' Marian questioned.

'I do,' Josiah answered. 'I have it on me now, but it is a bit worse for wear.'

'I would love to read your letter, even if it is not finished,' Marian said, and Josiah reached into his trouser pocket to retrieve it. He passed it to Marian, who stared at the worn sheet of crumpled paper. For a moment, her eyes were fixed on the faded ink words before she looked up at Josiah. 'It is the most beautiful letter I have ever received from anyone,' she said, with a small laugh to choke the tears streaming down her face.

'Then there may be a chance in the future that we might become more than just friends?' he asked, holding his breath as his heart pounded in his ears.

'You truly are a foolish man,' Marian laughed. 'I have been smitten by you from the first moment I laid eyes on you. But you were always timid in my company, as if you were frightened to tell me what was in your heart. But I have come to realise that is a part of your wonderful nature, and I love you, Josiah Steele. I know I always will, and I suppose I am to be the foolish woman who waits on the docks for the man she loves to return to her.'

This was the happiest moment in Josiah Steele's life.

Josiah spent New Year's Eve with the Curry family. Every minute with Marian was precious as news of the defeats of British troops by the Boer commandos were reported in the newspapers. The Dutch farmers refused to bow to the military might of the British Empire and fought for their independence. The swiftly moving irregular Boer commandos were well armed with efficient small arms and each man was an expert marksman and horse rider.

Five days into the new year, Josiah boarded a ship to steam to Natal. Marian stood on the dock, tears streaming down her cheeks as she waved her soldier lover goodbye on a bleak, chilly mid-afternoon.

EPILOGUE

Majuba Hill

February 1881

Now a lieutenant with his beloved Scots, Josiah led his old platoon with Sergeant Peene in a night march under Major General Sir George Pomeroy Colley's overall command. Colley had decided to seize the high ground of Majuba Hill, reinforcing the British position, whilst politicians carried out talks of cessation of the rebellion with Boer political representatives.

Josiah had fought in a small but vicious battle at Laing's Nek at the end of January, prior to advancing on Majuba Hill. Sir George Colley had sent a message prior to the battle to his counterpart, Piet Joubert stating,

The men who follow you are, many of them ignorant, and know and understand a little of anything outside their own country. But you, who are well educated and have travelled, cannot but be aware how hopeless is the struggle you have embarked

upon, and how little any accidental success gained can affect the ultimate result.

Without waiting for an answer, Colley led his Natal Field Force of over fifteen hundred troops, supported by artillery and Gatling guns, to a strategic pass on the Natal–Transvaal border.

The attack went in against the Boer positions in the Drakensberg mountain range with British infantry and cavalry units, but they were heavily repulsed, with the deadly accurate Boer marksmen causing one hundred and fifty of the attacking forces to be shot down. Amongst the many dead were the officers of the British units, and Josiah thanked his father for the advice not to stand out as a sword-wielding officer.

Now Colley's small force had ascended to the peak of Majuba Hill, overlooking the main Boer positions, despite breaking the truce with the Boers during peace negotiations.

Josiah's platoon had been reduced by five at the disastrous clash at Laing's Nek, but morale was still high. Josiah was vaguely aware that this was not a righteous war, but one forced on the independent Dutch farmers by businessmen with power and influence in the British government. But he was a soldier, and whatever political or economic forces guided this attack meant little to him.

The morning arrived and Colley's small force were masters of the high ground overlooking the vast expanse of the African veldt. It had been an unresisted ascent to the heights and Josiah's men stood on the skyline waving their fists and shouting insults at the Boers on the veldt below, confident below nothing could dislodge them from the mountaintop. On Colley's command, a heliograph signalled to British units a distance away from the hill, proclaiming the victory. But he had been presumptuous, and when the Boers saw the occupation of the hill, they immediately swung into action, advancing up the slopes, using dead ground as cover while taking deadly aim at the defenders. The superior Boer sharpshooting soon took its toll on the exposed defenders. Within the hour, units of Boers had reached the summit, where all hell broke loose.

Josiah was forced to fall back on the use of his pistol as the bearded civilian farmers swarmed over his position, causing his remaining men to flee in panic. As Josiah attempted to rally his men, he felt the impact of something slam into his head. He had not seen the big Boer militiaman attack him from behind and Josiah fell into a darkness without dreams.

General Colley was shot in the head attempting to rally his command and fell dead on Majuba Hill. He had seriously underestimated these farmers, who were born with a rifle in their hands and had not read the doctrine of British military tactics.

The British survivors fled back down the hill, and the defeat at the hands of these Dutch farmers would echo for many years until two decades later, when Boer and British would face off again in the Second Boer War that carried the world into the twentieth century.

Ninety-two British soldiers, including Sergeant Peene, lay dead on the hill; one hundred and thirty-two had been wounded and fifty-six surrendered to the Boers. Josiah's surrender was presumed as he was unconscious after the hill had been taken.

Boer casualties amounted to one killed and six wounded.

★

Josiah, along with the others captured on Majuba Hill, were briefly imprisoned by the Boers but handed over when a treaty was signed recognising the Boers' independence. Josiah felt a deep shame for how many of his men had fled in panic, but eventually reconciled himself to the fact that he might have joined them had it not been for the rifle butt of a Boer irregular soldier.

He and others of the wounded British army were returned to England, where his troop ship was not greeted by cheering crowds. Instead, only the friends and families of the wounded men awaited them on the docks. Josiah stood at the railing and saw Marian waiting for him with an anxious expression on her face. With his head wrapped in bandages, Josiah waved, and Marian looked up to see his smile.

Josiah saw her lips move but did not hear the words she uttered. 'Please God, let this be his last war.'

But it would not be so.

AUTHOR'S NOTE

The Palmer River goldrush of the 1870s claimed more lives than we will ever know. Disease, starvation, banditry and drowning were rife, as well as armed resistance from the Indigenous people whose waterholes were destroyed and hunting grounds disrupted, and who resorted to cannibalism to survive. We did not condemn sailors from shipwrecks who turned to consuming human flesh for survival, and even as late as the twentieth century there were reports in the western world of similar cases. It was the case that the Indigenous people of the north lived in a region short of game to hunt for protein, and for some, cannibalism was their only option.

There are many great authors who have written about the Palmer River goldrush such as Hector Holthouse and Glenville Pike, who were able to tell us of the many colourful characters who walked the tracks of the Palmer.

One such historical character stands out in relation to the goldrush and that is Venture Mulligan. His story alone could fill more than one book and I recommend that interested readers research his life and times relating to the Palmer River.

The name Kandahar is familiar to many Australians who served in the recent twenty-year war in Afghanistan. The inclusion of the trek and battle in this story is of interest as history continues to echo into the present world of geopolitics.

The Colonial's Son is a work of fiction using the canvas of historical facts recorded by those who were there. It is meant to remind us that our ancestors led lives with the same emotions, desires, fears and aspirations that we experience today. Only technology and social attitudes separate us from the ghosts of the past.

ACKNOWLEDGEMENTS

The production of a novel is a team effort and as such I wish to express my heartfelt thanks to the following from my publisher, Pan Macmillan Australia.

My wonderful commissioning publisher, Cate Paterson, who has been with me from the very beginning. To my current editors Brianne Collins and Libby Turner, editorial assistant Grace Carter, proofreader Rebecca Hamilton and my publicist Ellen Kirkness.

In the logistics of the books produced, thanks go to Milly Ivanovic, Marsha Peters and a special thanks to Sam Haft whose wonderful voice is the first to reproduce the *Colonial* series into audio format for downloading.

As an author many people have an influence on my life directly and indirectly. The list of these people is long, but a few are acknowledged here. John and June Riggall, Peter and Kaye Lowe, Mick and Andrea Prowse, Kristie Hildebrand,

John Wong (the real one!), Larry Gilles, Chuck and Jan Digney, John Carroll, Rea Francis, Pete (keeps my computer alive) and Pat Campbell, Dr Louis Trichard and Christine, Betty Irons OAM, Bob Mansfield, Rod Henshaw and Anna, Nerida Marshall, Lynne Mowbray, Geoff Simmons and Ken and Barb at the *Outback City Express*.

For my extended family of Tom and Colleen Watt and my nieces, Shannon, Jessie, Charly and Sophie. For my sister Lyn Barclay and husband Jock and my nephew, Jules, and niece, Anna. My brother-in-law Ty McKee and Kaz and family. The Duffy clan of Tony, Greg, John and Robert and their families. For Virginia Wolfe and her family, Maddy and Mitch. Tim Payne and Danny Payne and his family. For Monique and Nate as well as Mila and Reiah.

To the memory of those passed this last year, my beloved Aunt Joan Payne who served her country as a WRAAF in WWII. My old police and army cobber Kevin Jones OAM who was a major influence on my volunteer emergency service life. I will also mention my much-loved cousin Luke Payne who passed far too young.

My thanks go out to Rod and Brett Hardy who still fight for the television adaptation of the *Dark Frontier*. My Texas, USA, correspondent Peary Perry.

And to my colleagues in the Gulmarrad Rural Fire Service Brigade who are another family to me and a tribute to their seven-month deployments in the 2020/19 bushfire crisis. For my friends in the Maclean RSL Subbranch, 1/19 RNSWR Association and Northern Rivers Retired Police Association.

Amongst my author cobbers I would like to single out Tony Park for his wonderful support over many years. For Dave Sabben MG and Di for their friendship. Not to forget my old mate, Simon Higgins, and Karly Lane and Greg Barron.

Despite many years of struggle to establish a legacy for all emergency service volunteers across Australia we have finally overcome all obstacles to establish VESL – Volunteers Emergency Services Legacy. When I first brought the idea to a group of very talented people it seemed impossible, but we persevered and now are ready to launch.

Most of all my thanks to my wife, Naomi, who has the tedious job of reviewing the original manuscripts to ensure that I try to get the romance aspects of the book right for female consumption. Remember, I am just a typical and simple Aussie bloke!

MORE BESTSELLING FICTION FROM PAN MACMILLAN

The Queen's Colonial
Peter Watt

Sometimes the fate for which you are destined is not your own . . .

1845, a village outside Sydney Town. Humble blacksmith Ian Steele struggles to support his widowed mother. All the while he dreams of a life in uniform, serving in Queen Victoria's army.

1845, Puketutu, New Zealand. Second Lieutenant Samuel Forbes, a young poet from an aristocratic English family, wants nothing more than to discard the officer's uniform he never sought.

When the two men cross paths in the colony of New South Wales, they are struck by their brotherly resemblance and quickly hatch a plan for Ian to take Samuel's place in the British army.

Ian must travel to England, fool the treacherous Forbes family and accept a commission into their regiment as a company commander in the bloody Crimean war . . . but he will soon learn that there are even deadlier enemies close to home.

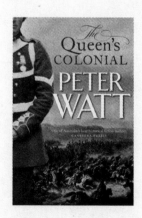

'One of Australia's best historical fiction authors' *Canberra Weekly*

The Queen's Tiger
Peter Watt

Peter Watt brings to the fore all the passion, adventure and white-knuckle battle scenes that made his beloved Duffy and Macintosh novels so popular.

It is 1857. Colonial India is a simmering volcano of nationalism about to erupt. Army surgeon Peter Campbell and his wife Alice, in India on their honeymoon, have no idea that they are about to be swept up in the chaos.

Ian Steele, known to all as Captain Samuel Forbes, is fighting for Queen and country in Persia. A world away, the real Samuel Forbes is planning to return to London – with potentially disastrous consequences for Samuel and Ian both.

Then Ian is posted to India, but not before a brief return to England and a reunion with the woman he loves. In India he renews his friendship with Peter Campbell, and discovers that Alice has taken on a most unlikely role. Together they face the enemy and the terrible deprivations and savagery of war – and then Ian receives news from London that crushes all his hopes . . .

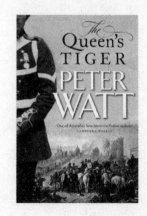

'Watt has a true knack for producing captivating historical adventures filled with action, intrigue and family drama'
Canberra Weekly

The Queen's Captain
Peter Watt

From India to America and New Zealand, action, intrigue and family drama.

In October 1863, Ian Steele, having taken on the identity of Captain Samuel Forbes, is fighting the Pashtun on the north-west frontier in India. Half a world away, the real Samuel Forbes is a lieutenant in the 3rd New York Volunteers and is facing the Confederates at the Battle of Mission Ridge in Tennessee. Neither is aware their lives will change beyond recognition in the year to come.

In London, Ella, the love of Ian's life, is unhappily married to Count Nikolai Kasatkin. As their relationship sours further, she tries to reclaim the son she and Ian share, but Nikolai makes a move that sees the boy sent far from Ella's reach.

As 1864 dawns, Ian is posted to the battlefields of the Waikato in New Zealand, where he comes face to face with an old nemesis. As the ten-year agreement between Steele and Forbes nears its end, their foe is desperate to catch them out and cruel all their hopes for the future . . .

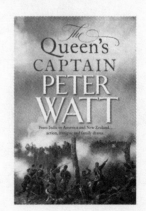

'Australia's master of the historical fiction novel' *Canberra Weekly*